By Harvey Swados

NOVELS

Out Went the Candle (1955)
False Coin (1959)
The Will (1963)
Standing Fast (1970)
Celebration (1975)

SHORT STORIES

On the Line (1957)
Nights in the Gardens of Brooklyn (1961)
A Story for Teddy, and Others (1965)

NONFICTION AND ANTHOLOGIES

A Radical's America (1962)
Years of Conscience: The Muckrakers (1962)
The American Writer and the Great Depression (1966)
A Radical at Large: American Essays (1968)
Standing Up for the People: The Life and Works of Estes Kefauver (1972)

CELEBRATION

A NOVEL BY

Harvey Swados

SIMON AND SCHUSTER | NEW YORK

3/1975
Am. Lit.

Library of Congress Cataloging in Publication Data

Swados, Harvey.
    Celebration.

    I. Title.
PZ4.S969Ce [PS3569.W2]   813'.5'4   74-23733
ISBN 0-671-21951-0

For Felice, Robin, Sandra, and Marco, with love

CELEBRATION

I have lived so much that someday
they will have to forget me forcibly,
rubbing me off the blackboard.
My heart was inexhaustible.

But because I ask for silence,
never think I am going to die.
The opposite is true.
It happens I am going to live—

to be, and to go on being.

Pablo Neruda, "I Ask for Silence"
(translated by Alastair Reid)

April 1975

APRIL 15   Dreaming. Dreamt I was dreaming. Not surprised that I was small, a child. But amazed that my mother was so young, so beautiful. She came tripping toward me in her pointy-toed white patent-leather boots, fluttering the pigeons from the stones of the Piazza San Marco. The starched flounces of her jabot, crisp as peppermint candy and carved in the same frozen swirl, bounced on her breast as she hastened toward me where I stood, alone and defiant, at once frightened and happy to see her. Did I know why I was frightened? Yes, but I couldn't admit it to myself. Most of all I was overcome by her beauty, the grace of her arm as she gathered up her ankle-length skirt, the tininess of her waist, the sparkle of her deep, laughing eyes.

"Samuel!" she cried. "To run away on your birthday!"

I dug my high-button shoes into the ground to keep from throwing myself into her arms. I could not hide the cornetto, so I brazened it out, licking at it openly. Nothing bad can happen, I said to myself, it's just a dream, why else would she talk to me in English, not in Italian or in Russian?

Bending at the knee with the grace of a waterbird, Mama brought herself down to my level so that she could stare directly into my eyes. Her touch, as she brushed back my windswept hair with her gloved fingers, belied her stern look.

"I was so worried," she crooned, smoothing the wrinkles from the white-starred collar of my new sailor suit. "Why did you run away?"

"I had this money," I lied boldly, "the lire that Nanny gave me, and I did so want a gelato. I was afraid that Papa—"

"Finish, quick! If he finds out you ran from the celebration he makes for you . . . terrible, don't ask."

Delicious conspiracy! The thick rich vanilla mingles in my

mouth, seemingly, with my mother's Roger and Gallet scent. She won't tell, she'll put back the money I took from Nanny's baguetto.

Around us, while she wipes the corners of my lips with her tiny lace-edged cambric handkerchief, the clapping of pigeons' wings as they alight before a stout purple-nosed German tourist, straining the seams of his red-piped waist-coat, grunting "Ach ja, ach ja" as he sows peanuts from a paper sack. All of my senses are alive at once, the campanile is bonging the hour behind the whirring of the pigeons, and through the gray fluttered veil of their weaving wings I see the giggling English girls gathered in a group for a pose, before the pockmarked Italian photographer with a spotted red ker-chief tied round his sweating neck, adjusting his tripod, clenching the camera bulb in his fist, and above my mother's goddess smile the sun glittering on the rampant Venetian horses frozen in flight and the clouds racing across the blue sky, and it is all delicious, delicious, delicious. . . .

How reluctant I was to awaken! I almost found myself waving goodbye to my birthday dream, as if I were a reluc-tant passenger on a rocking gondola, borne away against my will from the dock at the foot of the Piazza San Marco. . . .

I must have been smiling when I opened my eyes. Rog Girard, bending over me with passionless solicitude, was half-smiling himself. His familiar fine-cut features were obscured in the gloom, his black, black eyes all but concealed by those hooded lids—like the drawn blinds protecting me from the glare of the afternoon sun—but his thin lips were curved and parted, revealing almost reluctantly the astonishing white teeth that contrast with his smooth olive-skinned complexion. Sometimes I think he believes smiling is immoral, or reac-tionary.

My falcon secretary. I wish my vision were better if only so I could see him more clearly. He thinks he sees through me, doesn't he, like an X-ray man. No, more like a surgeon doing an exploratory, groping through my guts for signs of . . . Well, what he does see he sees better than most.

"I thought you might want to shave." Friendly but deprecatory, he tends to address me as if we were fellow UN delegates. He is reminding me indirectly of two points: First, that I can no longer see to shave by artificial light, and can do a decent job only when the sun is angling through the bathroom window onto the mirror over the sink. Second, that I have a horror of being unshaven, even before my own wife. Parading before Jennifer, even after ten years of marriage, with my white stubble sprouting I think of as almost as humiliating as letting her see my empty gums.

He knows that Jennifer will be driving up from New York with one or both of those television men, and that I will wish to be shaved and dressed to greet them properly. Facts. What he doesn't know is that I am eaten up with unease. That dream: Was it a true recollection, did it really happen, am I succeeding, in my old age, in calling up incidents from the remote and forgotten past? If so, it can make more bearable some of the indignities, the losing of more recent names, places, dates. How delectable, to be reunited with your sweet-smelling young mother after an entire lifetime! On the other hand, supposing it *was* just a dream? Could it be only an invention, a fable, to ease the stupid burden of being old?

That writer who came for a season or two at the Sophia School to teach my students, and seduce them too, used to say that after he had rearranged some incident of his earlier life into a short story he could no longer distinguish what had "actually happened" from what he had "made up."

Is that where I am now?

No one to answer such questions for me.

In a sense that is why I am starting a diary at the tail end of my life. For a man nearly ninety, perhaps it's a ludicrous operation. I will not look back on it (whether with rue or without) in years to come, because it is highly unlikely that there will be many of those. I can hardly see to sign my name any more. But for some little time I should be able to touch-type like this, if Rog gets on with the correspondence and the daily reading sessions. All I aim to do is what this first entry has already done—tell myself the dreams and memories that no one else could understand.

I have to be careful too. The television men may try to draw just those things from me; so I should set down here certain things I don't wish to be made public by interviewers, even for my ninetieth birthday celebration. Mama and me in Venice . . . if only that were all.

APRIL 16   They came, the two of them, accompanied not just by Jenny, but by Larry Brodie. Well, the whole idea of having me tell my life story to the TV cameras was his. Jenny accepts it, it brings me back in the public eye, painlessly, it'll increase her pride. Rog goes along too, seduced by the prospect of such a huge forum to promote my eccentric notions.

They're all so eager to get me to talk! Or to write! From the way they carry on, you'd think I had secrets, arcane wisdom, God knows what. The world's appetite for revelations is insatiable. Now they're dying to find out what I type in here when I'm alone, wondering whether I'm writing something.

Well, I am. And I want to settle up accounts in my own way. I want to say not how I feel about each of them from day to day—after all, I have nothing to "hide" from dear Jenny . . . except maybe (aha!) my sometimes reservations about Larry, the Great Disciple—but most important to me, how I feel about *myself,* now that I'm getting to the end of the line. Clear the tracks, Eternity, here I come.

The most remarkable thing about those TV men, supposed bearers of instant immortality, is how *ordinary* they are. A producer, a correspondent, between them they earn, I gather, several hundred thousand dollars a year. How else do you measure success in America? Celebrity status? By the mere act of celebrating people like me, correspondents like Dick Wells become celebrities themselves.

When they talk to me, when they begin to ask the "probing" questions, it is pitiful. The producer, Gabriel Gibbons, the older man, is rumpled and unassuming and perfectly pleasant, betraying nothing of the battles he must have been through in order to make it to the top. A family man. He speaks with pride of his children. More significant, he betrays no effects of having been exposed to accomplished and remarkable human beings. He is as deferential as if I were the first well-known old man he has ever met. For one awful moment I thought he was going to call me to my face the Father of Progressive Education. In caps. But he stopped short of that. I guess someone told him about Dewey. His hair is gray, but whose isn't, except for politicians and personalities like Wells, the correspondent, who have to pander to the youth cult? Even the grooves, one on either side of the smiling mouth, prove nothing much other than that he is a nice fellow.

As for Wells, he was far more courteous than I would have guessed from watching him bait people in his dogged, humorless way. But he gave no slightest hint that he or his researchers had a clue as to what questions might elicit some hitherto unrevealed truth.

There are to be at least three more sessions after this, one for each season of the year. Then the whole thing will be edited for posterity, or the instant oblivion of an hour-and-a-half "special." They all seem prepared for me to be iconoclastic, witty, skeptical, amusing, maybe even a bit shocking. Is it still possible to shock?

What they won't get out of me, no matter how hard they try, are the private things, the most important things. Dick Wells has lived in this world for forty-eight years or so (maybe more, it is hard to tell behind that jet-black hair, that healthy tan, that professionally clear-eyed gaze), but he is apparently still under the youthful delusion that if you ask enough questions you can find out everything there is to know.

Maybe he is just doing his job, as the others are doing what they think is best for me, fulfilling the assignment of presenting the "human" side of an inhumanly deified old man. Should be a simple task for a professional humanizer, if the subject is at all cooperative.

Just the same, I can't help but think that what Jung said about Richard Wilhelm would be utterly beyond Wells's comprehension. I had R. look it up to refresh my memory, but couldn't bring myself to quote it to Walter. Getting soft? It belongs here:

"Whenever I attempted to touch the actual problem of his inner conflict, I immediately sensed a drawing back, an inward shutting himself off—because such matters went straight to the bone. This is a phenomenon I have observed in many men of importance. There is, as Goethe puts it in *Faust,* an 'untrodden, untreadable' region whose precincts cannot and should not be entered by force; a destiny which will brook no human intervention."

Suddenly tired. When I started, I thought I could type for hours. Simple eye strain and fatigue? Or something called up by old Dr. Jung, who was so wise—and such a credulous old fool?

It wears me out just to think of how to keep this in a safe place. To say nothing of going on with it.

APRIL 17   This television business is not as simple as I had thought. Certainly they all tried to make things as easy for me as possible. The technicians drove up unobtrusively in two crammed station wagons and practically tiptoed around the house, even though they had what seemed to me like tons of camera and sound equipment. Nice men too. The Italian cameraman a sloppy-looking fellow, rumpled, big belly, but a sensitive face. And the sound man, a survivor I saw as soon as he took off his jacket and revealed the tattoo on his forearm.

Gibbons must have gone over my daily habits with Jenny and Rog, because he asked if I had any objections to having Dick Wells accompany me and my old coonhound on our walk to the post office and then to Walter and Lily's on the way home with the mail. It struck me as a bit artificial, what with de Santis and Freedman, one with a cigar, the other with dark glasses, tracking us; but that's where Wells knows his trade, putting you at ease.

"What's the dog's name?" he wanted to know, and when I said Lincoln Steffens, he laughed and remarked that he was going to remind me of that later, when we get to my muck-raking years.

Matching my slow step, he kept me company to the post office, questioning me on the way about my routine. After I threw the mail in my bookbag, I took him over to the Honigs', since that's where I stop to catch my breath for the mile-long walk back here. Lily had been baking, the house smelled delicious, we all four had some of her strudel with hot coffee and talked about neighborhood things, indigo, wildflowers, vegetable gardens, spring planting.

Only when we were back here and relaxing in the living room did Wells lead me into a conversation about my child-hood. The idea is for viewers to see me as I live now, here in the country and maybe in the New York apartment, while they hear me discuss my life. After they finish with me, after Wells and I have walked and talked three or four times in the course of the next few months, Gibbons will boil it all down to maybe two programs of an hour and a half each—rather like having someone take mountains of notes and do a two-volume biography of you, only with you posing for it. And, in a way, controlling it.

Didn't try to conceal the fact that I was afraid of my father. But who wasn't, eighty or ninety years ago?

Wells kept trying to get me to reminisce about the early days in Florence and my parents, "Philip Lumen, the bearded expatriate painter, and Marta, the beautiful young

Swedish-Russian wife he'd met and married there." Romantic enough, but how much has it to do with my turning into a general hell-raiser, a schoolmaster, and an advocate for children who couldn't speak for themselves? Wells was eager to bring out (rather crudely, I thought) the connection between my "exotic" origins and my becoming what I seem to be now. It's people like Wells himself who are responsible for glossing over the in-between—the hell-raising—or at least sanitizing it.

Partly it's a function of my being old. In this country if you live long enough your sins—in my case, bohemianism, radicalism, a jail term for subversion—are converted into cuteness. If you're the oldest living hoodlum they promote you as a onetime Robin Hood, or a symbol of the Old West.

Anyway, I did point out to Wells (and as with certain children, I could see the idea slowly taking root in his mind) that far more significant was the fact that as a little boy, like my father before me, I had had an old man for a parent. He was asking me about those years, the early 1890s, playing on the floor in a corner of my father's studio while he painted those forgotten landscapes, etc. etc., when I said, "My father was a charming old man."

"Don't you suppose your father was charming as a young man?" he asked with a touch of the sharpness I'd been led to expect from him.

I thought my answer to that was fair and honest and I am putting it down here because how do I know what Gibbons & Co. will edit out in the final version? I said,"I never met anyone who knew him as a young man. My own mother never set eyes on him until he was almost fifty, a bachelor of fifty."

Bells went off in Wells's head. He was dying to get me to say that I had become a substitute father for generations of kids because I'd been a young child with an old father. I told him the simple truth, that late marriage runs in our family, as in some English households. My grandfather, old Sam for whom I was named, was forty-seven when my father was

20

born. Sam was born in 1789, the year Washington took the oath of office. I added, with a certain satisfaction, "The memory of that family history gave me the confidence, in 1966, to marry a woman more than fifty years younger than I." "Well," he said, "it's true she was a young woman, but Jennifer Lumen is your third wife, isn't she?" I changed the subject.

But all that will turn up one day on television. What matters right now is reminding myself that the greatest threat to my integrity does not come from Wells or Gibbons, much less from those decent technicians, de Santis and Freedman. If anyone subverts me, inside the household or out, it will be because I want them to.

At supper, after Wells & Co. had left, Rog asked if I still felt up to a reading session or if I'd rather skip it. Jenny reads to me occasionally, things that take her fancy, but it's irregular because she is away on assignment so much of the time. I get great pleasure from R.'s reading—he knows just how fast to go, how much to inflect, even how to stop gracefully when I get drowsy. It's a real bond between us, his steady voice and my listening, and I dislike missing it, even when I'm worn out.

"What shall it be?" he asked, and was startled when I told him to find Dostoyevsky's *The Possessed*. He knows I can't keep long novels in my head any more, and I usually leave it to him to pick out salient passages from new books that I want to know about.

I told him that he needn't worry, I had no desire to go all through that novel again, I just wanted to recall Dostoyevsky's narrator's description of a famous old writer (couldn't remember his name, but I think it was a portrait of Turgenev) who turns up early in the narrative in the provincial town of the story. It took some hunting, but R. is quick. He found Dostoyevsky's shrewd commentary on how rapidly some "geniuses" fade in old age, which goes like this:

"It happens not infrequently that a writer who has been

21

for a long time credited with extraordinary profundity and expected to exercise a great and serious influence on the progress of society, betrays in the end such poverty, such insipidity in his fundamental ideas that no one regrets that he succeeded in writing himself out so soon. But the old grey-heads don't notice this, and are angry. Their vanity sometimes, especially towards the end of their career, reaches proportions that may well provoke wonder. God knows what they begin to take themselves for—for gods at least!"

I let R. read on to the end of the scene—a charming one in which the flustered narrator almost stoops to pick up the Great Man's coyly dropped reticule—before I stopped him. But R. is no fool. He said, "That's not you. That could never be you."

"Don't be too sure," I said. "Just leave the book on the desk on your way out."

APRIL 18 Today, that first moment of breathtaking mildness which does not last, but simply breathes upon you briefly, like a sudden soft kiss on the neck. My God! I thought, sniffing the air on the back porch looking out over the meadow, I've lived through another winter and it's *still* good to be alive, to look forward to one more summer!

I stood as silent as I could, clenching the head of my cane. I didn't even want the boards to creak for fear of signaling my presence to J., who was crouching with her camera, long-legged and intent, like some exotic bird, tracking the life that must be springing from the earth but that I can no longer see. It seemed almost as though that penetrating puff of warm air had brought her to me as a gift—she is often in her Manhattan studio, or on the road, in search of flora and fauna, with those elongated lenses like monstrous bug eyes. I dared not look too pleased for fear that if she did glance up she would observe my joy and feel guilty that she is not here more often to give me pleasure. She knows I am happiest when she is doing her photography here, home, rather than elsewhere. Maybe she even knows that I like to think of her being here, or even just coming here, long after I am gone.

I continued to stand there for a while, sniffing the air, after her tan jacket had slipped from my view below the slope of the meadow. Found myself thinking not of her but of my mother and father, seated across from me in the railway carriage en route from Florence to Genoa and the ship that was to take us to the United States.

It was the spring of 1894, Father had been "wiped out" (I had no idea what that meant, I thought it had to do with what he did to his canvases and sketch pads) by the collapse of his railroad investments in the Panic of 1893. He sat heavy-bearded and heavy-browed, hands folded stiffly in his lap, tense (I think now) from not having pencil or brush to clutch. Mother sat beside him, her fingers tearing at the little handkerchief. He made no move to comfort her, nor did I, since I didn't know the source of her tension. But I asked, and when she assured me that it was simple weariness I felt complete release from fear, even from uneasiness.

Indeed I was free to revel in a kind of elation, much like what I felt at watching Jennifer float through the meadow below me. I remember no unhappiness, quite the contrary, only the most intense delight at the greening poplars and vineyards drifting by as we chuffed through the Tuscan spring, with me sucking on peppermint sticks from a white paper sack, whose shape is as sharp and clear as if I held it in my hand at this moment, rolling onward to a great voyage, a new land, a new life. . . .

But then later, while I was dictating letters to R., Jenny came in, apologizing for intruding, excited. Larry will be coming back tonight from Washington.

I know she sees L. in Washington and New York. She knows I know. The excitement wasn't on her account, it was on mine. After all, he was just here, he arranged the TV thing and stayed to see that the first interview went off all right. Now what?

She won't say, but we'll see soon enough. I do resent the

23

idea that they are all involved in activities having to do with me that are being kept from me, then revealed only in bits and pieces as if I were a child, to be protected from both good news (he'll be overstimulated, he won't sleep well) and bad (the shock will be too great, why should he have to know about such things?).

APRIL 19 It all came out last night. Larry was bursting with it, charming, laughing at himself, for his clumsy impossible excitement. It's no wonder he couldn't settle for being a psychology professor. Or that J. is so taken with him. How could she resist the charm, added to the combination of his being my "first disciple," as he proclaims it, and a presidential adviser?

He tried to be grave, stalling, insisting on telling it his way. OK, we all enjoyed it around the dining-room table— Jenny and me, Walter and Lily, Rog, Mrs. Hoskins in and out with her special pork and rice in honor of the occasion.

Larry's chunky body radiates a ferocious kind of energy. He saws the air with his squarish hands (when he greets me he is careful not to squeeze too hard), shaking his thick shock of graying curls above the broken nose that makes me think of a Roman head in the Forum. He has not turned out to be handsome as I expected he would, in his schoolboy days, before life's shocks altered his features. But he's enormously attractive all the same. And no matter how much I kick against his having built his career on me, from the Ph.D. thesis on the Sophia School all the way to this bureaucrat's job, I must admit that he not only speaks to me with love, he speaks of me with love.

J. leaned forward over the round oak table, her shoulders shaking with laughter, the tail of her tied-up hair swinging free as she shook her head in mock dismay.

Walter and Lily were smiling too, as much out of happiness for me, I am sure, as at Larry. Lily's invincible air of

24

sweet gentility I always associate with reliability. I doubt that she was ever wildly desirable to Walter in all their forty-odd years of comfortable marriage, but I can't imagine her ever letting him down. And Walter with that lawyerlike pensiveness, his impeccably clean fingertips making a steeple even during the dinner-table joshing. In the glow of the three candles Jenny had lit I could see the precise part in Walter's gray hair, his pink scalp gleaming.

And then Rog. He has always intrigued me at dinner by sitting quite far from the table—so far that, especially when it is candlelit, he is almost entirely in shadow, his back to the fireplace, his facial reactions all but concealed from those around him Perhaps because of his dark saturnine complexion I almost expect him to do the opposite, to lean right into his plate, rolling up the rice into little balls between his fingers and popping them directly into his mouth without that Western pretense of distance from what you fork up and convey to your insides. I could feel him withdrawing further and further as Larry told how he had described my first interview session to his boss.

The President, Larry said, was most impressed—especially since his own childhood had been nothing to brag about—with my recounting to Wells the story of our days on 28th Street. He looks forward to seeing the interview: me explaining how I, the gently raised son of an expatriate artist, adapted to the shock of being one more kid on the streets of New York, minding the counter and the register of my mother's sweet shoppe when she went off to give piano or watercolor or sketching lessons to the daughters of those who could afford to hire a European gentlewoman.

My mother's gallant courage enthralls him—the contrast with my father, contracting consumption and going off to the Adirondacks to bring up blood into his starched handkerchiefs while I was being beaten up by neighborhood toughs.

"Anyone would be impressed," R. murmured in his even way. Then he said to Larry, "I wonder, though, what your

25

employer"—he said that word politely, even amiably, but none of us could miss the cutting edge—"is going to make of the Lumen contribution to native radicalism."

I liked that, even if the others didn't. Larry accepts the totality of my life, he has tried to deal with it in his own way, but it is true that in his hands I come out as a Lovable Old Guy. And I am not. God damn it, I am not. R. is the one man who knows this.

This was the moment at which Larry's horseplay ended. He said quietly, "I believe I have an answer to that. Sam, the President wishes your permission to name the National Children's Center for you."

Well, my God! Jennifer was glowing. I have never seen her more beautiful. Mrs. H. waddled in with a tray of brandy and glasses to go with the coffee, Walter Honig was on his feet with a toast, Lily was kissing me on the cheek, even old Steff roused from the hearth, wagging with happiness for me, and began to bark.

I must admit here, if not to anyone else, that ever since I was first consulted on the planning and design of the Center I have suspected something like this was in the works. I muttered that it would be more seemly if they'd wait until I was dead.

Larry rubbed his hands as if they were extended over the fire and said, "It all has to do with your being so alive, Sam. We'd like you to consent to a brief formal ceremony. You know, we really do hope that the building will be ready for use by the time of the bicentennial."

I said, "I really can't see myself doing that playacting."

L. cut me off. "I know, I know. The President said to tell you that if you think the trip is too much, or whatever, he'll come to you. But he wants the dedication to coincide with your ninetieth birthday."

The logs were snapping and the glasses were clinking and everybody was talking and laughing. I was suddenly exhausted. At that moment I caught sight of something in Rog

Girard's face that was absent from the others' . . . and I realized that there were going to be impediments to my playing the Great Old Man game.

I used to think that the unique quality of great age lay in its beautiful challenge to refine, to purify, to discover simplicity. Now that suddenly I am terribly old, I have the uneasy feeling that I had been romanticizing, out of ignorance. Because nothing seems simple to me now. Everything is complex, mysterious, impure, starting with my own motives and conduct. . . .

APRIL 20 I think perhaps I shall never be happier than I was yesterday at our little dinner party. Or that I shall never again be happy in quite that way. I can only think of the dream that followed it, after I had typed my diary and gone to bed, as a kind of presentiment. My dreams lately have been so full of charm that they seduce me into sleep. What if that changes, and they become dreadful?

I was seated on a little platform in the mall at Rockefeller Center. Behind me, although the weather was balmy, the giant Christmas tree was ablaze. At the lectern, Dick Wells, the President of the United States, natty in his red, white and blue outfit, was reading from a text to a huge crowd gaping up at us. His First Lady, seated near me, was Jennifer. Although she was naked, her legs were modestly crossed at the ankles. Her bearing was regal, her smile demure, as the President sang my praises. I was suffused with happiness as the crowd responded with bursts of applause to the President's recital of my career. Fathers held their children on their shoulders so that they could catch a glimpse not only of their President but of me.

But then I observed that Jennifer was holding the Vice President's hand in her naked lap. It struck me as poor taste considering that the Vice President was Larry Brodie. A series of little annoyances began to obtrude—a certain restlessness in the eddying currents of the crowd, a swaying motion of the temporary platform on which I sat, a sudden glint of envy, yes, outright envy in the usually mild and temperate eyes of Walter Honig, in the front row below us.

My happiness began to fade. This was only a show, it could not last. The crowd was beginning to melt at the edges, restless, bored. Suddenly my keen eyes (sharper than they have been for twenty years) spotted Rog Girard at the outskirts of the crowd, arms folded while the President's words boomed out over the tinsel-decorated loudspeakers. His enigmatic smile became a grin, then a leer, and I felt mortified, as though it were not Jennifer but I who sat there naked, as though it were not her lovely body but my shrunken, sagging flesh that was being exposed to public mockery. When I saw the man at Girard's side panic overwhelmed me. Young, slouching, heedless of authority, he commanded a band of youths—toughs, the motorbike gang type who sneer at everything worthwhile, every decent effort even when it is in their behalf.

They were going to break up the meeting. The police who ringed the Plaza would do nothing to stop them; they too were grinning. Even while rage and fright commingled in my chest and rose to my throat, I strained to see who he was, that young agitator. When finally I recognized him after a searching stare in which our eyes met, a scream choked my throat. I awoke sweating and trembling, convinced for a moment—until the terror subsided and I had oriented myself to the familiar confines of my solitary bedroom at four o'clock in the morning—that I was on the verge of a coronary.

Of course it can all be explained. Most of it, anyway. The dream of encountering yourself as an antagonist is hardly a unique experience. In my case it has to do, I am sure, with the fact that I haven't allowed anyone but Jennifer to photograph me in the last decade. The TV cameraman, de Santis, has been the sole exception. I suppose I think of my pre-

Jennifer face almost as belonging to someone else, instead of to me, the old man she married.

And the TV thing no doubt triggered it off. Before our dinner party had ended Larry elaborated on his announcement. The President thinks it would be wonderful if my television biography could climax with me accepting, on behalf of children everywhere, the Center named for me as an extension of national gratitude.

Who knows how hard L. has had to work at selling this idea to the White House? What mattered publicly was the result. He has won, and I am to have my apotheosis. He has annihilated Rog's fear that I am being exploited by those who never shared my outlook. While I . . . well, what the dream was trying to say, I think, is that I am terrified of being found out. . . .

APRIL 21   Already Rog is preparing his case. "They're after your papers," he said to me. No word of congratulation, only the cynical explanation that Larry's coup includes the acquisition of my papers for the Lumen Center.

I reminded him that Walter helped me make out a very careful will. It's no secret, W. is to be the administrator, Larry is to be co-executor with Rog. I didn't add that one of my secret pleasures is thinking of the future battles over my bones between those two. The money will go to Jennifer, who will distribute half of it—with W.'s help—to the appropriate children's agencies.

"But the papers," R. said patiently, "the papers. Every university, every institute in the country has been after them. I spend half my time putting them off."

It's partly greed on my part, partly fear of obliteration I suppose, that makes me hang on to all those cartons of old letters from people long dead for the most part, some of them obscure, some once distinguished and now forgotten, some still famous (those are probably the ones everyone is after). And the files from the Sophia School, accounts, correspondence with parents, and all the rest. But when Larry brought me the news from Washington I felt in a way that the problem was being taken out of my hands. Was that wrong? Would I be doing wrong?

I asked Rog if that was what he was implying. He said, "Well, it's a trade-off. You're giving them priceless files and they're giving you immortality American style—your name on a marble building."

How deflating R. can be! But there was something else. I had the feeling that it wasn't simply the eventual disposition of my papers that bothered him. He is mistrusted by Walter and Larry: when I am gone and the papers are in Larry's government agency, what role will there be for him, an outsider who doesn't even have federal clearance, after his career in the peace movement?

But that's the way the others see him, power-hungry, using me to satisfy his own political appetites. I prefer to believe, basing myself on the purity of his devotion to what's best in me, and not just what's most popular, that it's me he's worried about. I gave him an opening, but I couldn't get him to say anything more.

So Rog put himself in the worst possible light with me, as he so often does with others, and we called it a day.

It is getting warmer. R. left the window open for me, and even while I type I can sniff the air as it gently disturbs the white curtains. I am going to go for a little walk with Steff.

APRIL 22   Funny visitors today. I want to set this down because the girl triggered off certain reactions in me which I can't tell anyone about.

She was the more determined and aggressive of a couple that R. brought in, after some dull academic brainpickers had left. She did all the talking. In a husky, phlegmy voice which intrigued and irritated me (I was on the point more than once of asking her either to clear her throat or spit into a handkerchief), she asserted that if it had been the only way to get in to see me she'd have camped out on my lawn all night long.

"People have been known to do that," I said. "But when they got in they took sick from disappointment. Caught cold and fled."

She didn't laugh. She pushed on. "It's not just that my mother always told me what a great man you were. I discount ninety per cent of what she says anyway, she comes on so strong." Then she threw back her head and laughed. The kind of person who laughs at her own jokes, not at yours.

But as she laughed I became fascinated by her throat muscles working, and her free breasts leaping alarmingly under a thin half-buttoned blouse. They were large, longish, heavy breasts, freckled no doubt like her throat. They seemed to have a life of their own, stirring about from side to side.

"It's my *grand*mother," she said in that throaty gurgle, "who really turned me on about you. She was a great lady, not like my mother. In fact she was a big lefty in her day. She used to tell me you inspired her in the raising of her children, even though she didn't send them to your school. You were like a hero of hers. So I thought, if I could have the memory of meeting my grandmother's hero, I could pass it on to my daughter. You know, like continuity."

That word came oddly from this buxom, blond, big-breasted peasant type who stood foursquare before me, smiling.

"That's her, with Chris."

Her companion, skulking about restlessly during our conversation, looked misshapen. Now I saw that what I had taken to be a humpback was a baby carrier not unlike the one I had helped to popularize some forty years ago. The scrawny youth, whose long hair was gathered into a pigtail with a rubber band, did not have an affliction, but a baby riding his back.

31

"Her name is Amber." The girl explained, "She's a blonde, which is not surprising—her old man is blond too, right?"

It took me a minute to realize that her old man was young Chris, who had been photographing the two of us with one of those tiny Minox cameras.

"I know we're not supposed to have cameras," the girl said. "I hope you're not mad. Mr. Girard scared us when he warned us about no pictures and not tiring you out. Is he an Indian or what?"

"You'll have to ask him that," I said.

She nodded very earnestly. "I wanted pictures to show Amber some day. And to prove to my grandmother that I got up the nerve to come see you."

"Your grandmother is still alive?"

"She's very old. She's over sixty." She arose and shook back her hair, her breasts slipping here and swaying there, boats bobbing at anchor in the bay of her blouse. How I wished that I could see them! She reached out to touch my hand. "You don't know how grateful I am. There's one more thing . . . I just wonder if you'd tell me something before we go."

I waited for her to explain what it was. But it wasn't anything specific, she didn't want to know how many hours I slept, or if I slept alone. Not at all. She simply wanted words of wisdom to take home with the photos. "You know," she explained, "like advice or something. Anything at all."

I held her hand in mine, her fingers plump and blood-warm, tingling like breakfast sausages fresh from the pan. "I'll tell you," I said. "You make me think of Lorelei Lee. Those are my last words."

"Lorelei who?" she asked, puzzled and pleased. "Gee, who's that?"

"That's for me to know," I laughed, as I looked frankly down the front of her blouse, peering deep into lucky Amber's playground, "and you to find out."

So it wound up with me being as foolish as the girl.

She didn't make me think of dumb blondes. I believe I blurted that out in order not to say the truth, she made me think of fucking. Fucking young wives like her, young mothers too, encumbered with feckless mates like ponytailed Chris, who had never pleasured them properly. Or so I used to rationalize during those dark wild middle years.

How could I have foreseen that now, when I can barely raise this mottled hand to tap these keys, I should be haunted by those ghosts of those young women who brought me their children to be liberated, and ended up in my arms?

And worst of all, that demonic voice whispering, as I stared hungrily into Lorelei's open blouse, I bet even now, I bet . . .

Enough.

APRIL 23   Jenny has gone to New York. And then on to Bermuda, she says, for some underwater photography, now that the weather is right and she doesn't have to worry about me and the cold. I feel a little relieved. Not that I don't miss her, it's just that it distresses me to think of her staying around on my account.

Stopped in today at the Honigs' for Lily's fresh-baked strudel. W. gave me a sharp look. "You're uneasy about that honor, aren't you?"

"Wouldn't you be?" I asked him.

Walter brought out his pipe. "I can hardly visualize myself having buildings named after me—not even a county court-house."

"Honig Hall," Lily said softly as she poured me a cup of tea. "That would be nice."

"For what?"

In her marvelous prim way Lily said, "For a home for wayward girls. Walter, I want to revise my will."

"Nonsense," W. said. "There's no such thing as wayward girls any more."

Lily was confused. "What do you mean?"

"They're all wayward," W. answered with satisfaction. "Just like everybody's radical nowadays. You needn't fret, Sam. This building won't tarnish your image."

Pretty shrewd. He added, "You really should try to rid yourself of the notion that Larry and Girard are contending for your immortal soul. After all, they're both a little lower than the angels."

I told him then what Rog had said about my papers. He didn't brush it aside. He assured me that he would reexamine everything very carefully.

If I can't trust Walter Honig whom can I trust? But I know that behind his vest and watch fob, or the cardigan he wears at home, beats a heart far more attuned to Larry's world than to that of the ill-bred troublemakers Rog keeps reintroducing into my life.

"You want my opinion?" he said. "Girard worries more about being shunted aside, once you're canonized, than he does about your papers."

"Is he so wrong?" I said. "He doesn't want to see me tamed by the present of a mausoleum. Where will I be then?"

"In the Pantheon." W. took a careful bite out of Lily's strudel. "Accept it gracefully."

"It's not my way," I said. I could tell from L.'s face that I was getting loud. "Larry wants to wind up this TV show with me leaning on my cane, smiling gratefully at the President, with the wind ruffling my hair and Old Glory. Jesus Christ, Walter!"

W. sipped his tea and murmured, "It's a trade-off. In return you get to tell an audience of millions all the terrible things that you feel about the state of the world. Isn't Girard pleased for you about that? I have a hunch," he wound up, "that that fellow is going to try to gum up the works. You'd better keep your eye on him."

Annoyed, I grabbed up my stick and shuffled on back here. The trouble is, I can't move fast enough to demonstrate high

34

dudgeon. I must seem merely cranky and querulous. God damn it.

APRIL 24   Rereading yesterday's entry. Walter understands. And yet he doesn't, not at all. He wants me to be reasonable, like he is. Also grateful. Also mistrustful. That's like telling a child to eat his cereal because elsewhere innocent kids are starving to death. I spent the best years of my life prying kids free from that middle-class guile and gratitude cycle. Am I supposed to play such a game now that I'm old and practically helpless? On the other hand, who am I to look a gift horse in the mouth?

Feeling sorry for myself. Time to stop.

APRIL 25   Have the feeling someone has been poking around my desk. Can't prove it, no one goes near my things but Mrs. Hoskins. Bless her black soul, she would rather die than spy on me. Rog? I can't believe that. Never mind what W. says. He'd *like* to know—they all would—but that's hardly the same thing.

After R. ushered out today's last visitor (a dullard doing research on a Rudolf Steiner lady I'd forgotten), I asked him instead of reading to me to sit down so we could just talk, before he got on with his phone calls and letters and check-signing.

Immaculate, attentive, he sat facing me, linking his aristocrat's fingers around the knee of his whipcord trousers.

I said, "You know I've started keeping a diary."

"If word got out that you were writing something . . ."

I interrupted him. "I don't want word to get out. There are a few things I would like to keep to myself, and I am putting you on notice that this is one of them. Jennifer understands this, but I'm not sure that you or Larry do."

R. did not seem hurt. "Let me try," he said. "There are

some areas of your life that you wish to keep inviolate. Some, from the past, you don't wish to discuss with interviewers or strangers. Others, in the present, are simply your own business—such as what you type here when you're alone."

That sounded like what I had in mind. Except . . . it was what he did not say, what he implied about Larry, that disturbed me. As if it was L. and not he who was bent on intruding on my privacy. But L. would have no way of getting at this diary. Or would he? Would J.?

"Larry has known me," I reminded him, "since he was a kid. It's only natural for him to want to popularize those aspects of my life that have been more or less in the mainstream."

"Of course." R. nodded politely. "At the same time we want to preserve the balance. It's hardly just, to celebrate you as someone who used to be, once upon a time, a force for good. You still are. Every time you express yourself it matters. Why else do all of us care what you write here, in privacy?"

I felt he was confusing two different issues. Before I could say this, he went on, "No matter how freely you speak out in that next interview, the appearance of the President may overshadow your words, leaving people with an inaccurate idea of you."

"What can I do about that?" I asked him. "Turn up my nose at the Children's Center, after all my years of agitating for it? Refuse them my papers and my name too?"

"If you wish to reclaim your autonomy—" He seemed to hesitate. Then he got up. At the door he said, "We'll have to consider how we can liberate you from that embrace."

Liberate me? Celebrate me? I suppose there is a part of me that wants both—maybe I've tried to have it both ways. But here at least, in the privacy of these final pages and before it's too late, let me know myself. And never mind what they all want for me. Or from me.

APRIL 26   Told R. yesterday that I wanted him to get hold of some books on old age. He was moderately surprised—he's used to keeping me posted on problems of youth, not on those of decline—but he promised to do his best. For a start, he dug up a number of social science volumes. At random, I picked out one for him to read to me, a book on the Abkhasians published a few years ago by a lady anthropologist. Astonished to hear that many of their old gaffers had a history of youthful continence. Virgins until they were twenty-eight or thirty. Connection?

Was reminded, I told R., that George Bernard Shaw supposedly remained a virgin until he was twenty-nine and had a long red beard. When he came to the school to look us over and give us his Shavian seal of approval, he was so ruddy, so blooming, I remember saying to myself, "Maybe he knew what he was doing!"

Thinking back, I have never really examined the extreme slowness of my own sexual awakening. I didn't get into that with Wells, but it seems to me now that I must have spent a good part of my young manhood in avoiding any acknowledgment of the existence of sex.

Of course it was much easier to do that in those days. Dear beautiful woman, my mother never knew how to instruct me. She labored like a truck horse from dawn until late at night, not even taking time to tell me to work hard and behave; she simply assumed that I would.

She must have been in touch with Father about it, though, because he did make the effort—a disastrous one—when I went up to the sanatorium, alone, to visit him one Sunday. What I told Wells about Father was, I think, true. It's what I didn't tell. . . .

I implied, without putting it crudely, that Father's sex drive must have been modest, to judge by his prolonged bachelorhood and his epicene pre-Raphaelite paintings. He loved Mother devotedly, but not, I think, passionately. They were drawn to each other by their differences rather than their similarities. And I was the product of those differences. My father must have been bemused by me.

Parent after parent used to come to the Sophia School convinced that, having learned through his own suffering at the hands of a stupid, insensitive, or sadistic father, he would not reenact the tragic paternal folly. By bringing his off-spring to me, he was demonstrating his intention of breaking the endless cycle. He was ready to release his child from bondage, he was going to be warm and permissive, loving and compassionate, forgiving and understanding, supportive and self-limiting. But as the semesters went by I discovered that the damage had already been done, and that I could do little more than bind up the wounds, like a relief worker after an earthquake. Finally I realized that even relocating the stricken village to the other side of the mountain might only incline the volcano to erupt that way next time.

When Wells "probed" my childhood, he asked me if I thought my father would have been proud of me. I told him, after some reflection, that in my opinion my father would probably have puzzled over me, over my disorderly and im-moderately ambitious life.

But I did not tell him about the trip to the sanatorium in the Adirondacks, because it is nobody's goddam business.

APRIL 27 That trip. It is my business.

Up the Hudson River valley I jounced, along with the Sunday travelers, eating Mama's heavy European sandwiches and feeling unobtrusively for the dollar bill she had pinned to the inside of my suspenders. The day before, I had been waylaid by a gang of toughs from south of 14th Street who stole my newspapers and knocked me around. I had not told Mama, but was aching to pour it all out to my father.

It was not to be. Hastening through the brown slush and the strangers' hubbub of the station platform, past the frost-rimed handcart, colliding with red-nosed ladies awkward in boots and fur muffs, skirting frozen clumps of horse manure, I clambered into the trap of the burly tobacco-chewing cabman. The drive to the sanatorium was a wind-whipped blur. Suddenly there was Father, immobile in a wicker solarium porch chair, wrapped to the armpits in a plaid steamer rug, bearded but pale, two spots of color, splotched, startling, on those sloping cheekbones.

He inclined his old man's head, unsmiling, not for a dangerous embrace but simply in acknowledgment of my arrival along with all the others on the porch at visitors' day.

"I hope you had a pleasant trip," he said. His voice was dryer than I had remembered and even more precise, as if each word had the potential of shaking something loose in his chest. "I must say, Samuel, that you are looking well."

Could I tell him that I had been beaten up not twenty-four hours earlier and was afraid, not just of that, but of everything? His very tone was a reminder of how paltry my problems were in this place.

Falteringly I unstrapped the Gladstone which still bore the labels of a world he had left for good. I drew forth Mama's gifts. A jar of dill pickles, green as spring grass in the clear shadowless light of the solarium, another of Crosse & Blackwell's marmalade, a bright muffler newly knitted by Mama God knows when (perhaps when I was sleeping and she was not), a bundle of mail tied with twine, and some art journals on which Father laid a blue-veined uncertain hand.

In return, he gave me advice. It was all he had to offer. Sitting there frozen and helpless, wishing I could clap my hands to my ears, I could only think that it was ugly and awful. He spoke of "purity" and "tender affection" and "pollution" and "degradation," his normally grave voice lowered even further. I remember wishing that he would stop, stop, stop.

And then he coughed. It was the moment I had dreaded (not realizing that I had been sent on this voyage for a sex lecture), but it was still shocking. Just as he was speaking of

39

the female cycle, he stopped, shuddered, and the fleck of blood appeared at the corner of his mouth, bubbling in the sunlight between graying moustache and beard for an instant before it was caught up and removed by a snowy square of handkerchief held in that spare immaculate hand.

Everything fell apart under the impact of that tiny drop. Behind that tiny bubble of blood coursed streams; no, oceans. In the unacknowledged instant of its existence, briefer than the life of a bluebottle fly or a fluttering moth, it made an empire of crushing demands upon me, rendering me helpless with inexpressible horror. And hatred too, for in the cheerful babble of that sunny room, I felt that everything coming from my father's thin whitish lips—everything but his life's blood—was a lie or an evasion.

Gathering himself together, turning from the unpleasant dutifulness of the topic just abandoned, Father asked why I was not doing better in civics. Then, when he saw how desperate I was to be gone, he said something to the effect that he would like to think that there was another man in the family for my mother to lean on.

Why weren't you there when I needed you, I wanted to shout, why weren't you there when Mama needed you? Why do you sit here in the sunparlor like some giant parasite, spitting blood into your handkerchief and giving me advice that I didn't ask for? Who are you, old enough to be my grandfather and less than a man, to try to tell me to be a man?

My God, a lifetime later, the old man's fine cloud of beard now not even a handful of dust, the memory of it still makes my fingers tremble.

All I set out to note, so I thought, was what I did not say to Wells—that maybe there is some connection between my long life and my belated introduction to sex. Who would have wanted to roll in the hay with some wench after that scene with Father? Not I. I continued to dream of touching a girl's sleeve and suddenly feeling it turn to warm flesh and then exploding, awaking wet and guilty. Even after high school, as a scholarship boy at Williams, I had neither money for sexual exploration, nor time for courting girls of my own class. Dick Wells wanted to know about intellectual influences, athletics, whether I'd been bothered by being big and rawboned. Yes, he asked whether I had had any luck with girls, and smiled when I said they were like passing clouds, lovely but unattainable—unthinkable, even.

He didn't ask, nor did I tell, how I went for my initiation half-hypnotized, half-horrified, to the factory girls of North Adams, learning from them in the dank hallways of mill-workers' tenements, but never losing my spiritual virginity. I told him instead that the turning point in my young life (not to think of the sanatorium or the subsequent funeral) was the Panic of 1907, for I had to leave college a semester before graduation to help Mama. Having to face up to a new kind of reality, I told him, I became a man—and discovered what I was going to do with my life.

Splendid. What I did not say was that after Mama died too, worn out by the struggle, I was ripe for the affection of an older woman.

APRIL 28   Is all that stuff really true, about the bubble of blood?

I think I am sliding into dark waters. Walter peered at me over his half-glasses yesterday and said that my concern with my papers, with what he called "the dead past," was unlike me. A strange thing for a lawyer to say. On the other hand, maybe I am slipping loose from my mooring, turning from the future, like all the old, getting ready to die.

Jenny phoned yesterday from Bermuda. After the usual, she too urged me not to fret about "minor matters," meaning R.'s reservations about Larry's immortality program. Her voice, assuring me yet again of her love and her pride, came floating over the sea and through the air.

And I feel drawn to the past more than to an unimagin-

41

able future. It wasn't *just* vanity that drew me into the TV interviews. I begin to see that I was seduced by the invitation not simply to declaim to the young, or to charm the public, but to recall. Just to relax and recall. Dreaming of my mother and my childhood, I thought it would all be peaches and cream, say. But now I feel the awful pull of those dark waters.

APRIL 29   The visitors and the callers and letter-writers evidently see me as cogent, controlled, thoughtful, modest. If they only knew that it was hopeless! Every time I turn around I give myself away. Surely others must see that. An hour ago I was going to write something down here, I forget what already, but instead I drifted off with the large-print *New York Times* in my hands.

I was reading the obituary page, what else. Suddenly I sat upright, my poor eyes bugging at a small headline that leaped out from the center of the page: *LUMEN DEAD AT 90*. The unsigned paragraph began, "Samuel Lumen, lifelong champion of children's rights, died yesterday in his ninetieth year. He is survived by his wife, the photographer Jennifer Austin, and a . . ."

I dropped the paper, frozen with terror and rage. Dead? And only one lousy paragraph? No biography by Alden Whitman? Furiously, I threw down the paper and awoke, sweating and trembling.

And here I am, alive to laugh at the obviousness of it, to be ashamed of myself, and to wonder—are all old people so vain and foolish? I am no better than I was seventy years ago. Worse! And if I were to confess it to, say, Dick Wells, he would smile wisely at the anecdote as another instance of my modesty and wit. You see, America, how simple and lovable old Sam is?

APRIL 30   A phone call from Larry Brodie. Breezy, self-assured. Things go well in Washington. I must stay well, I must be alert for the apotheosis when the President and I will clasp hands before the building bearing my name. The last of the bureaucratic hurdles is being overleaped by Larry's bright young staff; they await my definite acceptance.

I said, "Larry, this is all so much baloney," and he laughed indulgently.

"I'll pass your message on to The Boss," L. said. "He'll be happy to be assured that in this rapidly changing world we can still count on the distillation of your folk wisdom."

I thought for a moment, and then said, "You know something, Larry? There's no fool like a young fool."

But we were cut off. Or maybe he'd already hung up.

May

MAY 1   I still can't believe it, I can't think what I am going to do, I don't know which way to turn. Why didn't I foresee this, why didn't I prepare myself? But how? What could I have done that I did not do?

And that dream of the other afternoon! Is it possible that it was not just *Galgenhumor,* laughter from the edge of the grave, but a prevision? Why else did I throw away the obituary page and awaken just as I was reading, "survived by a . . ."?

Let me put it down as carefully and coolly as possible. Maybe that will help. Nothing else will.

Everything began, everything went on to happen, in the most banal fashion. R. asked me if I was ready to receive visitors or if by chance I wanted to take May Day off. He knew I wouldn't do that, not when people had come all these miles. It was his own dry little joke. He brought in a group of ladies, liberals, who had driven out from Northampton to ask if I would serve as honorary patron of some children's festival or other. I forbore to ask why they couldn't simply have written (I knew the answer) or why the kids couldn't have organized their own festival (I knew the answer to that one too).

Out they went and in came a delegation of young people. There were, as I recollect, five of them—several more than necessary to state their case, but I am used to that.

Let me try to be precise. They numbered two girls and three men. One girl was an Indian; Linda Something. She enunciated her tribal name (a pretty one, but I've forgotten it already) very proudly. The other was a black, polite but combative, I don't recall her name.

The young men: A fellow with carrot-colored Raggedy

47

Ann hair and steel eyeglasses. An angular young man who might have been laid out on a drawing board with T square and triangle, name of Grebner (I remember it because he was the spokesman, and they kept nudging: Grebner, tell him this, Grebner, tell him that). And a tall, thin, somber, bearded chap who said nothing at all, but sat back in the shadows. Nonetheless I had the feeling—and this is not just hindsight—that he was the morally dominant one and also in some indefinable way the *physical* force behind them all.

Clenching his fingers, cracking his knuckles, the angular one said tensely, "I'm Grebner."

I said, "I'm Lumen," and he nodded without cracking a smile.

Chopping the air with his narrow bony arm as if it were jointed like a crane, he said nasally, "We began as an ad hoc task force to counter the Establishment's cooptation of the American Revolution."

I wanted to ask him to talk English, but I had promised myself not to be rude, so I waited for warmer words, a message I could recognize. They did not want my money (not right away, anyway—although sooner or later people usually do) but my active support for a cause combining anarchism with activism.

His nostrils flaring as if he were sniffing ammonia, Grebner explained that my visitors, who called themselves the Children of Liberty, supported the American Revolution, its ideals, and its scholar-statesmen. "In 1976," he announced, "the celebration of the Revolution of 1776 will be taken from Washington's hands. We, not they, will celebrate the bicentennial."

"Well," I said, "that's nice. How?"

"We shall expose next year's fictions—like the so-called Children's Center now going up in Washington—and this year's monstrosities."

I think I knew at that moment that I was not going to be solicited, I was going to be pressured. I looked around the room for Rog to learn who had put them up to this, but I could see no sign of him. Why wasn't he here? Instead, my eyes encountered those of the silent, sardonic young man in the corner. He was examining me with a cold curiosity, as if I were some kind of specimen. It gave me a tremor.

Grebner glanced at him, too, then went on to explain how the Children of Liberty are going to appeal to patriotism and demand protection of the helpless young from the foulness of bourgeois materialism. The rattlesnake flag, *DON'T TREAD ON ME,* is to be raised over movie houses showing war and horror films, knicknack shops peddling plastic garbage, supermarkets selling mislabeled nonfood. They will center their attack on redemption centers, where stamp savers pick up artificial birds and artificial flowers in place of those destroyed by blacktop.

"The occupied redemption centers," Grebner said, "will become the *real* children's centers, unlike the Tomb of the Unknown Child going up in Washington."

"You're talking about a building," I told him, "that is a realization of my lifelong dream."

Then the Indian girl put in boldly, "It's a perversion of your dream. Everything those people do is a perversion."

"The Center will exist long after they're gone," I said. "I'm not concerned with them, any more than I'm concerned with myself, because I'll be gone soon, too. But *you* are, aren't you?" I added. "Who decided that it would be a good idea to come here and beat me over the head?"

There was a moment's silence, and then the bearded one in the far corner spoke up for the first time.

"I did."

I got up and approached him. "What did you say your name was?"

"I didn't." His voice was low, musical, amused. "It's Fox." Then he said the surname for a second time, and it came out harshly, as if it had been stuck in his throat and he wished to expel it. "Seth Fox."

49

I felt myself growing dizzy. "How old are you?"

"Twenty-nine."

"There was a Seth Fox—"

"In Oregon? I am from Oregon."

I would have fallen if he had not reached out to grasp me. "We have never met," I heard him saying, "but you seem to know me."

I could do no more than wave feebly with my free hand. Alarmed, the redheaded fellow and Grebner ran out; I could hear them calling for Mr. Girard while the two girls helped me to my sofa. They were frightened, guilt-stricken. Not so Fox, who stood by grave but expressionless as the girls opened the neck button of my shirt, held up my head, offered me a sip of water from the carafe on my desk.

R. came in then, swift and efficient, bearing spirits of ammonia. He waved them all out. Then he turned back to me and said, "I'm calling Dr. Harrison."

"You can call him," I muttered, "but on two conditions."

Surprised, he paused with his hand on my desk phone.

"First," I said, "go catch up with those people. Tell Seth Fox that he must not go away. Second, don't come back in here. I want to be alone. If you have to call Harrison, do it from someplace else."

Shortly after he left, I was able to sit up. I began to type. But I can hear Harrison in the drive, and I haven't gotten to what I must say. Maybe, if I can pull myself together, I'll say it to Seth.

MAY 8   A week. I find it hard to believe. I remember things, but not much. Harrison and his mumbo jumbo, his bag of tricks from Miracle Drug U. And those vulgar, supposedly reassuring jokes about how I have a constitution like a horse, and why didn't they call a vet. I told him it's harder to get rid of some doctors than it is to get rid of their patients. He laughed heartily. But I'm stuck with him. He doctors

Walter and Lily, and Jennifer trusts him. Jennifer. I heard her voice, too.

R. says Yes, he has been in touch with Seth Fox, who is in Boston. (Why Boston?) Seth will come when I am "ready." I said, I'm ready. R. said, Harrison doesn't think so, he hasn't allowed anyone—and won't, until there have been several days without fever.

Whose life is without fever? Snoutnose Harrison. How could he know why I "took sick"?

MAY 9   Apologized to Jennifer. No sooner had she gotten off to Bermuda than they made her chase back here. Her fun, her work, everything sacrificed because of a feverish old man. And without a word of complaint.

But has she read this? I barely managed to get it under the mattress when that ass Harrison came bustling in. I was furious with him and R. for notifying her, but Jenny insists that they have standing orders to get in touch with her when anything at all goes wrong.

"Wrong?" I said. "There was nothing wrong. A touch of vertigo, that's all."

J. cocked an eyebrow. "That's all?"

Couldn't tell if she was referring to my health or to Seth turning up.

How much has R. told her? Maybe Mrs. Hoskins found the diary under the mattress and gave it to her? Maybe she found it herself? I can't remember putting it back in the desk drawer.

Two things: (1) Sooner or later J. must be told about Seth. Some of it anyway. Half? By me. Not by Larry, or Walter. How to begin? (2) There's nothing in here about Seth anyway, except for what I typed so feverishly before Harrison showed up.

If I go on, I'll have to find a better place for this. I *must* have my privacy. Seth.

MAY 10   A little scene with R. Felt it was high time he explained how those Children of Liberty had turned up here. The whole thing, he assured me, was quite "normal" and "ordinary." He had no idea that the meeting would be so upsetting to me. "As I told Mrs. Lumen," he went on, "if I had been able to foresee what would happen, I would never have scheduled an appointment."

"Whose idea was it?" I asked.

"Seth Fox has taken the responsibility." R. added, "But he was not the one who made the original contact. I went back through our files—it was that chap Grebner, and he came well recommended. Believe me—"

I told him I believed him. R. is cool but uneasy. I can't push it too hard, not before I have talked alone with Seth. No question, R. has been feeling the pressure from Larry, who has been phoning every day, they tell me, to find out how I'm getting along.

Apparently I threw a scare into everyone. If only they knew what a scare was thrown into me. Or maybe they do?

MAY 11   Feeling stronger. J. says Harrison has been stuffing me with antibiotics for some kind of infection. Forbore to observe that my kind of infection will not be cured with Harrison's bag of miracle drugs.

Pleaded with her to pack up her gear and get back to her work. At first she insisted that I am still too weak. Even when I told her I am going to need her, not now, but later on, before Dick Wells returns with his crew for the summer installment of the TV interview, that didn't work. She already understands that the prospect of my having to talk aloud not just about the School and my public activities, but about Luba, Sophia, Hester, and all the rest makes me very uneasy —but she says she'll be around then anyway.

Only when I brought up my unfinished business with Seth did I see that I had struck the right chord. I didn't even have to come out and say that it would be easier to have Seth here if I were quite alone. J. is remarkably sensitive to such things. To my moods.

"Listen," I said to her, "I realize I owe you an explanation about Seth Fox."

J. smiled and shook her head slowly. "You owe me nothing. You've always told me as much as you wanted to, and it's been enough."

"So far," I said, "but from here on out . . . I'll try to explain this to you when you get back, after I've seen him. All right?"

"Of course." She underlined that last word.

Maybe it was the underlining that made me feel I should say something more. The one thing I didn't want her to see was that just sparring around about it made me feel dizzy, as though I'd been exposed to a hot sun. I tried to be casual, but it was like tiptoeing barefoot on a bed of hot coals. "I've told you about my boy Philip, and how he met this girl Louise before he went off to war—"

"Yes," she said, "I remember."

"Well, Louise's last name was Fox."

She didn't say anything about remembering that. In fact she didn't say anything. I guess I was grateful for her silence.

"I started to keep a diary last month," I said, "when those fellows Gibbons and Wells showed up to do me on TV. I think I wanted a place to hide, you follow me? If I could tell Dear Diary, I wouldn't have to tell Dick Wells."

J. gave me one of her marvelous grins. "You are too much," she said. She smoothed down my hair with her cool hand. "You really are too much. Don't you think we've all been listening to you pounding that machine and wondering what in hell you were doing?"

"It's just possible you'll find out," I told her. "That is, unless I decide to burn it. There's a lot I'm ashamed of."

"Aren't we all?" she said.

And we let it go at that.

MAY 13 J. left today. Cool, handsome, all in white as if she were already back in Bermuda striding to the glass-bottomed boat and the scuba diving—short-sleeved wool sweater that zippered down the front, ducks, sneakers and no stockings, her bare ankles trim and pretty. She kissed my forehead—will she ever do that again, when she knows?—and hopped into her car, ready to retrace without a frown the whole tedious trip.

After she left, I told R. to get in touch with Seth and invite him to come and stay in the guesthouse. Mrs. Hoskins fixed me a cup of broth and I sat out on the porch, sniffing the spring air. Suddenly, out of nowhere, I've remembered a nightmare that had come upon me at some point during that feverish week of illness. Curious how my mind had suppressed it until J. left.

I was back at the Sophia School with a classroom of children. I was teaching in a way that I had always discouraged in others—at a blackboard, gesticulating with a pointer, harshly, overbearingly. And teaching for a reason I would have thought inconceivable—to make enough money to escape from the children. Naturally the students disliked me. Each one had a microphone, a teaching aid, at his desk, into which they kept crying, "You're too young! What do you know that we don't?" In the midst of this disorganized scrimmage a father tapped on the door and brought in one more child to add to my troubles. As he closed the door behind them and turned to confront me, the sunlight touched his young face. He was beautiful, like a god risen from the sea, with innocent sea-blue eyes and a mass of damp curls. But the boy at his side was frightening, threatening. As I opened my mouth to protest that the class was already too large and unwieldy, that they were knocking at the wrong door and

54

that, anyway, this was not even my métier, the child reached into his shorts and exposed himself. Instead of a boy's little pee-pee tube he brought forth a man's parts, hairy and monstrously disproportionate. I wanted to shout, to stop this outrage, but my tongue was sticking to the roof of my mouth. The classroom bell—my telephone—saved me.

Now that I have set it down, I wonder why I told J. about the diary. This is not for her eyes. Or anyone else's.

MAY 14   Walter came in today while I was napping. I arose stiffly, waving him aside, and felt among the clothes hooks on the wall for my black cardigan. I was shaky, and startled. W. apologized for barging in, explained that R. had gone off on an errand. At once I suspected, as I groped anxiously for the damned sweater like an old man feeling for fruit on a wobbly ladder, that that was precisely why he had come in at this time. When I found it, I raised it carefully from the hook so as not to tear the loop, and then lifted first one arm and then the other to slide them into the warm sleeves.

W. had been standing there patiently, holding a gift, Lily's grape preserve, with the label pasted on the jar and the waxed paper sticking out from under the screwed-on lid. She always uses too much pectin.

"You and Lily worried already about my being alive?" I said. "Jennifer's hardly left."

W. took it with a smile; he's used to me. But I know him too, and I could see that something was on his mind. He couldn't just come out with it. He had to go on and on about the postmaster, the weather, who was I going to get to cut the south field this summer. I waited him out. Finally he said, "I understand Seth Fox is coming."

"He's been here already." I was purposely playing dumb; I didn't want W. to see that I was agitated. "He showed up the day I took sick."

"You make it sound as though there wasn't any connection between the two." W. was disbelieving, but not exactly sarcastic. "Anyone would have been upset—startled—at his turning up unannounced."

"So I was startled," I said. "But I'm ready for him this time."

"Are you?" W. looked stern. "Are you aware that the Foxes were both killed in a plane crash near San Diego several months ago?"

The Foxes. I used to think of them as the Little Foxes, sitting out there in Oregon, accepting my checks every month and never acknowledging them, never sending one word about the boy. I said, "Tell me more, Walter."

"Mr. Fox had retired. He and his wife were visiting cousins. Seth had to return to Oregon to arrange for the burial and to help settle the estate. Apparently they had never told him anything. Not one solitary thing." For some reason, W. smiled when he said this. "Of course, when he went through his . . . through the family papers, he discovered that they'd been banking the monthly check from me." Then he stopped.

"Go ahead," I said, "tell me more. Tell me first where you learned all this. Did he look you up?"

"No." W. shook his head. "But as soon as I learned he'd shown up, I instituted an inquiry."

After all these years, Walter still lapses into that kind of legalese from time to time. I try to bear with it. "Listen," I said, "what you mean is, you got hold of Larry in the White House and turned the spies loose on Seth. Right?"

W. said with mild indignation, "Larry is very discreet. And he's about the only person around who knew Louise Fox. And of course Philip."

"So you did go to him."

"Well . . ." W. shrugged. "After Seth had turned up with that outlandish group, I thought it would be better to play it safe and find out what I could."

56

"What else did you find out?" I didn't expect that he'd tell me everything, but since Seth is my problem I felt I was entitled to know.

"Not too much. It wasn't sheer happenstance that he paid a call here with the Children of Liberty—by then he must have been reasonably sure that my checks had originated with you." Walter smiled encouragingly. "But he's not in their inner circle. He came to them through a friend of his, an Indian girl named Linda Running Water. Apparently she —or they, collectively—felt it would be a bright idea to try to enlist you in their madness."

Implicit in all this was of course W.'s disapproval of my toying with young radicals. I didn't want to get sidetracked on that today, so I pressed him for more on Seth. There wasn't much forthcoming.

"I can understand your eagerness to see him, Sam," W. wound up. "I'd feel the same way if I were you."

Could he? Can the childless ever understand such things?

He added cautiously, "I just wanted to point out, though, that he did choose an odd way to establish the connection. He could have written, or come alone. Instead—"

"I know, Walter," I said. "I know what you mean."

And that ended that.

Now we'll see.

MAY 15   Well, he's here. I told Rog to have Mrs. Hoskins install him in the guesthouse when he arrived. But R. didn't tell me he'd arrived until I awoke from my nap. Decided to go out there and see.

When I got to the guesthouse no one was there. Nothing on the little porch but a hunk of basswood lying on the glider. One side was incised with a marvelous kind of relief which I could feel with my fingertips almost better than I could see it, an animal, a fox head, I think, carved as if it were a small totem.

Holding it in my hand, I rapped on the screen door. No answer. Went on inside and saw evidences of occupancy—backpack, some magazines—but nothing strewn around. I sat down on the bed and discovered a Bible by the pillow, open to the Book of Job. It was pleasantly cool, I hadn't been in here in quite a while (once upon a time I had used it as a workroom), and as I sat there sniffing I wondered to myself, What is he like, lying here, waiting for me, reading the Book of Job?

Then suddenly he was in the doorway, slender but so tall that he seemed to fill it, featureless with his back to the soft sunlight.

"Is the screening all right?" I asked him. "The mayflies can be very bothersome."

He smiled. He really has a very gentle smile. "It's very comfortable." Then he said directly, "I take it you're ready to acknowledge that you were responsible for the checks Walter Honig sent my folks every month for twenty years."

"Your folks?"

He gestured impatiently. "Since they raised me and adopted me, I always called them Mother and Dad. They never told me about those checks. Why not?"

If I had anticipated the question, the suddenness of it was upsetting. So I temporized. "They didn't approve of me, I suppose. Many people didn't in those days."

"But they never spoke of you." He sat down rather heavily in the canvas captain's chair across the room. "And they never used the checks."

"That's not possible," I said. "I would have known. The canceled checks—"

"Dad deposited them in a special account for me," he said. "When I went off to college he apparently decided to use the account to finance me. So you're responsible for my college education. Does that interest you?"

I assured him that it did.

"Then why the secrecy?"

"On my side," I said, "advice of counsel. Walter Honig suggested that it would avoid complications. On the Foxes' side . . . I never met them in my life. You should have asked them, perhaps."

"Well, I can't now. They both died in a plane crash, you know." He added painfully, clapping his hands together and twisting them as though he had captured something and wanted to crush it, "The same way my parents did, when I was an infant."

So they had lied to him about that too. Lied all the way from beginning to end. Well, it was understandable.

"I learned about the special account only last month," he went on, "when I had to go back out there and sort through the papers. What I want to know is, why did you send those checks?"

It was hard to believe he hadn't figured that out. "I felt a certain responsibility for you. For the same reason he did."

"You mean my grandfather."

I nodded.

"So you are my grandfather, too. I wanted to hear you say it."

But I hadn't said it. And now that the moment had come— as I suppose I had always known that it would—there was no tenderness in it. We were being businesslike. Man to man.

"I think it's my turn to ask a question or two," I said.

He raised his eyes from his clasped hands and surveyed me coolly, measuringly.

"You didn't come alone, the first time. You came with a committee. Did you want to claim me as a relative, or just to embarrass me?"

He sat still for so long that I began to think maybe he hadn't heard me—or that I hadn't really spoken, but had only imagined, in my old man's way, that I had uttered the words. But at last he said, "Let's say that my motives were mixed. Like yours."

We had a lot to find out about each other, but suddenly

I was desperately tired. I pushed myself to my feet and asked if he could stay on for a while so that we could sort out our motives. He arose politely and held open the screen door for me and my walking stick. "Yes, I can stay," he said. "I'm free as a bird." Then he added, "At least we've made a start, haven't we?"

Is it wishful thinking on my part, or was there a note of pleading in his voice?

MAY 16   Jennifer phoned, sounding fresh and happy. Not a word about Seth.

After she said goodbye I sat here wondering what he was doing out there. Thinking about me? How strange. I was putting off doing anything because I wanted to keep his nearness in suspension. And because I was terrified of making a slip.

Finally I picked up my stick and stomped up the drive again with old Steff. Seth was bent over the basswood on the porch, whittling. Was that all he had to do?

He looked up, tilting his head against the inclination of the sun, putting it behind my back so he could get a look at me. He said neutrally, "I've been waiting for you." Then, as if aware that that might sound rude, peremptory, he added, "Last time I barged in, it really shook you up."

"That was different," I assured him. "Unexpected. Things do get to me—I have to take them with a certain caution. If I get *really* sick I'll die, right?"

He made an odd face, pulling down the corners of his mouth. It was almost as if he were shrugging with his face; but I couldn't be sure. I hadn't intended to play on his sympathy.

I sat down on the glider and we talked. Impossible to get it all down. What I came back here with was most peculiar: a combination of suspicion and rapport.

For example, when I asked him what he was doing, he

60

repeated after me: *"Doing?"* adding a certain mocking quality to the word.

"I'm between lives," he said, and then added more graciously, while patting my dog, that he'd be glad to tell me another time about the earlier lives, those I knew nothing about.

There is to be a quid pro quo. He is desperately eager to be told everything that had been withheld from him about Louise and Philip. Perfectly understandable—and quite impossible. What I did was to let him coax from me certain facts that, while harmless in themselves, I could not have brought myself to discuss with Dick Wells in front of his technicians, de Santis and Freedman. Such as:

What his mother was like. He seemed willing to take at face value my assertion that since I only met her once (oh, thank God, thank God, that he did not press me for details), I cannot say much more than that she was shy, charming, bright, and very much in love with Philip.

Philip. That's what he's really after—news of Philip. Understandable. The Foxes had memories of their daughter, some of which they must have shared with him, and mementoes—photograph albums, college term papers, whatnot—that he must have hunted up over the years. But they had refused to speak of Philip.

I couldn't very well avoid that. I said that Hester and I had named him for my father, the painter, as my father had named me for my grandfather, the merchant. I told him the innocent stories about Philip's difficult boyhood as the son of the Sophia School's founder, with me and his ill mother. I have promised to show him photos; but when I suggested that Larry could tell him a good deal more about those days the next time he comes up to Twelvetrees, he shook his head with a certain grimness.

"I want to hear it from you, not from him."

"But he was Philip's closest friend," I said. "All through the thirties Larry and Phil were inseparable. It's one reason

Larry has remained so faithful. He's like a member of the family."

I think that was too much. It was insensitive of me. Seth turned quite hard. "Brodie is not my kind of person," he said. And that was that.

For today, anyway.

MAY 18   It seems that Seth Fox is not Larry's kind of person either. Long talk with L. on the telephone. He is "honestly and frankly" worried about me and Seth. Why?

Because he thinks that the circumstances of S.'s turning up with that committee of his are sinister. I tried to reassure him, said that S. hasn't uttered one word about that group. But L. remained agitated. He worried about their "cooking up" something. "I'm afraid they'll try to take advantage of your generosity," he said.

What scares L. is that S. may rock the boat he is rowing to glory, may somehow queer the Samuel Lumen Children's Center before the public announcement, the final commitment by the administration. So he fears and mistrusts Seth, sight unseen.

"Larry," I wanted to say, "think of Philip! Why don't you come to Twelvetrees and embrace him?"

But no. I have never been able to tell Larry the truth. There had been moments, in those horrible days just after Philip's death, and then Louise's, when I wallowed in the ultimate degradation—nightmare visions of Larry returning from overseas to confront me with his knowledge of what I had done, to curse and condemn me.

Of course nothing like that ever happened. Quite the contrary. When L. did turn up, still in his army officer's uniform but eager to get into graduate school, he was his old vivacious self, bursting into my life once again to jar me out of reclusiveness and my depression with the news that he was determined to do his doctoral dissertation on me and the

Sophia School years. From that day forward, he became like the son that Philip might have been. He was the one who dragged me before the public again, made sure that I was not forgotten, insisted that I renew my commitment to children, this time on a larger scale. When I complained that I was pushing sixty-five, he was the one who said, "Nonsense, that's irrelevant," and hauled me off to Japan with him to focus public attention on the Hiroshima children. And then, a year or two later, to Korea.

People can make jokes about L. building his career on me, as I'm sure they do, as I'm sure S. does, and I suppose they even scoff at me for allowing myself to become a stepping-stone for L.'s undisguised ambitiousness. But he returned my life to me at a moment when I was ready to give it up, and that is something I wish I could explain to Seth.

Without ever having met, they dislike each other. For what they would call political reasons, I suppose. Is there any way I can resolve this, now that S. has come into my life, without telling them everything—and running the risk that they will make it up with each other at my expense, discovering a common bond in their contempt for me?

I am romanticizing. There is no more reason for them to like each other because of me, because I tell them to, than for them to dislike each other because of me.

Still, I wish . . . How handsome Seth is! There are moments, when he becomes very animated, that he seems quite beautiful to me—like a last gift—and I long for the courage to caress him.

He has not come. I am going to go to him.

MAY 19   I thought, Well, if I can hardly tell S. everything that weighs on me, surely he should be able to tell me what weighs on him. So I asked him, straight out, about the Indian girl and the Children of Liberty.

"I had a feeling that would be eating at you." He smiled

63

in his slow way. "Linda and I are good friends, but no more than that. As a matter of fact, I met her through the girl that I'm going with now."

I said nothing to that.

After a while he explained, "Linda's passions run to politics. I've been through all that already."

I felt I had to be careful. "Do you mean," I asked him, "that you aren't really involved with these people? Or only through this Indian girl?"

"I'm not unsympathetic." S. was serious now. "I can understand why Linda should be so committed. But I'm going to be thirty years old, and I'm a little—" he smiled again, whether at me or at himself I could not be sure—"dubious."

I told him he was raising more questions than he was answering. He twitched his neck about and his nostrils dilated, and there was something so fine, so tense, about those involuntary gestures that I was put in mind of a nervous young racehorse.

"If you want me to say," he said, "that I'm sorry for startling you that day, then I'll say it. It was foolish of me. I should simply have written you, or come on my own."

"In all sincerity," I assured him, "I'm glad you came, no matter how. You cannot imagine how often I have thought of you." I would have said more, but I desisted—not so much from shyness as because I did not want to divert our conversation from the business of why he had chosen to come with those people. And I told him that, bluntly.

"I told my friends about you," he said. "I mean, that I had found out about the checks . . . when I went to Oregon for the funeral and stayed to settle the estate. You understand, I was curious, and disturbed, and anxious to learn what sort of man it was who had . . . Not the public man everybody reads about, but the person who had sent me money every month for twenty-one years." He looked up at me at that point. "If in fact it really *had* been you. I wanted to be sure. That's the way I put it."

64

"I can understand that," I said. "And so they said, Let's all go see him? Let's see if we can hit him up for support?"

"Something like that," S. said rather uncomfortably. "You make it sound a bit—well, crass. That's not how I felt at the time. Believe me, if I had thought my turning up would send you into such a tailspin, I never . . . It would have been crazy, to jeopardize your health and ruin my chances of talking with you like this."

Reasonable enough. The next move is up to me, isn't it? To talk. To explain! Certain things you can't explain. They simply *are*.

I didn't want any more at that point, I can only handle so much at a time. I told him I had to get back to my work with Rog, and a flicker crossed that sensitive face.

I am always eager for the approbation of young people. But *his* approval, *his* admiration? I think I would give anything for it. Anything, to have him regard me the way Jenny does. The way Rog does. And to see that mistrustful flicker . . .

"What's the matter?" I asked him. "Don't you believe me?"

"Oh, of course," he said rapidly. "I know you have work to do."

I would not walk away without his telling me. Finally he said something about Girard "stage managing" me, or seeming to.

I was upset, but dared not allow myself to show it, or to become involved in a discussion about R. I stood there leaning on my stick, while old Steff scratched himself and arose for the stroll back to the house, and suddenly it struck me as funny that Seth should be talking about R. in almost the same terms as all the others—when they dislike him because of his post, and his involving me with silly and subversive young people like the Children of Liberty.

"We'll talk about that another time," I said finally. "For now, I'll just say that I need the stability he gives me."

"I can see that." S. nodded gravely. I couldn't be sure that he was serious. But I let it go.

Stability? A word without meaning for the young. And justly. As for me, I think I must seem like a big snowman to youths such as Seth and his friends. Imposing, a bit pompous, one hand extended palm upward in the teaching gesture, the other clasping a scroll, an honorary award carved in ice. As the spring sun rises higher, I shall begin to melt here and there, until one day everything will collapse in a puddly heap and nothing will be left but a carrot, some buttons, a few chunks of soft coal. . . .

MAY 20   Seth came up to have lunch with me, companionably, leisurely. He turned down Mrs. Hoskins' cold cuts, took nothing but cottage cheese with honey and several glasses of milk. Still, we talked like two dining companions, slated together aboard ship.

My comparison amused him. As a boy in Oregon, he had been mad for ships. By the age of twelve or thirteen he not only knew everything there was to know about barkentines and frigates, yawls, sloops, ketches, but he was drawing them very well and turning out what he called "acceptable" marine watercolors. His teachers urged him to consider art school. Career number one, he called it.

Like me, he has had a number of careers. I am dismayed that as a man pushing thirty, he has no apparent need at the moment to do anything but whittle on the porch of the guesthouse, while waiting for me to turn up and resume our conversations. Is it my fault, I wonder, is it a consequence of what I did or did not do, this aura that he gives off of suspension, of indifference to prosperity and getting on with the work of the world? I must not importune him about this, it could jeopardize everything. Anyway!

In high school he turned to mathematics, had two papers published before he was eighteen, and went on to Reed as a special student in math, doing graduate-level work before getting his degree. Career number two. He got as far as the first semester of graduate school at Berkeley before the student movement caught him up. He then went the route of activism, agitation, voter registration in Mississippi. "I thought of myself as a professional radical." Career number three.

Eased out by the blacks, he turned his back on politics. He "blew a couple of years" with the flower people and drug cultists before he took up the trade of cabinetmaking—career number four—and moved into a commune (oddly enough, not too far from here), which might almost be considered a career in itself. Bored, he shipped out to sea as a carpenter ("regression to infantilism," in his words).

In Cambridge, at loose ends, he met Susan, his current girl friend, and her roommate Linda, who was deeply involved with the Children of Liberty. He seems half-amused, half-impressed by their passionate dedication. Yet there was a cynicism in his account, an implication that one of these days he'll drift on elsewhere. It shocked me.

I must have registered a certain dismay. "What's the matter?" he asked, almost tauntingly. "Do you think it's time for me to settle down? How old were you when you settled for stability? Sixty? Seventy?"

I was embarrassed. Not at his calling attention to my own vicissitudes. I am willing to answer for those, to him if not to Dick Wells. But at my seeming to be censorious about his own life choices, when I had not earned the right. As he implied, who was I to talk?

Before I could quite recover, he flung at me, casually yet sharply, one of the questions I had been dreading. "I can understand your being curious about what's been happening to me. But why," he demanded, "did you wait thirty years to find out? How come all you ever did was to send money?"

By then we had done a lot of talking. He knew how I had loved Philip, who had made an early decision for one career instead of many, one that led to an early grave. And how

Philip had brought Louise to visit me before completing the voyage from Twelvetrees to his death. And how I had become reclusive until Larry pulled me back into the mainstream.

So I said, "Maybe I didn't want to know. Maybe it was too much for me to handle. My school was closed, my two wives were dead, my two children were dead, even my son's girl was dead. What makes you think I was ready to cope with you, when I could hardly bear to go on living?"

He didn't answer. He didn't even raise any of the obvious questions. For the moment I am off the hook. But how long will he go on believing (if indeed he still does) that nonsensical story of Louise's accidental death? If he suspects his mother killed herself in a moment of melancholia after his birth and his father's death, he's closer to the mark, but there's more, there's more. . . .

Supposing he finds out that she died hating me, and leaving him like a curse on the doorstep of her parents? Supposing, worse yet, that he already knows?

Then he is leading me on. Getting me to spin more and more lies, wrapping myself in a shroud of my own falsehoods so that when he is ready he can dump me in a grave of his own devising. He sits there stroking that silky beard and smiling with those eyes impossibly like Philip's. But then I say to myself, maybe it's not impossible, maybe he does have Philip's eyes after all?

MAY 21 Request from social studies class in Madison, Wisconsin: "Dear Mr. Lumen, Our class is doing a unit of American history. We voted to study the history of education. Since you have done everything from exposing child labor to running a famous school, we would be grateful if you would tell us your philosophy and what you think young people can do to be better citizens. Yours truly, Janet Fishbach."

"Dear Janet," I dictated to R. He sat ready for anything, from a platitude to a wave of the hand meaning, You do that one. But something stopped me. Seth? Dick Wells, coming back next month for more?

I started again.

"Dear Janet," I said, "We must never be allowed to forget that the world is full of suffering people. We must always be alert to new ways of helping others who are in pain, or deprived, or unhappy. While we are learning we should be doing. Thank you for helping me to remember what I was in danger of forgetting. Gratefully yours—" I opened my eyes after saying that and looked at R.

He nodded appreciatively, but I was glad when he went away and left me alone.

MAY 22   A sunny cloudless day. I was out in the back garden, peering here and there to see if Fred Hendricks had been taking proper care of the new annuals Jenny had set out. Suddenly, a shadow across my path. Steff barked. Before I could say anything, Seth's voice: "I'm going to have to be leaving."

I felt a sudden twinge in the small of my back. I gestured over to the deck chairs under the white lilac at the edge of the lawn. S. followed me silently as I made my way through the still, silver-damp grass and eased myself into one of the chairs. "Just like that?" I asked.

I was confused. Unprepared. I was afraid that he would read relief on my face when what I felt was a kind of terror at being abandoned.

He was eyeing me keenly. I said, "Aren't you happy here?" and he made an impatient gesture.

"With me gone you'll have one less threat to your stability."

I couldn't deny that. "Even if you leave," I said, "you won't really go away." I tapped my head. "Not from here." I didn't dare tap my heart.

His smile was not what you would call heartfelt. "Well," he said, "that's where you say I was before I turned up."

"From time to time," I said in all honesty. "But now . . ."

He must have surmised how I would feel. I said, "Here I was, just growing accustomed to the pleasure of your company . . . I would hate to see you disappear. Have you gotten what you came here for, is that it?"

"Quite the contrary. You gave me money, an education, and I never even knew it. Now I thought—because you were so anxious for me to come back—that you'd give me a miracle, a father." I froze, but he went on heedlessly. "Instead, you gave me tidbits. Commonplaces. So I see no point in hanging around."

"All I can say," I said (rather weakly, I suppose), "is that I'd like you to feel that this is your home, and that you're free to come and go as you please."

"With Susan?" he asked, cunningly.

"But of course." There was no other reply I could make.

"You seem to be under the impression," he said, "that we can be friends."

"Maybe I even hoped for more."

"That's hardly possible." The dog twitched and recoiled, as if S. had kicked out at him. "Not when it's clear that you look on me as some kind of wastrel who's come here to threaten you. An ingrate. Well, maybe I should be grateful that you've concealed yourself from me for thirty years."

"I haven't meant to be censorious," I said. "I've tried to answer your questions."

He laughed. "And pretty cagey you were."

I am not used to being talked to like that. S. slouched in the redwood chair with the sunlight splaying around his bony shoulders and glittering in his thick dark beard. He held his hands clasped; the stigmata of his last career were clear even to me on his knuckles and fingertips, which were spatulate, scarred, and already more workworn than my own, although mine were curled and knobby as the head of my walking stick. I stayed quiet until the impulse to fight back receded.

"I'm not faulting you for being old. You can't run around the world the way you used to, or take up all the causes."

I should have said goodbye and wished him luck. Some self-destructive imp pushed me to demand of him what I must have known he would say.

"But you've allowed your entourage to arrange this whole scene—" he extended his arm to take in lawn, garden, meadow, house, barn, guesthouse—"like a stage setting. No, like a tableau. Everything frozen into place, and you in the center of it."

I had a sudden recollection of my reverie of myself as snowman. He was saying, "It's all too pat. The genial old genius with the beautiful young wife. Beloved by all. People make pilgrimages."

"Including you?"

"Perhaps. But I also thought I was giving you an opportunity."

"You've been giving me more than you know."

He ignored that. "You've got it both ways."

"How so?"

"You're a national monument, so you can get away with playing like an outsider. But you haven't been put to the test for a long, long time, have you?"

"Your tests may not be mine." His smile angered me. "What would satisfy you, short of my proving that I'm in my second childhood? As it is, whenever Rog Girard makes a statement in my name, I'm charged with that."

"Every old man is. I think you know what I mean even though you pretend that you don't. You're safe and you want to stay that way. Why take chances with your sainthood? Maybe people like Walter Honig think Girard is a dangerous influence. Well, to me he's just part of the decor."

"All you're telling me," I said, "is that I've had it. Don't you think I know that far better than you?"

"Now you're asking for pity. Plus loyalty." He was so hard! "But, you see, I don't want to be one more member of the entourage."

He owed me nothing except hatred, which I had been—I admit it here—desperately trying to avoid. "I think maybe you pitched your expectations too high when you came here."

"I came to test your greatness."

"Which doesn't exist. If you insist, I'll talk about the things I don't tell the TV people, the researchers, the visitors who are not my flesh and blood. If I told you how filthy I have been with my wives, how rotten I have been to my children—"

I had the feeling that for the first time he was startled. He demanded, "Then what?"

"Then," I said, "you'd hardly think me capable in my ninetieth year of surpassing myself."

"It's not a question of surpassing yourself. Everybody, great ones included, has done rotten things. Absolutely everybody. If the saints didn't have to conquer their evil habits," he said, laughing now as if pleased with the conceit, "there wouldn't be any trick to becoming a saint, would there? You could get beatified just by going about your business of doing good and achieving your quota of miracles."

"But I'm not a saint," I protested. "I'm trying to tell you, I'm a sinner who has had the luck or the shrewdness—if that's how you want to interpret it—to surround himself with a claque. Surely you don't think I could purge myself of sins I'll never be able to tell you about."

"That's exactly what I think."

"Then you're crazy," I told him. "Plain crazy."

"Better crazy than servile," he said. Then he added, leaning toward me almost confidentially, "I really didn't come here to make you suffer. Or to add to your private suffering. Nobody can do anything about that. So I'll be on my way."

As far as I know he is still out there. But I don't know for how much longer. And I don't know if I want him to stay and haunt me, or to go away and leave me in peace. Which I will never be again.

MAY 23   Supposing I were to tell him? No, it's ridiculous even to think of it. I wouldn't know how to begin. And, long before the end, he would do what? Hit me, or spit at me, or laugh at me and turn away and leave forever? Maybe I could write it out and read it to him as poets do, trying out their verses on their wives or girl friends.

Meanwhile the painters have come with all their paraphernalia—gallons of paint, brushes, torches, extension ladders hauled out from the interior of their panel truck. Not worth remarking, it's so ordinary, and yet I can remember the first time Hendricks and his boys (men now) parked the truck in the circular drive and I said to myself dramatically, The end of an era, no more ladders for me, when you can't paint your own house you know you're old. Old! I was virtually a kid then compared to what I am now. If you got rid of the self-dramatizing, you'd say to yourself, Thank God I can afford to pay Hendricks to keep me from wasting more precious hours on that mindless work.

Actually, what's more interesting is what this biennial renewal ceremony (or is it triennial? I'd have to look it up, not worth the trouble, but it does warn me how I can't always seem to remember ordinary current matters) reveals about Jenny and me. Because if it weren't for her I wouldn't bother, I'd let go unless the Hendricks boys got after me and embarrassed me into keeping my contractual obligation to them. And even then, I'd be apt to say, Let's try a cheaper paint this time, or, Why the hell don't we paint the place a putty color and do the shutters in a pale rose instead of that same old black? Maybe it would be fun for a change, maybe it would last longer and look cleaner than the white?

No, she's the one who is determined to keep the place spotless and glistening, even when she isn't here. I think that must have been her first image—idealized a bit too, in retrospect, the way those things tend to be—when she drove up here ten years ago, fresh out of Sarah Lawrence, nervy, insisting on taking pictures of me, not just for another eightieth

73

birthday story for *The Village Voice,* but "for a strong anti–Vietnam War piece." I remember her saying the words and my heart pinching and then swelling for her wholesome young idealistic beauty.

And she must remember the stark white New England country house, gleaming incredibly in the morning sun rising over the Berkshires, and the solid sturdy handsome white-haired man (sexy, she said afterward!) standing in the doorway to greet her as she hauled her equipment from the back seat of her rickety, chipped, dented Volkswagen.

No more chips or dents for her. And no radical breaks with tradition, no putty-colored paint. She wants it as it was that first morning and as she imagines it must have been for so many years, generations, before that. And me too, as I was. If only I could do that for her!

The least I can do is to let the Hendricks boys do it her way. It gives her great pleasure, and it makes her feel too that she is coping, I think. Every day a few people show up, it should look just so for them, even for the bearded and bedraggled who couldn't care less and would never notice; and certainly it should conform to the already existent picture in the minds of the expectant—the Gabriel Gibbonses and Dick Wellses who come to take pictures and fix me forever in the doorway, framing me in the whiteness and purity of tradition. Probably she is more right than I, she usually is. My weariness with tradition, with keeping things up, may be simply a function of old age and the clogging up of all those little streams that used to nourish the brain. My acceptance, my uncaring neglect, may be akin to the readiness with which I'd settle, if it were not for Jenny and the others, into never changing from slippers into shoes again, never sending out the ties to be rubbed clean of the spots made by my palsied hands.

Fastidiousness is a fixation of middle age. The young couldn't care less—Jenny didn't when first she drove up in that beat-up VW—and the old are letting go, preparing to leave.

MAY 24   I was right. When Jenny phoned today I told her about the painters and she was pleased as a kid with a new pup. Really pleased, genuinely. "Oh boy," she said, "I can't wait to see it," as if it would look any different from before! And then she asked if the Hendricks boys were bothering me, upsetting my routine. I told her truthfully that by the second day, once I'm over the shock of realizing that the painting time has arrived again, it's as though they weren't even there, burning, scraping, rhythmically sweeping their brushes across the flank of our house.

MAY 25   Much rain. No Hendricks boys today. Instead, an oceanic sense of peace and growth. It seemed to me I could almost hear the ground opening to receive the moisture. Steady, sustained, persistent rain that I find it exquisite to be surrounded by; on days like this I am glad I continue to summer here. It is possible to sit in that apartment and not even know that the rain is coming down. Here I feel almost as though I were standing in it, beautifully drenched, renewed. And in the distance, between the folds of the hills, the mist rising, as in some vast, infinitely unfolding Japanese print.

I spoke of this to Rog when he came up to me as I stood at the glass doors, entranced. He seemed startled—it was almost as if there were no mist out there for him—and for one awful moment I thought, Oh my God, my cataracts are tricking me into thinking there is beauty where there is nothing. But then it occurred to me that even so, what's wrong with that? It's as worthy as a lovely dream, isn't it?

Anyway, I think now that I had simply caught R. unawares. He appears distracted these days; his mind seems to be elsewhere. No point in taxing him with it, as long as he's taking care of everything well.

Was on the verge of asking him about Seth, when I was

spared the trouble (not trouble, really—the fact is, I just don't like to bring it up with Girard). Because suddenly I saw him plunging across the lawn, taking a shortcut out to the guesthouse. Hair and beard streaming, rubberized raincoat glittering in the glazelike light.

So he is still there. It was on the 22nd that he said he would be on his way. I suppose he'd stop by to say goodbye, he is polite and well brought up in the old-fashioned sense, but I can't help wondering whether he is delaying his departure to get me to say more, maybe even commit myself, or just to put some pressure on me.

MAY 26   Jennifer has finished. Before she rejoins me here, some darkroom work at the apartment, she says. That means Larry. It is disgusting, the secret pleasure I take from their rendezvous. If they knew, they would be humiliated, crushed. On the other hand, doesn't a good portion of their pleasure come from the need of stealth, and doesn't that need arise from their connection with me? So it works both ways, doesn't it? If not for me, I bet they would have tired of each other long ago.

Supposing I were to tell him that his mother was not killed in a crash, but committed suicide shortly after giving birth to him. Just that, nothing more. Wouldn't that be a kind of binder, a token of my willingness to tell him what Mr. Fox never told him, to hurt him, if need be, in order to show him that I am willing to give him what he came here for? I have the letter, so I can prove it if he chooses not to believe.

Then I can destroy the letter, which I couldn't bring myself to do thirty years ago, and instead kept hidden like one of those delayed-action bombs his little group must be toying with. One less bit of melodrama in my life. But I mustn't be rash. If he accepts the tragic news about Louise, won't he want to know why she destroyed herself? Will he accept my telling him that it was simply melancholia? He is shrewd and brilliant, but enough of a romantic to accept that, even to be seduced by it. Isn't early suicide in fashion in certain quarters? A new and darker image of his ill-fated mother.

I used to think that I was undeservedly lucky in having my only son die without learning the full scope of my betrayal. That I was promiscuous, he knew, all through his adolescence; I could only hope that he understood and forgave. Certainly his last letters were friendly, if not bursting with filial affection.

Now my luck has run out. Maybe everyone's does, if he lives long enough. The sun comes out, and the snowman melts into a dirty puddle. Think what would have happened to Lincoln, Roosevelt, probably even Kennedy if they had lived on. Debunked and revealed—certainly to themselves, most likely to the world.

For a while, I think up until this very spring, I kidded myself along with the help of my entourage. (Seth's word.) Now even my dreams fail me, and if I live on I may live to see them all fighting—not politely, like civilized people, as they are now, but like maddened dogs—over my miserable remains.

MAY 27   Gabriel Gibbons and Rog have set a date for early June. Dick Wells is to come back with the crew (I don't mind them, in fact I wish I could just sit and talk with them), and we will stroll about, doing the muckrake period, my antiwar agitation, my imprisonment, and the great years thereafter with the Sophia School.

It all sounds so easy. Even Rog the cynic is almost enthused about the thing.

"When Gibbons said summer," I said, "I thought he meant July or August. Why did you agree to next week?"

"They're eager," he said. "The schedule is a bit more advanced than you may have understood. By September, or early October, they'd like to come back and do the autumn

77

sequence. Then Gibbons hopes we'll be ready for the final shooting over the Christmas holidays. At the apartment, if we're there."

"Or anywhere," I said. I was beginning to get the feeling that if they wanted to rush it a little it was because they'd been consulting Dr. Harrison, or the handiest life-expectancy chart. "I'm not superstitious," I reminded Rog, "but I refuse to make plans that far ahead. I'm not a goddam orchestra conductor."

"I made that clear. But I couldn't stall them on next week. They are in touch with Brodie in Washington, they know you're expecting Mrs. Lumen back from Bermuda in a day or two, and Gibbons has to commit Dick Wells elsewhere during the summer months. Also to give him his contractual vacation time."

Whenever you complain that you're being imposed upon, it turns out that you're making things difficult for someone else. Never fails. Doubtless they think they're doing me a favor, giving me the chance to rattle on about the good old days. And brag a little, in the bargain.

This is evidently what Rog has in mind. "I do feel—" whenever Rog begins with that phrase, I know he's going to be in there punching (fortunately he's too clever to use the expression with anyone but me). "I do feel," he said, "that we should take maximum advantage of this opportunity. Mr. Wells wants to devote most of the time to your early career as a crusading journalist—"

I reminded him that I hate that expression.

He smiled politely. "—and to the founding of the Sophia School and those years of educational pioneering."

"I hate that too," I told him. "Why don't you leave that kind of talk to Larry? Wells is going to try to draw me out about Luba and Sophia. My private life. I know what those people want. Sensation. Revelations. Confessions."

"Wells has promised," Rog said, "that this session will be even more open-ended than the first. You'll have ample opportunity to talk objectively, historically—and to draw parallels for the new generation."

Which is what Rog wants me to do. I'm willing. But he can't possibly know how once you put the soup on the stove it stirs up the old memories, not the best, but the worst of them. They all think it's the strain of seeing people, the cameras, the wires, all that nonsense. They haven't got the imagination to understand how painful it is to dredge up the dead, and the incidents that are better buried—and that could with luck stay buried, if it weren't for people like Dick Wells. And Seth.

Even dear Jenny can't possibly understand. How could she? Not only hasn't she lived long enough to suffer in this rich protective country, she hasn't had the opportunity to do things that one day she'll hate herself for. . . .

MAY 28 Dinner with the Honigs last night. Lily knows I can't take crowds, not at the end of the day. Walter came and got me, and then brought me back. It was very pleasant, the three of us in their kitchen. I can understand their not wanting to entertain Rog Girard, and Lily was diplomatic enough to invite me when she knew Rog had to go off to New York.

Lily really fussed over me. I had admired her garden extravagantly before dinner, but no, she said it wasn't that, it was for Jenny's sake: She wanted me to be in a good mood when Jenny comes back. They really do love Jenny. Even from the beginning, when I told them I intended to marry her, they were kind. They didn't roll their eyes or warn me, much less did they call me an old fool. They simply took her into their lives—inevitably like a daughter or a grand-daughter, but nevertheless like an equal.

Only when Walter brought out the port (he knows I prefer his Remy Martin, but he refuses to serve it, he doesn't want responsibility for my spending a sleepless night, over-

79

stimulated) did he reveal that he's been on the phone to Larry. Or vice versa. It seems the White House wants to make arrangements for a brief meeting of me with the President. Gibbons and crew will be there to televise it, for tape, like these other segments, to be integrated into the portrait of me when they get around to editing it. I had the feeling they want to speed this up so the President can shake my hand before I'm dead, but Walter laughed and said, No, both the White House and the producer want to be sure they have this, just in case there's delay in construction work on the Children's Center and they can't get a formal segment of me and Number One clasping hands in front of the new building. With luck they'll have both, but for sure they want this. It sounds reasonable.

Why didn't they go through Rog? I didn't have to ask. Walter comes in very handy to Larry as a way of getting to me without having to involve Rog. Walter volunteered that there are a few legal problems in connection with this televised meeting with the President. "Which you'll take care of for me," I said. Walter nodded casually.

He was just as casual when he asked after Seth. Lily put in, "You know I would have invited him too, Sam, I'd have been delighted, but Walter felt—"

Of course Walter felt. He could hardly have brought up the White House thing with Seth there, could he? And, as he pointed out with as much tact as Lily, "I gather the two of you have been more or less feeling your way."

I said that was a fair description of the situation. One of these days, I said, he'd be leaving; and I wasn't sure if he'd be back or would be in touch thereafter, any more than I was sure whether I had any claim on him, or ought to pursue it. "I'm trying to leave it up to him," I told them, "whether or not he wants to have me as a relation."

Lily looked at me incredulously.

"I should think he'd be thrilled." A childless woman. I can remember when I used to feel sorry for her! having to

80

make do with occasional visits and Christmas cards from two nieces and their children. "I don't mean because you're you, but just to discover that you're not alone in the world, that . . ."

"He doesn't feel that he's been alone, I take it." Lily is always honest with me; I had to add, "I really don't think he's thrilled. For a while I think he was fascinated, but now he's thrown it back to me: Do I want him for a relation?"

Walter was the only living person (Lily too, no doubt) who knew of the checks he'd mailed off to Mr. Fox every month for twenty-one years; I'd already told him what Fox had done with them, and he'd shrugged and said, "They didn't go to waste, did they?" Now he said, "You don't mean he's giving you the option of pretending he doesn't exist?"

"Well, yes, I suppose he is," I said. I wasn't eager to explain that he was giving me conditions, but Walter is not dumb, and when he came back with exactly that, I couldn't in good conscience deny it.

"Walter," I said, "I'm getting pretty tired," and at once Lily began to fuss at him to take me home.

Walter was his usual polite self, helped me into the car after I'd kissed Lily good night, but as we were crawling along the mile of road that separates their house from mine, he went right back to the matter as if we'd never stopped talking about it. "Sam," he said directly, "what does he want?"

"You can guess," I said. "He wants me to accept him. All of him."

"Not his politics? That would be a little ridiculous, wouldn't it?"

Right away I knew two things: that this was what the whole evening was all about, even though I was practically home and in bed, and that Walter knew something and was uneasy. Which meant probably that Larry was, too. As if I'm not!

"Listen, Walter," I said, "are you trying to pass along a little message?"

He laughed, but didn't answer directly. Not that he had to—the laugh said it all.

MAY 29   Seth came in yesterday to say goodbye. Apologetic for disturbing me, almost deferential; yet at the same time arrogant. All qualities that I recognize terribly well—he comes by them honestly. I couldn't believe that he was going to take himself out of my life as abruptly as he had come back into it.

"I feel that I should bow out at this point," he said. "Your wife is coming back, and you have to do that TV interview."

"And you?" I asked him. "What about you?"

"I have things to do too."

I felt the most terrible arthritic pains in my elbow. I sat there rubbing it with my fingers. Finally I told him that I didn't think his going away would "solve anything for either of us." I said that from now on he would never be far from my conscious thoughts, no matter where he went. It was ridiculously inadequate, but at the moment it was the best I could do.

His smile was so sad that as I sat there clutching my elbow I almost felt that he was feeling sorry for me. And maybe he was. He said, "I've come to the decision that if I stayed on any longer it might be misinterpreted."

"By whom?"

"I don't give a damn about anyone else." He waved all that away with his hand. "I meant you. I don't want you thinking that I'm pressuring you to take some kind of stand."

"Your friends were pressuring me. They still are."

"They have that responsibility," he said in a tone that left me uncertain as to whether he was dissociating himself from them. Then he added, "They haven't been here these last few weeks. I have. You're tired, you're full of aches and pains. Maybe you're entitled to pick up the medals and go out with a flourish of trumpets. And if I stick around, as a kind of reproachful presence . . ."

I let go of my elbow. I said, "I don't feel guilty about you." I wasn't lying. I don't.

He said cruelly, "You sure as hell feel guilty about *something.*"

"Who doesn't? Don't you?" But as soon as I'd said that, I regretted it, just as I regretted rubbing my elbow. "If you want to know, I feel guilty about Philip. And Louise."

Having gone that far at last, I was trembling. And almost terrified that he would ask why. What would I do then?

But he didn't. The arrogance came out again. "They say all parents do. I wouldn't know. All I know is, I haven't got anything to feel guilty about as a son, do I? Anyway, those things can be taken care of."

His sudden crudity was preposterous. "What are you talking about?" I demanded. "Psychoanalysis? Sensitivity sessions? I don't believe in mental health. There are just degrees of mental illness."

"And talking about problems doesn't help." He had his head bent to one side and was stroking his curly beard as if it was hard to cope with the enormity of my statement.

"Help?" I found myself imitating his intonation, mocking his use of the word. "Help? Some things help, some don't. I simply don't believe in cures. I don't believe that guilt for cruel behavior, or whatever, goes away simply because you've dragged it out and talked about it."

"Well," he said, "if you don't handle it in one way you handle it in another, right? I mean, look at all the stained-glass windows, or in our day the graduate-studies centers, named after their dead parents by guilty children with enough dough to buy absolution. You yourself did it in reverse, way back when you named the Sophia School for your first child, didn't you?"

I was on the verge of calling him a son of a bitch. But for

what, for saying the truth? I said carefully, "I suppose every parent who survives his own child has to feel a certain guilt, regardless of the circumstances. All survivors do."

"And if you can alleviate it by immortalizing the child, why not? I don't think there was anything wrong in your naming the School for that little girl."

"Thanks," I said.

He smiled and got to his feet. "Just because I'm leaving doesn't mean I'm withdrawing my offer. I guess there's still a little time left if you want to make one grand gesture, the way you did with the Sophia School. Not much, though."

"Not much what?"

"Time." He took my hand and said, "Girard will know where to reach me."

MAY 30   Jennifer back. Strange, now that I can no longer desire her (although I continue to get enormous pleasure from contemplating her, thinking about her even), she is as much like my own child as she is my wife. I find myself worrying about her in that way, taking that kind of pride in her looks and her accomplishments. And despairing, as if she were my child, of her ever understanding me. A lot of this has to be my fault. After ten years of marriage I still haven't told her a fraction of what I know and remember (and wish to forget) about my earlier life. And she comes up sporadically—like Seth—with that voracious hunger for news of the past. What was it like? Was it exciting, thrilling, awful?

I made her unpack and wash her hair before we sat down to tea together. But then, relaxed, practically the first thing she asked about was Seth. Was I upset, she wanted to know.

I was no more upset by his going away than I had been by his turning up. "Everything is painful," I said, and added with little hope of being understood, "but at this point dreams and memories are more painful than realities."

"Poor dear," she said. "I don't want you to be upset. It's just not good for your blood pressure. Dr. Harrison—"

84

"Fuck Dr. Harrison," I said with a certain satisfaction. "He's immersed in reality, like a pig in clover. What catches me up these days is the way reality has of evoking things that are only real in my head. Things that would be nothing more than dust if they weren't stirred up."

But I just don't believe Jennifer had lived long enough to comprehend that. She's sensitive, she's clever, in fact I think she's brilliant, but you can't expect her to see into what perhaps only an artist could, say a Rembrandt or a Rodin. I suspect she senses that—it could be that that's why she's shifted from taking pictures of people (including old people, like me or Walter) to photographing marine and animal life, which she does wonderfully well.

She said, almost wistfully, "I remember you used to say that one of the pleasures of growing old was the increasing sharpness with which you could recall those you loved a long time ago."

"Sometimes sharpness can prick you," I told her. It was sententious, I know, but I wasn't quite sure how else to explain that I desire the sweetness of memory without the sourness of guilt. An impossible desire. I see now that it is all too like my desire to remain in the swim without paying the price of being nipped at by the other fish. To say nothing of all that tempting bait dangled before my greedy eyes.

"You can't have it both ways," I mumbled, half to myself. "I got away with it for a long, long time, but now it's beginning to catch up with me."

Jennifer stared at me, alarmed. I really think for a moment she was frightened that I was losing my marbles. I'm trying to remember if I used to worry that all of a sudden, before my eyes, an old person would turn childish, or at any rate unreasonably irascible. Don't think so. My father was old— at least for me he was—but I worried about other things with him; and he was dead almost before I had the chance to observe him carefully.

"I'd like to have Seth here," I explained, "a family member. But you can't just *acquire* a person. You have to cope with the baggage he brings with him. The memories he awakens in you of others, the convictions he is entitled to even if they are not yours."

Jennifer put her hand on my arm. "I can't believe you didn't accept him in that way. I know you too well." She chuckled in that self-confident way that has never ceased to delight me—it makes me think of so many kids, so many of my students, when they had done something they were pleased with, solving a problem or playing a sonata well. "After all," she pointed out, "I walked in that door once myself. And I *know* how you accepted me."

"Very different," I said. "You accepted my advances"—I love that word—"partly because it was the most outrageous thing you could think of to do to your parents."

"I fell in love," she protested. But she blushed as she said it. Everything about our early meetings rushed back to her as it did to me—not just the sex, the crazy business of the old man and the young girl, but the earnest talking thereafter. She had proposed more than marriage, she had threatened to move in without marriage, and she had sworn never to ask for money, or children, or anything more than the pleasure of my company. And I had thought to myself, After I'm gone they'll forgive me. How was I to know that I'd outlast her parents?

It is fantastic not just that she kept her promises—I felt that she would, I prided myself as much as Walter or anyone on my ability to judge character—but that it worked out so marvelously for us both. And yet sometimes—now, for example—I feel that the worst thing I could have done to her was to accede to her wishes. She isn't even aware of it, she'd swear that she's happy, that she's fulfilled herself, that she's never for a moment missed the children she forswore.

I know by heart the whole litany of the liberated woman, including the one who swears that she has not felt the need of offspring. And God knows how many unhappy mothers I've commiserated with, yes, and slept with too, battening on their unhappiness. But I still feel today, rotten and destructive parent that I would have been myself, that there is something *different* about people who have never had a baby, never raised a child. Jennifer is proud of having been my confidante for almost ten years; but how could I ever tell her this? It's not a selfishness in the childless exactly, because some of them (like Jennifer herself) are exceptionally sweet and generous and thoughtful. Rather, it's an inability, like a shortcoming of the imagination, even to grasp the many-sidedness of certain problems. It's not a matter of fault, you don't say of a tone-deaf person that it's his fault that he gets nothing from music, but you can't pretend that it doesn't exist.

"Anyway," I assured her, although I don't know if she wanted to hear this either, "Seth will be back one of these days. Or his committee. You remember his committee?"

"Oh Sam," she said reproachfully, "you're not going to get involved with that. Not because of him."

"If not with that," I said, "then with something else."

I can't even tell her that I'm a swine, because she wouldn't believe me. She'd laugh indulgently and pat my arm. And if I persisted, and told her why, she just might leave me. And I couldn't bear that.

June

JUNE 2 Skipped some days. And all because of what may have been a chance remark of Jennifer's.

I was working on the screen porch with Rog, trying to pay attention to some communication from UNICEF and to the answer he'd composed for me. I was distracted not because of the loveliness of the day or the profusion of butterflies and bees whizzing in and out of Jenny's flower bed—I'd wanted to sit out on the lawn, but Rog said the mayflies were still too thick and nippy. (This was the day before yesterday, did I say? I think the flies are disappearing already.) What distracted me was the continual need to get up and shuffle over to the little john just off the porch. When I'm alone in my room it's not so bad, at least I don't have the feeling that people are watching me and keeping score.

If I had known before the operation that I would be stuck with this degrading business, I really don't think I would ever have let Jenny talk me into it. I would never have allowed Harrison and his crew of butchers to take the prostate. I think I would have decided to keep it and take the consequences. For them my precious life is all that matters, keep me alive and kicking despite everything. They don't have to undergo the daily humiliation of hanging over the bowl, waiting prayerfully to void a couple of drops as if it were a goddam holy fount you were sprinkling in order to avoid the shame of wetting your pants.

Anyway, on one of my miserable trips I all but bumped into Jenny, who was dashing around getting the house fixed up. She wasn't just making up for some weeks' absence, she was positively prettying things up for the TV boys, who are due here in a day or two. She was all over the place like a storm, bossing Mrs. Hoskins around (Mrs. H. loves it), dusting this, moving that, cutting flowers, filling vases. I said rather grumpily, "For Christ's sake, why don't you slow down a little? What are you knocking yourself out for, Dick Wells and his cameraman?"

"I want the place to look nice," she said reasonably, and then added, maybe because I had bumped into her and jolted her into a spontaneous reaction, "and besides, so do you. I know you think I'm childish, but that's the way we childless women are, isn't it? Putterers, that's all. Fussy housemaids. So you just let me fuss."

She laughed, to take the curse off it, and went on about her business, leaving me standing there outside the john, shocked. Absolutely shocked.

I am still trying to settle in my mind whether it was one of those casual remarks that you have to guard against over-interpreting, or whether our collision had jarred her into revealing a resentment that could only have come from reading this diary. She hasn't been back all that long, but already she's been through the house like a whirlwind. Nothing is impossible.

Which is what I thought to myself about Rog Girard. He is so quiet and contained, he could have memorized what I've written down here and never revealed anything about it. And he's had more opportunity to be in here than anyone else—and at least as much reason to want to know what I'm writing as anyone. Except maybe Larry—and he must surely have told Jenny how anxious he is about me and my tendency to go off half-cocked.

Maybe, though, suspiciousness is simply leaking out of me like urine? It's supposed to be a sign that things are letting go, like those first telltale spots on the tie. I swear to myself that I'll fight against it. But then that little voice whispers, Suppose there's warrant for it? Who's the sucker then? Can you go on playing the innocent while they all wheel and deal, swooping around you like vultures? Look at Seth. Why did he stick around here so long? To find things out, you can't blame him for that. By the same token, he had as much reason as anyone to find out what I tell myself in these pages, things maybe that I wouldn't tell him. And he had as much opportunity as anyone. Who the hell knew where he was all those weeks when Mrs. Hoskins was off, and I was down at Walter and Lily's, or wandering in the meadow, or out for a ride?

I begin to get a crazy feeling, maybe everyone has read this, when I sit here thinking that no one has. Maybe they all know things I can hardly bear to admit to myself alone. Maybe I ought to go all the way, put down everything here, including the fact that I know they're all reading it. You're all reading it, all right, here are some things that will curl your hair!

No. That's paranoia. It's terrible to give way to what people are watching for in you, maybe waiting for, with mixed hope and dread.

JUNE 3   They'll be here any time, Wells and his crew. I heard Jenny on the phone with Gabriel Gibbons yesterday, settling last-minute details, while I was writing down that last entry which I really should scratch out. Either I'm going to use this thing like a toilet or I'm not. And if not, then I stop right here. Period.

But I don't wish to stop. Quite the contrary, I feel a desperate need for it this minute, now, to save me from saying things I should not reveal to Wells and his machines. I said to Rog, Please, let me rest and compose myself for an hour or so before those fellows come.

All right, I'm composing. Myself. The windows are up, the sunlight streams in through the maple leaves and the metal screens, and I can hear faint sounds—a tractor clambering up the south slope, those kenneled beagles yipping up the road, an occasional station wagon that fortunately doesn't slow down or turn into our drive, bearing cameras, cables, microphones, truth serum. Not yet. . . .

What I want to do: Anticipate Wells's personal questions.

Answer them here, now, so that when he does open his mouth I will be poised, calm, reflective. Impersonal.

Listen: I can be honest about the public questions. I can knock him dead with the truth. I'll tell him that when I left Williams in 1907 it was with great reluctance, not with eagerness. That I was terrified of having to support my widowed mother instead of vice versa. That I was job-hunting after the Crash and fell into the journalistic business of muckraking the exploitation of children because a relative of my mother's gave me a note of introduction to Norman Hapgood at *Collier's*, not because I had ever given the matter any serious thought. That I quickly discovered two things: I had a marketable talent for a racy and rather shrill prose, and I would have to become a specialist in order to survive once muckraking had faded away.

Just what he'll want. The real Lumen. Salty, self-deprecatory, gruff exterior to hide that golden heart. Sir, you're trying to put yourself down. You were more than an opportunist as a young man, you gained a national reputation as an authority on child welfare even before World War One.

That's where I can do the radical thing, make Girard happy, show the kids that I am not just honest but idealistic too. And it's only the truth, that as I wrote up those things I became personally involved, felt a stake in them—Dewey and Jane Addams and Ella Flagg Young in Chicago, the first White House Conference on Child Welfare in 1909, the first Children's Code Commission, in Ohio (1911, wasn't it?), the first law authorizing assistance to needy mothers, in Missouri. And the establishment of the Children's Bureau in Washington. And the Supreme Court knocking down all those new laws, one after the other. How all that radicalized me once and for all. How whenever I feel myself getting stuffy and impatient with the young, I think of how those self-satisfied, self-righteous old men tried to bar the way to the most elementary protection for the most helpless element of our population, the children.

Yes, how one thing led to another and I found myself walking the picket line of the great textile strike of 1912 in Lawrence, Massachusetts, next to Luba Lefkowitz, the woman who finally opened my eyes and freed me forever from my lingering ties to my father's class.

She bore your child. That's right. The little girl after whom you named your famous school. That's right. And then you were divorced, after your return from prison in 1919 for opposing the war. That's right. *But I will not tell him any more.*

Once, I tried with Jenny, and she stared at me so blankly, so uncomprehendingly, that I had to turn away. The surface stuff she could get, I could see from the shine in her eyes that she even found it romantic. The big, hulking, tousle-haired young journalist-agitator, sexually unawakened save for a few furtive encounters, mourning the mother who had worn herself out trying to see him through college and out into the world. And the tiny Russian Jewess, a daughter of the working class, four years older than he and a million years older in knowledge of the world, a sewing machine operator in a firetrap loft but a free woman, drenched in Shaw, Strindberg, Maeterlinck, as well as Marx, Kautsky, Babel.

"She was opposed to the institution of marriage," I told Jenny, who stared at me, big-eyed, trying to understand that there had been girl rebels before the 1960s and 1970s.

"But she married you."

"Only after she became pregnant. Only after I went to her comrades and pleaded with them to intercede, not just for me but for the baby."

But when I tried to go on from there, to explain to Jenny how I had not only failed Luba, but betrayed her, I could see that she refused to accept it, like a child who compresses her lips and shakes her head firmly at a new dish, knowing without sampling it that she won't like it.

And maybe it was just as well, because if Jennifer had been able to come to terms with my intellectual arrogance, my wild pride that I thought to be based on "logic" and "scientific socialism," then I would have had to go on and re-create that scene which I have never had the courage to describe to another living person. But when I explained to her that it was Luba who had opened my eyes to imperialism, Luba who had brought me to the antiwar elements in the Socialist Party, she could not see, she simply could not understand, why Luba should not have been proud and pleased when I was arrested for sedition and sentenced to prison for opposing the war.

"In a way Luba was proud," I said, "in a way she was pleased. If I had been only a friend, a former lover, that would have sufficed. But she had my child, an asthmatic baby, and she had bad lungs herself. She was in no position to afford my pacifist posturing."

Jennifer protested. "How can you call it posturing? You stood up for your principles. And they weren't just yours, they were hers. You said yourself, she was responsible for your beliefs."

"And I was responsible for her and the baby. Or should have been. She counted on me, she needed me more than the peace movement needed a martyr." I could see that I wasn't getting through. I added, "Besides, I was a damn poor martyr, throughout all that ridiculous, long-drawn-out trial. By the time I went off to jail, hardly anyone was paying any attention."

"But jail!" she cried, as though the word represented some unheard-of horror. "My God! That took courage."

"Less than it would have taken for me to forsake my socialist principles and live up to my personal commitment." I looked at her stubborn countenance, which I could see was stubborn not just because she wished to stand by something her husband had done long before she was born, but because she is of that generation reared to worship at the churches of logic and rationalism. "There are time when logic isn't enough, when your heart should speak," I said, and let it go at that, not without a certain relief.

Relief, because I was freed of the need to describe what happened not to my body but to my heart during those tedious months of incarceration. I thought of myself not (as one might think) as abandoned, or betrayed into stupid confinement by my wildly idealistic wife. No, I could not relate myself to her in that way; after all, she had replaced my mother, to put it crudely. Quite simply, I thought of myself as a damned fool—and I was desperately eager to get back to Luba. And to Sophia, that exquisite, delicate child.

Getting off the train after commutation of the sentence, I was confused, excited. Simultaneously elated and depressed, I recall, by the heedless hurrying crowds at Grand Central. Hard to describe; maybe only someone who has been locked up could understand and explain. They bumped into me and charged off without apologizing or looking back. Was this what I'd been sitting in the cell for? I hadn't expected a band or a welcoming committee, but someone from among those who had followed the trial might have been at the prison, or here, to ease the way a little.

I hastened to the subway, falling into lockstep with the crowd just as I had done in prison. I was beginning to be frightened, sat uneasily on the edge of the wicker bench until the train approached my stop. I was at the door and out as soon as the conductor pressed the button. Then awkwardly up the stairs to the open air, my valise bumping against me, hastily stuffed with one change of clothing, the books I had been reading, the articles I had been writing, and half-running the two short blocks to our apartment.

I think I knew at once. The three dark rooms reeked, stank, of emptiness. From Luba's letters I had half-expected to find that Sophia was not in the apartment but in the hospital on Second Avenue; but where was her crib? The empty corner gaped at me like a giant wound, a hole torn in my heart.

"Where is she?" I howled. "Where is she?"

Then at last, peering like some wary beast into the darkness, I saw Luba crouched in the closet among overturned valises of children's clothing, crayon drawings on coarse yellow paper like that I had pasted on the wall of my cell (a smiling circle above four sticks for arms and legs, entitled MY DADY), a tin bathtub boat with a wind-up key sticking out of its yellow stern, a Raggedy Ann doll with a torn dangling arm flung across its orange-spotted cheeks.

"Dead, you miserable bastard! You poor miserable bastard!" Luba's achingly familiar voice emerged in a thin high wail. "Dead! Dead!"

That's what I won't tell them. Let them figure it out for themselves.

And they're here, I can hear all the polite noises out there. Soon they'll be tapping at the door, or sending Jennifer to ask sweetly if I'd come out and go into my act. I really don't see how I can go on.

JUNE 7 The afterglow persists. When I think of what might have been—nagging questions about Luba, prying questions about the financing of the Sophia School or the years with Hester or the other women—I am so relieved! It was almost a party afterward, I drank more than I should have, I teased Wells about his reputation for ruthless interviewing, he teased me about my subtlety in disarming him with my ruthless honesty. "You made me feel that I would be a rat," he said, "if I let you get away with all that self-deprecation."

"There's no question," Gabriel Gibbons said, reaching up to his ear with his index fingers to twist a coil of hair in what I can see now is a tic, something left over from when he was a little boy, twitching unhappily at his classroom desk, "you gave one of the greatest performances I have ever seen."

That made me uncomfortable for a moment, but de Santis and Freedman were laughing too and praising me, and even Rog was relaxing with them, pleased that I had come on strong—without interruption from Dick Wells—for freedom for the young and power to the young too, relating the struggle of then to the battles of now.

And Dick Wells said comfortably, grinning, "Yes, you know, you put me in a position where I felt I had the responsibility of reminding our viewers that you weren't at all what you said."

"You just said I didn't lie," I said

"I said you were self-deprecating. You kept explaining, when you spoke of your early days as a muckraking journalist, and your imprisonment, and your founding of the Sophia School, and your visits to Russia and discussions with Lunacharsky, that you're just like everyone else, only worse."

"But that's what I believe!" I insisted.

"And I believe," Wells said, "that you're just like everyone else, only better. That's what makes you so important to the new young people as they grow up. You have their common humanity, and at the same time you inspire them with a sense of what they could be."

"That's very beautiful," Jennifer cried. "You mustn't protest, Sam, there's simply no getting around what he says. And I'm so glad he responded to you in that way during the televising. It had to be said."

For a second I had the uneasy feeling that if it did, I had forced Wells to say it. But although he was saying something to that effect, I really don't think he was bright enough to understand fully its implications. If he did he wouldn't defer to me so; and I don't think he's being deferential just in order to do a couple more interviews with me later in the year. I've sold him a bill of goods, apparently, as I have Gabriel Gibbons and all the rest. And Rog, even Rog, was pouring booze for the boys and positively glowing over Wells's tribute to me; it went the way he wanted it to, and if he's going to be unhappy about the presidential thing, we'll take that as it comes.

But listen, meanwhile I did feel I had to explain some more. I always feel that—does it arise from guilt, or from the simple human desire to be understood? Anyway, I persisted. "You see," I told them, "I just can't get used to being old. It's a condition that I was unprepared for. Still am. And that teaches you humility. I do think I used to be more vain when I was younger. Now I keep wondering why people speak to me with such respect when I'm only a little boy like the ones I used to worry over, and write about, and defend, and teach. You look at me and don't see me, a mere child. What I once was, and thought I had stopped being so long ago, is really what I have remained!"

A kind silence then. I don't think they understood.

Just the same, a quite joyous evening. Gibbons and Wells stayed over (slept over was the way the kids used to put it), and the next morning we had a delightful leisurely breakfast together out on the porch. I felt good, strong and free of the damned arthritic pains, and took Wells for a little walk in Jennifer's garden. De Santis photographed us as we went, but I didn't mind.

JUNE 8   Came in yesterday from a walk, was going to do some work but didn't want to disturb Jennifer, who has been in and out of her darkroom. On a hunch, just meandering, did something I haven't done in a long time. Picked up Jenny's guest book that she keeps on the dry sink in the front hall, put on my glasses, started to read. I have a feeling that I was looking to see what if anything the TV boys had written on this occasion. There they were, all right, the most recent entries.

"This is not an assignment," Dick Wells wrote, "but a privilege."

Gabriel Gibbons, the hair-twirler: "I look forward to this second visit with even more keen anticipation than the first." Or words to that effect, as if he couldn't compose an honest sentence without the help of an intelligent secretary. He certainly looks and talks more sympathetically than this. Well I remember telling Jenny, when she first put the book in the hall and asked Rog to have visitors write in it, "There are some people who are going to be embarrassed and confused by this. It's like asking them to pose for a picture." And she laughed and said, "Maybe that's why I want it. I think strangers who are prepared to take up your precious time ought to have to pay some kind of dues before they enter our club." "To see the pin-headed boy, right?" But she just laughed harder at that, and rubbed my head.

Underneath those fellows, the cameraman, de Santis, had scrawled (almost illegibly), "I don't feel like I'm working here. I feel at home. Marvelous." And Freedman: "God bless Mr. Lumen." Doesn't hurt to have a blessing, I suppose, if you don't take it seriously.

Then, leafing back, comments from young people. At least I would think they must have been written by young people, who don't use phrases like "looking forward with keen anticipation." One fellow was defiant, big block letters: "NOBODY KNOWS THE WHOLE TRUTH, NOT EVEN SAM LUMEN." What's so bold about that? Anyone would agree, from Larry's boss, the President, down to . . . me. And a girlish handwriting, tilted backwards in a way I didn't think young women affected any more—coy, bending away from carnal contact: "I meditated for a long time before gaining the courage to come here."

Rubbish, meaningless stuff. It made me tired. Keepsakes for Jenny after I am gone. I was about to slam her book closed when my eye lit on a late April entry—I have a suspicion it's what I was looking for in the first place. It said simply, "I am here. Seth Fox."

So I went back to my room and lay down to think about that, and first thing I knew I was asleep. I was a student again (how often one dreams that, all the way into old age—maybe if young people were made aware of this early in life, they wouldn't try so hard to become ex-students??). Seated in the very middle of a large classroom, doing a writing exercise.

Our teacher was called Miss Boatwright. I looked up, sure enough, it was Hester. I wasn't startled, just mildly surprised, the way you are in a dream when you meet someone you had thought to be long since dead. So that's what she's up to, I thought, and bent to my task, which was to write a composition on the theme "My Dreams for the Future."

I don't know what I wrote, but I was pleased with myself and full of anticipation when Hester called "Time's up!" and we passed our papers forward for her inspection. She sat at her desk, marking the papers and looking exactly as she had before our marriage, when we first met, at the protest meeting for Sacco and Vanzetti: very lean and aristocratic, like a fine mare, silky hair drawn back into a bun and throwing into relief the large pale forehead, high-ridged nose that ended in flaring nostrils, and extraordinarily long, curving neck. The throat where that pulse beat so rapidly. The eyes that were, when she looked up and stared through you as though she were transfixed by something remarkable just behind you, so blue, so protuberant, so coldly passionate that later I was to marvel at how I had been unable to see the madness in them at our first meeting.

"Samuel Lumen," she called out in that high, clear, every-syllable-enunciated voice, so high and so clear that it was pitched just this side of hysteria, "step forward."

I came to her side, breathing in the familiar hyacinth toilet water, thinking to myself that I would never be able to erase from my mind the echo of that voice, frightening in its wild intensity. With sick fascination I watched her long white index finger stabbing at my composition.

"Look at your *i*'s," she commanded, "look at your *o*'s. Do you see how old-fashioned they are? How out of date? And you take pride in this? You are a pretentious underachiever."

These last words were so preposterous that I was tempted to laugh. But as she raised her eyes to mine, they glared at me with such desolation that I was struck dumb with shame and terror.

I awoke trembling. Sweating. All the satisfaction of these last few days suddenly wiped out. I can account for Hester's turning up in the dream, and indeed dominating it; after all, I did talk about her, our marriage, our son Philip, her help with the Sophia School, her illness, with Dick Wells. And I think I can even explain to myself that business about my *i*'s and my *o*'s (*i*'s and *me*'s? *ohs* and *ahs*? *p*'s and *q*'s?). What baffles me is the terrible depression into which the dream has plunged me.

Why should this be? I can see that it should upset me, bother me for a minute to admit to myself, say, that I am dated, out of it. But why the terrible depression, persistent and so overwhelming? I must think about it. Maybe in thinking I can overcome it.

JUNE 9   I think it's this. I think the dream, or my extreme reaction to it, is telling me that I can't get away with the stories I told Dick Wells for the interview. I mean that even though no one else may complain, no one else may say, "You're falsifying, you're leaving things out," I know it, and my conscience will plague me.

There's something silly about that at this late date, like kicking yourself forty years later for not laying a girl who had more or less indicated her availability. What's done is done, what's not done it's too late to do anything about. Or is it? If I went into detail about the Sophia School and all the rest—not with Wells, that would be impossible, but with someone else, with Jenny, or even with Seth—would that relieve me of this immensely heavy burden? I don't know. Even here, alone with this notebook, I hesitate.

Jenny is the only person I've ever told how I suffered at the hands of Hester. That's a metaphor of course; it wasn't her hands that caused the pain, although I think they were the first thing I noticed about her. In contrast to the stubby fingers of my poor Luba, scarred by a hundred needle pricks,

Hester's were the hands of a lady, pale, tapering, unblemished by the battle for existence, which she had not had to wage with her bare hands. They fascinated me, it's true, lying in her lap at the Sacco–Vanzetti protest meeting, so contained, not clenched and battering like Luba's (that was only to come later).

Jenny was unsympathetic with my dreadful loneliness after Luba left, and with my being attracted to someone as different as Hester Boatwright. Even with my stupidity in not seeing just how different she was, in not suspecting, despite her alternating moods of wild gaiety and black despair, that she was psychotic. And J. understood perfectly, that was her word, "perfectly," how I had been forced to turn to other women after Philip's birth, when it became clear that our married life would not be a life.

But that was all part of my pitch to get J. into my lonely old bed. How she pitied me, the vigorous innovator at the peak of his powers, condemned out of gratitude to go on living with the sick, mad creature who had given him a son and a school, named for the dead daughter of the former wife.

There was one little thing J. didn't know (she could have tried to worm it out of Walter Honig, except that he doesn't know quite all of it, and besides would be too gentlemanly to reveal a confidence). That is: my deal with the Boatwrights to sell myself and my little boy down the river.

I shouldn't have been surprised. No doubt they'd always thought of me as little more than a radical jailbird, with a consumptive expatriate for a father and a foreigner for a mother. Not only were they unmoved by my growing reputation, they undoubtedly thought it bad form to be too well known—and they made damn good and sure that Hester was not going to sink the family funds into my experimental school.

They couldn't suppress her enthusiasm for the idea, or her use of her own funds to buy the old farm buildings in New Jersey and hire our first faculty, just as they couldn't stop her from marrying me. In fact I doubt that they even wanted to do that, because they knew far better than I how barren the years after her graduation from Radcliffe had been for her, and how close she was to being an eccentric spinster when I turned up. But they were damned if they were going to let me get my hands on her inheritance. Or put her away.

When Henry Boatwright summoned me to his Boston office, it was not long after the Crash and I was desperate, both for the future of the School and for the future of my son and myself. Henry knew it; there wasn't much that man didn't know, although he had less understanding of human beings and their aspirations than a newt or a salamander.

It was like something out of Dickens, or maybe Howells. Taking the tiny, trembling wire-screen elevator up to his third-floor Park Street office. Being ushered into his presence by an obsequious old retainer with sleeve guards and a green eyeshade, who backed out of the mahogany-paneled office as if retreating from the royal presence.

Henry had his sister's pallid complexion and protruding eyes. His hands too were like hers, narrow and tapering. I remember how they lay on his desk blotter, his fine hairless wrists extending from those white starched cuffs. He raised one hand to indicate the vacant chair before his desk; he did not offer to shake my hand.

"I see no need to go into details," I said to him, "about Hester's condition. There may have been episodes before our marriage that I was never told about, that I'm still not aware of. But her state now makes it impossible for me to raise our child properly. To say nothing of running the School. We never know when—"

Henry silenced me simply by moving his long thin head up and then down. He was agreeing with me. Also shutting me up. He raised his thin hand to adjust his spectacles, which caught the light as he turned his head sideways to me, and said in that incredibly well-bred voice, "Our family is quite aware of your problems. But we shall never allow you to have

Hester in-sti-tu-tion-alized." That last word came out as though he had just devised it to fit the situation. Every time I hear a made-up word like *finalized,* I think of Henry Boatwright telling me that Hester would not be institutionalized. The expression *put away* would never have passed those thin pursed lips; and of course in retrospect, you understand, what's funny is that no doubt he thought he was the moral one, dealing the best way he could with an irresponsible reprobate.

I told him that it was up to me to determine that, and my legal responsibility when it came to signing commitment papers. But he had anticipated all that, and he barely took the trouble to smile. "We see no need for that kind of extreme action," he said to me, "not when there are resources to handle the situation. Hester is entitled to round-the-clock care, of at least comparable quality to that which she would receive in a . . . nursing home. Your child is entitled to a governess in the event that his mother is distracted, or incapable of looking after him properly. And you, sir," he concluded dryly, "as a loyal husband, faithful to his marriage vows, are entitled to the economic security that would be yours if your wife remained in a position to continue underwriting your educational experiments."

All very high class. The Boatwrights agreed to cover the household and school overhead, both substantial, in return for my keeping Hester under my roof indefinitely. If I didn't agree, the School would go down the drain, and they'd start legal proceedings to take Philip from me as an unfit father. Henry was very delicate, but he indicated that he was aware of my sleeping with other women. He even indicated that I could go on living this dissolute life as long as I maintained a certain discretion—and would not commit Hester.

Dear Jennifer, I can hear you commiserating with me. I can hear you saying, But Sam, you had to do what you did. Well, it didn't seem that simple to my boy. Do you think Philip was impressed by the fact that Bercovici and Komroff, Eastman and Untermeyer, Henri and Bellows, were visitors, teachers sometimes, at the Sophia School? No more than his Uncle Henry Boatwright was. Do you think he enjoyed growing up knowing that his father was screwing his schoolmates' mothers, the visitors, anyone at all in fact who was available? I suppose I had to do that too, lay all those women, because I couldn't sleep with a madwoman and I didn't have a mistress and I was in my forties and panicked.

Never mind. I have to admit, although I have barely been able to bring myself to this point, that I subjected Philip also, over the years, to a mother who would interrupt a poetry reading to demand of the visitor, in her clear, well-bred voice, with her head flung back and her neck arched, that he admit his fraudulence—and then proceeded to drown him out with her own recital of Rossetti and Swinburne. To a mother who would turn up at a fire drill on a sunny afternoon clad in raincoat and galoshes, and insist that the children take up pick and shovel for a massive hole-digging against the imminent arrival of the Russians. To a mother who, clad in the white peignoir that I had bought her in more innocent days, would seat herself at the main-hall piano at four o'clock in the morning to play Chopin with all the power that her steely, crazed fingers could command, awakening the children with the Revolutionary Etude, fortissimo, head flung back to reveal that swanlike neck, eyes fixed on her vision beyond the ceiling, oblivious to the gaping children clustered behind her in the doorway.

I retreated from one cowardly lie to another, telling Philip that Mommy had terrible headaches, Mommy was more sensitive than other people, Mommy saw things that other people didn't, Mommy had to be left alone if she sang to herself or played the piano for six hours. Until he was old enough to understand without my having to explain that Mommy was a loony, that her freedom to roam the school grounds had something to do, somehow, with the freedom of his fellow students, and that everything painful and shameful and degrading had to do in some mysterious way with freedom.

You might even say that Philip was a lucky boy, to have

had the Second World War come along so providentially to free him from all that freedom. He was a good boy, bringing his girl out to meet me after his mother had died and it became clear that I was going to have to close the School. And he was a smart boy, to get himself killed before having to cope with my final betrayal.

Have I said enough at last? Too much. My hands are trembling, maybe from exhaustion, maybe from shame. Maybe from both.

JUNE 10 I am tempted to tear this up. At least yesterday's entry—such a collapse into hysteria. It's a wonder I didn't fall into a weeping fit, throw myself at Jennifer's feet, put my head in her lap, demand that she . . . It is possible that she reads this from day to day with a certain distant fascination, keeps it to herself, and engages in that smiling placid dissimulation so familiar to the relatives of a man unaware that he is wasting away from cancer. The very old tend to die much more slowly from malignancy, Harrison once told me, than the young; for some it is a part of the whole ageing process, keeping them company, so to speak, as they move slowly toward the grave. And malignancy of the spirit?

On the other hand what if Rog is the one? I am morally certain that someone besides me is putting his hands on this, and if it is Girard I am putting myself in his hands in more ways than one.

Half an hour ago Larry was on the phone from Washington. "Have you been minding your p's and q's?" he asked me and I was so stunned that for a moment I could not reply. I was convinced that he had read—or that Jenny had read to him—my dream of Hester rapping me across the knuckles. But it was his way of being cute.

He did not seem to expect an answer, since he went right on to tell me, much excitement in his voice, of the way the

Children's Center is shaping up. "We're knocking down the bureaucratic hurdles," he said, "kicking them aside. Ruthless! I swear to you, by next year, by the bicentennial, the dedication, we're going to have everything in there we ever wanted."

"Don't swear," I said. "You'll put the evil eye on the whole thing. Besides, if I know Washington, you'll have everything in that building except children."

"That's where you're so wrong. It'll have offices, sure, it's going to bring together a flock of disparate agencies. But the open part, the public part, is going to be like a big funhouse for kids. They'll come from all over the country—" he was getting more enthusiastic by the minute—"the world, in fact, and they'll get involved in everything from a science-and-art fair to a multimedia children's history display that they won't just look at, but participate in."

"The head swims," I said.

"You won't laugh when you see the plans. I want to come up tomorrow with Diederich and Hayes—you remember them, the architects. They're eager to show you the final floor plans."

"I met them three years ago," I assured him, "in case you think my memory is failing. We went over the preliminary sketches and models. They were pretty good."

"Pretty good!" he shouted, laughing. "Come on! You were all excited. Now it's going to be your building, we hope and pray, the Lumen Children's Center, and they want your approval of the last-minute space allocations. The hole is dug, the pilings are in, but we've still got a few months for final interior redesign."

"Well, come ahead," I said. "I never knew that you needed a special invitation."

"Maybe not, but an appointment, Master, that's what I need for these fellows and me."

I said, "You could have cleared that with Rog."

"I'd rather not." The laughter fell out of his voice. "In

fact I'd rather Girard wasn't around when I show up tomorrow. I want to talk to you alone for a few minutes before Diederich and Hayes show up."

"Now what?" As if I didn't know. His opening crack about minding my p's and q's hadn't been for nothing.

"Let's talk about it tomorrow."

"Not if it's going to be more of your old griping about Rog. I'm perfectly satisfied with him." To take the sting out, I added, "Which is more than I can say about you."

"Maybe I'm overeager," Larry said, "but I've never used your name without your okay." He hesitated for a moment and then went on, "I just can't believe, despite Seth and all that, that you're going to let yourself get mixed up with those Children of Liberty. That stuff is murder."

Despite Seth and all that. That's what he said. I let it go, I told him I'd see him tomorrow, and I hung up angry.

I still am. Not just at him. At myself, at Jenny (who serves as his eyes and ears here), yes, and at Rog. I called for Rog right away, to get his story, but he's gone out, Mrs. Hoskins says. So.

I doubt that Larry would make it up. On the other hand, I just don't believe that Rog would commit me to those people without my consent. Everyone seems to know what's going on except me. Why in hell can't I control these situations?

The thing is, Larry has always known more than almost anyone. When he and Philip were kids growing up together at the School, he must have known what was going on with me and that procession of women. In fact I sometimes had the feeling that it increased his respect for me. I never asked him, but it is possible that Philip introduced Louise to him during the war; they did keep in touch until Philip was killed, and for all I know they managed to get together once or twice before they went overseas. Who knows but that Larry managed to figure out how I kept the School alive. If he didn't know it at the time, he could have wormed part of it out of Walter; God knows they've been thick enough these last few years, making common cause together against Rog.

Well, if Larry didn't understand that before, he does now —assuming it's Jenny who's been reading this. On the other hand, if it's Rog? And if it's true about Rog and that bunch Seth is mixed up with? Now that he sits in the White House, Larry has ways of learning all sorts of things about everybody.

When I try to say to any of them that I think I am entitled to some privacy, they protest fervently. All my friends. Each one is willing to point out (always subtly, never crudely) how it is the other that is creating trouble for me by trying to make capital out of my situation. I am going to put a stop to this. I am going to bring things out into the open.

JUNE 11   Larry should be here shortly. I wanted to have Rog's denial to confront him with, but Rog has not come back. Turns out he went to Boston. Frustrating. I know he had things to do, but it's as if he deliberately absented himself so as not to have to answer my question. And when I ask him he'll say that he didn't want to be in the way—quite right, too—when Larry Brodie came to call.

Had breakfast with Jennifer. I said plainly, "Do you and Larry know something about Seth and Rog that I don't? Or that outfit, the Children of Liberty?"

Her surprise was absolutely genuine. She had no idea what I was talking about. So all I did was make her uneasy—and for no reason, because whatever is on Larry's mind, it is quite possible that this time he hasn't taken her into his confidence. L. is cagey and has room for maneuver; in other words he can use J. when he feels the need and leave her out of it when he doesn't. I am convinced that this time she is out of it.

This despite my painful awareness of the extraordinary female capacity for dissimulation. I know there are women who are transparent, and (like J.) constitutionally incapable of theatrics or trickery. I am convinced, though, that women

111

are generally better at deception than men, not because they are meaner, but perhaps for obscure reasons that have something to do with the preservation of the species. I have seen it too often not to believe it.

Think of the time when I was screwing that young woman on the black leather couch in my office. She came in full of concern about her daughter, who had been such a problem at home. She wanted me to be frank, were they doing the right thing sending her to my school, it was a terrific financial burden, her husband was working fourteen hours a day to keep his business afloat. She leaned over my desk, pleading for reassurance, giving off a little eddying wave of heated perfume, granting me a tantalizing glimpse of the valley between her breasts. I took her quivering chin in my hand and kissed her gently, reassuringly. Her mouth opened wide, as if she were parched, and in an instant she was all over me. We staggered to the couch. I had scarcely begun to fumble when she was flat on her back, legs high, sliding her panties off. She was in no mood for preliminaries. I rammed it in, crazed by the surprise of the situation and the sudden sight of that white flesh against the black leather. She reared up against me with astonishing force, as if we were long-separated lovers marvelously reunited.

Scarcely had I come, quite unable to contain myself, when I heard the door opening behind me. I was up in an instant, I have never moved so fast; and when I turned to confront the two boys at least my zipper was up and my shirt inside my trousers, even my face was contorted into calmness. But the woman had no need for contortions. Slithering like a snake, she slipped from the couch to greet the boys, her skirt sliding smoothly around her knees as she arose, her hand extended graciously.

"This is your son, isn't it, Mr. Lumen?" she said, indicating Philip coolly. "There is a resemblance. And the other boy . . ."

The other boy was you, Larry. A new boy then. Do you

remember? You would become aware of the others, I am sure, of some of them, anyway; so even if that freshly fucked female was a shade too fast for your heedless clattering entrance, there would be those who were not. That one strolled out with you for a tour of the grounds, leaving me with sweating armpits and a soaking crotch—and, as a souvenir, her panties stuffed under the cushion of my sofa.

So, if not her, then another. And if you were aware, how could you have devoted so much of your talent and energy to puffing me up? Has it really been to build a career on the sand of mine, like a city built on the ruins of its predecessor? Weren't you ever bothered by your hypocrisy? I can hear you answering: Not any more than you. Well, if I wasn't before, I am now. And besides, what kind of career can you build on a life that you know to have been false, corrupt, and rotten?

Surely you know better than Dick Wells, who said to me solemnly, while Freedman and de Santis captured us for a credulous posterity, "With all the pain and suffering of those years, with all the economic problems too, you must still look back at the Sophia School with a great sense of personal gratification." And he clutched in his hand the sheaf of testimonials from the international fraternal order of my alumni, furnished no doubt by Professor Larry Brodie of the White House—including one, I should not be surprised, from the girl (now a distinguished middle-aged lady lawyer) whose mother I had mounted in my office.

The more I think of it, and of that white marble building Larry is so eager to decorate with my name . . . it is all such a lie.

And what Rog wants of me—that I should be "true" to my old name for radicalism and libertarianism . . . isn't that just another lie?

How can you make a hero out of an opportunist, unless you yourself are an opportunist, too, willing to build another legend on a lie?

I wish Seth were here. Maybe I would be able to tell him

everything. Even if he were to run away, with his hands over his ears, maybe I could make a fresh start.

JUNE 12 Everything happened backwards yesterday. Or maybe that was the way Larry had outlined it, and I had misunderstood him. Or chosen to misunderstand.

Anyway he arrived, not before but with the two architects, the machine-gun-talking Swiss and his black partner. Quite a team. They were even more enthusiastic than Larry, if possible, and I must say that they have something to be enthusiastic about. The best of both worlds, the artist's and the man of affairs'—the joy of creation and the intense pleasure of knowing that what you have made will really be there long after you're gone, giving pleasure to others, whether they know who you were or not.

And my *soi-disant* disciple, the developmental psychologist, has reason to be proud, too. L. worked very hard with those two men for a long time, backing them up when they came in with a new concept, stiffening their resolve when they weakened; he's entitled to be excited. So I didn't begrudge him the satisfaction of pulling Jennifer into our session, or the glow in her eyes when she surveyed the models they carried carefully out of the back part of the government station wagon and set up on the porch table along with the working drawings.

It was only afterward, when Jennifer was seeing the architects off, that I began to feel that old feeling. I had chipped in with a few suggestions, and I had to admit to Larry that it had been fun talking with the architects, who didn't stand around fawning but were businesslike and practical, in the way I've always observed that true artists are when their own concepts are being put to the test and they are involved in having things come out *right.*

Larry leaned back, happy, on the porch glider and put up his feet. He began to swing slowly back and forth, just as if

114

the day's work was all done and we were both relaxing. "I told you this was going to be a tremendous experience. And they were pleased, more than pleased, I could tell. You validated their big decisions—"

"Your decisions, I think," I said.

"Well, to an extent. I've had a part in it all along, and I'm glad. And I was going to add that you helped them today, maybe even more than at your first meeting several years back."

I said truthfully, "I was a little hesitant. I'm no architect. And I'm not sure but that my ideas about enclosing space for kids may be dated."

"Baloney. You don't really believe that. Even if you do—" he laughed his familiar hearty laugh—"you're wrong."

He rocked and I sat in my favorite chair, the one with the fat corduroy cushions that are kind to my bones; and for a brief while I was under the delusion that I had helped in a good day's work, and was perhaps entitled to a fraction of the excited fulfillment of Larry and the architects. But then L. made his pitch, and I saw that everything had been a prelude, that he had purposely set it up so that the excitement, the scale models, the drawings, the consultations had come first, to charge me up, to make me see how grand, how inspiring, the project was. Not just a stained-glass window, but a culmination. If I behaved myself.

"It would just be one hell of a thing," he sighed, "if we let anything get in the way, in these final months."

"Nothing is going to stop them from putting up the building," I said, "short of some catastrophe. And even catastrophes usually don't keep the construction workers from earning their pay."

L. smiled at me amiably. It was as if the smile saved him from going into a long harangue. I know the game you're playing, it said, you know the stakes I'm playing for.

"The building goes up," he said. "It goes up the way we want it to, with virtually every inch of it testifying to your vision and your genius." He held up his hand to stop me from protesting at his use of those last words and went on, "I want to make certain that it goes up with your name on it. As it should."

The whole thing is silly, isn't it? I mean, I'd have to be the worst kind of damn fool to deny that the Children's Center is going to be a beautiful thing. It almost makes me cry to think of it—and L. knew that when he brought the architects up here. But what am I supposed to do to earn this going-away present, promise to be a good boy? At my age?

So that's what I said. "At my age," I said, "you can hardly expect me to shape up."

"Your lovable eccentricities," Larry said, laughing at me in the way he has, "are a part of your persona. I wouldn't dream of trying to blackmail you into behaving like a—well, like a Walter Honig. But you can hardly expect the President not to be worried when he learns that Rog Girard has been engaged in clandestine negotiations with a group of anarchist extremists."

"Where did he learn that from?" I asked. "From you?"

"No sir, not from me. You know perfectly well that there has to be a full security investigation before any President throws his arm around somebody."

"Thanks. But foreign dictators are all right, they're safer than American radicals, aren't they?" In my heart I knew the answer, it was the one Seth had implied: You're safe, too, in fact you're tame, all that stuff is dead and buried. It even adds a touch of glamor to think that once upon a time you sat in jail for subversion, once upon a time you marched and demonstrated, once upon a time you ran a far-out progressive permissive school. As of now you're just a lovable old duffer.

And the only thing that would reawaken any sense of unease would be the notion that I was being used, that I was lending myself to the exhibitionistic game of a group of kids in a wild effort to assert my second childhood. That alone could lead to my being ignored instead of honored, gently passed by instead of saluted before I passed on.

I tried again. I said to L., "What's the price? Firing Rog?"

"I didn't say that." He folded his fingers, turned them inside out, and cracked the knuckles. "I know what he means to you."

Of course. In a way, even Rog is an asset—he enables me to be painlessly radical. Except when he goes too far.

"But you're going to have to get him in line," L. said. "You're going to have to insist that he leave off signing your name to things, involving you in ridiculous and degrading—"

"I'm going to have to?" I interrupted him. "Listen Larry," I said very coldly, "when I was in the federal pen during World War One I met a Wobbly who told the screw in our cellblock, 'There's only one thing in this world that I *have* to do, and that's die.' "

Larry flushed and did not reply. But he had made his point, and I had been able to cut him off only with a corny bit of folk wisdom.

After a while, he changed the subject. He knew that I wasn't going to be able to get that beautiful building out of my mind.

JUNE 13   Mrs. Hoskins says Rog called to say he wouldn't be back until tomorrow. I was annoyed, but I couldn't honestly say that there was work waiting here for him. Just me, waiting for an explanation.

After Mrs. H. took the call, Jenny said, "You seem very quiet."

I said, "Would you feel very bad if the Children's Center wasn't named for me?"

She was startled. "I can't imagine . . . Larry seems to think it's practically all set, the dedication ceremony even. . . . Why . . . ?"

"Why? Larry may not be able to persuade the Great White Father that I am politically reliable. I can hardly get to the john and back without help, but I'm still regarded as just a little bit dangerous. In a way that's flattering, isn't it?"

"Oh, Sam." That was all she could say. "Oh, Sam." But the expression on her face was almost sickening. It made me feel like a swine.

"I didn't say it won't happen," I assured her. "But I don't want to have to crawl—well, no, not crawl, but do anything against my grain—in order to make it happen."

Jenny was staring at me. "I can't think of anyone who would want you to go against the grain. Certainly I wouldn't. But then I'd know better, I wouldn't dare stir up that stubborn streak."

"Jenny," I said, "believe me, I'm aware of what a blow it would be to Larry if this thing didn't go through. I know how long he's worked for it, and how closely it's tied up with his own career. And I'm not eager to embarrass him out of mere spitefulness or crankiness." I said, finally, since she was just sitting there thoughtfully with her chin in her hand, as if I had been talking about her flower garden or a novel she'd been reading, "I think I know too how painful it would be for you. I mean, if you ever felt that I was messing up Larry's career, putting my own reputation ahead of his honest aspirations—for me as well as for himself."

"It's you that I'm married to," Jenny said very quietly. "You, not Larry. Your welfare comes first."

JUNE 14   Had a dream. I was back at Williams, it was now, streets full of autos instead of buggies, but I was still young. Didn't surprise me, I took it for granted, the way you do in dreams.

What I didn't take for granted was that I was going to be awarded a prize at chapel, before the entire student body, for being the top student. I was bowled over. I thought, how proud my mother will be! If only my father had lived for this moment! My friends were slapping me on the back, teachers and acquaintances were waving and winking as I walked across campus to the dean's office.

The dean turned out to be Lily Honig, looking just the way she does now, except that she was wearing academic robes. I had assumed, waiting to be called in to her office, that she was going to tell me the details of the prize, or simply congratulate me in advance. Instead she smiled that sweet gentle smile that I have always found so endearing, leaned across the desk, and murmured, "Isn't there something you want to tell me?"

She must know something else about me, I thought, as I sat before her with my tongue dry and useless in my suddenly parched mouth. I couldn't look her in the eye as she waited patiently for my answer; her fine fingers were raised from the blotter, ready to drum if I took much longer to reply. How could she know about the waitress at the Williamstown Inn, whom I watched furtively, staring at the great mass of black hair piled up high on her head, her ankles flashing (sometimes even a glimpse of calf) as she scurried in and out of the kitchen bearing trays heaped with steaming dishes, her body swelling here and there, making me squirm, sending me home to my bed where I called up unspeakable visions of her with the sheet pulled all the way up over my burning face while I masturbated, slowly and voluptuously? How could she know about my cheating? My not answering all of my mother's letters, with their funny little European turns of phrase? My smoking when I was not supposed to smoke? My stealing the gloves from the haberdashery shop?

"Well?" Lily demanded, her fingers ready to fall. She repeated her question, "Isn't there something you want to tell me?" and I tore myself from her steady fearsome gaze, tore myself into wakefulness to save myself from the dream that had begun so delightfully and ended so nightmarishly.

It all seems very pat to me. I only wonder if that is to be my only escape. Waking up, I mean. Is death a kind of waking up? In the dream, I remember, I raised my eyes and looked out the window behind the dean's (Lily's) head: freshly fallen snow in the field stretching away to the north beyond the building, white and untracked, and for an instant I thought of bursting through the window and running through it, away, far away, to where no one would be able to follow and ask me if there was anything I wanted to say. I think I would have run off if I hadn't awakened.

JUNE 15   After that dream I had a talk with Rog. But I wasn't in shape yesterday to go on writing about it as well. Makes no difference.

I called him in and said bluntly that I wanted to know what he's been up to with the Children of Liberty. He wasn't in the least put out or uneasy. He said casually, "It's interesting you should ask that, because that's one of the matters that took me to Boston."

I said, "It seems to me the least you could have done was to tell me something about it."

"I told you some time ago," he said, "that they'd asked for another appointment. Perhaps you've forgotten."

I assured him I hadn't and that in fact I didn't want to see them, didn't want to get any further involved beyond the inescapable fact that Seth had first turned up here as one of them.

"But that's just it," Rog said. "That's why I couldn't let it go. And that's why I had to go to Boston—to see Seth."

"I'm disappointed in you," I said. "I never thought the day would come—" Because I didn't want to sound petulant, I stopped. Besides, I owed it to him to give him the chance to explain.

"First of all," he said very quietly and earnestly—none of that cajolery Larry comes on with even when he is broaching serious matters—"I want to assure you from the outset that I have done nothing to compromise you, I have made no commitments in your name, absolutely none."

He flashed me a glance with those big dark Oriental eyes (whenever he looks at me like that I am reminded of those old illuminated Persian manuscripts), and I waved at him to go ahead.

"Those people began to exert pressures through Seth, pressures that I'll get to in a minute," he went on. "I felt it was my obligation to respond to them, since they were in the broadest sense political, without disturbing you, or upsetting you. I think I ought to add that everything I have done has been solely for your welfare and your good name."

"God damn it," I said, "that's all I hear. Everybody is trying to do nice things for me. What do you take me for, Rog?"

He was very cool and very dignified. "I can only say that I have nothing to gain personally by what I have been doing in your behalf."

"I never said you were a careerist. But you have political commitments. So don't play games with me. There isn't a person around me, you included, that isn't grinding his own axe."

"Until this minute," he murmured, "I assumed that the axe we were sharpening was our common property. If you're going to repudiate it . . ."

I saw red. First it was Larry telling me what I had to do, now it was Rog. And each one threatening me. "Let's get something straight—" I was trying to keep my voice down but it was coming out cracked and cranky—"I worried along somehow, for eighty years or so, before you turned up."

Rog smiled. He didn't even have to answer. He knew perfectly well that I hadn't taken him into the household simply on a whim; I was as conscious as an old man could be that I was being manipulated not just by Larry but by a host of lesser types, and that I needed him desperately if I was to pull away from the liberal embrace before it smothered me in love and honey and destroyed me.

"There are times," I told Rog, "when I will not submit. There are things I will not submit to, even when they're put to me in the name of love. Or esteem."

When I had told Larry that I didn't have to do anything except die, he backed up. But R. didn't back up after I said this. He nodded vigorously, as if he was in complete agreement with me. As always.

"That's almost word-for-word what I told the Children of Liberty," he said.

"You said you went to see Seth." I wasn't conceding anything, I was just uneasy. Maybe even a bit frightened. "Was it on account of those kids?"

"In a way. It was me they were pressuring. I really saw no need to involve you."

"Pressuring for what?" He has me asking the questions. It's one of the things about R. that arouse such intense resentment in Larry and the others; they can't understand (a) why he isn't more deferential, and (b) why I put up with it. But how many ass-kissers does a man need?

"They were getting insistent about another appointment with you." Rog actually grinned. "I know some people believe I take a perverse pleasure—or is it a malevolent pleasure?—in bringing people like that here. They don't know, as you do, that there are times when I have to push the extremists away. You had already made your feelings pretty clear about the Children of Liberty. What clouded the picture, and gave them some leverage, was Seth."

He stopped again. And again I felt that bad mixture of chill and frustration, as if all around me were Lilliputians pricking at me, jabbing at me, pinning threads to tie me down, bind me, deliver me over to those who wanted to enslave me. I said angrily, "Can't you just tell me what happened?"

"Grebner, their spokesman, became very annoyed when I told him diplomatically that your schedule was too heavy for his group to pay a return visit. I won't bore you with our political discussions. The gist was that I was a fink, in fact a laundryman."

That was a new one on me. Rog clarified it for me: "Washing away your right-wing sins, so to speak, with my radical soft-soap."

I laughed, but not for long, because then Rog told me that the C. of L. were threatening, if he couldn't secure my cooperation, to use what they knew about Seth and me.

I felt myself turning cold. "How does that make them any better than the wheelers and dealers they were so scornful of?"

"I didn't see any profit in pointing that out to them," Rog said. "It seemed to me more practical to go and have a talk with Seth."

I asked him to tell me about that. I don't know if I sounded cool, but by then I didn't care how I sounded—I was desperate to hear.

"I found him living and working in an office building on Huntington Street, nor far from the Conservatory of Music. The building is full of music publishers, cello manufacturers, flute-repair workshops. Very lively, in fact noisy, at least by day. Seth has quite an elaborate setup—workbenches, power tools, pieces in various stages of construction. Several of them are very handsome, as you might expect."

"You were gone several days," I pointed out.

"Seth has no phone." Rog grimaced. "I left a note in his mail slot the first time I stopped by, but he didn't get in touch. I thought it would make more sense to stay in Boston and keep trying until I found him in. Which I did, eventually."

"Was he surprised to see you?"

"I don't think so. Although he claimed he hadn't seen my note, had thrown it out with a bunch of circulars. He's casual about those things. But he did ask after you—in fact, it was the first thing he said. He seemed genuinely concerned."

"But not to the point of getting in touch wtih me," I said.

R. made a face. "He has his problems. I really have the impression that he's . . . torn. I do think, though, that he's quite sincere about his feeling for you."

123

"But he hasn't been in touch since he walked out of here. You mean he's angry at me and worried about me, both at once?"

"Something like that."

As R. went on, I followed him closely enough—it was what I was hungry to hear—but I found myself constructing the scene for myself: Seth surrounded by his immaculate tools and his messy personal life. An occasional girl, no doubt, to palliate his loneliness, exclaiming at the beauty of this half-finished cabinet or that unfinished chest, sniffing the odors of fish glue, wood shavings, lemon oil. Glancing too casually at the curtained-off alcove, where the bleak mattress and box spring share space with two orange crates crammed with paperback relics of his earlier "careers," as he calls them—classical texts of Marxism, urbanism, urban planning. Discovering that you have to take a key from a peg next to the meticulously arranged wood chisels and walk all the way to the end of the long hall, past the cellists and the flute repairmen, simply to take a pee.

The loneliness of lying there in the dark, in a locked-up office building, steel beams, fluorescents, begrimed windows, deathly silence, surrounded by the work you have been chipping and sawing at all day. No escape from anything, not yourself, not the old man over to the west who was so cagey, so niggardly with his revelations and his affections.

Am I imagining too much? Isn't it like that at all? I'm not about to drive over to Boston to find out. I'm getting like a garden snail, the idea of simply crawling from the base of one grapevine to another is in itself exhausting. I have to steel myself now for weeks to prepare myself psychologically, like those global commuters readjusting their bowels to the weirdness of supersonic flight, just to get here from New York in the spring and back to the city in the autumn. No exploratory excursions to Boston for me.

"Is he sitting there sanding that wood and hating me?" I asked Rog. "Is that it? Is he in on this business of trying to force me to endorse those freaky kids?"

"Not exactly," Rog said. His voice was not reassuring. "I do think he regrets having told them—in a moment of annoyance, I think—just why he stayed on here so long, and what his connection to you is. He does not approve of what they're doing—that is, in relation to me and the business of getting back in here—but on the other hand, he will not completely dissociate himself from them. He thinks of it in terms of loyalty to a common ideal. And besides, he sees no reason why you shouldn't see them if you are sincere in what you told him."

I thought to myself, What did I tell him? I said so much. On the other hand, of course, I didn't say nearly enough.

"Well," I said to Rog, "it all sounds pretty inconclusive. And I'm tired. Let me think about it."

So he has left me, and I am thinking about it, and the first thing that comes to mind after having written all this is that I started out annoyed with R. and wound up thinking it over. Which is precisely what the others are always complaining about. Now in a way they could say that I am more dependent on R. than ever, since he is now a link—or has made himself into one—between me and Seth.

I am really tired.

JUNE 16 Feel much better. Slept well, even with the bladder and the arthritis. What would I do without Harrison's sedatives? Whenever I think of old Freud refusing narcotics to dull the pain of that recurring cancer, I am awed. That is not for me. What an amazing old bastard. I have an excuse (as always). Freud said to Stefan Zweig, I think it was, Better to think in torment than not to be able to think clearly. Since I have never had his confidence that I was thinking clearly, I settle for the dope and a night's sleep.

Anyway I have decided that it is up to me to get in touch with Seth. Since he has no phone I must write. Have worked out in my mind a number of ideas and came up with something like this which I am going to dictate to R. later today.

Dear Seth,

Rog has told me of his meeting with you. I wish it had been possible for me to be there. I would be so delighted to see your shop and your work in progress, but I have to content myself with secondhand descriptions.

I am writing to ask you to come back to Twelvetrees so that we can talk about the matters you discussed with R. Surely you can leave your work for a day or two? I promise to be frank and also, as the diplomats say, to be forthcoming as well.

Please ring me up collect and say yes. You can pick whatever day you like—this house is yours. Or the guest cottage, if you prefer.

Yes, let him come back. I'll explain everything to him that I possibly can. I'll try to be honest. There's no reason why we shouldn't come to a better understanding. And then maybe I can be freed of this paranoia, this gloomy feeling even on a cheerful sun-filled day like today, that they are all ganging up on me.

JUNE 17   Even while I was dictating that letter to R. I could feel the resistance in the air. He said nothing, merely scratched away in his book with his head down, but when I got to the end, instead of closing with "Love," as I had intended, I said, "Affectionately."

That didn't make any difference. R. closed his notebook and said, "I really don't think this will evoke any response."

"What do you mean?" I said. "God knows it's friendly enough. Is there something more going on that you didn't tell me yesterday?"

"I tried to make clear that he's in no mood to resume relations unless you commit yourself at least to seeing those people."

"Well, the hell with him then. I told you yesterday, I don't want to be shoved around by anybody."

"That's not his mood. I hope I didn't convey that. He was really disturbed by the way they've been using him to get back in here, so to speak. But he feels just the same that you ought to—as he puts it—'live up to your reputation.' "

He said those last words as though there were quotes around them, and they made me acutely uncomfortable, as if it were Seth himself uttering them.

After a while I said, "I'm willing to talk to him about that. Doesn't the letter convey that?"

"Yes, but I don't think it'll bring a response. He says there was a stalemate when he left, and it's my impression that sending another letter won't—"

"God damn it, send it," I said. "I didn't ask you for your impression. It's my impression that you're still trying to get me to endorse Seth and that pack of nuts. If the letter goes against your principles I'll type it myself. I'm still capable of doing that, you know."

"I'm sure you are," he said. "The impression is widespread in fact that you're spending a good deal of time composing a kind of private summation of your experience."

"And that's nobody's damn business either," I pointed out.

But after he'd gone I was left with the old question: Has someone been reading this?

And then, later, still upset with R. because of his attempting to discourage me, I found myself wondering whether it wasn't all a put-up job, as we used to say. How do I know for a certainty that things are as R. says? It is possible after all (I don't set myself up as the greatest judge of men) that R. is manipulating me, as Larry and the others intimate. . . . Well, I'll have a better idea after I've talked with Seth.

JUNE 18   Remarkable experience!

Ferocious rain and windstorm last night. Most unusual for this time of year. I lay in bed for a long time listening to it lashing against the panes. As the wind whipped the long

127

fronds of mock orange and forsythia they squealed horribly against the clapboards, like small children or animals in pain. I even thought at one point that the bed was swaying, as if I lay in a ship's cabin in a storm-tossed sea. And then of course the whole experience of being in such a storm came back to me with extraordinary vividness, the way I had lain in the bunk with my feet braced to keep from being thrown to the deck, my thigh muscles aching, fighting back nausea as the bulkhead came up to meet me, then receded. The water sloshing about in the carafe above my washstand. The vomit in the passageway. The wild wailing of the wind in the rigging as I made my way to the wretched saloon.

On what ship? At first I thought, lying there in the dark, that it must have been on the voyage to Russia in 1928, when I sailed from Edinburgh to Archangel on that inspection trip of the Soviet experimental schools. But no, that was during the summer when the Sophia School was closed for vacation, and it had been a smooth voyage. To the Far East, then? No, when I went to Japan after the War, and to Korea in 1953, I traveled by air. Memory's tricks.

It had to be back in 1915, the peace trip before my indictment. The beginning of the trouble with Luba. No wonder I suppressed it. It had been a rotten trip anyway, I was lonesome for Luba and Sophia, the trip was a ludicrous failure. I had turned around and come right back.

But then I couldn't get back to sleep. Too many thoughts had crossed my mind, I became anxious, uneasy, thinking that the roof would blow away, or the day would never come, or I would not live to see the sun again. No one but the insomniac can know that terror.

After peeing, I took my bathrobe from the hook and scuffled on into the kitchen. I put up the kettle, thinking to myself, A hot cup of tea will be the next best thing to chicken soup. But when I turned to reach for a tea bag, I all but collided with Jenny, who must have tiptoed in to see what was going on.

I was startled, I let out a cry, Jenny took me by the arm, we sat down at the kitchen table. "It's only me," she said, "I thought I heard something."

"You did," I said. "Clumsy me. I didn't mean to disturb you. I couldn't sleep. The storm . . ."

"It woke me up too," she said. "It wasn't you."

She was too diplomatic to say that she had been worried about me. I'm sure she must sleep very lightly, listening for my footfall, waiting for me to return safely from my frequent trips to the bathroom.

She brushed aside my apologies as we sat there in the half-light of early morning, sipping the tea that she had made. Then she said, very softly, "Come back with me to my room. It's too early to be up, and I don't want to go back to bed alone."

It was the first time in a long while that I'd been in her bed. I'd almost forgotten how warm, how blissful it can be to lie enwrapped in a woman's arms. And how strange that, when I am sitting here alone, as I am now by my own choice (indeed, at my own insistence), or lying alone in that high old narrow bed, it is seldom the picture of Jenny, soft, heated, enveloping, that I call up in my confused and blurry erotic reveries, but rather other women and other times. And yet none of them, none, ever did for me a fraction of what Jenny did just last night. A kind of miracle.

Later, after the rain had let up and the sunlight came pouring through in a golden, glorious mass, Jenny pinned up her hair and pulled on a pair of blue jeans and ran out for her gardening tools. I sat on the porch watching while she threw herself furiously—it's her way, it's one of her charms for me —into the work of weeding and hoeing and spading her garden patch. It was as if not I but she had been regenerated by our dawn encounter. I felt inexpressibly peaceful, watching her bending lithely and furiously to her work. And I thought to myself, Why can't it always be like this?

Because then, I suppose, I would want to live forever. And

what would the young do if we refused to let go? Just the same, I am not ready yet to let go.

JUNE 19   J. announced that she is off to New York. Work to do there, appointments to be kept, a Pinter play to see. I thought, with my vicious cynicism, Well, my dear, I can practically chart your cycle by your trips to the city. I really am an ingrate. But I can't help thinking that maybe her lovely hospitality of the early morning before freed her from any possible guilt at the idea of leaving me once again for—I was almost going to write, for the fleshpots of New York.

Seth has not phoned yet. Maybe he will write. I think I would not feel so funny about J.'s leaving if he had gotten in touch.

JUNE 20   I was thinking how convenient for all concerned that Larry's former wife and kids live in New York. When I recall how he came out here and wept, just before the divorce! I tried to comfort him and he got drunk and told me I've always been like a father to him, like a grandfather too, he said (knowing that would please me in a funny way), and then passed out, and Jenny and Mrs. H. (because it was too much for me, even then) struggled together to put him to bed. Next morning J. brought him juice and black coffee; sometimes I think that was when it all started. And now that years have passed, it's so neat and convenient for one and all. Indirectly, I suppose even *I* benefit from L.'s domestic arrangements.

Dick Wells looked around the living room (I keep coming back to those interviews) and remarked, as others have before him, how I am surrounded by the mementoes of so many former Sophia students—watercolors, figurines, poems, odd postcards—and how comforting it must be "to have a world full of children." That was the way he put it, and it's hard not to respond affirmatively, when you know that it makes you sound good.

The truth is, though, that I wonder now what all that adds up to (couldn't bring myself to say that to Wells). The school that bore my little daughter's name is long since closed, it's only a childhood memory to its aging former students, and an item in the history of American education. The fact that some of those people like to keep in touch with me speaks well for them and I suppose for me, but are they really family? I am no Mr. Chips.

I couldn't hang on to my parents, they got sick and died; I couldn't hang on to my wives, they divorced me or went crazy (until Jennifer); I couldn't even hang on to my children, they died or were killed (even if Philip had not been killed, I think I'd have lost him, one way or another). So I have always thought of family as being young people. Not necessarily students, but the kind who still seek me out for one reason or another. Yes, even like Grebner's group. Or especially like Grebner's group. It's possible that when I drew back and told R. not to give them any more of my time, I was subconsciously influenced by a desire for respectability in the eyes of Larry, my bridge between the two worlds.

Still no word from Seth. It gnaws at me even when I am distracted by visiting delegations, phone calls, other decisions big and small. R. says nothing, why should he, he advised against my writing in the first place. All he has to do to be vindicated is to sit tight.

I think I will talk to Walter about it.

JUNE 21 Walked over to the Honigs'. Lily had gone shopping, as I'd hoped. Not that Walter won't talk it over with her later—that's what marriage is all about—but sometimes I just like to talk to a man (or a wife) without the partner's presence.

"First day of summer," I said to Walter. "I figured we ought to celebrate it together."

Walter was pleased. "Isn't it interesting, Sam, that the more solstices and equinoxes we've experienced, the more significant they come to seem. Let's have a glass of buttermilk on it." And he laughed—he knows I detest buttermilk —and poured me some lemonade Lily had made, knowing I'd be parched and even a bit wobbly from that one-mile hike.

"Depends on what kind of significance you're talking about," I said. "I hate to admit it, but the coming summer serves to remind me of its going. I guess that's why I prefer spring, and the promise of summer."

"You're one of those who always look forward, Sam," Walter said, maybe a bit uncomfortably. "You've always been younger than me—always will be, too."

After a while I worked things around to Seth. We were sitting out back, under his willow, by the pond he and Lily had dug so many years ago that I've forgotten just when it was—back when they had livestock, in any case, and used it for watering them, as well as for waterfowl, and skating in winter, when they were up here over the holidays and could get the snow plowed off it for fun and games. We're all too old for that now.

I knew Walter would not be particularly sympathetic to Seth, certainly not to the Children of Liberty; but I was unprepared for what he threw at me.

"How do you know Girard sent your letter?"

If it had been anyone but Walter I would have been outraged. As it was, I made no bones about my anger: He was implying that I didn't have any more sense than to be led about by the nose, that I would be unable to see it if it turned out that my secretary was dishonest, deceptive, and unworthy even of being entrusted with a letter.

"I didn't say he *didn't* send it," Walter said coolly, with his lawyer logic. "I merely observe that you don't know for a certainty that he did. You don't even know for sure that his version of his meeting with Seth is correct. You don't even know if those young people did pressure him to arrange another meeting with you. Or if Seth really was of two minds about that—assuming it did happen as Girard asserts."

All he was doing, as far as I could see, was trying to poison my mind against R. Which was what Larry had been working on for years, without success. The harder they try, the more preposterous it gets.

"You don't think," Walter asked, "that Girard hasn't been trying to turn you against Larry?" Against all of us, was what he meant.

"He knows better," I said. "He knows you don't disrupt friendships that go back thirty and forty years. If he has reservations about some of Larry's ambitions for me, so do I. And you know it, you know the distinction. It's a political one. Just because Larry loves me doesn't mean I have to love everything he does. Or put myself utterly in his hands."

"I assume the same goes for Girard," Walter said. "You wouldn't simply accept on faith all the things he wishes you to be involved with."

"We talk them out," I assured Walter. "You of all people should know that I wouldn't let myself be manipulated."

But I had the feeling that he thought my vanity was being pandered to by Rog, who is in his view constantly feeding it with fresh supplies of young radicals. Why can't he see that it is Larry who is always trying to bribe me with sweets from his new establishment?

"You're just not being helpful," I explained, "when you keep at me about Rog. At the moment my problem is not Rog, no matter what you think. It's Seth."

"I don't think you understand me," Walter said, but very politely, as always. "I am simply suggesting that you test out the entire situation instead of sitting around stewing about the boy. Have Girard get hold of those Liberated Children, or whatever they call themselves. I gather," he added, a little bit snide, "that shouldn't be too difficult. After you've heard them out, Seth should be willing to come back and more or less make a fresh start with you. That is, if Girard's version is as correct as you seem to believe."

Well, I could hardly believe my ears. Here was old Walter urging me to do what the young ones were demanding. I stared at him. "Do you really want me to give in to those kids? You're worse than Rog!"

He smiled at that. "Not at all. I think you ought to call them in and tell them in no uncertain terms what you think of their kind of adolescent blackmail. Then see where Girard stands—whether he in fact does wish to protect you against them, which I think should be his primary responsibility, or whether he has been conspiring with them, and people like them, to use your name for—"

"For what, Walter?" I couldn't help teasing him. "Subversive purposes?"

"Well, I do think the matter could be clarified if a disinterested observer were to sit in on your discussion with those young people."

"Who? You?"

Walter shook his head firmly. "No doubt they regard me as a class enemy, or whatever they call retired lawyers nowadays. I was thinking perhaps of Jennifer. Everyone recognizes that she puts your interests first."

"No sir," I said to him. "I will not drag Jenny into this business. I have my life and she has hers, which is very, very different. And besides . . ."

Walter was patient, and I should have stopped where I had intended to. But finally I had to go on, "And besides, the whole matter of my relationship with Seth is a problem I'm going to have to work out on my own. You ought to be able to understand that."

He bowed his head. Then he said, "I was thinking in terms of protecting you."

"From young people?" I was pressing him rather crudely.

"Never that. As you said, I of all your friends know you too

134

well for that. Let's say, from being abused by young people—
or by those who make use of young people, including Seth.
Don't you think," he demanded with a fervency that did
more to shake me than anything he'd said up to then, "that
I know how badly you want Seth back?"

As always, when he feels that he's treading on personal
ground, Walter not only dropped the subject but changed it.
Like a number of family counselors and general practitioners
that I've observed, men accustomed to advising on financial
and family problems of the most trying and intimate nature,
he is basically a prude, and uncomfortable in areas where he
suspects that he himself may be inadequate—or impoverished.

It wasn't a standoff, though. As I assured him when he
backed his car out and drove me home, I am determined to
take his advice. Which means taking Rog up on his challenge
—Seth up on his—the Children of Liberty on theirs. Without giving in to anybody, I promised Walter.

Or am I in the process of giving in to everybody?

JUNE 22   Told R. I've waited long enough, and to
go ahead and get those kids here, on condition that Seth
either comes with them or shows up here thereafter. He gave
no indication of triumph, but then he wouldn't. Have no
way of knowing if this was what he wanted all along.

Now that this little die is cast, I find myself hideously
uneasy.

It's Seth. How long was he here—three weeks, a month?—
patiently waiting for me to be honest with him. He was right
to get out, to hole up in that fish-glue workroom in Boston
and turn his back on me. It's not those silly Children of
Liberty. He must suspect—he *surely* suspects if he got his
hands on this while he was here—that I did not come clean.

It is just possible that if I did come clean Seth would take
it with utter calmness, not as something disgusting or horrifying but as an incident hardly worth making a fuss over.

After all, just because I continue to receive young people as guests and visitors, as favor-seekers and autograph hounds, does that mean I have any idea of how they feel about sex in the 1970s? I imagine our notions about free love sixty and seventy years ago must seem incredibly naive and romantic to them. Dear Luba's dream of the free feminine spirit, untrammeled and uncorrupted, would probably be seen as naive fantasizing by those tough pill-popping females who seem to be thinking (if that is the word) not in terms of partnership but of abolition of the other sex.

But do I have the nerve to take a chance on finding out? Could I bear it if he were to react as I fear? Maybe it would depend on the way I told it—whether coldly, or lightly, or with all the detail that still haunts, or simply as a statement of a long-ago occurrence.

You see, I could explain to Seth, Philip did not come out to see me when he returned from the European theater. I can't say now, with hindsight, that I blame him, but at the time I was extremely upset (maybe because I felt guilty at what I had subjected him to during all his adolescent years at the Sophia School). It hurt particularly that he had made the choice of spending his brief leave with Louise, who had also been waiting for him throughout the war years.

I really had to choke back the urge to rail at him when he phoned me and announced, "I'm being shipped out to the Pacific. I have no time to get home, this'll have to be it."

You mean, I thought, you don't even care enough to show your war-weary face? You can't stand to see my face? I listened, hurt and enraged, when he asked if Louise might come out instead in a while, alone, to make my acquaintance.

I had to say, Yes, of course, you know she'll be welcome here whenever she's free; and when Philip said, "She's very shaken up by my being redeployed, she had counted on my being back for good," I had to reply, "I understand," without shouting that I felt that way too, how did he think *I* felt?

Those were the last words we ever spoke to each other. I

said that I understood, but he didn't tell me that he did. After he left, Louise had arrived unobtrusively, even timidly as I recall, taking the bus out to Jersey and then a cab to the School, so that she wouldn't disturb me and make me squander my gas ration stamps on her. I was surprised by her timidity because, since she was older than Philip, I had envisioned her as an aggressive woman, a college graduate determined to marry a boy who had not yet been to college and had a mentally ill mother. And then she was a licensed commercial pilot too.

But there wasn't a trace of flamboyance to her. Short, slight, she edged into the house almost fearfully, despite my urging that she regard it as she would her own. She was uneasy, she told me after a while, not because of Philip but because of me.

"I knew so much about you," she said. I began to see why Philip had been attracted to her. The wings of her smallish, flattened nose flared sensually when she spoke. Her birdlike, somewhat swollen upper lip—which reminded me at once of all those thumb-sucking children who had been brought to me over the years—lifted to reveal her upper teeth, very even, white, and sharp, like those of a creature that might eat from your palm, but would leave scratch marks.

I remember how she drew breath to go on, her breast rising beneath the plain oatmeal-colored cardigan. "Long before I met Philip," she said, "I had been hearing about the Sophia School. I majored in psychology of education at Smith, and you were kind of a hero while I was in college."

"No longer?" I was kidding.

She said seriously, "I think you've done wonderful things. I've told Philip more than once."

"There's a lot he hasn't told me," I said. "I imagine you can understand that."

"I think it must be terribly hard," she said, "being the child of a famous man."

"I don't know about famous," I said, "but it's been rotten

137

for him being the son of a man like me. By the time I was ready to try to make amends for what I'd put him through, he was in the army and the War was on."

She said with that earnestness that only the young can muster up, "He doesn't dislike you. I hope you don't think that."

"I know he's been trying not to," I told her, "and I'm grateful for that. And for his sending you. And to you for coming. I half-expected you were going to fly in!"

She laughed. "The flying is fun, but it's just on account of the War. And Philip. What I really want to do is to work with children, the way you have, when Philip is in college. Shouldn't I be able to get a teaching job of some kind, wherever he decides to go to school?"

Don't you believe in our dream? she seemed to be pleading, while she nervously pulled at the pleats in her skirt, Don't you think we'll live happily ever after? When she raised her plain brown eyes from her lap, they had grown large and brilliant.

I gave her what reassurances I could, and then asked her to have lunch with me, and a glass of wine. I had thought she would be coming to me in pity, partly because she was (as Philip had promised) a kind person, anxious to improve the bad relations between her fiancé and his father, and partly because I was surely for one of her generation a relic, the designer of a defunct school, dropped from sight during the War like a stone cast into a well, dabbling with his memoirs like all the has-beens who don't know of any other way to fill the empty days.

When Louise told me simply that she had been awed by the thought of actually meeting me, I was encouraged to believe that she was not patronizing me after all. And encouraged to hope, therefore, that the book I was working on might turn out to be something more than a time-killer. So after we had eaten, and polished off a liter of wine over her protests, I took her into my study and into my confidence, bringing out the chapters I had completed, and the table of contents, and asking her for her opinion of what I ought to include that would be most useful for people of her generation.

Flushed and pleased, Louise fingered the typescript pages carefully. "This is going to be such an important book," she said. "Once the War is over . . ."

"My dear Louise," I told her, "you make me feel that I too had better try to survive. And it's been a long while since—"

Without warning she began to cry. It was so quiet, so barely noticeable, that I think my first awareness was the sight of a tear dropping through the air and falling onto my manuscript. With a swift angry gesture she wiped the page dry; but she was shaking, and when I bent over the chair in which she was seated, I observed that she was clenching the pages as fiercely as though they were a life preserver.

"What is it?" I asked. "Have I said something wrong?"

"It's not you. You've been so nice. I didn't want to admit it, to say it."

"To say what?"

"I don't think Philip is going to survive. Europe was different. I can't explain why, but I just knew he'd come back from there. When I wrote him that, it wasn't just to reassure him. But now, the Pacific . . . well, it's simply asking too much, it's beyond reason." She was biting on her knuckles. "I didn't want to burden you with this. Please believe me. I know how much he must mean to you."

Her shoulders were quivering under my hand like a tired dog's flanks as I drew her to me. She relaxed for a moment, slack and yielding to the fatherly touch, then turned stiff as I tightened my hold. In that instant I learned, I was positive, that Philip had told her not just about his crazy mother but about his overardent father. All about me. My endless series of sexual triumphs, the legends of which had brought more women to my room, each one easier, not so much because of me as because of the power of the legends. So Louise had come, I thought, filled not just with fear and unease because of who I was, but with curiosity as well, eager like all of them, to see the great lover in the flesh.

While I held her, easily, with one arm about her shoulders, I assured her, as I had before lunch, that she had done the right thing.

"It's really all right," I said. "And you mustn't be afraid or ashamed to let go." But she remained rigid. "Listen," I said insistently, "this is why I wanted you to visit me. Life in these times is a waking nightmare for all of us. For each of us. We have to take what we can and cling to each other."

I made no further move until I felt her grow loose under my touch. Even then it was she who moved, who raised her head to demand, "Do you really mean that?" bringing it close to mine. Her lashes were damp, sticking together as she blinked. Her lips were parted.

I bent forward to erase the last few inches that separated us, and kissed her gently. Now how is it that, of all the dozens of women, the hundreds of times, I can recall this with such clarity? The one encounter, such a brief flashing moment in my overlong life, and yet more vivid than the years of nights, the countless couplings with Luba or Hester. Is it a kind of bonus, that if you get down on your hands and knees and peer into the fireplace of the past, you can still feel your face heating from the glow of those old coals? Is that heat intensified by a guilt as live as that which drove me forward on that quiet afternoon just thirty years ago?

Guilt, pleasure, the inextricable confusion of the two, whatever, I can recall as though it were thirty minutes ago how I slipped my tongue between those sharp little teeth as soon as the tips of her breasts touched my chest. At first tentatively, almost accidentally, as a hand may fall not onto a wristbone or elbow but by chance on a fleshier area; then I drove it quickly, decisively, deeply through the parted lips.

The inside of her mouth was soft and wet. For just a fraction of a second, a sliver of time that pricks me even as I write this, her tongue responded to my tentative probe, then to my desperate surge, before it doubled upon itself like a fish recoiling, too late, from a barb that pierces its cheek and holds it fast. In that effable instant I knew I had her. Triumphantly I bore down upon her, spurred on by her hoarse incoherent cries.

She fell beneath my weight like a tree toppled by a woodsman's axe. The unfocused swinging of her arms, the clawing of her hands, did nothing to halt my progress; the helpless thrashing of her legs only heightened my pleasure. I remember that she was wet between the legs, I remember that even her shrinking from me, her contracting, served to spur me on. Wildly we moved, as though the house had fallen around us and we were alone in the world.

Later, before my eyes, she put her finger down her throat and vomited up the lunch I had given her. She said things to me that I cannot bring myself—what lovely shyness! what maidenly pudency!—to set down here. But having gone this far I will note that I said in reply, "I am fifty-nine years old," as though that could possibly have any meaning for her, whether by way of explanation, expiation, or pathos. And that her last words to me, as I dropped her from my station wagon at the terminal before the loiterers, were: "I should spit in your face."

So I have said it, Seth. I am soaked with perspiration. But I cannot say that I feel purged. It occurs to me that if you come upon this you may not even believe it. The old buzzard, you may very well laugh, fantasizing about screwing my mother. Well then, ask yourself why I sent a check to your mother's parents every month for twenty-one years. And if you think it was to compensate for my son's never having the chance to marry your mother before you were born, ask yourself why the poor little Foxes lied to you about both Philip and Louise, lied to you about the way she died when I know for a fact that not long after giving birth to you she took out a plane and rammed it into a mountainside?

They told you a part of the truth, as we always do with

questioning children and grandchildren. As I am doing now. I don't even claim to know all the truth now. Maybe you are Philip's after all, and not mine.

But aren't you still mine, whether one generation removed or two? And isn't the guilt as great in either case? So we go to our deaths, streaked with guilt, as we come into the world smeared with blood.

JUNE 23   What pomposity I ended with yesterday! Who is to say that Seth will be the one to come upon this—supposing it is Rog, or Jenny? Or even Walter, if one day I don't wake up and they call in the Old Family Counselor to go over the papers?

By then I'll be out of it anyway. No reason to turn away from this or tear it up. Let them fight it out among themselves. People always do anyway, assuming to the close that it's from the highest motives.

Miserable piercing pains in my knees all night. No matter which way I turned it didn't help, not even when I lay on my back and drew up my legs, or finally sat up and dangled them. So at last I got up to take some aspirin and relieve myself, and walked around in the dark until the pain subsided. I was pleased that J. wasn't here to be disturbed and worry about me.

Shuffling around in the dark, I felt the rotten rheumatic pain transfer from knees to elbows. I told myself that it must have been the way I had been sleeping, arms over the head or something, but what difference does it make? Pain is pain, and by the time it subsided somewhat I was wide awake, sitting in the rocker and staring into the dark and wondering why I am still alive and why I persist.

Why hasn't death claimed me? One of those questions to which there is no answer. They're all gone, the people who helped me set up the School, the pedagogues, the artists, the intellectuals. Why not me?

People say it is because I love life. Romantic baloney. Didn't my son and my daughter, and all the countless millions who have died before their time while I continued to breathe, eat, fornicate—to do what they never had the opportunity to do—didn't they love life? It could be that those people who say I go on because of my attachment to the young are closer to the mark.

There could be something creepy about it, vampirelike. Maybe I am drawing not only sustenance from the kids who come in, but nourishment too. Wouldn't it be gruesome if everyone whom I touched died before his time?

Today R. brought in a nice bunch, with their teacher, a lovely chap named Kukudakis, or something Greek like that. Burning blue eyes that made me think of the Aegean on a summer afternoon, and a halo of black curls. A fan of mine. He brought his students here at his own expense, it seems, as a present for having worked hard at their American studies; this is final exam week, graduation, etc. They asked intelligent questions; coached in advance no doubt by young Kuku, but still they did make me feel not just that kids are nice as ever when they are not too corrupted by society, their striving parents, etc., but that I still have something to offer them.

Who knows, though, whether among themselves, away from the idealistic Kuku (a blameless radical who obviously respects Rog as much as he hero-worships me), they don't think of me as an old bore, the way we used to think of the GAR veterans they used to wheel out on the stage at our high school assemblies, before we sang "America the Beautiful"? Christ! The tedious tales of hand-to-hand combat at Antietam, or Chancellorsville! We were bored, nothing more, by the garrulous and uncomprehending survivors of one of the most bloody and glamorous conflicts of all time.

It could be these kids will recall me not just as garrulous and irrelevant, but worse: a fink, a poseur. After all, there is something to the American idea that you become a phony simply by outstaying your welcome. I was never captive to the faith of so many cultures that just because by genetic or other accident you happen to live a long time, you automatically become a sage. I have known too many old frauds and old farts for that. Have tried to assert this a number of times, in print and *viva voce*—but I get the feeling that even when people like Larry grin and nod, they are taking the path of least resistance. Maybe even saying to themselves, The old hypocrite, he puts down respect for the old, but it doesn't stop him from playing guru.

Well, what can I do about that? All this is by way of nerving myself, I know, for tomorrow's meeting. It would be just one more meeting with some young hotheads if it weren't for Seth.

And all those pressures.

JUNE 24   I sometimes think

JUNE 25   I feel so embarrassed. Not only can't I remember what I was going to say yesterday, I can't even remember why I stopped in midsentence. Did the phone ring? Was it Rog? A caller? Did something else strike me—as when I go to the dictionary stand or the *Columbia Encyc.* stand to look up something and then get lost in reading? Maybe I simply had to go to the toilet, that Goddamn bladder pressure. The worst possibility is that I dropped off, dozed off, and when I came to got involved in something else—that could only mean that I am losing the one thing to which I have been clinging. My wits. Not my physical powers, not even my dignity. Just my wits.

I really wouldn't want to live if that happened. But how am I going to know? That idiot Harrison would never tell me whether the senile can be intermittently aware of their senility—I doubt that he knows himself. Old Lincoln Steffens would still sit here at my feet or tag along to the john as faithfully as ever, even if I could no longer remember his name.

Nature protects people. The fearful generally don't know that they are dying, I think. The brave do. I've seen it. Human capacity for self-deception is enormous, though. The bubble of blood—did my father know? I have often wondered. He didn't say that day, it might have been stoicism, it might have been a desire to protect me, or maybe he was deluding himself. Can you be stoical about your own senility? Almost too gruesome to contemplate.

Just occurred to me: C. of L.'s session postponed from yesterday to today (any minute in fact), and maybe that's what I had in mind when I started that entry yesterday and dropped it in midsentence. A useful interpretation anyway— it gets me off the senility hook. I remember I was upset when Rog brought the news and disturbed my train of thought. Some train! Must have been a slow freight.

JUNE 26   It was interesting after all. I felt alert and ready when R. showed them in, not sleepy or confused. My old self.

We didn't congregate on the porch, around my favorite chair, because one of the Hendricks boys has been fixing the railing. He makes a production out of it, dropping nails from his teeth like a horse dropping hay, slamming away with his claw hammer as if he were building a pyramid; so they trooped into this room, where Buddy Hendricks is somewhat muted.

The original four—minus Seth brooding in the corner. For just a moment, when Rog said they were here, I had a flash of hope (or fear) that he might have come along. But no. The beautiful black girl spoke first, and coldly at that. "We're disappointed," she said, with what I took to be a heavy irony (I was noting that she no longer wore big hoop earrings—no longer felt like getting dressed up for the occa-

145

sion, no doubt). "Disappointed that it took so long for this session to be arranged."

"Well, you're here now," I observed. "Never mind about there being demands on my limited time. Let's get to what concerns you."

The Indian girl started to speak but was interrupted by the one I think of as the nicest of the bunch, the eager red-headed fellow with the shaggy bangs. "We've been having a good many planning sessions. Also coordinating meetings with our affiliates, people around the country. We thought you might be interested in a brief report on them."

"Not wildly," I said frankly. "Probably not even mildly. I really don't want to be rude, but—"

"What I want to impress upon you," he rushed on desperately, "is that we come to our decisions democratically. Even when we decide on extralegal courses of action, the decisions themselves must be arrived at democratically. That's a basic reason, see, for our growing attractiveness to young people. They're fed up with *anybody* ordering them around, including radicals and activists. If they're starting to trust us, it's because they can see that we trust them—even though one or two of them might be agents or informers."

"Wait a minute," I said. "Aren't you getting involved in a hopeless contradiction? As soon as you announce your intention of traveling on an extralegal road, you invite infiltration not just by informers but by provocateurs. And as soon as you have provocateurs in your ranks, you have no way of knowing whether or not some of the most brilliant and daring suggestions aren't coming from some government police bureau that wants to egg you on in order to bust you—and then wipe you out."

"You've put your finger on the basic problem," the black girl said coolly. "That's exactly what we've been discussing. The dilemma itself is what drew Seth Fox to us, after his involvement in other kinds of movements. And he's been a big influence on us and on the younger kids, in our arguing out possible solutions, or resolutions."

I was stopped. And fascinated. I was sorely tempted to ask what she obviously wanted me to: What was Seth's attitude, what were his conclusions? But before I could say anything, the redhead had cut in.

"We were hoping, you know, that you could be of help to us too. Like, you know, in thrashing this out and coming to a principled conclusion."

"That's not the impression you gave me," I said. "If you weren't giving me an ultimatum, you were at least hinting that you expected my public approval for whatever it is you're up to. Or into."

All this time it was Rog, not Seth, who was sitting quietly in the corner, not participating, leaning his chin on his left fist, occasionally jotting something in a pad on his lap. I was damned if I'd ask him to bail me out; I wouldn't give anyone that satisfaction.

Anyway, it was at that point, I think, that Grebner spoke up and took over, as I'd been expecting him to do ever since they filed in.

"Let me tell you, if I may," he said, "how we've resolved this provisionally, or theoretically—partly thanks to Seth, who couldn't be here today—and then what we think it means in very practical terms for next year."

"Go ahead," I said. "Go right ahead. I really am interested."

"We started with the proposition," he said in his nasal, logic-chopping way, "that conspiratorial behavior and activity on the part of a national, public organization like ours would be ludicrous. It would invite disaster. On the other hand, we were all convinced that for a variety of reasons I won't go into now, but which we think are grounded in reality and not in fantasy, it is impossible to achieve significant change in our kind of society without recourse to defiant behavior. And at least the threat of violence, if not actual day-to-day violence. That's the contradiction you put your finger on."

"Okay," I said. "I'm listening."

"Well. To put it simply and quickly, we decided—in fact

we voted—to make basic policy decisions publicly, and tactical decisions privately. When we visited you before, I told you we thought of ourselves as having a public face and a private face. Now we've carried that concept over into the area of legal and extralegal behavior. That is, we won't decide on occupying a redemption center or a shopping plaza without thorough public discussion. Once we do decide, the task force, together with the target area, will be selected by delegated groups much less susceptible to penetration by the police."

"You hope."

"Well, of course." Grebner actually smiled. It wasn't something he could do as readily as the redhead with the glasses. "But in any case, those who support us or participate in our public meetings will not bear responsibility for subsequent extralegal behavior."

I was about to ask him what made him so sure of that when he anticipated me by adding, "We also have supporters in the legal profession with experience in civil disobedience cases."

The whole thing began to look a little different from what it had when they'd first showed up. But I wasn't sure how much I was being influenced now by the knowledge that Seth was in on it.

"We never expected to involve you in active civil disobedience," spokesman Grebner said. "But we felt—we still do—that we're entitled to your support, on the basis of our adherence to your ideals and to all the things you fought for throughout your life."

It didn't all fit together. For one thing, there was no talk, no implication even, of threats about me and Seth. But even if they'd decided that that was unworthy of them (which I still wasn't sure of), there wasn't even any mention of the Children's Center. I decided to try them out one at a time, starting with the business of threats.

They all started talking at once, all eager to explain. But Grebner took command with a wave of his skinny arm. "Our position on personal pressure is analogous to our position on physical pressure. We discuss and vote on whether it's applicable. If we agree that it's necessary, it will only be applied by the activist committees."

"Are you people an activist committee?"

They were smiling at me. With the possible exception of Grebner (and he can't help the way he looks or talks), they are a charming bunch, highly charged, idealistic, confident of their aims if somewhat nervous.

"Well," I demanded of them, "if you are, how come you're not threatening me today? You were certainly resorting to that kind of thing in order to get back into my house."

"Two different issues," Grebner said. "There seemed no other way to get you to listen to us again. But now that you are, we'd much prefer to persuade you intellectually that we deserve your backing. You've got a long track record—of civil disobedience, defiance of improper authority, disregard for sacred cows. As for us, we've hammered out an attitude and a program that we feel are worthy of your support. I'm not minimizing the importance—if you permit us to use your name, it'll be a terrific help to us all over the country."

"Let's just suppose I refused. Then what?"

"Then we're authorized to threaten you."

It's hard to take offense when you're talked to like that. I mean, I was a little taken aback, but as I looked around at the two young women and the two fellows I couldn't find it in me to retort harshly, maybe because I was afraid it would make me look foolish. To cover myself, I reached out to pat Steff and asked Rog if he would have Mrs. H. bring us in some of her good homemade lemonade and anise cookies.

"You see," the redhead explained with becoming nervousness, "since Seth Fox is involved in that, uh—"

"Contingency," Grebner supplied.

"—yeah, contingency, he decided it would be inappropriate for him to come along with us today. You know what I mean?"

"I'm afraid I don't," I told him.

"Well—" the boy was stammering a little—"like, it was as much his concept as anyone's that we'd discuss such problems fully, and then abide by the majority decision. And he was bothered that you were taking so long to see us again, but still he was opposed to using personal pressure on you. I mean what you call threats, to get another appointment."

I could feel my heart fluttering in my chest. It wasn't exactly painful, more a kind of breathlessness, a premonitory notice of what it would be like when everything stopped for good.

"All right," I said, very calmly and very patiently. "Now you got in to see me again, so he should be satisfied on that score. So why didn't he come along?"

"Because he also voted against our putting pressure on you to persuade you not just to see us but to issue a statement in our behalf."

"But he was outvoted on that too."

"That's right."

"And yet he still supports you."

"That's right."

"I'm sorry," I said, "but for me there comes a time when you have to say no. It's fine to be a member of the team, it's fine to be a big democrat, but supposing the team votes to do something that goes against everything you believe? You people don't remember Adlai Stevenson and the way he degraded himself at the U.N. during the Kennedy administration. Well, I do," I assured them, "and after that I had no use for him."

"The difference is," Grebner said, "that Seth still approves of our goals. And he believes as we do that it is hopeless to expect something more than crumbs from the Establishment. We don't want crumbs, we want a new society. And I'd like to discuss that with you."

I told him to get specific. To stop talking ethics and ideals and start talking reality. What about the Children's Center?

Could he honestly say it was bad? Didn't he realize it was going to be a realization of dreams we'd had for decades?

"What about the price you pay for it?"

I started to get mad. A bad sign: Often it indicates that I'm not sure of myself, or that my *amour propre* is being tweaked. A typical parental response—when the kids really get under your skin, yell your way out of it. But knowing this has never enabled me to control it; old fools truly are the biggest ones.

Grebner had good control. Too much, in fact; it was his sticklike rigidity that I found so unpalatable. He just wasn't as real as the others—but they were right in simply flushing, or grinning, and letting him be their spokesman.

"We're shocked," he said, although he didn't look it, "that you could even consider lending your name to the administration."

I tried to look past Grebner, at the others, but they were unified; whoever had qualms, like Seth, hadn't come to see me. They were all clear that I would be lending my prestige to the Establishment and not to them, and that it had to be one or the other. Anything short of that was liberal straddling. It's an old tune, isn't it? Sometimes I get the feeling that certain problems, certain confrontations, never change and never will; it's at those moments that boredom threatens to overwhelm me. And I know in my bones that if anything will finish me off it will be boredom—you can see it in all those old and withered Florida faces when they're just on the point of letting go.

"Don't you think I'm the one to be shocked," I tried a new approach, "that young people like yourselves should be so crass and manipulative with me? You complain about the administration—all you want to do is borrow some prestige from me in order to make yourselves look respectable. Don't you see the difference between the administration and a building, a concept, an open door for kids, that will outlive us all?"

Grebner was cool. Cold, even. "We want your support

only if you withhold it from Washington. If there's one thing we are agreed on, it's that *we're* not going to be coopted."

"Bully for you," I said. "Nobody's forcing you. But you want to force *me*, right?"

"To take a position, yes."

"That's a little arrogant, I think. I've been taking positions for a long, long time now. I've fought for all kinds of causes in all kinds of ways. It's possible," I said, surprising myself with my own words, "that I might want to get out and fight for yours, if I were convinced that it would be nonviolent and truly international. But even if I were to go to bat for you, I wouldn't necessarily want to dissociate myself from the Children's Center. I'd hope that the world would be big enough for both—maybe for even more than both."

"So you want it both ways." As soon as Grebner had said that, though, the others began murmuring. My concession that there could be circumstances in which I might come out for them had immediately achieved something I hadn't counted on. It had split them, and before my eyes they began whispering among themselves, heatedly too.

Well. I pressed on. "I want to know about these threats of yours."

The Indian girl grinned at me. Before Grebner could get cracking on that, she said saucily, "We're not going to tell you that. We were saving that for a desperate scene, like if you got really *mean* with us."

"Now you don't think I'm being mean?"

"Mr. Lumen!" she laughed. "I think you're a wonderful man."

"I'm wonderfully tired," I said. And before I could add anything to that, Rog was on his feet and hustling them out of my room. I mean hustling; I haven't seen him move so fast in quite some time. In fact I had the suspicion—I would have taxed him with it, but he was smart enough not to come back after he'd gotten rid of them—that he wasn't as concerned with my exhaustion as he was with the situation. That is, that he thought it a propitious time to break off the discussion, even though (or maybe because) nothing had been actually resolved.

Whew! Maybe I was alert when they came in, but now I am really whipped. Feeling my age. I will have to nap and then begin to sort this thing out. I'm not through with those kids yet. To say nothing of Seth.

JUNE 28   Rog came in to read me *The Times,* and before he started I asked if there'd been any word from (a) Jenny, (b) Grebner, (c) Seth. He shook his head, said something about things being pretty quiet, and shook out the second section, ready as usual to read me the news summary and index. I could pick out what I wanted him to read to me. But I wasn't ready or willing to settle for that. I didn't want to just find out if anything had been happening while I was taking my nap. He was the one, as I pointed out, who had taken charge of the Children of Liberty and gotten them out of here, and I hadn't heard boo about their reaction to our meeting.

"I really think they were very pleased," Rog told me. "You could see that they weren't all in agreement on how to react to your position. Grebner, their spokesman, had obviously been hoping to persuade you to dissociate yourself from Washington—"

"Everybody hopes to persuade me," I said.

Rog accepted that and went on "—but I think he was all alone on that. Or pretty nearly. The rest of them were impressed by your willingness to listen and maybe consider a statement in their behalf. The girls particularly thanked me. And they did worry about overtaxing you, I'll give them that." He was actually smiling.

"Would you please tell me," I asked him, "what I can expect next from those young people? Grebner was still talking of threats."

"I doubt whether he could get the rest of the group to back him on that. Not after you promised to consider—"

"To consider what?"

"To reconsider, then."

"Listen, Rog," I said, "how long can this go on? I don't want to whine, but I like some peace of mind. I want you to realize: Everybody, absolutely everybody, is vulnerable to threats." He glanced at me quickly, sharply, as if suddenly he was the one being threatened (and it gave me to wonder: Suppose Larry gets something on him? or . . . vice versa?). I wound up not quite as I had intended, speaking generally. "There hasn't been a distinguished person I've known, from Franklin Roosevelt to Martin Luther King, who hasn't done something he's regretted, or doesn't want publicized."

"Honestly," he said, "I got the feeling as I showed them out that the pressure is off for now. Not that it was ever on, except in the sense that you were justifiably upset at having young people—"

I waved all this aside. "Come on, Rog," I said, "this wasn't all in my head. They had something specific in mind, even though they skated around it, and I still wish I could have dragged it out of them before they went away."

"I don't think they made any secret of that," he replied. "It had to do with you and Seth."

"I know that," I said. "The question is what. And to what extent Seth was involved. The only other person they could have learned anything from is Walter Honig. And that's a little unlikely, isn't it?" I hesitated, and then added, "Unless it was you."

It seemed to me that Rog paled. He opened his mouth to answer, but just then the phone rang, and I nodded to him to answer it. He stood there at my desk, above me, the little white phone cupped in both his long dark slim hands, murmuring into it, then listening, the corners of his mouth drawing down as if in surprise at what he was hearing. He glanced down at me. "It's Seth. He'd like to know if he can come out, around the first of the month."

154

"When is that?"

"Just a few days."

"Let me talk to him." I took the phone from him and said into it, "Seth? Of course you can come. I told you, you don't have to ask. I've been waiting to hear from you."

"Complications," he said tersely. The sound of his deep voice was so familiar that it hurt, like a piece of music you haven't heard in too long. "What I really want to know is can I bring a bunch of equipment out and store it?"

"Certainly."

"The rent is due here, and I don't want to stay on."

"You can stay here as long as you want, you know that." He didn't respond to that, and I added, "There's one thing."

That got him. "What's that?"

"Be ready to do a lot of talking."

He laughed easily. "You were the one—"

"I know," I said, "I know. I'll be here."

After I hung up I told Rog that I didn't want to hear the news. Not today. Too much to think about. So he excused himself and left me here. I'm going for a walk, maybe to Walter's; first, I wanted to put this down.

It occurs to me: It's not unlikely that Rog is keeping his own diary. Won't it be funny someday when someone compares his version of this business with mine?

JUNE 29   Jenny returns tomorrow. It will be so good to have her back. I thought I'd better tell her about Seth, and she said, Great—the way she always does. It will be exciting, having them both here.

Walter thinks I am allowing myself to be "taken advantage" of. He "assumed" that Seth would be turning up and gave me his cool gray smile—made me uneasy, as though he were mentally linking that assumption with the taking-advantage business. But he said only that he "doubted the wisdom" of my seeing Grebner's group without someone else present, and without obtaining a commitment that they stop harassing me. About Rog, he said nothing at all this time. Sometimes Walter's silences or omissions are more significant than what he says. Somehow I could tell from the way Lily bustled about that Walter had been talking to her about me, and that she was a little embarrassed about it. I do love her.

JUNE 30   I was sitting out under the apple tree, more or less hoping J. would turn up (she hasn't yet), and I guess I dozed off. Next thing I knew I was playing charades, which I haven't done in a good many years—mostly, I suppose, because J. doesn't care for party games, and Walter and Lily, who are so often here, are getting a little old for physical foolishness.

But we used to play it quite a bit back in the Sophia days —as a teenager Philip loved it, and even Hester would join in, at those rare moments when she was in good health and spirits and disposed to turn up at our parties. And I guess in the dream I was back at the School, although I didn't seem to be any younger and I didn't recognize the room. What was interesting was the group: John Dewey—my God, how long it is since I've thought of him!—looking shaggy and stooped and somewhat forbidding, watching the game more than participating; a woman painter (she didn't look like Georgia O'Keeffe, but I thought of her because when it was her turn she pantomimed painting a picture, a flower, and I was the one who guessed that her charade was *gilding the lily);* some parents; and several students, looking like today's students— blue-jeaned, sloppy, sexless.

With the exception of old Dewey, we were all gay and animated. Spilling beer, crumbling pretzels, making a lot of noise. We were playing partners, and when it came the turn of my partner, a rather sexy-looking woman, she threw herself into it with great verve, planting herself in the middle of the room and waving her right arm around in such energetic circles that her big breasts heaved with the effort. "Paddle!" someone yelled. No. "Wheel!" She shook her head, perspiration flying from her forehead.

Instinctively, I knew. "Crank," I said, and she nodded in delight, then proceeded to imitate someone writing furiously. "Letters," I said, and she flung her arms around me in delight, squashing her breasts against me.

But suddenly, as I glanced up, the pleasure of the little victory faded away. One of the students, a pinch-faced boy with granny glasses and an American flag sewn to the seat of his jeans, had flung himself weeping into the arms of the old philosopher. Dewey patted him clumsily but with genuine affection, and glared at me with such contempt that I tore myself free from the dream and awoke, sweating. My hat had fallen from my head and the sun was pouring down on me.

I picked up my hat, staggered to my feet, and made my way back to the cool of the kitchen, where Mrs. H. was sitting at the table and entertaining Old Man Hendricks with one of her interminable stories about her childhood. She gave me a cold glass of lemonade and I took it in here, to await Jenny in the shade and puzzle out the dream.

The key of course, aside from my consuming sense of guilt, was crank letters. I've been too busy (and disinclined) to write them—not that the household would ever let me—but of course I've gotten my share; every well-known person does. Why should I feel guilty about getting a crank letter? It's not my fault. Is it that Jenny never let me answer them, even when I thought I should, when she was handling my correspondence? Or Rog either, when he joined us here?

Then it came. I never cease to be fascinated at how the recent past and the old days are conjoined in our dreams. Those letters go back to the days when I was running the School, maybe forty-five years ago. They were sent by a former student, from Hartford Retreat, where he had been committed. No wonder I awoke sweating, frightened, guilt-ridden. I can't remember the name of the boy, or his family name, but all the rest is suddenly now as clear as if in fact he were one of the Children of Liberty, and it had all happened yesterday. The boy strolled into my office, Eric, that was his name, to discuss a couple of things one day. Nothing unusual in that. He'd been involved (and doing very well) with our tutorial program, in which the older kids like him took over as teachers and preceptors of the little ones; in fact I'd asked him to look over a paper I'd written on the program and make suggestions, which, of course, he found flattering. The little kids had looked up to him and followed his lead partly because of his enormous self-confidence.

"I understand you're going away," he said to me.

That was true. There was a meeting of some sort at the University of Chicago that I was scheduled to address.

"I'd like to take your place, Sam," he smiled. I wasn't surprised at his calling me by my first name; in those days most of the younger ones called me Uncle, and many of the older ones, just Sam. But something in his tone made me sit up. Despite the smile, he wasn't kidding.

"I've made arrangements already, Eric," I told him. "But I appreciate the offer. Everything will be in good hands while I'm gone."

"I wish you had taken it up with me," he said. He was a handsome fellow, poised and charming. He leaned over my desk and tapped on it with his forefinger. "I plan to run a school when I leave here. I could have made good use of your absence."

"I'm sure you could have," I said. "But you have lots of time." I tried to be light. "There is still that little matter of college ahead of you."

He waved that aside. "I may go into medical administration instead, if education poses too many barriers. You remember when I had my tonsils out last year, Sam? Well, it was perfectly obvious to me, within twenty-four hours, that I could do a better job of running that hospital than the administrators." He nodded at me with that charming confident smile. "I'm counting on your support."

158

My blood ran cold. It was Hester all over again. I made an appointment for him with our staff doctor, on the pretext that they could discuss hospital administration together. Within an hour the doctor was in my office, telling me to get Eric the hell out of the School before we had real trouble.

"He was going on and on about the family butler."

"He comes from rich people," I said. "There probably is a butler."

"A butler who murders people? The man had been in the family forever, Eric said, he'd been entrusted with absolutely everything. Then they found out he'd murdered his mistress with an axe. He told me the story as proof of trained medical incapacity to diagnose properly. I had one hell of a time administering sedation. Now you'd better get his folks on the phone."

Boys like Eric don't have folks. There was a mother in Connecticut, around Wilton, and a father in Manhattan, on the Upper East Side. The mother was barely civil.

"What do you mean, Eric is ill?" she demanded irritatedly. "Don't you have adequate medical facilities?"

I explained that it wasn't like cramps or appendicitis, and then I made the mistake of mentioning the butler story.

"My dear Mr. Lumen," she drawled, practically laughing at me, "what Eric says about Rogers is perfectly true. It was a shocking experience for all of us."

I tried to put the doctor on, to get her to understand that her son needed help at once, that she had a responsibility, that she should come and get him. But that was the whole point, she didn't want him, she was going away on a trip, just as I was, and she did not wish the responsibility any more than I did. I gave up on her.

The father was in conference. When he did call back he was in a barely controlled rage—I couldn't be sure whether it was at his ex-wife, his sick son, or me. But at least he did come and take Eric away. I thought that was the last of it.

Then came the letters. I forget how long afterward they

started coming or how many there were. They were a mixture of pleading and arrogance, of simple reasonableness and shrewd cunning. It was his mother, Eric insisted, who had had him committed, in order to spite his father and keep him from obtaining custody. I was the only one who could help. I had betrayed him and it was my obligation to free him. No one would take him back but me. He couldn't get into college without graduating from the Sophia School, and no other school would have him, out of the state hospital. He would comport himself with decorum. He would become invaluable to me. If I didn't help him I would regret it for the rest of my days.

Do I regret it now? I wasn't unwilling to take him, or at least I was ready to consider it. But everyone insisted that I would be borrowing trouble. You're not running a clinic, they said, you're trying to maintain a school. That was true, but what repute I had was built on the love and trust of the children—and here was one pleading, whispering, yelling, threatening—and as his mother coldly observed when I urged her to hurry down and take over, I did stand in loco parentis.

I put the letters away unanswered.

But nothing goes unanswered. Here in my last days, practically half a century later, I try to compose a reply to Eric. An apology, when it is much too late, for him and for me. Eric, I am sorry.

I think I hear Jenny coming! Thank God. I was beginning to feel abandoned.

July

JULY 1 After taking a shower and putting her hair up, J. fixed herself a gin and tonic and brought it out to the screened porch, where I was playing solitaire, waiting for her.

"Well," she said, stretching her long legs out on the chaise, "I want to know all the terrible things you've been doing while I've been gone."

I told her life had been full of exciting diversions—arguing with Mrs. H. and Old Man Hendricks about the porch railings (J. is pleased with them now, she says), grumbling about the bad news in *The Times* as read to me by Rog, listening to my old Budapest recordings of the late Beethoven quartets, meeting some more young people dragged out by their schoolteachers to see the old statue, eating gourmet meals with the Honigs.

"But you know I don't mean to be mean," I added hastily. "Lily is always wonderful to me, she's like a devoted younger sister. And I'm grateful that I can still enjoy her food—I'm aware of the men my age who sit in nursing homes lapping up Wheatena. And that I can still enjoy the walk over there."

"If I didn't think you could," Jenny said, "I'd never go away. And what else is new? I only ask to be polite, you understand—I'm dying to show you some of my new proofs, but you come first."

I had a hunch she was waiting for me to tell her about the Children of Liberty, but I just didn't feel up to that, not with Seth due to arrive momentarily. So instead, maybe because it had just happened and was fresh in my mind, I told her about my charade dream.

No, that's not exactly honest. That's the reason I gave her; I think the real reason I told it to her was to relieve myself of the responsibility of telling it to anyone else (like Seth, or Larry).

Anyway I wound up by commenting on how odd it struck me that John Dewey should turn up as a father figure in my dream, and that someone of my age should still be uneasy and anxious for the good opinion of a father who has been dead and turned to dust for better than seventy-five years.

"And what would you think if you were, me," Jenny laughed, her head back on the chaise and the muscles working in her long tanned throat, "and you always dream about your husband? And you couldn't be sure if he was really supposed to be your husband or a father figure?"

"Nobody asked you to marry me," I reminded her. "Not even me. It was you who insisted on it."

"Well, I'll be damned," she said, still laughing, "if I'm going to pay some shrink to tell me whether it's you I dream of, or somebody who looks like you but is supposed to be my father."

One of the few things about J. that irk me—and that I can't bring myself to complain to her about—is the way she always refers to psychiatrists as shrinks. I know some of them do it themselves, especially the younger, hipper ones, but to me that doesn't make it any more palatable.

Besides. I suspect she is being too lighthearted about her refusal to acknowledge the legitimacy of psychiatrists. If she isn't seeing one now to ease her mind about me and Larry, I'd bet anything she did when she was an adolescent.

But I said, "The point isn't the father thing so much as it is the persistence of guilt. Nobody leads a blameless life, but if I'd tried to do something for that boy, I wouldn't have him on my conscience fifty years later, would I?"

"And you might not even be here. With his delusions of grandeur, and of persecution, he might very well have attacked you. Maybe killed you. It's been known to happen."

"Callousness has been known to happen too," I said. "My school was supposed to be a place, don't you see, where kids could at least have the assurance that they wouldn't be abused in that way. That they wouldn't be fucked over, isn't that what they call it nowadays? Well, I fucked over Eric, and it was all the worse because he'd been given to understand that I was at least on his side, in contrast to his parents, who had dumped him on me, and then continued to dump on him."

"I'm sorry," Jenny said stubbornly, "but I think you've developed a kind of habit—it's almost become a reflex—of thinking badly of yourself. Maybe it's because you flinch from praise, it's part of your modesty, you can't stand prosperity, but whatever . . . you're always putting yourself down. If that boy had not been kept under treatment he might have jeopardized everything that was going on, that you were trying to do, at the Sophia School. I don't think he would have been worth it."

"But who can make a decision on something like that without knowing the facts of the case, the real history of Sam Lumen and the School? When Dick Wells asks me about the Sophia School he doesn't even know of the existence of a boy named Eric who wanted to run the place and be a master and for his pains got locked up in a nuthouse, like Russians who labor under the delusion that they are poets when they've not been duly licensed?"

"I don't think that's a fair analogy," J. protested.

"Maybe not, but my point is that people like Wells come around and milk me for great-man anecdotes and it never seems to occur to them that maybe there are other kinds of anecdotes that I'm too cowardly to tell anyone but you."

J. grinned reassuringly. "Maybe you get a certain special pleasure in confessing to me. If you're really so worried that people are going to think too highly of you, and that I won't spread enough scandalous anecdotes, why don't you write your autobiography, unvarnished? God knows enough people have been after you to.

"How do you know I haven't been?" I asked her. I meant

165

only to tease, as she was teasing me, but maybe I was also digging a little.

"Nothing would surprise me about you," she said. "People are always asking me what you're up to, in New York, everyplace. Even when I was in Bermuda. I tell them you're on a secret project. I figure that would tickle your vanity—"

"It does."

"—and besides," she laughed, "it's true, isn't it? Isn't it?"

"Listen," I said, "I've got this paranoid feeling that someone is sneaking in and reading what I'm writing."

She gazed at me in mock speculation, her eyes big and innocent. "Maybe it's a publisher's spy."

"I'm not writing anything for publication."

"But they don't know that. As long as it's words on paper . . ."

"But it's just for myself," I insisted. "And I don't like having the feeling—"

"But Sam," she said, "it's such a simple matter. Just put it in a desk drawer and lock the drawer."

"I have been," I said. "I've been doing that ever since I began feeling funny about tucking it away. But I still think someone is taking the key from my ring, or has had one made."

"Oh, Sam!"

I felt somewhat embarrassed, but now that I'd said it I couldn't exactly back out. "Well," I said, "what do you suggest, that I wear the key around my neck on a chain, like a cross or a mezuzah? I mean to say, if someone wants badly enough to see what I'm writing, he'll find a way, won't he? And not even my dearest and closest ones are willing to let me be, are they, to let me think my own thoughts in my own way?"

She came over and kissed my head. "I am," she assured me.

"Yes," I said, "I guess you are."

"And I'll try to see to it that no one messes with your room."

I was just as willing to drop it at that. So when Mrs. H. came bustling out with a trayful of summer salad and crackers and fresh-picked vegetables, I was relieved. Still, during lunch J. asked casually, her mouth full of biscuit, what was happening with the C. of L. and whether I'd worked it out. I said something about taking that up with Seth, who would be turning up any time, and she seemed satisfied.

I told her that I thought I'd lie down for a while after lunch, so she decided to write some letters. Actually I didn't feel like lying down; I just thought I'd set this down before Seth turns up and distracts me from it, maybe for good.

JULY 2 Big surprise, when Seth drove up yesterday in a rattling old flatbed truck he had apparently bought for the occasion. It wasn't all the stuff he had lashed down in the back, I was more or less prepared for that (although there was more of it than I'd expected). It was his passenger.

He hopped out, very limber, and waved hello to me, to the kitchen doorway where I happened to be standing with Mrs. Hoskins. But instead of coming over to shake hands he went around to the other door, reached in, and helped out this girl. A small chubby thing she was, half his size, with freckles on her face and a sunburned forehead.

"Meet Susan," he said. "She's my helper. She carries the light stuff, but she's stronger than she looks."

The first thing I thought was, How are we going to talk with this Susan hanging around? And the second thing, I suppose equally silly, was, Don't parents ever get tired of naming their daughters Susan?

She turned out to be a jolly and seemingly rather simple girl. Maybe I'll alter my early impression, but she strikes me as being open, friendly, a decent sort, and not terribly bright. I don't mean to sound patronizing. Not everyone has to be bright. Still, in the back of my mind I guess I had had other expectations for Seth, who is hardly an adolescent.

I had Mrs. H. call the Hendricks boys to get one of them to come over when he got off work at five and help Seth with the chests of drawers and the heavy equipment, since neither Susan nor I (to say nothing of Mrs. H. or Jenny) could be of much assistance with that. Susan asked if it would be all right for her to have a bath, as she'd gotten all steamed up from the last-minute packing and the trip across the state.

"Maybe you'd like to try the creek," I suggested. "We've dammed it up. The water is pretty cold, but in the hot sun it feels good."

"Oh boy," she said, "lead me to it!"

"I will," Seth said. "I haven't tried it yet myself, it was too cold when I was here last. But I'll leave you there while I come back for a cold drink, okay?"

That was sensible on his part. When the two of us were settled on the porch, Jenny came out, very cool but friendly, and after kissing Seth said she'd go down to the creek and meet Susan. Sensible on her part.

"Well," I said to him, "I wasn't expecting a girl."

"You don't mind, do you?"

"Not at all. I was just surprised."

"I can understand that. I used to know her in one of my earlier careers. But then, I told you about that."

"No," I said, "you didn't."

The look he gave me was a little embarrassed. At first I thought it was because of the girl, Susan; only after a moment did it occur to me that his embarrassment was not of that order at all, that it was not for the girl or himself, but for me and my old man's forgetfulness. I wanted to say, Now wait a minute, I know what you told and what you didn't, and you never once mentioned this girl to me. But since he wasn't making an issue of it, I couldn't very well, without being prickly.

Besides, supposing he was right?

"Well," I said to him, "what are your plans?"

Seth cocked his feet up on the porch railing. "Immediately?

I have to finish dismantling my Boston headquarters. I'm going to drive back to Boston in the morning, leaving Susan behind—if that's all right with you—and pick up another load to bring out here."

"Of course you can leave her. I meant a little further ahead than tomorrow," I said.

He laughed. "How about the day after tomorrow? That's the third of July, I expect to be back here by then, with the last of the heavy pieces."

"And then—"

"And then comes the fourth. What I was going to suggest was that if I still have some stuff left in Boston—and I probably will, cartons of books and things like that—you take a ride back there with me. The two of us, so we can relax and talk and see a little scenery."

That made me stop and look him over. Thin, wiry, pale was what I could see. Little tufts of hair on the joints of his fingers and of his bare toes, sticking out of old leather sandals. Denim jeans and shirt very faded and bleached, but clean. Does he look like us, the Lumens? They were bearded like him, my father and grandfather, but it's hard to say. Maybe a certain piercing, almost disconcerting sharpness in the glance of those light eyes.

"You don't seem to remember," I reminded him, "that I'm a very old party. I think it was Somerset Maugham who used that expression in his declining years. It took my fancy, I decided to save it up for myself."

"I didn't forget," he assured me. "I wouldn't bounce you around. The pickup really rides very well, if you don't push it too hard. We could leave it off with the guy in my building I borrowed it from, rent a car—with you as security—and drive it back here."

"Thanks a lot," I said.

"No, seriously," he insisted. "I've been sort of looking forward to driving around with you."

"How about walking around with me?"

"That too. But if you can walk, you can ride, right?"

The idea did appeal to me, partly because it would outrage those who were always wrapping me in lap robes whenever they took me for an outing, and partly, I suppose, because it was Seth who had made the offer. But I temporized, saying, "I'll see."

Seth laughed, a low deep snort. "That's what my folks always used to say when I was little. Then I'd say, 'I'll see means yes, doesn't it?' "

His folks. I took a peculiar satisfaction in the thought that he had not stayed out there in the Northwest after their death, but seemed anxious to settle down here, next to me; I had the feeling that he'd stay around here even after my departure.

"We'll see," I said. "Is that better than I'll see? You take me by surprise. I've been concentrating on how I'd answer other questions from you. And on the questions I want to ask you."

"Like about the Children of Liberty. I know. I thought we could go into that on our ride." He smiled at me with a certain malicious mysteriousness. "That's one of the reasons I want your company. I promise you that by the time we get back here we'll understand each other better."

We had no chance to go into that because Jenny was bringing the girl, Susan, back up from the brook pond. And after that it was social small talk and drinking and dinner, all very pleasant, but not worth the effort of my writing about.

Except that sometime during dinner it came out, I don't recall how, that Susan had had a child.

I was a bit surprised, she seems such a carefree girl, and then Seth said, with what struck me as the most extreme callousness, "Well, she lost it anyway."

At that I was really shocked. Seth saw it, and added quickly, "But I was sure you knew that. She lost custody to this guy, her former husband, because his folks had the dough and the lawyers. I'm positive I told you about that last spring."

I glanced at Jenny, and then at Rog. Their faces were set, almost frozen. I could read nothing there except a desire to change the subject.

Later, after Seth and Susan had turned in, I turned to J. and R. "What is this," I demanded, "about my knowing those things? Did you ever hear a word about that girl, much less about her having a baby?"

No, they hadn't. But each felt constrained to observe that I was the one who had had the long talks with Seth. And that neither of them knew all the details of those talks. Stalemate.

Seth was up and on his way very early this morning. I am a light sleeper, and as I stood at the window in my pajamas I watched him jockey the truck around the drive and on out to the road. No sign of the girl, who didn't even turn up for breakfast.

Now to catch up on routine matters with R. Maybe I'll get a better idea of what that girl is like at lunch. I must say that the business of the baby shook me in more ways than one.

JULY 3 Seth should be back any minute. Have decided to go to Boston with him tomorrow. Consternation as soon as I made this known to J. and R.: What would Dr. Harrison say? I said I didn't care, as far as I'm concerned Harrison is an old maid. If I feel up to it, it's my business. Period.

What made me decide to go was a longish session with Seth's girl. I have known a lot of kids over the years, but this one is (as they say) something else. She is perfectly pleasant, jolly if anything, laughs easily. She comes from a lower-middle-class family in Colorado Springs, where her folks ran a resort motel, and after that failed, a laundromat. I get the impression she has drifted from town to town and job to job; somewhere along the line she met and married a solemn graduate student who was, she says, into Eastern philosophy.

They must have been a strange couple. He liked to pick fights (again, her words), and she took off when it became

171

clear that he wanted to hurt her, which scared her particularly because she was pregnant. I shouldn't wonder, although there's a contradiction between his philosophical passivity and his alleged sadism.

Anyway, she went home to Col. Springs and had the baby, which she left with her folks because there was nothing for her to do there, not even to help her father in his unprofitable business.

"What were you *doing* when you met Seth?" I asked her. I wanted to see if I could form some mental picture of what had attracted him to her. I don't mean by that that she is physically unattractive. Quite the contrary. She has a nice body (although I bet her mother runs to fat), large plump cushiony breasts, an engaging grin and perfect teeth, a throat that ripples when she throws back her head and laughs. The kind of girl you could go to bed with as easily as you'd bite into a candy bar, and with as much innocent pleasure. Afterward, a Coke or a cup of coffee, and you're on your way. Not only no hard feelings, but barely any memory of it an hour later. So I was anxious, for Seth's sake, to find out if possible what he'd seen in her.

"I was doing some non-events and some anti-events," she said, and then, seeing my bewilderment, added, as if it would explain everything, "in coffeehouses. That's where we met, in a coffeehouse."

I decided against trying to learn what anti-events were, and settled for simply inquiring when this had been.

"I don't know," she replied, with absolute candor. "A while ago."

It took me some time to see that each event in Susie's life is quite unconnected with what has gone before, to say nothing of what might come after. Kids in recent years seem to have little time sense; this may be more our fault than theirs, and not even a question of "fault" but of such things as their sense of simultaneity because of the mix of instant worldwide TV transmission and historical pageant-dramas. If I am going to see Susie as typical at all, and not simply a freak, I have to cope with her as an extreme example of the type. A true spawn of the tube, perhaps even conceived halfheartedly while her parents were "viewing."

The more we talked, the more I saw that if you try to communicate with someone like Susie in terms of time intervals, you are doomed to not communicating. As long as you stay in the here and now, things go fine, she grins and talks winningly about this and that, how "great" it is around here, how "great" my wife is, etc. etc. But she is obviously as uncomprehending as a three-year-old when you speak of next year or three years from now; and stranger yet, when you speak of last year or three years ago, she gazes at you with the blank, turned-off stare of a teenage captive at a lecture about nineteenth-century politics, sixteenth-century painting, or something equally remote and "irrelevant."

I would not call her unfeeling, since she speaks with genuine enthusiasm of "beautiful" people like J. and "beautiful" things like J.'s viburnum and foxglove, or even stupid, since she seems capable of picking up and absorbing various kinds of data as she drifts through life—which defines her (for me at least) as no more ignorant than many young women. But I have this crazy suspicion that for someone like her all the "beautiful" things are undifferentiated in quality and degree, and float in an undefined present, unconnected to anything that ever has been, or will be. And that there is no such thing as growth, or decline. I can see her, in short, not only making love as casually and lightheartedly as if she were a rabbit or a butterfly, but as utterly unable to make a connection between it and what can happen (and in her case has happened) nine months later.

I thought it would be unwise to mention the child, to say nothing of how she came to "lose" it, after depositing it with her parents. But that's one more reason for me to go to Boston with Seth; I want to find out (I confess to bafflement) how he fits into all this—at the risk of his telling me it's not my business, or reminding me that I have had my own deficiencies in this regard.

Anyway, I can see Susie gaily picking dandelions, a healthy ornament to our lawn, and later on, blueberries. And one day disappearing as naturally as she turned up here alongside Seth in the truck. What I can't see is Seth, who gives off these radiations of being all intensity, all principle. Am I misjudging?

Will go Seth's way tomorrow. Must take along a cushion and a backrest. Just realized it will be the 4th of July. Was he aware of that?

JULY 10   When I think back on this last week I can hardly believe any of it. Or know where to start. What I mean to do is set down the day of our outing first. Then I'll try to catch up later; it will be impossible to write it all down at one sitting.

J. was worried about our driving on the 4th, holiday traffic, etc. I felt more exhilarated than I have for a long time, setting off on what felt like an adventure from the moment I was hoisted into the truck like a driver's helper or a hitch-hiker. I hadn't counted on the noise of the motor, which made conversation a little difficult. S. seemed perfectly willing to do most of the talking; he had carted out the last of his heavy pieces the day before and was in high spirits. He was going to return the truck, pick up the last of his clothing and books, and rent a car for the return trip. (Susie, he said frankly, had little more than the clothes on her back.)

I thought this was a good excuse to bring up the business of my reaction to the girl. S. was not angry, merely puzzled. "She makes no pretense of being an intellectual," he said. "It's true she lives by instinct, but her instincts are good, so what's the point?"

I tried to explain that it wasn't me I was concerned with, but him. He was the one who apparently intended to continue a kind of commitment. "I wouldn't have predicted a particular kind of girl for you," I said, "but given your insistence on certain standards of behavior—at least on my part —I'd have thought you'd be more at ease with someone like those girls you showed up with here that first time." I found that I was almost shouting.

He laughed good-humoredly. "Oh, they're not for me. Comradeship has nothing to do with erotic connection. Don't you agree?" He didn't wait for me to deal with that one, but went on simply, "I feel less lonely with her. If either of us felt the other was behaving really badly, we'd split. It's happened once already—but I've told you about that."

"You keep saying that," I protested, "and I wish you wouldn't. I think I know what you've told me and what you haven't. This Susan business is quite new to me. What about her baby, for example?"

He shrugged over the wheel. I felt it was a concealing kind of shrug, even though he went on to say, "She married this fellow at his insistence, in a moment of weakness. A rich boy who wanted to acquire her, the way he might have bought a painting, or a rare breed of dog. The way he did it was to get her pregnant and then marry her. When she saw what she'd gotten into, she pulled out. But he wanted a souvenir, and it was easy for him. I mean, he's got family and money, and Susie's got neither. So when she was busted on a drug charge he took over custody. Not a damn thing she can do."

Well, I thought, maybe. I couldn't keep from remarking that she didn't seem bowed down with grief at the loss of her child.

Seth did not snap back at me. "She's resilient," he said. "She bends, but then she continues to grow."

I did refrain from commenting that as far as I could tell, her growth had been arrested. If she seems to me like a wild and ragged shrub, that's not important; to Seth, she's a strong young tree. I have to believe he'll see her differently one day. He might concede that, but it wouldn't make any difference to her, or to their relationship right now.

We drove in silence for a while, going east on Route 2

across the upper part of the state that I like so well, in preference to the high-speed turnpike trip that would have been, S. pointed out, hard on my nerves. After a time he turned to me, the wind from the open window blowing his hair. His devilish smile should have forewarned me. "Go ahead," he said. "Ask me some more. After that I'll ask you."

I had to laugh. It's one of the endearing things about young people like him and J. Very mature, always interesting to talk with and listen to, and then at unexpected moments they turn into kids again. But I couldn't *not* ask him any more.

"Let's get to the Children of Liberty," I said. "One reason Susie confuses me is that I can't visualize her as having the slightest interest in them."

"She doesn't."

"But you do." I touched his right arm. "You were ready to blackmail me into sitting down with them again."

"I have different expectations from you than from Susie. Shouldn't I?"

I had to grant that he should, but I felt I had the right to know more about the depth of his commitment.

"They're trying," he said. "They're trying, and they're principled. That's enough for me—and from what I had learned about you, I would have thought it was enough for you too."

"No," I said, "it's not. If they decide to commit outrages, even if it's by majority vote, that's not for me, and I don't know where you got the idea—"

He cut in on me, suddenly quite cold. "Oh yes you do. You don't have to come on all righteous with me."

I was caught between anger—who the hell did he think he was?—and terror. Maybe he knew who he was? So I could say nothing, not one word, but simply sat there in silence, bouncing my old bones on the cushion, hanging on to the door sill as if it were a life preserver, and staring out the bug-spattered window at the countryside, which as we talked had been gradually giving way to the creeping sprawl of suburbia. I am not exactly certain of the sequence of events after that. I know I dozed off for a while and awoke with my mouth gummy and a slight headache from the unaccustomed jouncing; I know too that we talked again, this time about the Children of Liberty, but I can't think whether it was before or after my nap. Whichever, the substance is clear.

I brought up the question of nationalism, of young "radicals" identifying themselves not as internationalists but as nationalists. It's something I hadn't gotten into with Grebner and his group, and it struck me as particularly odd, if not obsolete, for someone like Seth to associate himself with flag-waving. I said, "Last I heard, young people were only waving the Viet Cong flag, or the black nationalist. Am I supposed to take this seriously?"

Seth's eyes grew narrow, as if the summer sun slanting through the windshield were bothering him. "Yes," he said. "You are. These people have concluded that you don't make progress in this country by being anti-America. The ordinary people whom they want to influence love this country, with all its shortcomings, and will never listen to anyone who doesn't."

"So they simply voted to love America, too?"

"Ridicule won't help you to understand." He said this not in a wounded tone, but flatly. Then, when I didn't respond, he went on, "They're neither fools nor cynics. They made a decision to rescue Americanism from the primitives. If you had asked them, you would have learned that they see no contradiction between their kind of patriotism and your kind of internationalism. They're in the process of rescuing our original revolutionary heroes from the textbooks."

"And of making them into folk heroes for kids today?" I asked.

"Now you're into it. Do you think it's so crazy?"

"No," I said, and I wasn't just being polite. I had to add, "I wouldn't have any difficulty endorsing that. But—"

He cut me off. "But once it stops being amiable, innocent, theoretical, you don't want to get mixed up with it. What would you have done in 1776?"

That kind of aggressive rhetoric annoys me, and I told him so. He grinned a big grin—it's one of the things about him that make him endearing—and reached out to touch my arm as I had earlier reached out to touch his. He said, laughing, "Maybe I do want to take you off that pedestal and put you on the spot. But I'm not out to tie you to the stake and touch a match to the faggots."

"Thanks a lot," I said.

"Oh, I don't deny that I think it's high time you got a dose of reality. You've been pretty well insulated for a long time now."

"What I'd like," I said, "is just a glass of water. Could we settle for that?"

He glanced at his watch. I remember how casual all this was. He said very easily, "We'll turn off to the shopping plaza at Newton, if you can hold out for just a little while. Then I'll get you a soft drink." I think he even went on to say something about the fact that we should have taken along a thermos of lemonade.

Next thing I knew, we had coasted off the road and into the shopping plaza. As the truck slowed the breeze died down and the heat came blasting at us, suddenly baking down on the metal roof and glinting through the glass of the windshield. I felt not only parched now but a little faint and somewhat frightened by these physical sensations that the people who loved me had been taking such pains to protect me from. I was about to say something like this, and it occurred to me too that maybe Seth wouldn't be able to find us an open refreshment stand in the plaza on a holiday, when my attention was captured by a crowd that had gathered at the far end of the blacktop.

"What is that?" I demanded of Seth. "What's going on?" As he eased the truck forward in low gear I was able to see

178

that those at the fringes of the crowd were hopping up and down from time to time, trying to see what was going on in the center, while those at the center seemed to be engaged in a kind of dance, a hoedown, or a hora.

All these people, mostly youngsters, were gathered in a loose circle around an open truck whose bed was filled with what looked to me like barrels. A girl with long loose hair that flowed down the back of her denim shirt was standing among the barrels, laughing and waving to the crowd. Every so often she would bend down to take something from people who had formed one of those human chains, and toss it into a barrel. Splosh! Water leaped up from within, her whole front was drenched, but the sun was beating down on her and she was laughing, and so was the crowd, which began to applaud every time she threw another object into a barrel.

Seth was bent down over the steering wheel, squinting up in order to see something atop a corner building that I couldn't see. "Look up," he cried, "look up!"

I couldn't. It was hard enough for me to make out the girl in the truck, the crowd kept getting in the way.

"Let's get out." In an instant Seth was out and around on my side, helping me down. I felt giddy, as if I were trying out my land legs again after a long sea voyage.

"Now look up," he said, holding my elbow and pointing with his free hand.

Several young men were standing on the roof of the building before which the human chain had formed. It was one of those redemption centers for trading stamps, the front door was wide open, and the human chain extended inside. The fellows on the roof had unfurled a flag. They hauled in the Stars and Stripes, and in its place up went their flag, which looked oddly familiar to me, but I couldn't place it at first. I turned to Seth, who had shoved his dark glasses up onto the top of his head and was laughing.

"Don't tread on me!" he shouted.

It was only then that I realized what he had gotten me

into. Perhaps I should have earlier, but my perceptions are no longer that sharp. I could sense a crowd of young people and an atmosphere of excitement, but it was hard for me to make out the details of the scene. On the other hand maybe I am still, over a week later, rationalizing my reluctance to concede that Seth could have planned beforehand—even conspired with the Children of Liberty—to bring me to the scene of their occupation of the redemption center and force me to confront it.

Of course, as soon as he shouted the slogan on the American Revolutionary flag that was being hoisted above the building, I realized what was up. All my senses were sharpened, my adrenal glands were pumping away, suddenly I could hear clearly a young man with a bullhorn who stood on the truck near the soaked, laughing girl at the trash barrels.

"Power to the people!" he was intoning, not solemnly, but with a deep chuckle. "Welcome to our Boston Tea Party!" Then, as the girl flung back her wet hair and tossed two objects that looked like ceramic birds into the water barrels, "Down with the junk, we're drowning the junk!"

The line of kids was working fast, passing things out of the store, merchandise I suppose you'd call it (I have to admit that to me it looked like the kind of useless garbage sold by the carload in all those suburban warehouse discount shopping centers), pink plastic rollers for women's hair, green plastic collapsible chairs, yellow plastic portable pools, white plastic place mats, striped plastic drinking glasses, fake-pearl steak knives and shishkebab skewers, kitchen clocks made to look like sunbursts, turdlike china candleholders, little animals like squirrels and chipmunks made up as bookends, transistorized gizmos to time TV dinners in ovens, junk, junk, junk, the mass-produced debris of our culture.

I wasn't sorry to see it go. I almost felt like cheering the kids on. I think I should admit this here, if nowhere else, that in another moment I *would* have joined them, if not in the pass-it-on line of destruction, then at least in applauding that wet, sweaty, laughing girl as she tossed their grubby loot into the rusty water barrels. But then a big blue-and-white van pulled up alongside Seth's truck, one of those mobile TV vans, and began discharging a crew that was scrambling, actually running with heavy equipment, to capture the scene.

"No more speeches!" the boy with the bullhorn was yelling. "Hurrah for a safe and sane Fourth of July! Dump the redemption center! Join the Children of Liberty, redeem the land!"

And the cameramen were zooming in on him, on the boys up on the roof with their eighteenth-century flag, on the line extending into the center, which I could now see had been broken into. Then the camera began to describe an arc, to capture the crowd in the lens—and it dawned on me, very late, but with sudden force, that I had been set up for this, that I would stick out like a sore thumb in this cheering crowd of holiday-making kids.

I felt trapped, entrapped, enraged. I shook myself free of Seth. I pulled open the door of his truck but could not get up into it unaided. The TV crew had caught sight of us and were swinging about.

I don't know if they had been tipped off, or if it was the sound of the sirens behind us that distracted them. While I stood there, helpless, trying to scramble into the truck (scramble, how ridiculous! I couldn't even lift my leg high enough to reach the inside), one squad car after another wheeled into the plaza like something out of a gangster movie, sirens wailing down as they ground to a stop in a circle around the crowd, blue lights whirling like some final visual fillip to the crazy afternoon's festivities.

"Get me out of here, you son of a bitch!" I cursed at Seth.

He stared at me, expressionless, his face almost vapid.

"You son of a bitch, don't just stand there, lift me into the truck." I must have been glaring at him.

Finally he moved, with what seemed to me to be agonizing

slowness. Maybe it was because he was uneasy about hoisting me or handling me roughly. But at last I was inside the cab; I took out a handkerchief to mop away the sweat, and kept it to my face in case the TV camera should be probing the windshield—I couldn't tell for sure.

Seth came around to the other side, jumped in, and eased out of the lot in reverse, as casually as he had swung into it.

When we were clear—I did think until the last second that we might be stopped by the police, but apparently they were intent on rounding up the young people and securing the garbage in the redemption center—I took the handkerchief away and said, through lips that were very parched, "That was a rotten, rotten thing to do."

He said, "It's the first time I ever saw you, or heard of you, hiding from the cameras."

I was holding on to the dashboard as he swung about. I really felt like hitting him, striking out at him. "What do you mean?" I demanded. "Just what the hell do you mean?"

"Did you go incognito to Russia in the twenties, to see what the Bolsheviks were doing for the homeless waifs of the revolution? Did you go incognito to West Virginia in the thirties, to see what was being done for the starving children of the miners? Did you go incognito to Japan in the forties, to see what was being done for the Hiroshima children? Or to Korea in the fifties? Or to Biafra? Don't tell me it's different now, don't tell me you're too old—you were in your eighties when you went to Biafra."

"Biafra?" I said. "How can you mention it in the same breath with this playacting? Who set you up as my moral guide? Who appointed you my Vergil?"

He glanced at me from the corner of his eye. "You did."

I can't write any more. I'm whipped.

JULY 13 So much has been happening, but I can't clarify this battling outside my door if I don't explain to myself how I came through that ordeal with Seth. When I think back on it I believe I was even more enraged at his equating the trash-in at the shopping plaza with Biafra than I was with his hauling me off by trickery to that dunking party—and that's what led me to reevaluate everything.

They knew, here, what happened even before Seth and I turned up. I have never seen J. so upset and angry; she had brought Walter and Lily over to await our return—all three pounced on Seth, they made me undress and lie down, they told me they had notified Larry Brodie in Washington.

When Rog tried to say something, they all turned on him. Walter said very coldly, "You should never have allowed him to make that trip."

"What makes you think that I knew where they were going to stop?" he asked.

They had no proof of that at all, and I can't believe he knew, I just can't believe it. I'm still not even sure that Seth had timed things so that we'd arrive there simultaneously with the TV van—but even if he did, I was having second thoughts about his "betraying" me or "tricking" me.

The reason for that is not so very complicated. After we pulled out of the shopping plaza, all the way into the city, where we turned in the truck and picked up a rented car, I was in a state of shock. It was partly physical and I think also partly nervous. Seth didn't say one word, either by way of explanation or of apology, but he made a silent decision to head for home right away rather than bothering to pick up the rest of his stuff at his apartment. He drove with a kind of concentrated grimness, glancing at me occasionally from the corner of his eye, I suppose to see if I was all right or was going to collapse on him.

It was only after we'd made the exchange and I was half-reclining, somewhat more comfortably, in the rented car on the turnpike heading for home that I got myself together enough to stop thinking back to Biafra and start talking with S. He reached under the seat and brought out a pint of whisky and made me take a snort. It made my eyes water, but it did quicken the blood in my veins.

"What kind of trick was that to pull?" I asked him. "And what kind of lunacy is it, to compare such an escapade to the suffering of hungry children, or bomb-blast victims?"

"You misunderstood me," he said flatly.

"May be," I said. "But I can only think how you must hate me to have exposed me to that."

"I don't hate you."

"Then you have contempt for me. I'd almost rather you hated me."

"I have contempt only for what those around you have been trying to make of you." At that point he took a drink himself from the bottle.

"And to the extent that I've allowed them to—"

"It's your responsibility. That's right. It isn't as if you were dead, or senile. You're still able to make your own choices. You did that when you went to Russia, and Japan, and Korea, and Biafra. You allowed yourself to be photographed, I've seen the pictures of you in those places, it's part of your myth. I even saw you on the tube, when you were at the airport heading for Biafra, and at the press conference when you got back."

I still wasn't sure what he was getting at, and I told him so.

"They're going to use those old stills and film clips in your TV biography, aren't they, while Dick Wells extracts charming anecdotes from you for the sound track?"

"I don't see what I can do about that," I said.

"In fact you like the idea."

"So I'm a vain old man," I said. "Is that what this is about?"

"Not quite." He offered me a kosher pickle from a jar, but the idea gave my stomach contractions. "All those times, you allowed yourself to be used, you submitted to publicity, not just out of vanity but because you were persuaded that the cause was just. So if you could help by looking into the camera, you would."

"That's not exactly right," I had to say.

"But it's near enough, isn't it? So why are you outraged now? Not because you might have your picture taken. It has to be because all those other experiences are safe by now, they don't make waves anywhere. Especially not in Washington. You don't want to go near anything that could, do you?" He hesitated and then added abruptly, "I thought I'd give you the opportunity to see something for yourself. Maybe to take one last chance. That's all."

I said, "Things always look different with hindsight. You don't take into account two things: I wasn't shanghaied into any of those earlier trips, and some of them were less popular and more problematical then than they might look to you now. But I was shanghaied into this one, I was taken advantage of, that's what I resent, and that's what you refuse to admit."

"I didn't force you into anything," he insisted. "I wanted you to see. If you didn't want to be seen you didn't have to. How does that make it different from your inspection trip to Biafra back in 1969? Remember, I'm talking about the publicity angle, not about the difference between starving babies and affluent kids."

It was true, I'd been thinking about those trips of the postwar years that had started, even before Hiroshima, with one to the DP camps, and ended (so I'd thought, anyway) with the physically and morally draining one to Biafra when I was already in my 83rd year and Jenny was terrified to let me go. And one reason I'd been thinking about them was that I knew Dick Wells would be talking with me about them. They were part of the substance of my life after the Sophia School closed down and I discovered that without the daily responsibility I was free to roam—not just sexually but geographically.

So I had started another life, not exactly methodically, but not exactly drifting into it either. It was a life about which I had—at least looking back on it—fewer compunctions or guilt feelings than about the School and what I'd had to do to keep that going; so it would presumably be easier to talk about with Wells than the earlier days had been. Well, easier for myself—less risk of ripping myself open, laying myself open to either insomnia or nightmares—but harder in the sense that as I get older even the "humanitarian" cause, the children's cause, seems less simple, more complex, than it once did.

I decided I owed it to Seth to explain some of this to him, if only to clear myself of his suspicion that I was simply greedy for adulation.

"We all like to have ourselves seen in a good light, don't we?" I said. "Maybe I am endlessly hungry for praise, maybe that's one reason I decided to go on with Wells's series about me—although I assure you it's already caused me a good deal more pain that I won't tell you about. But I want you to try to understand that I had other motives too. One of them was to try to get past this notion of me as a kindly old stuffed shirt, not for the sake of my own image (my God, how I hate that word!) but as a problem in intellectual rectitude. To take, for example, the Biafra trip, and show that what I got out of it was not another good-conduct medal but a profound sense of uncertainty. A sense that good and evil were so profoundly intermixed in the world, in me too, that even if I were physically capable—which I haven't been since Biafra, after all I'm not Superman—I would think twice before letting myself be used to promote anything other than the most universally accepted causes. I suppose you think that's just a rationalization for an increasingly encrusted moss-bound conservatism, but God damn it, I've tried to keep free of that incubus. Why else do you think I asked Rog Girard to join my household? Why do you think I wanted you to come and stay?"

When I stopped he took his eyes off the turnpike after a moment and said, "Go ahead, I'm listening. I've been waiting for you to open up. Tell me about Biafra."

So I did. I started with my insistence to the young people

from the group called the American Committee to Keep
Biafra Alive that all I was committed to, before seeing for
myself, was keeping Biafrans alive, especially children. And
with my calling at the Nigerian Consulate and being loaded
down with literature by a worried but polite young man.

"So you wanted to keep your nose clean," Seth said. "Get
specific."

"If I went into detail about the political lineup you'd say
I was boring you. But I had to do my homework in a hurry,
to get a sense of the politics of Nigeria since independence, to
see why it was that England and Russia and most of black
Africa were lined up behind Nigeria, with France and the
Vatican and the Portuguese and the South Africans, together
with a lot of assorted idealists, an odd combination, backing
Biafra. You don't care about that, do you?"

Seth smiled briefly. "I can read history books. I want to
know what you saw. Why do you keep harping on it just
because I stopped off with you to watch a redemption center
being trashed?"

"Fair enough," I said, although I knew he was setting
more narrow limits on me than, say, Dick Wells would.
"First thing I remember is the long flight from Lisbon down
to Luanda in Angola. The plane was full of young wives,
coming home from leave I suppose, with babies that they
bedded down in little hammocks slung from the ceiling of
the plane. Maybe I tend to fix on children. All I know is that
as I watched those women crooning to the babies in the
swaying hammocks, I felt the imperial lifeline more sharply
than if I'd been briefed, either by Portuguese administrators
or by the rebels who were fighting them down in Angola."

"When do we get to Biafra?" he asked.

"Don't be brutal," I said. "Humor me. By the time our
party took off, the sea access through Port Harcourt and the
other harbors had already been retaken by the Nigerians. We
had to fly up from Luanda to the island of São Tomé and
from there hitch a ride on one of the relief planes that were

airlifting supplies by night to a blacked-out airstrip in what was left of Biafra. It was on the island, a former penal colony, that I got my first taste of that seediness that always collects on the fringes of war areas, where there are dollars to be made as well as babies to be saved." And I told him about the young Frenchman who insisted on buying me drinks when I would awaken, still exhausted and enervated, from the midday siesta—a furtive little fellow who hinted broadly of his skills as a stealthy killer, skills learned in the back alleys of Algeria. He was of the type that become professional strikebreakers, foreign legionnaires, and here he was, drawn by a paycheck and the smell of blood to a land where idealists permitted babies to starve.

"But there were idealists too," Seth pointed out quite rightly, "who didn't permit the babies to starve, right?"

"There always are," I said. "When we got into the fighting area, I met them at Ubakulu Sick Bay, at Queen Elizabeth's Hospital, and in the courtyard of the Holy Ghost Order. That's where they took the films that you seem to object to.

"I don't want to weigh you down with the babies with the big bellies and that terrible knotlike protuberance that marks the onset of kwashiorkor, along with apathy, depigmentation, and a ghastly reddening of the hair. After all, I didn't have to go there either, to see them with my own eyes, in order to believe that they existed—and expired in the bush when their mothers and older brothers dragged them off the road to die. I could have seen them on the tube, as you and I have since seen other babies, in Bangla Desh. No doubt there will be more, after I've gone."

"Despite your efforts," Seth said.

I looked at him sharply to see if he was being sarcastic, but his mouth was firm and his eyes, behind the sunglasses, seemed fixed on the road ahead.

"In a public sense, Biafra was my last try," I said. "Yes, I hoped my presence would contribute something to spur the flow of food. But in a private sense, I'm trying to explain to you now that I went there to see for myself, not starvation, but evil. I wanted to discover, while I still had the physical strength, whether evil was abroad as it had been during the Second World War. There was much talk of genocide, of two million dead and more to come. I remember a poster fluttering on the plaster wall of the clinic at Ubakulu Sick Bay, a photograph of emaciated children not unlike those surrounding us, and captioned 'This Is Genocide.' But you see," I said to Seth, "after I'd been there some days I decided that it was not deliberate genocide."

I remember how Seth turned to me, surprised. "Do you mean to tell me that you didn't find the evil you were hunting for?"

"Not unless you think of stupidity as evil. And pride, and bullheadedness—on both sides—and of course bigotry. Bigotry was in large supply, along with starvation. What I'm saying is that after I'd tramped those dusty tropical roads and bounced through the roadblocks and listened to the impassioned young politicians denouncing their opposite numbers on the other side, I wasn't ready to come back here and assign all the blame for the bigotry and the starvation to one small group of villains."

"Is that what you're trying to sell me, that there are two sides to the question? Is that the wisdom of a lifetime?"

Was he impenetrable? A feeling of desperation was overcoming me. And along with it, a fear that I would die, then and there, that hot sultry frightening afternoon in the plastic-smelling rented car on the broad turnpike midway between what we had seen and what was back here in my quiet country house.

"It was guilt that impelled me to go to Biafra, not only against the advice of Dr. Harrison, who advises me against everything, but against the wishes of my wife, who had the job of nursing me back to health when I came home wracked with dysentery."

I was ready to say more, but he said sharply, almost as if

I were annoying him, "What were you feeling guilty about? You already said it wasn't the starving babies. You had no responsibility for a civil war in Nigeria. Is this supposed to be one of those existential guilts that they like to talk about in college philosophy courses?"

"I wouldn't know about that stuff," I assured him. "I do know about the death factories Hitler built for the Jews. And I do know that while Jewish children were being gassed and cremated, I was fussing around with the closing of my school, and with even more selfish concerns." I wanted to say more, I really did, at that moment I thought the time had come to say everything; his head was cocked toward me, he seemed receptive and even kind; there was nothing between us but a trapped fly which finally buzzed loose and sailed out of the window on his side. But the words stuck in my throat. All I could manage was something half-articulate about how stupid and bestial men (meaning myself) can be, filling their bellies, emptying their balls, lusting after women and adulation at the very moment when utter evil is let loose and ought to be forced back into its cage.

Maybe something of what I was struggling to say did get through. When he spoke, Seth was no longer mocking or cynical. His voice was measured. "So you crawled on that relief plane and risked your skin and your guts to make sure that you wouldn't be turning your back on genocide—the way you had twenty-five years before?"

"Something like that." I felt grateful to him now, no longer angry, no longer abused (even though by now I was really exhausted), but I still felt I had to make my point with him at the risk of having him set his face against me. "I didn't want to go, really, Seth," I said. "But I didn't dare *not* go. I was old, but not so old that I could use it as an excuse to sit home. And when I came back, I pleased no one—not even myself, I suppose, because it's easy to be moralistic and righteous, and difficult to be unsure. And I was simply not convinced that there was anything to the genocide charges, even though I was sure that thousands of Ibos had been brutally slaughtered several years earlier, maybe even in one planned, concerted drive."

Then I went on to what was most important to me, hoping only that it would be to S. as well.

"I was left even more uncertain about the whole matter of pride—tribal, racial, patriotic—and its responsibility for increasing the sum total of human misery in the world.

"I can still hear those women at six o'clock in the morning outside the quadrangle of the Holy Rosary Order of the Missionary Sisters, squatting in the reddish dust that is everywhere in the Nigerian dry season, and chanting *Kene Biafra O Chuku*, over and over. God in the Highest bless you, bless Biafra, O God.

"And I can still hear the outrage in the voice of the minister of information when I raised the question of whether all his rhetoric, all his insistence on the foe's genocidal fury, didn't make de-escalation more difficult. 'You cannot negotiate with a people who want you exterminated!' he shouted at me, as if the shouting would convince me of what nothing else had. And now you . . ." I said to Seth, but could not go on.

"And now I what?" Seth demanded. "I want to betray you?"

I shook my head, and then I found words. "No, I don't think that any more. But I do think that patriotism, even though your friends may consider it a smart way, a shrewd way, to reach people, is not a moral way. You know," I told him, "I was a little encouraged, I was just beginning to feel that maybe young people were outgrowing patriotism. Enough of them volunteered to drop bombs on Vietnam to enable us to go on tormenting those people for years—but enough of them said no, for the first time, to make me believe that the patriotic slogans were wearing out at last. But then along come the Children of Liberty to appeal to the same old retrograde notions. Why? In the name of higher efficaciousness? And would I really be such a wonderfully brave and daring old man if I were to go along with that?"

S. didn't say anything. We drove on for what seemed such a long while that I began to feel maybe he wasn't ever going to answer. I think maybe I even dozed off again. I do remember, though, that at length I turned back to him and found him smiling.

"Well," he said, "you finally got to say your say, didn't you?"

"Not all of it," I said. "But some. I have this uneasy feeling that every time I open my mouth, words come out in the form of a speech. I don't mean them that way."

He said, "I know that. But I don't have to agree, do I? We can carry this a bit further another time, can't we?"

I said sure we could, and I meant it. I hadn't said the final word, but that wasn't for his lack of willingness to listen. And if he hadn't said even the first word, or apologized to me for what he still seemed to regard as an innocent bit of trickery, he was apparently ready to. In fact he did go on to deny that his friends were patriots in the sense of being simple flag-wavers or disingenuous radicals. "We're not trying to get kids involved in anything like war or violence under false pretenses," he said. "We're not using love of country to arouse hatred against another people."

"How about against people within the country?"

"Don't you distinguish between scorn and hatred?" he asked.

So there we were. And I was content to let it go at that for the time, and even a little pleased—so pleased in fact that I was unready for the way all hell broke loose when we pulled into the circular drive here. Next time, next time. I think this is the longest entry I've ever succeeded in getting down at one stretch.

JULY 14   Bastille Day. And everyone here except me seemingly in terror that the Children of Liberty will pull off another 4th of July coup and somehow involve me. But I'm rocking on my own porch, while the participants in the trashing are going before a judge, charged with breaking and entering, willful destruction of property, etc. etc. etc.

Why are they all so insecure? No, that is a silly question, even if I put it to myself rhetorically. Everyone has his fears and his fantasies. Those who have the most to lose must have the greatest fears, I should think; if you don't have all that much, you are not going to break out in cold sweat at the thought of some crazy kids taking it away from you, whether by water, by fire, or simply by conjuring.

It was not until some days after the Boston Tea Party that I began to see its true consequences. In that first flush of anger and excitement, of course, I had intuitively grasped the fact that I'd been entrapped by Seth and that I had to get out of it, even by ingloriously hiding my face. But then on the way home he and I came to some sort of provisional understanding; and after that I took sick and only heard in a kind of feverish way the heated arguments, the raised voices in the hallway, the comings and goings that I knew had to do with my exposure to the trashing at the shopping center.

My God, the outrage! I've been feeling the shock waves ever since I tottered out of bed, some days after that grueling trip, and Dr. Harrison let me sit on the porch and listen to the radio. By the time Rog was reading *The Times* to me once again, and I could concentrate on what he was reading, the Letters to the Editor columns were bloated with righteous indignation. Right here at home, they were as unremitting as they dared to be in their attacks on Seth, wanted to cast him out, evict him, etc., until I told them all to cut it out, that he was to stay as long as he liked if only because he was my child.

Yes, I said that, and they all took it metaphorically. An old man's whimsy or something of that sort.

But never mind me, and everyone's vested interest in me,

for whatever I'm worth to them. After all, S. has that interest too. What gets me is the solemnity with which they express their horror at the C. of L.'s behavior. The stuffy editorials you could expect; after all, my immediate reaction as an eye-witness wasn't all that different (even if it was more legitimate, since I was entrapped, almost labeled as a participant). But the way it has kept up, the demands for outlawing, the fear of contagion, of the thing catching on, of young people all over the place taking the bicentennial celebration next year as an excuse to express their destructive instincts!

Even cool old Walter joined in. "Never mind that they began with useless or ugly objects," he pleaded the other day, bringing me cookies from dear Lily, who herself has been somewhat knocked out by our hot spell. "What is to prevent them from rampaging in art galleries if they decide that paintings are a useless bourgeois corruption of the artistic spirit? Supposing they decide pianos are counterrevolutionary? Or libraries?"

"Walter, Walter," I said, "you miss the point. I can understand your reverence for property, it's the basis of your entire professional life, but there ought to be some recognition of their values. Don't we share their repugnance for mass-produced trash?"

"That's irrelevant." Walter was quite crisp, self-assured, and giving me to understand that in this matter at least he was on his home ground and I had better attend to him. "It does not follow that they have the right to destroy. Once you set yourself above the law and assert the arrogant infallibility of your own taste, you deny to others the right to assert their own preferences, whether they coincide with yours or not."

That business of setting yourself above the law is one of those phrases that set my teeth on edge. Just the same, he knew he'd stabbed at a weak spot and he pressed on.

"Let's grant that these kids are acting from the highest of motives. Let's grant too that their taste is impeccable and that they wish only to call our attention to the mountains of trash that surround us. Once we allow them the right to destroy, others will assert the same right, and perhaps even usurp their name, to destroy not what we despise but what we cherish."

I think I have it down right; if not, I believe I've got the courtroom flavor. When he's really wound up, Walter doesn't sound as though he's trying to propagandize an ignorant and gullible jury—no, he's a judge's lawyer, and at his florid best you can imagine him arguing his case before the Supreme Court.

"You know, Walter," I said to him, "you come over here with a crock of home-baked cookies, and you're wearing that faded blue sport shirt and sneakers, but when you let fly with that rhetoric you seem to me to be wearing your Tripler suit and figured tie and Clapp shoes."

He's a rubicund old gent, but I'll swear he flushed anyway, right down to the collar of that open-neck shirt. "It's unworthy of you to resort to ad hominems," he said almost sorrowfully. "I forgive you for two reasons—because you're so much older than I, and because I know it's a sign, an indication of your own realization of the weakness of your argument."

So we wound up laughing, the way we usually have done over the years. He knew better than to pressure me about Seth—besides, Larry has taken over that job, unabashedly, in and out of here, back and forth between here and Washington like a bee buzzing between the flower and the hive. And it was Walter who grabbed the phone and rang L. at the White House on the 4th, I know it for a fact. And he knows I know it.

Tired. Maybe I can come back to this after a little nap?

JULY 16 Peculiar dream yesterday, even more peculiar consequences. I was in Harrison's office for a checkup. He asked what was bothering me. I said, Nothing, nothing at all. (Should make clear that the voice was familiar but it wasn't Harrison's, which didn't surprise me, as I couldn't see him, being on my knees with my pants around my ankles on his examining table, squatting awkwardly on a fresh sheet of waxy paper like an old, inedible side of beef.) Well, he said, and I could hear him squishing his rubber-gloved fingers into a jar of Vaseline, let's have a look-see. A disgusting expression and a disgusting experience. Every time I think of it I wince, and I wonder how the greatest of men—a poet, say, or a president—can seem great to his proctologist or his GP. I know all the scientific reasons for the exam, but I am still reluctant to submit to the painful indignity.

Anyway: The interesting part of the dream was not that I broke into a sweat, which I always do when I feel those fingers probing deep into my asshole, but that the doctor cried out, Aha, here's the root of our trouble! and hauled forth some lengthy object, the removal of which left me feeling spent, drained, prostrate (I almost wrote prostate) on the cold repellent table. I wiped the grease from my behind with the paper squares he'd made available, pulled up my underpants and trousers with arthritic awkwardness, and turned to see that the doctor was Dick Wells. With a white jacket on, he looked like one of those kindly television doctors who are always solving problems.

In his gloved hand he was holding a string of pearls that I recognized at once. You know it? he asked me, and I said impatiently, Of course I do, I'd know it anywhere. I hadn't seen it since my mother's death, which means about seventy years, but then it's true that I had seen a reproduction of it in a sketch my father had made of mother wearing the pearls about her neck, seated on a draped chair in his studio in Florence. I don't care much for the drawing, but I did show it to J. when we were married before putting it away again in the attic; in fact the pearls had been a wedding present from Father to Mother, purchased during their honeymoon in Venice, just as a Bohemian garnet brooch he'd bought in Prague had been an engagement present.

I wondered briefly, on awakening, why I hadn't dreamed of the garnet. As I hastened to find Jenny to tell her of the dream—not the unpleasant details, just the principal part, which seemed so pat, so obvious—I was laughing at the thought of how painful it would have been for me if that TV doctor had extracted the blood-red garnet, with its baroque setting, from my rectum. You don't know when you're well off!

J. was working at her big drawing table, lips caught between her teeth, while she measured off a big undersea photo with T square and triangle, preparatory to cropping and matting. She glanced up as I came in and smiled at me. But when I opened my mouth to tell her of the dream, as silly as any dream I've ever had, I felt abashed. Not because of the circumstances, or the silliness, but because in that very instant of revealing myself, another revelation came to me. I was suddenly convinced, absolutely convinced, that I understood the true meaning of the dream for the first time, and that the "patent" or "latent" meanings were not even worth bothering with.

"Look here!" I burst out angrily.

J. lifted her long hands slowly from the drawing board, the smile fading from her face. She was not used to hearing such words from me, uttered in such a tone.

"Do you remember my saying to you two or three weeks ago," I demanded, "that I had the feeling someone was going through my desk? Reading my personal papers?"

She nodded slowly.

"Well, now I'm convinced of it. I've kept them locked, but someone's been at them. Someone has been reading . . ."

"How do you know?" Her question was a reasonable one, but at the moment it sounded to me as though I was the one who was not to be trusted, as though I was the one who would bear watching.

I repeated her question angrily, mockingly. "How do I know?" And then of course I realized that I had no answer. What was I to say, that I'd just had a dream which I interpreted as a warning? I could hear her replying, Oh *Sam,* and stroking my cheek with loving kindness. I couldn't bear that.

"If I were to tell you that I put a hair on the paper and that the hair was gone, what would you say—that it had blown away?"

She nodded coolly. "Probably."

I felt myself growing angrier, in the way that you do when you know that sense and reason are not on your side. The weaker and wronger I felt, the louder my voice became. I knew it was childish, I knew she would be, if not hurt, at least distressed by my unanswerable petulance, but all that only served to intensify my belligerence. I heard myself saying, as if from a distance, "Well, I think it stinks, when I can't even feel secure in my own home, when I can't even have one last private area in my life, without having people prying and poking around." I thought of the doctor in the dream and I winced—not for that, but for what I was saying. "Is it too much to ask, that I can be left this one last bit of privacy?"

"I've worked very hard at seeing that you have it," she said, very quietly. "All I can say is I'm sorry if you don't believe that."

"Being sorry doesn't help," I said, driven further into stupidity by the unanswerable nature of her statement.

My brutality stung her. "I can't take responsibility for guaranteeing you anything," she said, "if you and Rog sabotage my efforts."

"What does that mean?" I challenged her.

"If anyone has invaded your privacy it has been Seth Fox. What he did that day was appalling. I can understand your coming back with him—you had no other way of getting home—but inviting him to stay on after that . . . insisting that he stay on! It's beyond me, just beyond me."

"He's my child!" I threw at her defiantly.

"Your grandchild."

I retreated a little. "It comes to the same thing."

"He took terrible risks with you. He made you ill. I can't see that he has any scruples at all."

"Now I suppose you're going to tell me he's the one who's been reading my private papers."

"I wouldn't put it past him." No sooner had the words passed her lips than she bit down on them, but it was too late; I had forced her into saying something unworthy of her; and I felt a perverse kind of triumph, as if I had succeeded in proving to her that she could be as mean and irrational as I, given the provocation. Isn't it strange, how shaming someone you love, forcing her to admit her own weakness, can give you pleasure.

Then she said, much too late, "Not that I think Seth did it."

I wouldn't let go. "If you think he didn't do it, either you think someone else did it, or no one did it."

"If you're so insistent . . . I think no one did it."

"So it's all in my head."

"You don't seem to have any . . ."

"Proof?" I asked her.

"Well . . . Mrs. Hoskins may have moved things around while she was cleaning," she answered, but without any particular force, as if she hardly believed the possibility herself.

Her uncertainty encouraged me to say several things that simply weren't true: "I've already spoken to Mrs. H. about it, and she had no idea what I was talking about. And if you're going to bring up Rog Girard as a possible culprit, I already brought it up. Let me tell you what he said." I paused, and then went on, rather dramatically, I suppose, "He said, Oh, I don't need to look at your memoirs, if that's what you're writing—someday I'm going to write my own! And he laughed like mad."

J. was looking at me dubiously now. I had the feeling that maybe I had pushed matters a bit too far. If I were to tell her this had all started with a semi-comic dream about my anus and a string of pearls, would she have laughed until the tears came? Or would she have become even more upset with me, even more convinced that I was a senile old fusspot?

"Listen," I said with a certain sternness, "why are you so reluctant to concede the possibility that it could have been someone else?"

She sighed. "I really can't think who else there is around here, except me and the Hendricks boys. They're in and out, fixing this and that. But I doubt that they'd be interested."

She was humoring me, teasing me. It infuriated me. "I'll tell you who else is in and out. Larry."

She stared at me. "He's been in and out for thirty-five years! You talk about Seth being your child—Larry is much more of a son to you than he could ever be. If you're really determined to distrust Larry, you might as well distrust me."

"Can you swear," I said loudly, my voice creaking, "that you and Larry have never done anything, anything at all, that you wouldn't want me to know about?"

J. flushed bright red, I have never seen her like that, then turned very pale. She seemed to be fighting for self-control, she didn't reply to me for quite a while. She walked around her drawing table, folded her arms, then turned back to me.

"I really wouldn't have believed you capable of this."

"Maybe you *should* have been reading my diary," I taunted her. "Then you'd know what I'm capable of."

"I've just never seen you so . . ." she raised her bare tanned arm and let it fall helplessly to her side.

"I've never been so put upon," I said. "How would you react if you were me, an old bone being pawed at by a bunch of dogs? If Seth doesn't leave me in peace, neither does Larry. Or even Walter, for that matter. Walter got Larry on the phone the day of that trip, I still don't know how he found him on the 4th of July holiday, and the next thing you know Larry's helicopter is on the lawn like a God-damned general's and he's badgering me, nagging me not to let Seth stay on, not to let him into my life any more. The only reason he finally left me alone was that old Harrison practically threw him out. And as soon as I'd recovered my strength a little, Larry was back."

"Only because he's been dreadfully worried about you."

"Worried about recapturing me. His big trophy for the White House."

"I'm sorry, I think you're unfair."

"And I think you're prejudiced. Don't you think I know Seth took advantage of me that day? All I'm saying is everybody does. Nobody lets me be. Just be."

J. seemed to consider this for a while, then said very softly, "I'll try to see that you're not disturbed. We'll talk about this again when things have quieted down."

She walked out the French doors, on to the garden where she could wear down her agitation with a trowel and a hoe, and left me to her prints and her file drawers. I had no desire to look into her files; besides, she always left them open when she went away. I haven't run in many years, but I wanted to run after her and say to her, Jenny, Jenny, you were never willing to see me for what I am. Ever since that first day you walked in here, you took me for some kind of unsoiled hero. You were awed by my journeys to Japan, Germany, anyplace where children suffered, you were awed by my very name and my eighty years and my seeming immortality, and my willingness to enlist in the anti–Vietnam war movement. As if I wasn't eager to be signed up, to be where the young were!

Even after you came to me and insisted on sharing what was left of my life (who would have thought there would be so much of it!), you persisted in perpetuating that stainless image. When I went on that last trip, to Biafra, you were terrified but secretly overjoyed and proud at the confirmation of your radiant faith in my purity. My complicity in making Larry an essential part of your life, once he'd rid himself of that tiresome woman, was only further evidence of my saintliness and all-encompassing understanding.

Well, now you know better.

I wanted to tell her those things, but instead I stood rooted to the floor of her room, watching her detach herself from me with a smooth firm resolution.

JULY 19   Before I forget, a strange and (for me at least) terrible occurrence. The day after my long harangue at J., when I insulted and humiliated her, I was up very early. I don't think it was six yet, but of course it was bright daylight, gloriously clear, the sun glittering on the dewy grass in the hayfield to the east of the house. I went out to the kitchen to make myself some coffee before Mrs. H. would be bustling about, cooking up her hotbreads. I was sitting on the porch sipping my instant coffee and drinking in the view, thinking that I really didn't deserve it, when to my astonishment J. came through the screen door—not from her room, but from outdoors, where she'd obviously been for a walk. Her sneakers were soaked through, and for that matter so were her white denim slacks, the bottoms of which were festooned with damp blades of grass and hay.

Before I could express my surprise at her having been out walking at such an hour—and with no camera slung over her shoulder for an excuse—she smiled her incredible smile, and greeted me with a warmth as glowing as the sunshine in which I was basking. I wanted to say something about hoping that it wasn't my fault she'd gotten up so early, hoping she hadn't lost sleep over my accusations—I wanted to express some kind of left-handed apology, really, some wish to be forgiven for my meanness. But the words did not come, and I sat there hating myself as she bent over me for a brief embrace.

"I hope you managed to sleep last night, Sam," she said solicitously. "I was worried about you being so upset, it's not good for you. I looked in on you during the night, and you seemed to be resting all right. But you're such a sly one—you might only have been pretending!"

And she tapped my shoulder archly. Not only had she for-

202

given me, there didn't even seem to be anything left for us to argue about, or to straighten out. She was the one who had been worried and upset about me, not me about her.

It was almost as if she had read my description of our scene and come to a decision about it after a long walk through the dewy dawn. No sooner did the thought enter my mind than I recalled, as she bustled about behind me in the kitchen, her saying that she had "looked in" on me. Maybe it was then that she read the apology I had been unable to utter aloud?

As soon as I could, I made my usual muttered apology about having to go to the bathroom and hastened back here to take out the diary. There was absolutely no sign of its having been touched since I put it away yesterday after that awful scene. What was I to make of that? I sat here for a long time, staring at it, and all I could think was, Oh God, if she didn't read it and she still behaved as she did this morning out on the porch, then she has decided that my wits are going and that she is going to have to humor me, play nursemaid, jolly me along, accept my eccentric tantrums. What will I do if my wife becomes convinced that I am senile? How do you talk someone out of that? How do you disprove it?

The best I could hope for would be for her to tell people, He had a good day today, He was his old self, He was clear as a bell, There are times when you'd never know, when the clouds blow away and he's as kind as ever, as sharp and amusing and witty as ever. . . . Oh my God.

JULY 20 I wasn't going to write any more about Jenny yesterday, but I got carried away. And then it became so painful I couldn't turn to what I originally wanted to set down—had to stop instead. Now I have pulled myself together and want to attack this business of my household ganging up on me. Where to start?

Only after my recuperation did I discover that someone claimed to have spotted me in a truck at the site of the trash-in. Considerable uncertainty about who the "someone" was. By the time the press turned up here, J. had tucked me into bed, Harrison had given me a sedative and ordered that no one outside the family could see me, etc. etc. When Larry got here, he leaked word that the "someone" was one of the Children of Liberty, trying to claim me as a sponsor of their craziness, and that the story was unworthy of serious attention.

Seth was infuriated, saying that L. had no right to put the finger on the Children of Liberty, who already had their hands full with prosecution on half a dozen charges, without their having to disclaim responsibility for exploiting me.

That was only part of the noise I heard, swelling from time to time like unpleasant music from a neighbor's party. Rog had, as he'd often done before, given "Samuel Lumen's" statement to the press about the episode. Walter, backed up by Larry, confronted Rog for the first time (at least I never saw or heard him do it until this last week) and accused him of putting words in my mouth.

"Who authorized you," I heard him ask R., "to issue statements from Mr. Lumen's sickbed?"

Rog's voice was so quiet—as usual—that I had to strain to hear his response. He said something like, "I have never abused Mr. Lumen's confidence."

"That's not responsive," Walter snapped out, as sharply as if he were in a courtroom. He must have thought I was asleep.

"If you feel I've exceeded my authority," Rog said, "all you have to do is ask Mr. Lumen if he feels I've misrepresented him."

I knew it was getting sticky; Walter shrinks from this kind of thing. In fact, his response was inaudible to me. I had the feeling he was not only lowering his voice because he'd reminded himself of me, presumably sleeping in here, but restraining himself from accusing R. of being in cahoots with Seth. The worst thing for me was the conviction that old Walter was trying to forestall the possibility of R. and S. forming a syndicate after my demise, in order to misrepresent me as being a sponsor of whatever they happened to be involved with.

And Rog? And Seth? Same thing in reverse. I get the feeling they are determined to elbow Larry aside. If they can't do it while I'm alive, by means of the Children of Liberty or whatever else will make L. turn purple and drive him out of the household in terror, they'll pursue it after I'm out of the way.

Christ, what a bunch of vultures. If I brought them all in here and lined them up in a row they'd look at me the way J. looks at me. With love and pity. Poor old boy, it's a shame you're losing your grip. We'll bear with your paranoia for the sake of your good name and your past glory.

But it is true, damn it, taken separately I love them. And need them.

JULY 21   Rog came in with a series of folders. Correspondence, calls, queries, appointments. Harrison, he assures me, has OK'd a small work load—a little bit more each day, but portioned out, like exercise.

For a while it was boring but soothing, just what the doctor ordered. Then, after getting through some routine stuff and just before picking up *The Times* to read me the news summaries, he read me the statement he had issued in my name two weeks earlier, concerning the C. of L. and the looting of the redemption center. Casual but businesslike.

He was not halfway through it before I saw what the excitement was about. "Rog," I said, "I can understand your bypassing the question of whether I was actually there. I can see that if we admitted I was it would open the whole question of why, and of Seth and the kids, the whole works. But the way you wrote the statement it sounds as though you're balancing that off by denying that I was turning my back on them, much less fleeing from them, or hiding from them, or even attacking them."

He gave me an absolutely clear look—guileless, straightforward, even a bit puzzled. "But isn't that true?" he demanded, crossing his hands over the papers on his lap. "Isn't that a fair summation of the way things are?"

"Only superficially," I said.

"I don't think I understand." He bent forward over the statement. "I made no pretense of analyzing the organization or giving your response to its entire program. I thought it best to restrict the statement to a refutation on the one hand of the rumors that you knew beforehand of the group's plan —and on the other hand that you had condemned it in advance, and that they tricked you to get even."

"To make it short and sweet," I said to him, "you wanted to take the heat off me."

Rog's smile at this was not exactly a grin; it was more as if I had used an odd expression which caught his fancy. "I've always felt that was one of my responsibilities."

"Fair enough," I said. "But if you take the heat off, is it another of your responsibilities to add fuel to the fire at the same time?"

He stared at me, honestly puzzled. Or so it seemed.

"Why did you have to go out of your way to deny that I had refused to have anything to do with them?"

R. answered me with a question: "Isn't that another of my responsibilities, to knock down the idea that you are censorious of young people? Haven't you always urged me to bend over backwards in that regard? Even during the worst of the drug panic you insisted that we must never condemn young people's curiosity and spirit of experimentation. You've told me over and over: I never want to be cut off from young people—even when they're groping for strange things."

That was all true. Maybe the very fact that Rog was telling me that I had been using him to cover my left flank made me annoyed and irritable. Obviously he hadn't wanted to be put in the position of reminding me of the conditions of our relationship. Well, I didn't like his reminding me of them, either. So I struck back in what I suppose was a rather cruel way. "Didn't I just say," I asked, "that your summary of the situation was only superficially true?" When he inquired with his invariable politeness, "In what way?" I gave him an analogy.

"Suppose you had to squelch rumors that you have been having an affair with Jennifer." I could see him change color before my eyes. "I know there are such rumors. There have to be, given our household. If I asked you to compose a statement, what would you say? That it was nobody's business but ours? That it was a pack of lies? That would be true enough, but something more definitive would be expected from me. So maybe you would add that I have always been a supporter of freedom and equality for women, and that I never intrude into Mrs. Lumen's personal life."

By now R. was on his feet, scrambling rather desperately for the papers which had scattered about him as he jumped up. I didn't quit. "Wouldn't people say, and with some reasan, that even if all those things were true, they were only true in a superficial sense? So instead of killing the rumors, that kind of truth could only give rise to more speculation, right? I mean, cynics looking at my beautiful healthy wife could either wink, as they have for hundreds of years at the protestations of senile old husbands, or speculate about who else the lucky man might be, if in fact it wasn't Rog Girard, the faithful secretary."

R. started to protest, but I cut him off. "Let me finish. Cynics would also have to wonder about you, wouldn't they? What's in it for you, grubbing your life away for an old man with one foot in the grave, if you aren't even receiving his wife's favors? You're handsome, bright, obviously talented— in fact some of the cynics are claiming that you're the author of my late works, my sharp letters, my radical statements, aren't they?—and you're also very single and very unattached. How come?"

He really couldn't take any more. When I think about it now, I can hardly blame him.

207

"If you wouldn't like to be put in that position," I persisted, "then think a little about the position I'm in because of all these things that are imputed to me by you and Larry and everyone else."

"I do think about it," R. said, "I assure you I do," and then, muttering something about having promised Dr. Harrison that he wouldn't overtax me, he backed out. I think he wanted to slam the door.

I sat here for some time, wondering what had made me turn on him like that. It wasn't simply that Walter had finally convinced me that R. was abusing my confidence. I turn on Walter too in small ways, on Larry, on everyone. Why do they put up with it? Because they have more to gain by tolerating me? Or because, far from putting up with it, they're really planning and scheming to use me some more?

A funny familiar noise out in the yard roused me out of this nasty reverie. I picked up my stick and ambled on out, past the room R. used for an office (inside I could hear his typewriter clattering *furiously*—was he pouring his heart out to a friend? Bringing his own diary up to date? Writing more "truths" in my name? Maybe I should rifle his desk one day and find out how much truth there is in all of Larry's accusations). Was surprised to find, when I got outdoors, that Seth's Susie had set up the croquet game on the lawn and was banging away, pink instruction sheet in one hand, mallet in the other.

"Hi," she called out with her usual cheerfulness. "I found the set in the barn. Decided to take a whack at it."

"Why not?" I said. *"Faites comme chez vous."*

"What does that mean?"

"Have fun."

"I'd have more fun," she said, "if I had somebody to play with."

"Where's Seth?" That was what I really wanted to know in the first place.

"He went off to see those friends of his." She pouted. "Why don't you play with me?"

"It's been quite a few years," I said. "In fact, I can't even see the wickets."

Susie was more than nice about that. "I know what you mean," she said. "Like, I'm so nearsighted I can hardly see the lawn. Wait right here—don't go away!"

While I lowered myself into a garden chair, Susie ran off to the barn with the wickets, her fleshy hips joggling as she passed me. I sat there thinking about Seth, and our discussions since his return, which had been limited by my illness and recuperation. He hadn't said anything about it, but I had the feeling that my illness had been a good excuse for Larry and Walter to insist that he not spend too much time with me in my room. Now that I was up and about again I was determined to see more of him. Right now in fact I was anxious to find out if he had had anything to do with the statement about the Children of Liberty that Rog had composed in my name, so I was disappointed that he wasn't available—and a little uneasy at his going off to confer with what his girl called "those friends of his."

I was spoiling for another fight, I suppose. Maybe that was why I dropped off to sleep in the garden chair—nature's way of protecting me from the consequences of my own temper. Then I had one of those complex, involved dreams that they say can be completed in your head in something like four seconds.

I was going to visit Hester, who was in a nursing home at last, now that it no longer mattered, and dying of pneumonia. They'd tried penicillin, which was still pretty new, but she had an adverse reaction—so Henry Boatwright had told me as we walked down the corridor to her room.

Henry was past sixty now, as I was, and as cold and forbidding in appearance as ever. But he had become remarkably kind; as we approached Hester it struck me that for the first time he seemed as concerned about me and my feelings as he had always been about his poor sister. That was when I realized (the way you do in dreams) that Henry was really Walter Honig, so it was understandable that he should be looking out for my interests. Not only did he usher me into the sickroom with unusual gentleness, he even patted my arm!

Hester was wasted, but that I had expected. What I was unprepared for was her vivacity. No, not just that, her clarity. She raised herself up on her elbows and actually smiled at me in greeting. The veil of madness was gone: It was as if in dying she was being restored, her sanity was being returned to her . . . and she was returning to me, after all the long years.

I sat by her side and took her long white hand in mine. The fingernails were bluish, but her fingers curled about mine and she gripped my hand in greeting.

"I've been worried about you," she whispered, "so worried.

"You've had so much tragedy," she said. "My illness. The war. The School closing. Do you think I don't know how that must have hurt you? And then our dear boy. Our dear Philip."

I lowered my head.

"Worst of all, perhaps, his girl, poor Louise. Henry has told me." I felt my whole body shuddering. I wished I could awake from the nightmare. "He wasn't going to, but I pressed him. Sam, look at me."

I raised my head. "Luba has died too," I said, not quite sure why I was telling her, knowing only that I had to.

"Yes," she said, "I know. Do you know, this is the first time you've looked me in the eyes in so many years. How long? Twenty years?"

"Don't talk any more," I said. "Just rest."

"Nonsense. You mustn't let this get you down. Henry tells me you have been keeping to yourself. Writing book reviews, memoirs?"

"Something of the sort."

"You must get out. You must take up your work with children. Isn't it possible for you to get out into the field? There must be a way . . ."

I heard myself saying, "I've been asked to go to Germany. To the DP camps."

"What are you waiting for? For me to die? You've waited too long for that already. The best thing you can do for me is to get back to work. Don't sit out there and rot, pretending you're an old man when you're not."

She knows, I said to myself, that I am infected with guilt as if with some disgusting disease. I gazed at her splendid patrician features and said aloud, temporizing, "There's the school property to be looked after. The buildings, the grounds . . ."

"Since when have you been married to property, like some gatekeeper? Henry will sell everything for you, won't you, Henry?"

Henry tapped me on the shoulder and motioned for me to go, and when we were in the hall I was alone, which did not surprise me since I had not counted on his accompanying me any further, and in a DP barracks, which did not surprise me either since that's the way dreams are. I was asking myself, though, Is that the way it really was? Am I here among this swarm of survivors because of Hester, just as it was thanks to Hester that I had succeeded in making the Sophia School a reality? Had she really come back to me in her last hours, or was that just a soothing trick of the mind?

I had no time to reflect on this further, for I was caught up in the confrontation with a Polish Jewish boy who had just been trapped in a large-scale black-market operation. Like all youthful slumdwellers, he had the wary eyes and hunched shoulders of a shrewd little old man. He had been trading in typewriters, U.S. Army property, no laughing matter for one who was neither citizen nor soldier and so not licensed to deal in American taxpayers' dollars. The little businessman, his narrow furtive features turned up in a smirk, had already seen his parents go to the ovens; he was not likely to be cowed by me or by the exhausted and distraught social worker, who I knew would one day accompany me to Palestine and all the months of grinding labor there, and who now stood beside me, screaming at the boy in Yiddish. I started to cry.

I was weeping not for him but for myself. The lady looked like my mother, but my mother had so rarely raised her voice that I was intimidated by the shrill unfamiliar sound. "Who asked you to do it?" she cried. "Who needed it? Wasn't I taking care of us?"

She had been trying, God knows. I wanted to tell her (but didn't have to) that that was why I had gone out and gotten the paper route. And that was why the young Jewish toughs from the Lower East Side had jumped me, cursing me for invading their territory, mocking my fancy accent when I tried to plead ignorance, tried to explain that my father, like theirs, was afflicted with consumption.

"Who asked you to get beaten up?" she shouted in the European accent that was no longer charming, but hateful and embarrassing to me. "Who asked you to get your knickers torn? Who's going to buy you more clothes, hey?"

Struggling to free myself from the accusing cries, I willed myself awake. Wiping my wet eyes, I focused them on the figure before me, bloody-handed and triumphant in the summer sun.

"Hey there," she said, waving the wickets she had dipped in red barn paint, "you looked like you were having a bad dream."

"Mixed," I said. "Only some of it was bad. I just don't know whether I was dreaming of things that should have happened, or could have happened, or actually did happen."

"It's like reading some novels," she said surprisingly. "They're so real you think the author's been reading your mail. Or your mind."

There was more to Susie than met the eye. After she'd gone and gotten herself messed up with red paint, I couldn't refuse to play with her. And it was true, I discovered, once I struggled to my feet—I could see the wickets better, now that she'd daubed them. And I did enjoy myself with her, immersed in the sheer pleasure of the sunny moment as I haven't been in a long time. Watching her jump with glee when she made a shot, or bang her mallet into the ground when she missed, was utterly different from watching Jenny, whether at work with her camera or at play in her garden. J. is a cool, efficient, mature, beautiful woman; I love her and marvel that she is here, when she is here. Susie is a child, demanding as children are when they cry, "Play with me!" but otherwise demanding nothing of what the others do— my heart, my guts, the very fiber of my being.

I begin to understand what Seth sees in her.

JULY 24   Gabriel Gibbons "dropped by" yesterday on his way to a concert at Tanglewood. I wouldn't put quotes around those words if he were like, say, Jennifer's various relatives, who do actually drop by from time to time. They come unannounced, they sniff about, smiling and nodding, trying to conceal their surprise that I am still alive and that J. is still at my side. They never stay long.

But Gibbons did insist that he was on vacation and had no intention of talking business—i.e., Dick Wells's interview series—with me. He just thought it would be "nice" to say hello and sit on the porch with me for a few minutes, which was just what we were doing.

"If that's the case," I said, "where's your wife? Do you always go on vacation alone?"

I think he actually blushed, right into those deep grooves on either side of his mouth. He put the palm of his hand flat against his flushed countenance for a moment, and then explained, "My wife and I have separated."

"After how long?" Sometimes I can take advantage of my years to be very direct. If people want to be hurt, let them.

"Twenty-seven years," Gibbons said gruffly. "A long time."

"Then you're a God-damned fool," I told him.

"I never said I wasn't," he replied. I liked him for that, a whole lot better than I had before. He had struck me as just a little bit too show-biz, a manner I have never cared for, especially when it is combined with phony self-deprecation and exaggerated deference.

"What about Dick Wells?" I asked. "I haven't seen him on the TV lately."

"He's on vacation too, on the Vineyard." Gibbons smiled. "With his wife."

"How does *he* manage to stay married, with all that running around he does?" I hadn't thought about it before, but now I was curious.

Gibbons laughed out loud, a base chuckle. "My guess is, the only question Dick ever asks Laura is, What's for supper? He's a good interviewer, you know, finding out about people is second nature with him, but I've never heard him dig at Laura about her background, her motives, anything. Doesn't even seem curious about what she does when he's not there. And she seems to like it that way. She lives very comfortably, you know. And she runs a boutique."

As if I cared. I like both men well enough, but truthfully all that concerns me is what they mean to do with me. They're not youngsters, they're middle-aged men, and I'm not going to try to influence them to change their lives or attitudes or give up their astronomical salaries. I'm not even particularly curious about them, the way I suppose I might be if I were a novelist. It's my imagination (or what's left of it) and my life (and what's left of that) that worry me.

I did try to hint around with Gabriel Gibbons but couldn't get anything more specific out of him than that first fine flush—and I'm still not sure whether that arose in his seamed cheeks because of the break-up of his long marriage or because the Tanglewood story was an excuse for his coming here to press for a date for the next interview session.

He didn't press, he didn't even hint around with me, but I have no idea what went on between him and Walter, who just happened to come by (oh yeah), and joined us with Jenny for a cold beer. I think all of them (including Larry by long distance) were putting the squeeze on Rog to get him, in turn, to prepare me for another bout with Wells.

Was going to check with Rog to see if my suspicions are correct or are only more of my senile dementia, but couldn't bring myself to broach the subject with him. He still seems a bit miffed at our talk of the other day. I guess he's trying to keep his self-control with me. It's not as if he's my wife: One blow-up and we'd probably be through. So far, such a thing has been unimaginable, but who knows?

But you know what I keep thinking: Was that the way it really happened, my dream of the last reunion with Hester, on her deathbed? It's so frustrating, to be dependent on my own uncertain memory. I'm more firm about incidents in Florence and Venice eighty years ago, and more, than I am about things that may have happened thirty years ago or, for that matter, thirty minutes ago. What's maddening is not to have corroboration. If I should be confused about what Gabriel Gibbons did or did not say, I can always ask J. or Rog. But who can I turn to for confirmation of my dream about Hester? Henry Boatwright would tell me the truth, I'll give him that much, even if it were to my credit and his discredit. But he died in the fifties, when I was packing to go to Korea to see the refugee kids there. And now there's no one to ask, nothing to rely on but memories or dreams. And this jumbled diary.

JULY 28   Bickering and squabbling. Turned out I was not paranoid but was absolutely right about Gibbons; he did take Rog aside and urge him to urge me to prepare for another bout with Wells and the crew.

Rog did not tell me about it after Gibbons had left for Tanglewood because he wanted to spare me any undue excitement. As if that wasn't what keeps me going.

Seth was the one who told me about Rog and Gibbons. I

must admit that I thought S. was up to more of his tricks, but when I checked with Rog he said it was true, Gibbons had said to him on the way out, quite casually, that plans were well advanced for the climactic episode. Would R. please try to coordinate schedules with Professor Brodie in Washington as well as with G.'s office in New York?

How did Seth come to know about this? Rog told him. Why did R. tell him? It gets to be like one of those children's stories, Chicken Little and Turkey Lurkey, that I used to read to my little Philip and all the other kids, sitting on the Common at the Sophia School a thousand years ago.

So I got the two of them together and sat them down on the lawn with me. Seth's hands were scarred and stained, his hair was powdered with sawdust, giving him an oddly artificial, tinselly look, as though he were made up for a stage performance. A dried blob of wood putty lay along his cheekbone, forgotten like shaving cream. A dark channel of sweat plastered his blue denim work shirt to his back for the entire length of his spine that was visible; and his jeans were smeared, scarred, and worn thin. R. of course was his usual immaculate self, his slick black hair unruffled by the breeze, his Madras summer shirt looking as though it had just come from the shop. Just to look at the two of them together, it was hard to credit the stories of the others that they were conspiring jointly against me.

"As you know and as I have been explaining to Seth," Rog said, "at first I was rather enthused about the opportunity the Wells interview afforded us for expressing your views to a huge public. I did whatever I could to expedite the arrangements. It was only when I saw how that interview was being tied in with an effort to tie you in to the Establishment that I grew uneasy."

"Well," I said, "then what? Tell me the truth: Did you get so uneasy that you decided to go around me?"

"I hated to dampen your enthusiasm."

"What you mean is," I said, "that you felt it was no use arguing with me when my ego was so involved."

With his usual quietness, R. observed, "You're being unfair to yourself, more than to me. I did try to persuade you of the dangers involved in accepting Mr. Brodie's proposal."

"And you didn't get anywhere because I was seduced by the idea of having a building named after me. Was it you who brought Grebner into the picture, and the Children of Liberty?"

"I know that's been put to you by Mr. Brodie," he said. He added with surprising vigor, "I hate like hell to be put in the position of seeming to stand between you and your oldest and most faithful pupil."

No doubt he did, but he wasn't answering the question. I glanced at Seth, who hadn't said a word all this time, but simply sat there chewing on a blade of grass. I was beginning to wonder if he was enjoying Rog's discomfort.

"Never mind if I figured it out for myself," I told Rog, "or had it pointed out to me. Why don't you just tell me, among the three of us, if you went and got hold of Seth after you learned that the President was going to be my co-star."

Rog hesitated. He looked at me, then at Seth, opened his mouth, then closed it.

Seth said pleasantly, "I went to him. That's how it started, and I don't see why you or Larry or anyone else should make such a big thing out of it."

"If only I'd been told," I said, "if anyone had troubled to take me into his confidence—"

That was when Seth said, "You have a way of forgetting. I already told you—"

I didn't let him get any further. "Don't treat me as if I'd lost all my marbles!" I shouted. "I won't have it, do you hear?"

"Didn't mean it that way," he replied hastily. A kind of apology. "I'm simply trying to get Rog off the hook."

Now Rog tried to break in, but I said, "I'm aware of that. I'm also aware of all our earlier conversations. And nothing you said, ever, was a denial that Rog could have come after you just to get me involved with the Children of Liberty."

"Is that what you want? A denial from me, and Grebner, and the rest? Why don't you settle for one from Rog?"

"I'll settle for one from you," I told him, "if you can prove you mean it. I'm not interested on your getting Rog off the hook. That could just be a sign that you two are in cahoots after all."

Seth spat out on the grass. "In other words, heads you win, tails I lose. Whatever I tell you, you'll take it to mean that we've been ganging up on you. So the hell with it. Figure it out for yourself."

"You come back here," I said. "You moved in, with your girl. Was it simply to soften me up so I'd go with you that day? Did you have the whole thing worked out in advance with Girard, in order to scare off the White House?"

Seth remained sullen. "That's Brodie's version. You'd rather believe him anyway—you'd rather get your picture taken with the President than with some young agitators. You prefer the marble mausoleum to the respect of the next generation." A speech, no less.

"Larry Brodie has been in my life, in my family, for a long, long time," I said. "But he has no priority over you or your generation or Rog or the next generation."

"Prove it."

"I don't have to prove anything," I said. "You do."

But that wasn't exactly true, was it? This is a poor time for me to start leaning on my authority. He knows, Rog knows even better, that every time I wake up I have to prove to myself that I'm still alive. And there's only one way I can do it: by reaching out to the young, who gave me everything I've got . . . including a reason for waking in the morning.

That's why R. sat there coolly while Seth and I were gnawing away at each other so horribly and so stupidly. He understands the desperation in my need, which S. can only guess at, even if he doesn't realize (unless he's been reading this after all) that I am something more than foxy grandpa to S.

I say to myself what I couldn't say to them, sitting out there on the grass: If it comes to where I have to make a decision, I doubt that I have it in me to turn my back on the power and the glory. What Larry has offered—assured immortality—is something that only a saint could walk away from.

Rog has been trying to cope with this. Seth refuses even to try. So I wonder, what would happen if I told Seth? Would he turn away in disgust, deciding once and for all that I am not worthy of his soul-saving efforts? Or would he make use of the truth as, let's put it bluntly, a blackmail weapon? To ask the question is to admit that I do not know either him or myself.

August

AUGUST 1   Some days ago, maybe it was weeks, Larry sent me as a present a book of Jung's called *Memories, Dreams, Reflections,* which came out about ten years ago. According to the frontispiece, 1965. The date is important because, while it is posthumous, it is not a "new" book. For at least twenty years, maybe thirty, L. has sent me new books that he thought might not come to my attention otherwise and that he thought I would enjoy. But seldom old ones, probably because he feared I might take that amiss, as a reflection of my educational gaps.

But why this? Especially since he has always known how deeply I mistrusted Jung and refused to associate myself with his (or similar) brands of reactionary mysticism. I tossed it aside.

The other day, I think it was after that frustrating talk with R. and S., I lay down on the settee and for some reason picked up the Jung, meaning to read myself to sleep with it. I think my rationalization was that if R. is saving my failing eyes by reading *The Times* to me, I might as well look at something I wouldn't otherwise ask him to read to me. (What led to *that,* I may as well confess, was my wondering if R. was after all working together with S. to alienate me from Larry —whether R. has been so selective in his reading that he has kept from my attention news items of which I should be apprised. I finally discarded the idea, not because I doubted R. was capable of it—for my sake, to be sure—but because I am sure to be filled in on such things by Walter, or Larry, if not by Jenny.)

Anyway, here is what is interesting. My eye was led, as if by some magnet imbedded in the page, to words that seemed directed precisely to me, as if old Jung were attempting to

223

break down my irrational resistance to him, and to increase my respect for him. I want to copy them down because I no longer trust my memory for such things, and for another reason as well.

"It has become a necessity for me to write down my early memories. If I neglect to do so for a single day, unpleasant physical symptoms follow. As soon as I set to work they vanish and my head feels perfectly clear."

Extraordinary.

Then he says, ". . . all the memories which have remained vivid to me had to do with emotional experiences that arouse uneasiness and passion in the mind—scarcely the best condition for an objective account."

I'm not saying that I agree with him. But it's as though we understand each other, as though he were here in this room and I could communicate with him. He'd have no trouble in understanding my confusion about some of the "incidents" I've set down here (and some I suppose I have been afraid to set down)—take that dream about Hester on her deathbed, and my uncertainty as to whether it happened that way. There's no one here I can talk to about that, absolutely no one. I'll copy one last thing of Jung's:

". . . this has always been the case with me—that all the 'outer' aspects of my life should be accidental. Only what is interior has proved to have substance and a determining value. As a result, all memory of outer events has faded, and perhaps these 'outer' experiences were never so very essential anyhow, or were so only in that they coincided with phases of my inner development.

"I have guarded this material all my life, and have never wanted it exposed to the world."

Well! My situation is not his, not at all, but the conjunction can hardly be accidental. Larry arrives today, tonight rather. Ordinarily I would be asleep and would see him at breakfast. Now I can hardly wait to ask him what he had in mind when he sent me the book. He hasn't so much as

224

mentioned it since he sent it, hasn't asked for my reaction, nothing. For my part, I haven't said a word to him (that I can recall, anyway) about what I have been entering in this journal. But there is always the possibility that he has learned of it from someone else, that he is craftily nudging me, egging me on.

We shall see.

AUGUST 2   L. came marching in last night, gave me a big hug, complimented me on my recovery, asked me what I was doing up so late.

"Waiting for you," I told him.

He laughed. "After all these years?" I wasn't sure whether he was teasing me, or was really a bit annoyed at me for being up when he could have been alone with J.

So I told him about the Jung, and how it had charged me up.

He laughed some more. "You are really something, Sam." He gazed at me with admiration, as if he were admiring my physique or my hair. "How many people are there nowadays who would lose sleep over a book? Don't you realize that books are obsolescent?"

"It isn't a book," I said. "It's an idea. A group of ideas." I tried to explain the effect it had had on me, but I don't think L. quite understood me, because he seemed simply pleased at my reaction, nothing more.

"Well, that's just great," he said. "Somehow I had a feeling you'd respond to it."

"That's just what I want to talk about," I said. "What do you mean, somehow you had a feeling? Why should you have suddenly decided to send me that book?"

L. shrugged. He said, very casually, "Every once in a while you talk about memories and dreams, how inextricable they are, one from the other." I do? I thought. When? He went on, "I had a hunch this would make you sit up straight."

"Yes, but why?" I demanded. "It is because of the things I've been setting down in my journal?"

"How the hell would I know about that?" He seemed nettled. "If you liked it, great. But that's not what I want to talk to you about. I want to lay this whole business of Seth Fox and your secretary out on the table."

I felt like swearing at him. But there was no point, was there? It was my turn to shrug. "I'm too tired for that," I said. "We can take that up in the morning."

"Fair enough. Let's turn in. I had a long day in Washington before I got here."

I'm sure he did, but that didn't prevent him from planting the seed, did it? Or from turning away my question about the Jung book.

AUGUST 3   At breakfast L. was relaxed and hearty. That didn't stop him from going to work on me, with the help of a manila folder. As soon as Mrs. H. had cleared the breakfast dishes from the porch table, he stuck one of those vile cigars into his head and said that he wanted to talk to me frankly.

"Don't you always?" I asked him.

He blew smoke and laughed. "What I mean is that I want to get personal." He aimed the stogie at my face like a pointer. "I've more or less been a member of the household since I was a kid, right? So I think I owe it to you to bring up certain matters that are nobody else's business."

I kept my mouth shut. As if I didn't know what was coming. As if he didn't know I knew.

"Let me ask you a simple question." As he leaned forward the years fell away, and he wasn't a middle-aged man, but the boy I had felt such an affinity for—big-eyed, intense, intellectually eager and ambitious, innately kind and anxious to do good. How ashamed we are of our desire to do good! It has become a term of derogation, as if it were worse than

226

doing evil. Larry really is kind, he really does want to do good—and for me first of all, I have to believe that. (I even suspect that if I were ever to tell him that his association with J. is causing me pain, he would break it off.) Even his voice sounded younger when he said, "Is it because of Philip that you've allowed yourself to be taken advantage of by Seth Fox?"

"Larry," I said, "I can't answer that in any way that would satisfy you. I just don't think I've been taken advantage of. You've been hinting the same thing in regard to Rog Girard for a long time."

He ignored that. When he answered, I could see how he was trying hard to interpret everything in terms of my own benevolence and generosity, just as though it was thirty-five years ago and I was still running the Sophia School and he was still trying to understand why I had issued a seemingly arbitrary order. "Because if it's Philip who's on your mind and in your heart," he persisted, "I just want to say I can understand it."

"Thanks," I said.

He ignored that too. He was bent on being serious, on calling up our most deep connections, appealing to our profoundest ties. "I don't talk to you much about my children," he said. "That doesn't mean they don't matter—I've never felt I had to tell you, or to state my feelings. I always have the confidence that you understand without my falling into a verbal mush. I count on you."

"Okay," I said. I was beginning to feel a little embarrassed and hoping he would put an end to this kind of confidentiality. On the other hand, it was better than if he intimated, like Seth, that once upon a time we had talked all this out, but that I seemed to have forgotten all about it.

I hadn't forgotten Larry's mistake of a marriage, his bringing the young woman around for my approval, not thinking that maybe she would disapprove of me. Which she did (and which didn't dispose me to think fondly of her, since her distaste was obvious), and it was a bad omen, because in a sense I was what Larry wanted to become. Courtney had given him to understand—he was a young instructor then, at Smith, and she was one of his brighter students—that developmental psychology fascinated her more than anything else in the whole world. Children too. Myself, I felt from the very start that she was excited by the prospect of having a husband who would not be a stockbroker or a maritime lawyer (the primary occupations of all her male forebears) and who would not insist on saddling her daughters with family names like Courtney.

They did have a daughter, sooner than they had counted on, and named her Sarah, as close to Sophia as Larry could manage. And another one right away, to keep Sarah company growing up, in accordance with Larry's principles. By then they were having trouble, the details of which I was not privy to (although I could guess) since L. was far too busy to hang around here, what with the family and the teaching. They made the classic error of having another child in a last desperate effort to stick together; but although Courtney did succeed in producing a male—I suspect that she was more eager for one than Larry—they split up after several more painful years. It was after that that L. found his way back to me—and through me, not just to J., but to his new life as a public figure. His doctoral dissertation on my school (a logical enough project) became a popular book; he was not bashful about appearing on TV or consorting with politicians; and without the ties of home and hearth he was free to promote himself and his career. I don't mean to sound cruel, even when I am talking to myself. He has been very good to me, and very good for me—better than almost anyone else in the world. I leave out his virtue of steadfast faithfulness since that is open to interpretation not necessarily flattering to either of us. I am sure Courtney, when she pauses from her social activities to consider me, regards me as some kind of Svengali who schemed to destroy her marriage.

"Aside from the question of guilt, which by now I know I have to live with," L. said, rolling the ash from his stogie onto my nice bone china saucer, "I recognize in advance my own commitment to the future offspring of my three children."

"Aside from the question of guilt?" I couldn't help but mock him. "You mean you've managed to forget that Freud called guilt the most important problem in the evolution of culture?"

"Even if I wanted to forget, you wouldn't let me." He blinked at me rapidly, always a sure sign that L. had dropped kidding and was in earnest. "I'll always feel guilty about my kids and I know you always felt guilty about Phil, what with Hester and all the troubles Phil had growing up as her son."

"And mine."

"And yours. I'm trying to tell you that by now I understand better, even if I didn't when I was younger and Phil was my buddy, how profoundly you feel your responsibility not just to your son, or to his memory, but to his progeny."

When he stopped and put a fresh match to his cigar, I felt a premonitory shudder pass over me, as though I was going to be forced against my will to tell him what I had never been able to bring myself to tell anyone.

"What's the matter?" he asked. He must have seen something; he can be very keen.

"Nothing," I assured him. I had to say that, how could I tell him what I had not broached to Seth himself? Or to Jenny, for that matter. If anybody now alive has an inkling, it is Walter—and if I can be sure of anything on this earth it is that Walter has never breathed a word, not even to Lily. Certainly not to Larry, although he has always been fond of him, ever since he was a kid in the School, and has even managed to close his eyes to the business with J. That lawyer's code of Walter's is even more sacred to him than his Episcopalianism.

After a decent interval Larry went after me. "Well, all this is by way of preliminary for my need, no, my obligation, to tell you that no matter what you may think you owe to Seth because of Philip, there is no reason why you should permit him to abuse your hospitality."

"Larry, I'm not being hospitable," I said. I was beginning to think that, in spite of his having shared with Philip a knowledge of my affairs, maybe he had never suspected anything after all about me and Louise. So what perverse imp egged me on to near-exposure? I said, "This is his home. He belongs here."

"He's a thirty-year-old man. He belongs in his own home. Why, even if he wasn't your grandson, but your son, I should think he'd . . ."

I don't remember what happened at that point. I think I got to my feet, I must have had blood in my eye, because Larry broke off and came over to me and took me by the arm and eased me back into my chair.

"I'm sorry," he said. "I don't mean to get you upset, but facts have to be faced."

I wanted to tell him that I didn't have to do anything, if I didn't feel like it I didn't have to face facts; but words would not come.

"Are you all right?" he asked, and when I nodded, he said insistently, "I detest the idea of his capitalizing on his connection with you. And on your good nature. Moving in here—"

"At my invitation," I managed to say.

"—making deals with Girard, ganging up on you for the sake of a gang of sickies."

"You have no evidence of that."

"What do you think is in this folder? The two of them were conferring for months before the effort was made to drag you in."

"That's hardly a crime. And don't show me your eaves-dropping data. It's not worthy of you." In truth I didn't *care*. It's all so boring, so tedious. Why can't I make them understand that? "You've worked so hard at understanding children, Larry," I said to him, "that you haven't the faintest idea of what it's like to be old. You look at me and you say to yourself, The old boy looks well today, or, His appetite seems unimpaired, or, Except for his eyesight, his faculties are remarkably sharp."

L. put his cigar in the saucer and looked at me blankly. "But isn't that all true?"

"From one day to the other. And although I doze a lot, when I am awake I don't feel any marked decline of my intellectual faculties, not even after that stroke of four years ago. What you seem incapable of understanding is that I keep asking myself the same question Gide put to himself when he was eighty: What can I turn them to?"

L. knows when to hold back—and, after all these years, when to let me go on.

"It isn't enough for me to sit and doze. Or daydream. Or write my private reflections in my private diary. Or enjoy my beautiful and creative wife, her quick mind, her graceful bodily movements, her comings and goings. Or even to see myself fulfilled in you, even when your success is sometimes referred to—did you know? you must know—as my greatest monument."

L. looked away, as if he were suddenly ashamed. For himself? For me?

"I am trying to flee from the vanity of old age," I said. "From the obsessive concern with myself, my bladder, my toenails that I can hardly see or bend to cut any more, my reputation, my immortality. And you're not willing to let me. You appeal to my worst weakness, my vanity. You seduce me back to all the braggadocio about my accomplishments, those miserable accomplishments that I am trying to forget. What for? Presumably for my sake. But actually it's for yours, isn't it? For the career that you've built on a facsimile, a mummy labeled Sam Lumen that you prop up in front of the TV cameras like a commercial for Instant Wisdom."

L. had turned quite white. His bushy moustache stood away from his face, which seemed to have shrunk back into his skull. Finally he found his voice. He said, "I swear to you—"

"Don't swear," I told him. "It's unbecoming. Just consider, do I have the right to make a fool of myself, the way I did when I was young? Do I have the right to consort with fools, freaks, and nuts, if that's what I need to make me feel that I'm still alive, still wanted, still needed?"

"My only concern—"

"Your only concern is my welfare," I imitated him. Cruelly, I suppose. But I've had enough. "That's what they all say. Everyone is conniving for my benefit. I believe you, that even if it wasn't jeopardizing your pet project, the Lumen Center, you'd be furious with Seth and his friends for exploiting me. But that doesn't help me. Do you want to help me? Let me make a monkey out of myself if that's what I need to keep from curling up and dying. Let me do it, even if it means people will say you haven't been looking after my interests properly, even if it risks lowering your prestige. You're young enough to overcome a little setback. But I'll be dead any morning now."

Certainly I was being selfish. But if you haven't earned that in your ninetieth year, then when?

"Sam, you make me feel like a shit," Larry said.

That was what I had in mind. In my defense I ought to say that I don't usually have that in mind; I honestly don't think L. or anyone else could excuse me of habitually demeaning them. Maybe for that very reason L. was thrown back on the defensive.

"I'd do just about anything," he mumbled, "to keep you from feeling hemmed in, or pushed around, or bossed. Or exploited, don't you see that's as ugly to me as anything else that takes advantage of you? I swear, my whole adult life has been devoted to making the world appreciate you. As long as Girard is doing that too, in a way that gratifies you, fine. But you don't believe that's true of Seth Fox, do you?"

"Seth is different. He's not devoted to me in the way Rog is. Or you are. He's a very special case." I decided to let L. off the hook, or at least to feed him a little more line. "I've been frank with you just now, haven't I, about my grievances?"

He didn't reply but gave me that eye-blink message.

"I never questioned that you had my best interests at heart. But you haven't stopped to think that one side effect of your high-level huckstering has been to rub it in that I'm more dead than alive. And that you and Walter, and whoever else you enlist, from the White House to Jenny, not only know what's good for me but are ready to embalm me even before I've quit breathing. When you come down here, it's funny that just about everybody, not just Seth and his friends, but you and your snooping data, seems engaged in a conspiracy to persuade me that I'm senile."

"That's the last thing—"

"What are you going to tell me, that I'm paranoid, because I'm afraid maybe it's true after all, maybe all of you do know better than I what's good for me? I'm trying to tell you," I said to him, "that I've been involved with Seth in just this kind of hassle. You think I'm just putty in his hands, a foolish old man. Don't interrupt. He has a nasty way of referring to things that I've never known about, and then casually letting slip that we've already discussed them. Like those corny old plays where the evil husband is quietly trying to drive his wife out of her mind so he can collect the insurance or whatever. Believe me, I don't let him get away with it, but he's playing to my weakness, don't you see, just as you play to my vanity with all that crap about posing with the President and having buildings named after me. I would have scorned that when I was your age and willing to sit in jail for what I believed." I guess I took a breath at that point, once I had made clear that I had been as rough with Seth as I was now with him. And I wound up, "One way or another, you're all taking advantage of me. And I won't have it. I want to be left alone."

Of course that's not true. Or at least, it's not true all the time. Some of the time I want to be left alone, so I suppose L. (or Seth for that matter) could have said, How are we supposed to know when? Don't you insist your participation is what keeps you going? So I am a crank and a tyrant. God damn it, what else can I be? I have this house, this wife, this bank account, this secretary, this loving disciple, this boy returned to stay with me, but I have no freedom. Not from any of it.

Anyway, at that moment a look of great relief came into L.'s eyes. I was surprised, couldn't relate it to what I'd been saying. But then I felt a presence. I turned my head and there stood Jenny and Lily. And behind them, Walter. I don't know how long they'd been standing there, not long I would guess, but I can't be sure, can I? Anyway,

No. Too tired to write more.

AUGUST 5 Missed a day. Don't know whether to get on with it or finish up what went on that morning with L. Better finish up. Several things happened that I don't want to skip.

J. bent down to kiss me and I thought I could smell the sweat of uneasiness. That's the first thing. Was I crazy? She looked, as always, cool and poised and smiling. But even as she gave L. a friendly peck and asked him something innocuous about Washington, I caught her glancing at the manila folder he had tried to shock me with. She knew what he was up to, my dearest Jenny did.

In fact, so did old Walter. What else would he be doing on my porch so early in the morning? He hardly made any bones about it, accepted coffee for himself and Lily from Mrs. H., sat himself down beside me, and asked me how I'd been keeping.

"Alive, no thanks to any of you," I responded.

"My, aren't we waspish this morning," Walter said. "So this is going to be one of those days."

"Don't humor me, Walt," I warned him. "It wasn't one of those days until I realized everyone was going to gang up on me."

"Not me, Sam!" Lily Honig blurted out, and then turned very red. That's the second thing. She is so sweet and so transparent, I took it to mean that she had heard them talking about me, about me and Seth, what to do about it, etc.

"Of course not you, Lily," I assured her. I was tempted to ask her right there, before everyone, what they'd been up to, but she was embarrassed enough as it was. "But don't tell me you just stopped by to challenge Susie to a game of croquet, Walter."

He glanced back and forth between me and Larry. "If we're intruding on some sort of . . ."

"You know damn well what you're intruding on," I assured him. "Larry has been trying to show me evidence that Seth and Rog have been in league against me, and I've been trying not to listen."

"I didn't say in league against you," L. pointed out. "I said you were being exploited."

"And I said you were exploiting me too," I answered. "All from the highest of motives, on all sides."

"I assure you," Walter said to me, "that I have done my very best to explain to Larry that Seth has always been very important to you. Always," he underlined the word, "many, many years before you set eyes on him, or expected to."

"I can understand that," Larry said. "I simply resent his taking advantage of the connection."

"Isn't it odd," I said. "That's exactly what he says about you."

Everyone started to talk at once. I wanted to get up and leave. Jennifer must have sensed it, because she placed her hand on mine and said to everyone, "Please." Or was it simply because Mrs. H. was coming back with her cart from the kitchen? Whatever her motive, she did manage to quiet them all down.

"Darling," she said to me, "what do you think is the best solution?"

"That depends on what the problem is." I hadn't meant that to be funny; at least I don't think so, but it did set J. to laughing, if not the others.

"All right," she said, "you say. What do you think the problem is?"

"If I repeat what I was just saying to Larry," I told her, "that I just want to be left alone, you'll say that's no problem."

"But that's precisely what we're concerned with," Walter said. "I for one am very concerned about the unreasonable demands that have been made on you. And I tell you frankly, I tend to hold Girard to account for it. That was his job, wasn't it, to filter all those demands? As far as I'm concerned, he's botched it. To put the kindest interpretation on it."

"You mean, to put yours on it, Walter," I said. "Why won't anyone take my opinion, or my wishes, into account?"

I knew I was sounding petulant, I knew it. In a moment I would have tears of frustration and impotence in my eyes.

"If Sam is satisfied with Mr. Girard, Walt," his wife asked, "why not take his word for it? He's his secretary, not yours."

I had a hunch that Lily had already said this to Walter in the privacy of their home, but felt impelled to repeat it to him in public. So I was doubly grateful. How could Walter deny the reasonableness of this without intimating that I was no longer capable of looking after my own affairs? Or was he, pushing eighty himself—well, seventy-eight or so—going to join the pack and tell me that I was losing my marbles simply because he disapproved of Seth, after all these years?

In fact Walter was a little stiff. And defensive. And gave away the show a little when he said, "Lily you know perfectly well that is the argument I have advanced to Larry for a long time, myself."

"That's true," Larry said. "That is true, Sam. Walter has always urged me not to assert myself so possessively about you and Girard."

Which confused me a bit, but only until Walter added, "It's only since the appearance of Seth that I have been persuaded that Girard has overstepped the bounds."

"God damn it, Walter," I said, "they're my bounds, not yours."

"When he goes behind your back, as Larry has persuaded me, it's time for your friends—"

I cut him off. "It's my back."

"Now you're getting silly."

"I'm getting out of here." I pushed myself up out of my chair. I don't think I am stuffy, but I didn't like Walter saying that in front of people half our age.

It was Jenny who stopped me. Not physically, simply by fixing me with her clear gaze and asserting, "That will simply leave us where we were. The argument won't go away if you do."

But I wouldn't have to listen to it. I couldn't bring myself to say that, though, not to Jennifer. Before I could collect myself, Walter spoke up again.

"May I suggest," he said to us all, "that instead of going around in circles we call in Seth and Girard. We can all put our cards on the table, air our grievances, and see if we can resolve this tension. It should be possible to return to the kind of relaxed atmosphere that Sam wants and is entitled to."

"At the least," Larry observed, "we could set up guide-lines."

That really got to me. "For Christ's sake, Larry," I said, "must you remind us that you work in Washington? I'm going to be ninety years old, maybe, if I make it to next winter, but that's no reason for you to talk as though I was a bank or post office."

Jenny was laughing, even Lily was smiling. This wasn't a very good morning for Larry, but he had brought it on himself, flying in with that folder and trying to swarm all over me with his officialese and his snoop squad. Just the same, it was clear that he agreed with the rest that they had a good idea (I was beginning to wonder if it wasn't the idea they had planned on broaching to me beforehand). I felt myself panicking, although I wasn't eager to let on. How could I object to everyone getting together and talking things out? I couldn't very well say that there were things I simply didn't want to take up with more than one person at a time—and things that I hadn't even been able to take up with one person. What am I supposed to do, read them my private diary? All I could do was to stall.

I told them I had nothing against a get-together, I would always be in favor of Rog's sitting in on any session that had to do with me and my public interests, and I saw no reason why Seth shouldn't be invited to join in.

"Why not now?" Larry asked. He glanced at his fancy watch that shows the time to the split seconds, the day of the month, all kinds of fancy data for the busy executive. He wanted to get cracking; I wondered if he wanted to throw that manila folder at Seth and Rog before he helicoptered off to Washington.

"Because I'm worn out from all this," I said.

He drew in his horns at once. "Okay then, you rest up and we'll get in touch with them to see when we can all sit down together."

"Larry," I said, "listen to me. I want to talk to Seth myself first. He's not my employee, he's not like Rog."

"All the more reason."

"Please."

As soon as I said please, Larry caved in. He gave me a big grin and a hug and said, "We'll do it your way. I'll try to be available whenever you're ready—" he was kidding, now that things were settled and he didn't have to be solemn about things like guidelines—"for the historic Lumen Conference. I'm on vacation, as you know, but I'll make myself available."

238

"In the meanwhile," I said, "I'm sure you'll be talking to Gabriel Gibbons about the Wells interviews. That is, if you run into each other."

L. laughed some more. He enjoys being teased as long as it doesn't interfere with his plans. I knew he was going ahead with the next interview, and with the part of it that would include the President, and I just wanted him to know that I knew and that I understood that this was the real reason for his irritation with Seth, who would otherwise have simply amused him—or made him wax sentimental about Philip.

So I retreated back here, and I guess they broke up. Or perhaps they continued to talk about Seth and what to do if he persisted in hanging around and exercising his baneful influence on me.

I knew I had to talk with S. about all this, and about Rog, but I was not eager to. I was reluctant even to see him. Finally I did.

Next time.

AUGUST 6   Have been rereading some of this. One thing troubles me: A lot of it appears to be simply an attempt at an objective recollection of conversations with friends and relatives. So he said, so I said, so he said. Is that worth the expenditure of energy? After all, it is very wearing to set all of it down, and most of it could hardly come as a surprise to anyone who was there; maybe I'd do as well to turn on a tape recorder.

But then, that's just the point, isn't it? Those little variations, my rearrangements (not conscious, but determined no doubt by my personality) of who said what, in which order . . . and all slanted to present me in the most favorable light even though, I swear (as L. would say!), I am conscientiously trying to be painfully honest with myself—more so than I could bring myself to be in conversation with anyone.

Maybe that is why I put off seeing Seth. It all seemed such

an *effort*, not just talking with him, but assessing it after-wards. Sign of failing faculties? Or simply fear?

Certainly it would have been easy enough to say to Rog, Ask Seth to come here and see me. But I didn't, even after I'd explained to R. that there was going to be a sort of parley at which his presence was expected. I could have added that S. was expected, in fact needed, but I think I felt even at that moment that the invitation would be better coming directly from me, rather than from the man who was supposed to be his partner in conspiracy.

Anyway, R. took it without so much as the blink of an eye. He is a kind of intellectual butler. Not that I've ever had a butler, or even known one well outside of mystery books; I mean that kind of intellectual *savoir faire* that permits him to register nothing more than the faintest of smiles at the most outrageous assertion. It did occur to me that he already knew and was simply politely concealing that fact. But how could he have known? No one present in the morning (it was late afternoon when he came in to see me, I guess I'd been dozing a long time) was likely to have rushed off to him with the news, although it was possible that he might have been eavesdropping (mystery-novel butler), or inquired of Mrs. Hoskins what in the hell we'd all been up to.

Matter of fact, he accepted the plan with what appeared like genuine satisfaction.

"Yes," he said, nodding, "that should clear the air. As long as it doesn't overtax you."

"What overtaxes me is the bickering," I assured him. "The pressures. I'm half-convinced that you ought to sit down with the troop and see if you can smooth things over without me."

"I'm afraid your presence will be necessary to give the proper authority." He meant that without me they'd all be apt to gang up on him as a usurper of their old privileges.

Probably he was right. But it didn't keep me from asking, "What are you all going to do after I'm gone?"

His only answer was an enigmatic smile. You could take that smile two ways: indulgent, as if my dying was something unimaginable, or unspeakable; or wary, as if to say, Come on now, you know how long I'll last here without you—the others will have me out of here before your body is cold.

"Rog," I said, "you've been very good for me. Good to me, as well."

His smile faded. This time he spoke: "This has been the greatest experience of my life."

Those were his exact words. Often in these last entries I've had to make an approximation of what people told me, or a paraphrase, but those were R's exact words. And they really floored me, they were so out of character.

You can't have had much of a life, I was tempted to observe. But he hadn't earned that kind of flippancy from me, not at this stage of the game, with everyone after me to curb him, muzzle him. Besides, I thought, maybe there have been compensations that I haven't given much thought to—not just the daily gratifications of being my intellectual butler or gatekeeper or major domo (which I suppose are substantial enough if you're that type), but the expectations of a handsome reception from the left for having made me toe the mark (at least that was what his detractors were hinting), and worthwhile offers from here or there for his memoirs, his revelations of the last days, the life and death, whatever.

(N.B. He lets me go on about my coming demise, after all that's part of his job, to listen. But he never refers to it himself. Is he observing a taboo, or merely being diplomatic in accordance with that bourgeois custom which dictates that you are never to raise the topic of death with the very old?)

We didn't say anything more about this, instead we went on to take care of the most routine matters, even some bills Jenny had overlooked, but I had the feeling, which I believe was justified, that he was reassured that I would stand with him as long as I was physically able.

Oh yes. I am so intent on R. (Almost wrote *poor* R., for

some reason) that I almost passed over the matter of the bills. Several were invoices from the lumberyard where the Hendricks boys have permission to order material in my name for repair jobs around the property. But these were substantial and, as R. pointed out when I asked why, they were not initialed by any of the Hendrickses. Then by whom, I asked, and he answered, with every evidence of reluctance, S. F.

At first it didn't register. Then I said to R. that he might as well leave the slips with me, since I was going to be seeing Seth anyway. After he had left I found myself wondering whether the whole thing had been deliberate, a plant. On whose part? Jennifer's? I couldn't see her doing that; on the other hand, she is very methodical about household things, and it is unlike her to neglect to take care of even the most recent bills. Could L. have put her up to it, in order to call to my attention how I was being taken advantage of? It might even have been R., deciding for reasons of his own to dissociate himself from the man in the guesthouse. After all, Seth was not above letting me know that he thought R. a convenient tool for me to play at keeping the faith with the young and the radical.

I didn't get excited, I just felt the suspicion gnawing at me like a little rat. I know what I would have done when I was younger: I would have grabbed up the bills and marched off to Seth and said, Just what the hell do you think you're doing? Now I sat and let it all eat at me. Is it because I can't bring myself to distrust my own flesh and blood? Or is it something worse, another sympton of senility: inaction married to a festering distrust of everyone?

AUGUST 7   Seth. Before I write down our talk, though, I have to recount the dream that finally got me out of here and over to the guesthouse.

It started out as the same old dream of academic unpreparedness, going into the final exam knowing that I had not memorized the irregular verbs, that I had accumulated seventeen cuts and was unable to write an essay on matters discussed at length in the lectures, etc. etc. I think it must be fifty or sixty years easily that I have been afflicted with this dream (I am perfectly aware that it is a very ordinary, common dream and I claim no distinction, any more than does, say, the cigarette smoker, for being stuck with it); sometimes I think it's not just an affliction. It may have been one of the driving forces that impelled me to start a progressive school against such long odds. At other times, though, I fear it will pursue me into the grave, and that when they lay me out I will be dreaming, in a final convulsive brainwave or motor reaction, that I am unprepared to meet my Maker.

Anyway. It soon shifted, and I was no longer in Williamstown, no longer feeling the bluebook turn damp and wrinkled under my fear-sweaty fingers. I was the same age, nineteen or twenty, but it was many years later. It must have been about 1924, because I was accepting congratulations on the birth of my son, Philip. There was a huge pile of mail to answer (Rog was taking care of it for me!), as well as a regular queue of well-wishers. I was smiling and shaking hands and even passing out cigars from a box with a medallion of twin female heads, *Luba y Sophia,* when suddenly I was confronted with my father, unsmiling and elderly.

"Father!" I cried out happily. "You've been away so long, I thought . . ." I dared not finish the sentence. How can you tell your father that you had thought him dead?

"Yes, I have been away," he said. "After all, I am an expatriate, you know."

Then I knew, too, in one of those bursts of awareness that come to you in dreams with the force of religious revelation, that it was my *mother* who had died, and that I had refused to concede that it had happened by thinking that it was my father, obviously very much alive, who had passed on.

I embraced my father, confused not just by the odor of

243

Roger et Gallet (wasn't that my mother's perfume, not my father's cologne?) but by the conflicting emotions, joy at finding my father alive, sadness at realizing that my mother was dead (it flashed through my mind that she might have died of grief and shame, after all her sacrifices for me, when I turned up unprepared for my finals at Williams).

"You've heard the news?" I asked him.

"I think you're a bit young to have a son," he said in his grave way.

"But, Father—" My happiness was dissolving; resentment welled up in me from nowhere; I was tempted to ask him whether he hadn't been a bit old when he had become a father for the first time at fifty. I said sharply, "I'm almost forty."

"You don't look it." He was always correcting me. "Forty?"

"Well, thirty-nine."

He shook his head like a judge denying a defense motion. "You show no signs of being prepared to take on such a responsibility."

That gave me an opportunity to brag a little. I discovered that I was aching to tell him of my accomplishments during the years of his absence. "Father," I said, "I've gained a certain reputation in the field of children's problems. I became a journalist, I had something to do with the struggle against child labor. I'm starting a school, with the help of Hester, we've agreed that it will be dedicated to the liberation of children from—"

"From capitalism?" My father was openly sneering at me.

"Why not? And from parental domination, what do you think of that?"

Surprisingly, my father inclined his head in assent. "I approve. I hope you will begin by liberating your son."

I had a terrible fear that he was going to say something more, that I had already liberated my daughter from this world entirely. But he did not, and I was overwhelmed with the desire to delay no longer, to see my son at once. My son,

I realized, was not Philip at all, Philip had gone off to join my mother and I had only been fooling myself with this charade into believing that one of them at least was still alive. My son was Seth, and the only way I could get to see him was to free myself from the convulsive grip that my father had on me and to awake.

I wrenched myself into wakefulness and lay there for a moment, staring up at the half-shadowed white squares of the ceiling above me, stunned by the power of a dream to evoke faces, voices from a past now unknown to everyone but me. If I were the greatest genius of all time it would still be beyond my ability to reproduce the voice of my father, cultivated, deep, weary, drawling—and yet I had just heard it echoing in my ears with its precise, unique, matchless timbre, just as his solemn, refined, humorless features had materialized before me with more precision than my failing eyes could now summon up to see those who now live with me in this very house.

Well, that was what finally galvanized me to squeeze my swollen feet into my moccasins, to take up my cane, and to shuffle off to the guesthouse in search of Seth.

On the way over I rehearsed some preliminary talk. You've taken your time about dropping in, he might say sardonically. To which I could with justice respond, My house is open to you, I don't mean to insist on my great age, but after all . . .

But of course nothing like that happened. Seth wasn't lying around as I had been, waiting for me to make his pilgrimage to Canossa. In fact he was so absorbed in his noisy work that he didn't even notice my entrance until I came up close behind him.

He was naked, save for a pair of ragged blue jeans that he had cut off at the knees and a pair of ankle-high workman's shoes. Around his longish hair, to keep it from falling into his eyes, I suppose, he had tied a red bandanna. His thin wiry frame was running rivers of sweat as he bent over a drawer

245

which he was apparently sanding by hand and from time to time fitting into a bureau. When he did glance up he gave me a big grin, but did not immediately stop sanding.

So I looked about in the comparative gloom for a place to sit down, and discovered that Susie was lying on the bed in the corner, reading the movie section of the Sunday *Times,* or perhaps just holding it over her face to protect herself somewhat from the flying specks which were falling on everything and leaving a fine layer of dust on every surface. She put down the paper beside her, pushed herself erect, said, "Hi," her usual greeting, threw some articles of clothing from the rocker at the foot of the bed so that I might sit down, took my broad-brimmed hat, which I had almost forgotten I was wearing, and offered me a Coke which I declined. She shrugged but did not stop smiling; I have the feeling that she never stops smiling. It must be disconcerting to live with a girl, to make love to a girl, who never stops smiling.

I said inanely, not to her obviously, but to Seth, "You're working hard in this heat."

He flung back his head. "Spasmodically."

"What does that mean?"

Susie answered for him. "He means, when he feels guilty about not seeing his friends, he drops his tools and runs off to plot and scheme." From the way she grinned I gathered that she didn't object, even though she was apparently not included. "And when he feels guilty about falling behind in his work, he goes at it like a maniac, heat or no heat, for twelve hours at a stretch. Crazy."

I asked if I was intruding on this maniacal labor, and they both assured me that I was very welcome. So I sat there fanning myself in that dark dusty heat with my hat, which I had retrieved from Susie, and waiting for an opening.

Finally S. flung aside his sanding block, wiped his face and torso with a not very clean towel, and said, "I've been meaning to thank you."

"For what?" I asked, a little surprised.

"Well, I was down at the lumberyard looking things over, and when they found out where I was working they mentioned that you've got credit there. So I went ahead and used it—it saved me time and trouble. I would have had to go out and borrow the money to buy the stuff."

All I could think of in response was something to the effect that he should have known he could come to me for a loan if he was strapped.

"I've got a bad enough name already in your household," he replied, "without getting tagged as a moocher too. So if anybody asks you, you tell them I'm paying the lumber bill as soon as I finish these pieces, which are already commissioned. In other words, the money is guaranteed."

I was a little embarrassed for several reasons—because of Susie's presence, because I know I have something of a reputation for being an old skinflint (which S. was perhaps alluding to indirectly), and because I didn't want the relations between us, complicated as they are in ways that no one but I can wholly see, translated into family-finance terms. At the same time, it did give me an opening of sorts, certainly a better one than telling S. that I had just had a dream about him—which wasn't even strictly true, and which I wouldn't have felt like recounting to him in any case.

So I told him it wasn't money or mooching that was upsetting the people around me, it was what they conceived of as his malign influence.

He laughed and said, "I thought Girard was your resident bogeyman."

"If Rog has been tolerated," I explained, "it's because everyone conceded that he's been invaluable. And because I chose him."

"You mean you didn't choose me? Maybe I've imposed myself on you and the household, but it was at your invitation."

"Let's not rehearse old arguments," I said. "It's hot and I'm tired."

He shrugged. "You brought it up."

"For a reason," I said. And I told him about the decision to have a conclave, including him and Rog.

S. said to Susie, with her laughing all the while, like some kind of happy idiot, "How do you like that? The Grand Sachem is inviting me to a powwow." He turned back to me. "Well, I don't want to go."

I don't know what I expected, but I hadn't expected this, and I told him so.

"Why should you be surprised?" he asked. "Why should I have to account for myself to Larry Brodie or Walter Honig? What have I got in common with White House advisors and Establishment lawyers?"

"Me, for one thing," I said.

"Well, you've got a point there," he conceded. "Except that I was under the impression that our relations were between you and me. Do you think I'd have moved in here with Susie and all my gear if I knew I'd have to pass muster with those people? All I'm concerned with is whether you think my presence here is disruptive."

"I'm not sure," I said. The heat was beginning to get to me, and I began to wish it was over with so I could leave.

"If that's the case," he muttered, no longer smiling, "we can pack up and leave."

"But I want you to stay," I insisted. "I am not being morbid, simply realistic, when I say that I have no idea how much longer I'll be here myself, and I'd like you to stay as long as possible—even if you are disruptive. I'd prefer peace and quiet, and I've done my best to plead for that with the others. If you're not here, if you leave, I won't even be able to plead with you."

"You really are something. Consistency is not your strong point. Without me, presumably you'll have some peace and quiet."

"That's what the others intimate. I'm not so sure. Even if Rog were to leave and make their dreams come true, I'd be left with my inner . . ." I was going to say inner torments,

248

but I suddenly felt it would be pompous, talking like that to someone so much younger, so I stopped.

"You know," he said after a while, "I have the feeling that just by existing I disrupt your life."

"It's possible," I conceded, "but then that's my fault as much as it is yours,"

Should I have gone on to plead with him—Please come, defend yourself, not against me but against them? I couldn't.

S. leaned his thinnish but strong bare upper arm on the chest with the vacant drawer and peered out at me from under the piratelike red bandanna. He cocked his work boot on the bench and spoke into my silence.

"Isn't it true," he asked, "that *they* are disrupting your life?"

"Well, I think so," I admitted, "and I've been arguing with them. But they have certain, well, rights. They have a vested interest in my welfare, so to speak, and they honestly feel that they're not only looking after my best interests but promoting my cause."

"Maybe your secretary could say that, but the others? What cause are they promoting? Quietism? Self-congratulations? If I'm disruptive, it's only because I remind you of what you were when you were younger, and what you considered your obligations to be in those days."

"Oh, you remind me all right," I said. I glanced at Susan, but she had withdrawn into the anodyne of the starlet interviews; for a moment I was tempted to break out, to say it all. But I contented myself with observing, "When I was younger I could afford to be altruistic, to concern myself day and night with the troubles of others, all over the world. Now I have to concern myself with my own troubles—in a way you simply cannot understand—as a matter of self-protection. My vision has shrunk just as my body and my bones have shrunk."

"I don't believe it." He was looking at me almost crossly.

What could I say to that? It was the very basis for his

coming here, setting up shop, conniving with the Children of Liberty. And his refusal to believe, like everything else, came from the goodness of his heart. What was more, his appeal was to the best in me—that was why he was able to get at me through Rog, whom I had brought into the house, I could see now, because Seth had not been here.

I couldn't rail at him. All I could say was, "I would like to be what you still believe I am. In fact I try—that's why the middle-aged distrust Rog, isn't it?—but in truth it's impossible." This was hardly what I had come out here to say, but now it seemed inevitable. "I am not great. If I once was, which seems unlikely, I didn't know it because I was too busy to care. Now I care, partly because of Larry. I can only say in my defense that it's part of the shrinking process."

None of this, as I think back on it, was exactly calculated to bring Seth around to the powwow, much less to get him to call off the Children of Liberty and the attempt to emboss me on their flag. But then I wasn't exactly calculating—I was saying things I hadn't intended to when I went down to the guesthouse to see him.

"You want, and you don't want." He said this not contemptuously but more or less reflectively, wiping at the sweat which continued to ooze forth on his prematurely furrowed countenance.

"That's true," I said. "In fact I want to go on living and I don't want to go on living. You should be able to understand that."

"Why?"

I put my hat back on my head; the brim shaded my face from him. "Because you're my flesh and blood."

"Indeed?"

"You're my son, aren't you?"

After all my tiptoeing around, all my confiding of moth-eaten secrets to this diary as a way of protecting myself from having to utter certain words aloud, they slipped out as easily as if I were discussing the weather! But even more remarkable was the way Seth responded.

"Of course." He spoke with absolute calm, almost (could I possibly have imagined this?) with *indifference*. I fancied that he cast a glance, whether stealthy or casual I can't say, in the direction of Susan; but observing no reaction from that corner, he turned back to me and repeated exactly what he had said. "Of course."

No bafflement, no laughter, no shock, no demand— whether outraged or indulgent—for explanations. And greatest surprise of all, no surprise.

Was he the one, then, who had been reading these pages? Or had he been told by Rog, or someone else? Does everyone know? I cannot believe it. I know, many things that seemed to us appalling, startling, shocking—particularly those things having to do with sex—seem perfectly ordinary, uninterest- ing even, to younger people. But the matter of paternity, of who your father is . . . I cannot believe that this would be a matter of indifference even to the most liberated. When I reminded him that he was my flesh and blood and he replied, Indeed? was he questioning me or simply asking what differ- ence it made?

Stunned, I felt my way cautiously. "You know what I'm referring to?"

"I wouldn't have moved in here if I didn't."

I just could not bring myself to be more specific, to ask him just what he knew, or how he knew, or when he knew. Perhaps I didn't want to find out. If he was still taking the expression as a kind of metaphor (which was barely possible), I didn't have the strength to find that out either, or to reveal the reality beyond the metaphor.

I don't know how long I sat there like that, in the hot dusty shade, with my floppy hat brim drooping over my face. I heard Susan sigh, but only because, I think, she was settling herself into a more comfortable position on the bed.

Then Seth said coolly, "I regard myself as your legitimate heir."

Legitimate? That word was odd and old-fashioned coming from his lips, and I said so. Besides, I told him, there wasn't all that much to inherit. I tried to make light of this, more or less, by adding, "It's lucky for Jennifer that she has a profession, and that her own family is well to do." By which I meant to make clear to him also that she was my primary heir—if he had really meant to say legal rather than legitimate heir.

"I wasn't thinking of Jennifer," he told me.

I felt rebuked, as though I had been implying that he was some kind of fortune hunter. "I'm not thinking of the past," he said, "but of the future. If you're no longer concerned with it, but simply with refurbishing your past, then Larry is welcome to that. But I still claim the heritage."

I was sweating, unsure of whether I had escaped disaster— only to fall into another kind of trap.

"I don't enjoy the idea of being haggled over," I said, "as if I was something on a bargain counter. First you all try to push me this way and that, then you start haggling over me."

Seth folded his arms. He smiled. "That's precisely why I'm not going to the powwow."

"But you people will have to settle these things," I said, maybe a little desperately. "I won't have this going on any more."

He shrugged. I didn't even know what the shrug meant. I felt drained, frighteningly exhausted. I didn't want to confess weakness, but I had to; I asked Susan if she would lend me her arm to accompany me back to the house.

"Why sure," she said, jumping up. She grinned at me encouragingly. "You play croquet with me, the least I can do is walk with you. Right?"

I don't remember anything after that, not even getting back here.

AUGUST 10 Jenny is throwing a party. She decided, no doubt after consulting with L., to turn the conclave into a social event. "More pleasant that way, yes?" she demanded, and I could hardly say no, especially after she told me she was going to bake some blueberry pies for the occasion, using the berries she and Susan have been picking in their spare time. (J.'s polite way of putting it; actually *all* of Susan's time is spare time!)

"You wouldn't mind, would you," J. said very casually, "if I invited Gabriel Gibbons over from Lenox? He practically commutes between New York and Tanglewood, he adores the concerts, and I think he's a bit off his feed since the break-up with his wife."

"You never even met the woman," I pointed out. "He may be the most relieved, happiest man in the world. What you really want is to add his pressure to the others'."

She teased me about my suspiciousness (I don't think she knows how painful that subject is for me, even in jest—wait till she gets old and finds out she doesn't know whom to trust), and said something about Gibbons being concerned, after all, with the remainder of the Wells interviews.

"So why not ask Wells? And his wife? They're just sitting around Martha's Vineyard not doing anything except biting their nails and talking to Larry on the White House hot line."

"Well, it's a brilliant idea and very sweet of you. I'll bake an extra pie. We'll have the Wellses, Gabriel Gibbons, Walter and Lily, Larry, and of course Seth and Susan. With Rog and us, that makes eleven."

"Except that Seth won't come."

J. simply refused to take that seriously. "Nonsense," she said. I could hardly go into a long exposition of what passed between S. and me out in the guesthouse, but I did try to make clear that S. would not hear of a parley which would be a kind of trial, a defense by him of his relations with me.

"Then you put it to him the wrong way. Let me talk to him."

I couldn't very well oppose that without appearing to be an obstructionist. So off she went blithely. How long she was gone, I don't know, since I dozed off; when I awoke she peeked in on me, grinning.

"It's all taken care of," she said.

"You mean he's coming?"

"They're coming," she corrected me. "Seth and Susan."

I was going to ask her how she had managed to accomplish this, but before I could quite think how to put it, she added casually, "They are expecting a guest this Friday who may stay for a day or two—I told them to bring him along, it'll make an even dozen for dinner."

"A guest?" It struck me that the presence of a stranger might complicate things, or inhibit Larry—to say nothing of Walter. On the other hand, maybe that was what was needed, someone disinterested whose presence would serve to keep everyone in line.

"A friend of Seth's," Jenny explained. "Chap named Gary Grebner."

I couldn't believe it. I must have gaped like a fish. A poor fish. So Seth was ganging up on me after all. Or at least on Larry. He might say he was evening the balance. And Jenny, didn't she realize what was up? Or was she a party to the deal? Had she gone out there and made the concession, compromised with S. in order to get him to share a pipe at Larry's powwow? It won't be a peace pipe, that's for sure.

"Jenny," I said to her, "are you aware that Grebner is the fellow from the Children of Liberty who started the whole business?"

"Don't worry your head about it," she said. "I'll take care of everything."

How much is everything? Can she be aware of what she's getting us into?

AUGUST 11 Was awakened from my nap by raised voices. Confused. Thought at first someone was trying to get in to see me and was being intercepted by R. But then my head cleared and it became apparent to me that it was Jennifer I was hearing. I was really surprised, in fact upset: I can't think when I last heard J. raise her voice.

I thought to myself, Is she quarreling with R., has it come to that? I blamed myself, it was I who had set them against each other. But then, just as I was squeezing my feet into my slippers so that I might go out there and restore peace before it was too late and everything fell apart, I realized that I had not heard R., in fact I had heard no one but J. She was talking on the telephone. . . .

Fearing to embarrass her, I hung back. But I couldn't help wondering what it was all about; I suspected, but was unsure. When R. came in with the papers some little time later, I asked him straight off to tell J. that I should like to see her.

"She's gone off," he said. "I'll tell her as soon as she gets back, though."

"Do you know when that will be?" I asked as offhandedly as I could.

"She didn't say," he remarked neutrally. "She left in something of a hurry."

I had to let it go at that.

R. was eager to read me a draft of a piece under my name that had been requested some time ago by one of those new magazines that spring up like mushrooms after rain and have a vogue for a while. But as he began to read I grew baffled; when had we discussed all this? I had no recollection of any of it, not even the subject, which had to do with memory and childhood: At what age can memory be said to function, and how "reliable" is it in later years, as a descriptive tool, when the rest of the mental mechanisms begin to falter? It is a commonplace, the article observed, to remark on how in the very old inability to recall quite recent events is often accompanied with an acute sharpening of memory for the most remote occurrences, extending through childhood all the way to infancy. But the real question to be considered, it went on, was whether these "memories" of earliest childhood were in fact recollections of actual events, or whether the senescent brain might not be simply inventing, and also rearranging materials which had been presented to it in time past by parents or progenitors. In the opening pages of his auto-biography, *My Past & Thoughts,* Alexander Herzen tells us vividly how a drunken soldier tore him from the arms of his wet nurse—he was an infant, it was 1812, and Moscow was burning—and opened his baby clothes to see if there was money or jewelry hidden in them. When he found nothing, the enraged soldier tore the clothes to pieces and flung them to the ground. Recounting this tale from the vantage of his middle years, Herzen explains that it had been told to him over and over at his insistence by an old servant woman of the household, as he lay in his crib listening eagerly, pleased that he had taken part in the war against Napoleon. But—the article noted wryly—had Herzen lived to a ripe old age, and revealed the anecdote of his infancy only at that time, he might possibly have tried to pass it off as a "memory" spring-ing full-blown from the recesses of his own mind as it probed all the way back to the primal birth trauma.

I had absolutely no recollection of ever having discussed Herzen with Rog. Certainly not recently, when he must have been putting this article together from notes taken during our conversations. As a matter of fact, I can't recall having looked at the Herzen memoirs for a good many years. It was Luba, of course, who introduced me to Herzen, along with Bakunin and the rest of her nineteenth-century gallery of heroes, although I think it must have been well into the twenties before I got hold of the Garnett translation. Those early days before the war, before the birth of Sophia even, came flooding back to me—my arm around Luba's waist as we stood at the rail of the 125th Street ferry, crossing to Jersey in the summer breeze, walking hand in hand along the Palisades while she recited Pushkin to me and poured out her own dreams and passions in the Russian manner. . . .

R. must have seen my confusion. He stopped reading and inquired, "Is something wrong?"

I dared not confess that I had no memory of having discussed any of this with him, not even the Herzen. We are
close, he and I, but there are certain things I cannot confide.
And certainly it would not do to let him know that my mind
was wandering (all the way back to Luba!) while I was supposed to be following his transcription (the word is his, not
mine) of "my" ideas. So I said, rather gruffly, "Go ahead, read
on, read on."

"Do you like it so far?" he inquired.

"It's almost too likeable," I said. "I'm not sure about all
that wittiness, but I suppose you know best, you speak for me
better than I do myself."

He read on, pleased. I did try to attend more carefully,
and I remember thinking that if I were reading this instead
of being responsible for it, I'd be enjoying myself. Then
suddenly I was brought up short again, by an illustration
taken not from my earlier reading, but from my own
early childhood. It was not long after we had come to the
United States, and we were living in a gloomy house on 28th
Street. Father went out every day, "to see people," which I
suppose was a euphemism for visits to relatives and acquaintances in search of financial help. It must have been an agony
for him, since he was utterly unused to that sort of thing, but
he had been wiped out by the Panic of 1893 and had no
alternative. All I knew was that he had no studio any more,
that I had no friends to play with, and that Mother sat in
her strange shrunken room in this strange and surely ter-
rifying country, writing long, long letters. It was so quiet
that I could hear her pen scratching between the soft slow
throbbings of the wall clock. One rainy summer day something rose up in my throat, I could stand it no more, and I
crept into my mother's lap without asking her permission,
jarring her arm and startling her. But she did not object, in
fact she laid down her pen and enfolded me in her arms,
crooning to me, after a time, in a voice I hardly recognized,
singing a song I did not know at all. We were rocking together like that, warm and weeping, when the hall door

opened unexpectedly and Father stood there, staring at us. "Marta," he said in a quiet fury, "put that boy down." I tried to stand, but my mother was clutching me so tight that I could not free myself. "That is a disgusting sight," my father said. "The boy is almost eight years old. You hold him in your lap when his legs practically touch the floor—I will not have it!"

Well, the article went on, as R. read it to me in his deep, well-modulated voice, this incident has all the circumstantial material of memory, in addition to the obvious fact that (unlike Herzen) I was surely old enough for such a traumatic experience to embed itself in the recesses of my consciousness. And yet, how can I be sure that the incident "really" took place? Does it not conform a little too neatly to my own half-understood desires, then and for a long time thereafter? Could I not at some point in a long life have dreamed something very like this, particularly during that period in the twenties when I was profoundly affected (like most of my contemporaries and friends) by Freud, and was attempting to establish a haven for children despite two unsuccessful marriages and a lost daughter? And could I not, as the sole, and aged, survivor of the supposed incident, have transferred it from the realm of dream to that of reality?

How I managed to contain myself while R. read on, I do not know. I was tempted to stop him, by force if necessary, to compel him to tell me when I had ever told him that story, and if I had not, whether he had been rifling my private papers for something very like it. But I was in terror lest he should say to me, like Seth, Don't you really remember? It was only yesterday, or perhaps the day before.

So he read on to the end while I sat like a stone. He said something about suggestions or corrections, and I shook my head dumbly. At last I could stand it no longer and asked, "Isn't there a covering letter? You always have a covering letter."

He knew exactly what I meant. My signature sufficed to

indicate that the work enclosed was of my own authorship. I had never had any qualms before, but now, as he placed the letter before me and handed me my pen, I saw my mother's hand, and the long, sad, unfinished letter I had interrupted by creeping into her arms. I began to weep.

Angrily I brushed away the moisture and inscribed my initials.

"Are you all right?" he inquired solicitously.

"You already asked me that," I replied with some heat, and added gratuitously, "What's the matter, don't you remember?"

Flushing slightly, he retrieved the letter unobtrusively and slipped it into the folder with the article.

"Please go away now," I said. "I want to be alone."

I don't know if that was what I wanted. I do know that I could not bear to have him go through his daily routine of reading to me from *The Times* obituaries of men half my age. It's not his fault, he can't understand, how could he?

No one can. They are all dead and I have no one left to talk to. If I have to be betrayed by lachrymose incontinence —the worst kind, since it implies the collapse not just of the bladder but of the brain—I will face it alone.

AUGUST 12 Did I write all that? I hardly seems possible. At any rate, I feel a different person today. A long sound dreamless sleep. Awoke to the glorious quarrels of the songbirds in the maple outside my window and decided to go for a walk to get some air into my lungs.

They will not count me out yet, the ghouls. Not as long as I can breathe deep and clear my head of self-pity, that corrosive, destructive poison. When you think of it, I had reason to weep yesterday, and not just from self-pity. Why should a man apologize for weeping? Is it a consolation to be reserved for women? If they are taking over supposedly masculine prerogatives, let us appropriate some of theirs. It has nothing to do with being old.

Went for a bracing walk. After a while, though, I felt that the graveled edge of the county highway was hardly presenting a challenge to me. I hesitated for barely a moment, and then struck off through the brush that more or less separates our property from that of the Hendrickses—gnarled old half-fallen-down apple trees, struck by lightning and split by storms, blueberry bushes, wild laurel, and too many nasty pricklebushes.

Not easy getting through all that, even with my stick to push the stuff aside, but I was determined to get down to my grove of firs, planted by the CCC boys back in the thirties. How delicious it was to stroll by my lonesome through these cushiony alleys, protected from the hot sun by the tall intertwined pine boughs far above me. The low dead branches yielded easily, snapping off at the thrusts of my stick; and I didn't even mind the occasional ones that caught me unawares, flicking at my face and making me flinch as I pressed on.

After I'd passed all the way through several lanes, bringing me up against the rusty barbed-wire fence strung up by some earlier farmer, maybe one of the Hendrickses, to keep his cattle in bounds, I decided to descend to the older, steeper woods, to the maples and birches and shagbarks that fought their way up through the boulder-strewn brush, divided here and there by the runoff rivulets that join at the foot of our property to form our trout stream. It was the first spot I'd taken J. to in those early days when she'd come round first to interview me and then to persuade me to marry her.

It's been years since I've ventured down there alone. There has been a certain unspoken household agreement that those woods are now out of bounds to a brittle old man with failing vision. Reason enough for me to go, one more time. How invigorating it was to venture down, groping, fumbling, circling shoulder-high boulders, ducking under vines, testing damp spots with the stick, listening for the inviting chuckle of the stream, even though it is reduced in August to a trickling whisper.

I made it at last, winded but triumphant, and sat down at the water's edge to see what I could see (not too damned much, I admit), and hear what I could hear. I leaned on the stick Larry had brought me back from a vacation trip to the Blue Ridge country; I knew by heart what was engraved on the shaft between my fingers: *Hit's curious what a body sees walking by his lone, outlandish birds, beastes tracks, and traces in a stone.* . . .

Finally, regretfully, I braced myself for the rugged climb back up, buoyed by the chatter of the birds and a certain sense of triumph. I almost felt as if the birds were calling to each other, remarking on my temerity. Maybe even my courage?

But as I hoisted myself up, moving on what I took to be a diagonal in order to minimize the strain of the ascent, I grew dazed and weak and, finally, disoriented. That is a frightening sensation, and as I stood there I bethought myself of the children at the Sophia School whom I used to take on nature walks half a century ago, of how their high spirits would alter insensibly to a kind of awe as we penetrated deeper into the woods, and then—for those who would from time to time lose their way—to a tearful terror of the unknown and a weeping fear that they would never be found. They always were (our grounds were hardly primeval or particularly vast in area), and I knew that I would be if I chose to stand and wait.

But I did not. I had no desire to be found frozen to the spot. The day had been my own and I wanted it to conclude that way too. So I sat down gingerly on a monstrous huge tree that had crashed years ago and was now rotting, returning to its source. I did not want to sprain or break anything, and I felt that if I could regain my wind and my sense of balance I would make it back up on my own.

As I sat there, gripping the stick and pondering, surrounded by the odd little woodland sounds, the strange nestlings and rushings that are horrifying to the young and comforting to the old, I thought of what had been going on around me in my household—Jenny calling on Larry and having a scene with him because of her insouciance in the deal she'd made with Seth; Larry calling on what was his name (it took me a while to fix it in my head), Gibbons, the separated man, and Wells, the mellow-voiced interviewer; Seth being petulant but maybe rightfully uncompromising as he headed into his thirtieth year.

My fear, such as it was, faded away. I was going to get back home and take charge. The notion of all those people attempting to manage me, to rearrange me into something that would comport with the ongoing pattern of their lives, was one that I simply was not going to put up with.

But I think that what finally galvanized me was the sound of familiar voices calling my name. "Sam! Sam!" Then, "Where are you?" And, "Just stay where you are, we're coming!" That last, with its frightened, falsely hearty reassurance, set me on my feet once again. And on my way. I knew which way to go now, and moved on, slowly but firmly.

When I came to the clearing, to the blueberry bushes, the stone fence with its tumbled-down gap through which I could pass and the meadow which the Hendricks boys cut and baled while I watched from the sanctuary of my porch, I breathed deeply and passed my hand over my hair. I did not wish to appear winded or disarrayed.

They caught up with me there, several of them, chattering and crying out their alarm and relief. Jennifer, Seth, Susan, Rog, fluttering around me, not like birds or butterflies, more like geese.

"Are you all right?" Rog demanded. "Would you like to take my arm?"

"Is it becoming a habit of yours," I said, "to keep asking me how I am? When I'm dead I think the difference will become noticeable. Until then—"

"For heaven's sake, Sam," J. interrupted me, "do you have any idea how worried we were? Look at you, you're all bleeding." She put her hand to my face and dabbed at my cheek with her handkerchief. It came away smeared from where one of the dead branches must have lashed at me.

"Man," Susan said excitedly, "we had search parties out. Mr. Honig was driving up and down the road, Seth walked one way, I walked another, Mr. Girard and Mrs. Lumen were directing the operations. Like a manhunt!"

"I don't think I should necessarily be hunted down," I told her, "for whatever crimes I may have committed."

"Sam," J. insisted, "you must have heard us calling to you. Why didn't you answer?"

"Maybe I was too busy enjoying the solitude," I said.

By now the pleasure—even of having all this commotion —was dissipating. I was becoming annoyed, worse, upset. I didn't want them to see me as winded, scratched, bleeding. I had the uneasy sense that all of them, allies and opponents alike, were united in thinking that I had done something irrational, that I hadn't simply gone for a walk in the woods, but had succumbed to a suicidal impulse.

"Do you really think I didn't know what I was doing?" I asked J.

She closed her eyes for a moment. The movement of her eyelids gave me the feeling that she was trying to contain herself. Then she smiled. "Don't be silly," she said. "We were only afraid that you might have fallen, or injured yourself."

As she took my arm she gave me strength. I needed it, the final climb back to the house was almost more than I could face, but I would not concede. In fact, I could not talk, I needed all my forces to move my legs, pushing onward with Larry's walking stick with one hand, hanging onto J. with the other. When we got to the porch at last I dropped into my chair.

Lily was in the kitchen doorway with Mrs. Hoskins, Walter stood before me with his arms akimbo.

"Sam," Walter said, "you really are something. What were you trying to prove?"

"If I said that I'm non compos mentis, would that satisfy you, Counselor? You must have had clients before me who were off their rockers. Don't stand there looking at me as though I was the first."

"Very funny," W. said. "I wouldn't walk down there alone myself any more, and I'm ten years younger than you."

"Nine," I said. "And you're hardly fit to drive, much less walk."

"You had us all scared out of our wits," Mrs. Hoskins ventured. "Why did you want to go and do a thing like that?"

"To scare you out of your wits," I told her. "Go inside and bake something, or look up some recipes. I'm sick of being nagged at."

It was at this point that Lily said to me quietly, almost aside, as if she did not want all the others to hear, "I wasn't worried, Sam."

My heart was still pounding in my chest. I turned in my chair to look at her. It occurred to me that I had been taking her for granted for too long, thinking of her (when I did at all) as Walter's helpmate.

I took a deep breath and folded my arms so that she should not see how they were trembling from exhaustion (the ordinary tremor I can do nothing about any more, other than move about so that it will not be too noticeable). "Well, Lily," I said, "It seems as though you're the only one."

"That's possible," she said. "I could understand their worry, but I didn't share it." She hesitated, then added, "You won't take it amiss if I tell you that I think you're being overprotected?"

"Not at all," I said. "Not at all."

But I wasn't sure exactly how she meant that. And now that I'm alone again in my room, and free of all the chattering and the twittering, I'm still not sure, even though I've been pondering. And pondering.

AUGUST 13   Tomorrow is J.'s dinner party. She expects Larry shortly. I imagine they've made it up, if he was the one she was bickering with on the phone (and I'm reasonably sure it must have been). Anyway, the stakes are much too high for L. not to show up. Also Gabriel G. and Dick Wells. Has Grebner encamped out there in the guesthouse? I refuse to ask. Time enough for him to have a go at me.

Well, I'm ready. The women are cooking up a storm in the kitchen, the men are doing the same elsewhere, and as for me, I feel cool and confident. The eye of the storm.

. . . J. just stuck her head in.

"You're in the eye of the storm," I told her.

"Now what does that mean?"

"Oh," I shrugged. "just more senile babbling. Don't worry about me."

She stuck her tongue out at me and went away. . . .

AUGUST 15   It all began amiably and sedately. Rog tapped on my door to ask whether I was ready.

"Jennifer said to tell you that you should make a grand entrance, the Honigs are here with Mr. Gibbons."

I knew what that meant. She'd been busy with Mrs. Hoskins on the hors d'oeuvres, and she wanted me to help R. entertain. She also wanted R. to get me into a tie and jacket. He himself was looking quite regimental with an ascot at the throat and a natty navy blue blazer. I did try to temporize, telling him he could pick out a tie for me, and that I'd put in an appearance when Wells and his wife turned up.

"But they already have," he said. "They flew over from the Vineyard, and I picked them up at the airport and took them to the Red Deer Inn. They were renting a car there—I expect them any minute."

I was mildly curious about Mary Wells, but not curious enough to have invited her and her husband to stay with us— or for that matter Gabriel Gibbons, who was apparently a house guest of the Honigs. J. knows that I cannot bear to have anyone come to sleep in the house other than herself and Rog—and of course Larry, who has been coming and going for thirty years. I purposely fixed up the guest cottage —I really don't think I am inhospitable, it is just that I sleep so badly, like all old people, and am so sensitive to the least change—so that visitors who came and stayed late could sleep nearby without disturbing me.

But with Seth and Susan installed there, and whoever of their allies came in turn to visit them, I couldn't accommodate others. Nor would I be up to all the excitement and clatter, even the simple coming and going.

I think I am avoiding the facts of the matter. If I go on like this, what will happen is that I'll exhaust myself on trivia, my arm and my eyes will wear out, and I will have to stop without even having gotten to the party and what went on there. It is so hard to discipline yourself when you are old. You say to yourself, what's the point? If I haven't earned the right to indulge myself now, then when?

Well. I went on out to the porch with Rog, and by the time he had poured me my whisky ration, and I had shaken hands with Gibbons and Walter, and kissed Lily (she did smell as good, I told her—raising a blush—as the rest of us looked), the Wellses had driven up in their rented car, spitting gravel all over Jennifer's laurel as the brakes hit the driveway.

The talk was about children and young people. It developed that Gibbons had not only had a wife, but several children, about whom he spoke with a desperate smiling eagerness that touched my heart. The older, a girl named Emily, was in the process of obtaining her second divorce. She had been married first, in an apparent act of rebellion when she was an undergraduate at Barnard, to a black musician who lived on cocaine and sweetened breakfast foods. She had left him for a Vietnam veteran who had lost a leg in a helicopter crash and was resisting rehabilitation.

"I'm not certain," explained Gibbons, who, it was becoming clear to me, was certain of nothing save for his rather anachronistic love of baroque music, "whether Emily is really a strong person underneath all this floundering about. I mean, maybe it does take a kind of courage to free yourself from the consequences of a series of dreadful mistakes. What do you think, Mr. Lumen," he appealed to me, "isn't it better than if she had sunk into a kind of slothful acquiescence with either of those men?"

"Absolutely," I assured him. I did feel like consoling him, like giving him whatever reassurance I could that he was not responsible for all this waste and wreckage, that he too had done the right thing by convulsively wrenching himself loose from his long-time marriage partner.

But more was to come. J. had joined us, bearing food offerings, and she asked politely, "And what about your boy?"

"Eric?" Gibbons' ferociously defensive smile broadened; it was all but unbearable. "He took off for Sweden to escape the draft. He went to a crafts school there, but he fell in with a bad crowd. Adele and I went over several times to visit him, to express our moral support, and . . . well, you know. The fact is, it was probably there that Adele and I decided that our marriage was no good."

So much wretchedness, so little accomplishment! I wanted to put my arms around him. I was put in mind of the weeping parents who came to my office in the Sophia School, to plead with me to tell them what they had done wrong. And when I think of those days, how petty were the problems of those affluent children compared with the torments of this generation! What dreadful, hopeless, bleary, whisky-smeared scenes there must have been in that Swedish hotel room.

I do think that one of the differences between those days and these is that there used to be more feeling for privacy when it came to personal troubles. None of those parents at the Sophia School would have dreamt of making a scene in public; but here was Gibbons, a high-salaried producer and executive, accustomed to making decisions, not just about the spending of large sums of money but about what millions of people would and would not get to see on their television screens, standing before a group of strangers and all but weeping, confessing his inadequacy as a husband, a father, a man. He wasn't even drunk.

Walter's lips pursed judiciously, as if he were summing up the pluses and minuses of his house guest's confessions; it could be that I am unfair, but beneath W.'s appraisal seemed to lurk the self-satisfaction of the childless, free forever from such vexing cares. One thing I have never been able to bring myself to say to W. is that if I were a trial lawyer I would never want a client of mine to be judged by a jury of the childless.

But not Lily. I am led to think (there is no one I dare say it to) that childlessness was W.'s fault—or choice—and not hers. She gazed at poor old Gibbons with such compassion, her heart went out to him, as they say, that for a moment I thought she was going to burst into tears.

Very fortunately Dick Wells brought his wife in at that point, and introductions had to be made, distracting us all from the insoluble woes of the Gibbons family. Gabriel himself subsided into his gin and tonic, either because he did not make a practice of baring his breast before his colleague or because there were getting to be too many people for him to hold our continued fascination and sympathy.

Mary Wells is very ladylike. Reticent, well brought up, modest about whatever her capabilities may be (and I am sure they are there)—in short, very like those mothers of the upper class who began to bring me their children after the School moved from scandalously experimental to snobbishly correct. She asked me why I was smiling so broadly when her husband introduced me! I told her she reminded me of a woman I'd known a million years ago who had gotten me to stop smoking by promising to go out with me—could I have said, in front of her husband and everyone, that my leer came from the thought that there had been a time when her correctness and cool demeanor would have posed an immediate challenge to me to overcome?

That's all long gone now. But it still makes me smile to think of it. Secretly.

Well. Everything was going along innocuously, as people became lubricated and the social oils functioned. Larry had slipped in as unobtrusively as is possible for someone so hulking and magisterial, Mrs. H. was making the rounds, J. was relaxed and laughing and very beautiful, and then, the grand entrance, Seth and Susan and two others came up the drive and onto the porch.

"Who's the fourth?" I whispered to J.

"Grebner's date, apparently." J. smiled. "Don't worry, there's room."

"Young people don't have dates any more." Then I recognized her, as the foursome swept into my view: It was the black girl who had been part of the delegation on both occasions. She smiled at me, a bit uneasily it seemed, and accepted my outstretched hand as if it were made of china. I had the feeling she was surprised that I was still alive—at least she appeared to be staring at me as if she had never actually seen anyone so old outside the pages of a medical textbook.

"You're looking well," I said to her.

"So are you," she said, at which Seth laughed aloud, and Grebner seemed to color slightly (Susan was already at the hors d'oeuvres—that girl really is the glutton I had suspected at first sight). I felt they were sharing a private joke.

"You seem surprised," I said to her. "Was I supposed to go into shock after your little escapade at the redemption center?"

Grebner answered for her. "We heard you had taken sick after that drive with Seth. We were really concerned."

"I no longer travel well," I explained. "And then I thought I was out for a pleasure trip, not a field trip in the new civics."

Susan was in the usual gunny sack cum sandals, although I suppose it had been a concession on her part not to come over barefooted. Seth himself had gotten scrubbed up, washed and combed his hair, and was at least to my no longer sharp eye as neatly turned out as any of the others. And Grebner was Grebner, intense, contained, but voluble when the right button was pressed; he is the kind of serious, hot-eyed person whose clothing you tend not to notice.

Of course they were *different* from the others, and it wasn't just a matter of age (there cannot be more than a very few years separating them from Rog or Jennifer) or general appearance. Or even manners. I think if I had been only a casual observer I would have looked upon the scene as a pleasant family gathering, with some family friends included in the bucolic festivities. Everyone (except me) standing about, drink in hand, chattering; no splitting off into defensive and exclusive groups, not even men in one corner and women in the other. And yet I was aware, even with my impaired vision, that a chasm separated the guesthouse four from the others.

Why? How? I don't think it's just hindsight that impels me to say such a thing. Intensity, maybe? But no one could exude more intensity than Larry—it's his trademark. I think it resided more in the sense of radical grievance that lay, like lava within a volcano, beneath the smiling surface. There just wasn't anything like this among the others, no matter how dismayed they may have been at breaking bread with the younger set. When I put that down, it's the word dismay that jumps out at me: Seth and his friends (always excepting Susie, who is simply Susie) weren't just dismayed, they were pissed off. Does that do it?

Anyway. The bell rang, Mrs. H. shooed us in, and I was intrigued to see how Jenny had disposed of everyone between me at the head of the table and her at the foot. I hadn't given this any thought before—but she had placed Larry at my right hand and Seth at my left. Clever. Walter at her right hand and Rog at her left. Shrewd. In between, Lily and

Gabriel Gibbons, Susie and poor Dick Wells, Mary Wells and young Grebner, and the black girl whose name I just don't seem able to dredge up.

Thirteen.

The usual jokes were made about this, and J. said something about dusting off the extra leaves for our dining-room table. It suddenly occurred to me that I had been taking it for granted for a good many years that she was no more enamored of big dinner parties than I. But now, seeing her, flushed and pretty, ladling onto the old Haviland china the dinner she and Mrs. H. had planned between them, I found myself wondering whether this was just one more handy myth, something I had taken for granted simply because it suited me, an easily fatigued old man, to believe it. After all, we did have some large and amusing gatherings in the early days of our marriage; but I was a lad of eighty or eighty-one at that time, and far more sociable (and less easily exhausted) then than now. I even counted it a kindness on my part to free her from the embarrassment of having me doze off before guests at table; for years now she has made her own plans for eating, as for sleeping and other matters.

Well, if she has missed these parties it is too late now, as with so many other things, for me to make it up to her. I had the sharp feeling, even before the dinner was over, that— even though I was enjoying it myself and was therefore more alert than I am nowadays with large groups—this was going to be the last one of its kind, ever, for me. Maybe that very feeling, that foreshadowing of finality, sharpened the clarity of my own perceptions.

I think I was the one who triggered off the first explosions. During a momentary lull, just as Mrs. H. was wheeling in the blueberry pies, something made me say, "When are the fireworks?"

Some of the guests gazed at me innocently, curiously, as though they didn't quite understand. But I felt a stiffening on either side of me. They knew, my two boys.

"Come on," I persisted, driven by an urge I still cannot

271

put words to, maybe simply a desire to bring on the inevitable, accelerate the sluggish tide of disaster and get it over with. "Wasn't this supposed to be a confrontation, a clash of the hounds baying over this old bone?"

"You're overdramatic, Sam," Walter said from the outer end of the table. "What's wrong with a compromise, an accommodation?"

Seth muttered tersely, "Plenty."

"I see nothing irreconcilable among us," Walter insisted. "I know it's considered trite to say so, but we are nonetheless a group of civilized people." He raised his glass. "And we are united, after all, by affection and devotion to our hosts, Sam and Jenny Lumen. I drink to them."

As I recall now, those were the last lucid words of the evening. Or at any rate the last not spoken in anger or outrage.

I can't see the paper, not even the keyboard. Perhaps my eyes are tired, perhaps I am simply infuriated all over again by the recollection of what came after. But I will put it all down tomorrow, I promise, if only because I am determined to set down the record that will justify what I intend to do next.

AUGUST 17   Meant to get on with it yesterday but couldn't. Too much continuing commotion. They will kill me yet, all of them. I have to stick to my plan, regardless. And I will have to find an ally, I cannot go it alone—not because I lack the will, simply because I don't have the physical resources. I am not without ideas. I am not without resources. They have not finished me off yet.

I don't want to be unfair. Efforts were made. I made it sound yesterday (no, day before) as though J.'s dinner party was simply a brawl. It ended that way, yes; but people did try. Perhaps having difficulties making talk with young Grebner, Mary Wells turned to Seth and asked him what he did. Seth was very pleasant, telling her about his cabinetmaking;

I listened, learning things I hadn't known before. And Mary got all excited, in her ladylike way: It developed that she is mixed up with an ancient-music group, plays the clavichord, had one built for her by a man in Boston whom Seth knows well. Rapport. Well no, an exaggeration perhaps; Seth is a bit too ruthless to suffer ladies gladly; but they had more in common than dinner-table small talk.

And on my other side Larry was flirting with Susie. Sometimes you wouldn't know it, he is so eaten-up with ambition and so anxious to be the big shot, but he really is at his best with young people. I have to say that he didn't devote himself to child development for nothing. When he wants to be charming, he can be overwhelming—and Susie was batting her eyes at him and gurgling, and he was laughing as I hadn't seen him laugh in a long time. (I think J. was too busy with Walter and Gibbons to notice.)

What changed the tone of things was first my insistence on ending the bonhomie, and then Grebner's eagerness to pick up on it and demonstrate his intransigence. I remember particularly how he said to Walter, after W.'s toast, "Affection has nothing to do with principle."

Everyone froze. It is fascinating, how that word *principle* enrages the old, when it is uttered by the young. A dirty word. What do you *mean* by that? they asked, as if it were unimaginable, the implication that he should have principles and not they.

Grebner was happy to oblige. His didactic professorial way was calculated to set the old folks' teeth on edge. The black girl did try to soften it a bit, but she got pretty much brushed aside—he'd started it, not she.

Dick Wells seemed so honestly puzzled that I began to think maybe he hadn't been filled in by his producer, to say nothing of Larry. Seriously, politely, he asked Grebner and Nadine (that's her name!) to explain what it was about the interview series that disturbed them. Naturally, what they told him, he found hard to believe.

"I'm afraid I don't understand," he said, patting his lips with his napkin, "what right you feel you have to interfere. Mr. Lumen and I haven't even finished the interviews—"

"That's just it!" Nadine cried.

"—so you don't even know what the final result will be like on your screen. I don't even know myself."

"We know two things." Grebner stabbed the air rudely with his forefinger. I knew what he was going to say before he said it—that I was going to meet with the President in the final segment, and that the Children of Liberty were not being given the chance to refute the concept of the Children's Center or my endorsement of it.

When Wells opened his mouth to answer, Larry beat him to it. I could feel him beside me—if he wasn't actually trembling, he was giving off vibrations. He said loudly, "Your arrogance is incredible. You are taking advantage of Mr. Lumen's fondness for young people."

"May I point out," Grebner said coldly, "that Mr. Lumen is not your property."

At that point I think I put my hand on Larry's arm to physically restrain him.

"Suppose you tell us," Gabriel Gibbons demanded of Grebner, "what you think gives you the right to pre-censor a public affairs program?"

He didn't say it in a particularly mean way, but in a tone of genuine bewilderment—but Nadine told him he was being stuffy. "It's your crowd that are doing the pre-censoring," she said. "You're not giving us access. And I'll tell you why. Because if you did you might scare off the President. Right?"

I couldn't hold Larry any longer. "Access?" he yelled. "You've already abused the right of access to this house!"

Jenny was very pale. Seth was quiet. Walter and Gibbons both started to talk at once, but it was Dick Wells, with his authoritative commentator's manner, who got the floor.

"I'd like to know what would happen if you had what you

call access." Wells was turning on the charm, showing us why he was such a high-salaried performer. "Let's try to discuss that without histrionics. If you'll tell me first, Mr. Grebner, then we can hear from Dr. Brodie, all right?"

"We would expose hypocrisy," Grebner began.

"I'm sorry," Wells said very politely, "but that's hardly the purpose of my interview series with Mr. Lumen. Can't we focus on that?"

Nadine took over. "We want an assurance that Mr. Lumen will be given the opportunity to discuss us and our program."

"Discuss you?" Larry cried. "What you want is an endorsement."

"How do you know what we want?" she demanded.

"Because you're as crass as a soap manufacturer," Larry said. "You and your so-called ideals."

"Please," Wells pleaded. "One minute, Dr. Brodie. I want to find out if these folks would be satisfied if I questioned Mr. Lumen, during our next session, about his attitude toward such dissident youth groups as theirs. I myself would be happy to do that. It might add—"

Larry couldn't stand for that. He cut in, "All you'd be doing is giving in to their blackmail. Why are they any more entitled to free publicity than anyone else? Would you ask Mr. Lumen what kind of soap he uses, for God's sake?"

Gibbons turned to Grebner, "How about that, son?" Son was what he said; I haven't heard the word used in that way in a long, long time.

Grebner was ready. He shoved his dessert aside; he looked like the kind of boy who didn't care what he ate anyway. He put his hands flat on the table, palms down, and said, "We're not pleading for endorsements or begging for discussions, no matter what these people say. We want to see that Mr. Lumen is liberated from their grip before it's too late."

I said, "Thanks," but it was so noisy and tense I don't think anyone heard me.

"We want him freed from the Establishment clutch so he

can be the kind of hero he used to be for young people," Grebner went on. "We want that for the same reason we want to free young people from the gruesome commercial swamp that's dragging them down and choking them to death—the swamp that's epitomized by our television and our shopping plazas, our commercials and our redemption centers."

"You've made your point," Gibbons said. "Now, like Dick said, I'd like to hear from Dr. Brodie on this."

I think this was the point at which Lily said, in her lady-like, rather plaintive way, "I don't understand why we don't hear from Sam himself. It's his life you're talking about. Shouldn't he have some say?"

Another kind of tension. Maybe I could or should have said something that would have defused it. But I am human, too, and I was as irritated as anyone at the table. I said so. And I added what I still think was right: "Let it all come out," I said. "I don't want to add my self-righteousness to everyone else's."

Larry started to talk then, fairly quietly, but very intensely, about how absurd it was that I could be considered property, least of all his. "Just the same," Nadine said, "you act like you've got a copyright on him."

"Nobody copyrights Sam Lumen!" L. said. "But everyone honors him. What you people can't stand is that the President wants to honor him too." He turned to Gibbons. "I'm shocked that you and Wells should be willing to deal with these people. They're engaged in a wrecking operation. They'll do anything to keep the President from the program, they'll do anything to keep the Children's Center from becoming the Lumen Children's Center. I don't see why you should give them the time of day."

"You're giving yourself away," Grebner taunted him, "with all your shock and outrage. Is that the way you behave in the White House?"

"I don't have to endure provocation from blackmailers there," L. responded.

That got to Grebner. "I dare you to demonstrate black-mail. I dare you to demonstrate corruption. The great educator! No language is too low for you."

"You've been trying to blackmail Mr. Lumen. Why else did you insinuate Seth Fox into this house? You made a deal with Girard, you suborned him, you used Fox to work on Sam, you know it, and you know why."

Rog was on his feet at this, but before he could even speak Seth had jumped up on my left, knocked over a glass of iced tea, and was swinging at Larry. Somebody, I think Nadine, screamed, the men were tangling and thrashing over my head and falling behind me, others were rushing to try to disentangle them, Mrs. Hoskins came running in from the kitchen, Jenny came all the way from the other end of the table to shelter me and take my hand.

Well, I left them. I got out of there with Jenny's help and back into my room. That's when the worst thing happened.

She eased me into my chair and turned to close the door behind her. But even with the door shut, you could still hear raised voices, cursing, banging of fists on the table, rattling of cutlery and glassware. J. stood for a minute, her back pressed against the closed door, her hands over her ears to shut off the sounds. When she looked at me, her eyes were welling with tears.

"I'm so sorry," she said. "I never meant for anything like this to happen."

"Is it me you're sorry for?" I asked her.

She didn't notice the edge on my voice. "I made a mess of it, didn't I?" she said sadly. "I thought food and drink would soften everyone, make everything go well. Instead it turned into a nightmare. I was in terror that something might happen to you—I was sitting down at the far end of the table and I felt paralyzed, a million miles away. Are you sure you're all right?"

"I'm all right," I said. "You'd better get back to the company."

"The hell with them!" she cried bitterly. She rubbed her eyes dry with her knuckles. "Let them destroy everything. It's disgusting."

"It's only Larry and Seth, really," I pointed out. "The television men tried hard to get to the young people."

"I think Larry behaved abominably. I know how much he loves you, but I never dreamt he'd get so carried away, so outraged, that . . ."

"No," I said, "you didn't count on that, did you?"

J. cocked her head. Now she was hearing me over the party noises. "What do you mean?"

"Seth lost his head too. Why don't you mention that?"

"Larry is older," J. replied promptly. "He should have known better."

"You expected more of him."

"Of course." She looked at me. "Didn't you?"

"By now," I said, "I don't expect anything of anybody. But it does seem to me that you weren't just expecting Seth would lose his head—you were hoping he would."

"That's not so."

"When you said that you ruined the evening, you meant that Larry did, didn't you? If he'd only managed to control himself, and left the ugly aggressive misconduct to Seth, you both would have been home free, right?"

J. was gaping at me. I wanted to hurt her, I wanted her to be enraged like the others. Like me.

I said, "Because then I would have had to get rid of Seth and the troublemakers once and for all. And everything would have been smooth sailing for Larry and the President and the Children's Center, the whole thing."

"For God's sake, Sam," J. cried, "I wanted smooth sailing for you, just as I always have. Is that so awful? What's wrong with wanting to protect you?"

"If you'd wanted to protect me," I said, "you wouldn't have exposed me to that."

"I told you I was sorry. I never intended . . ." She stopped when she saw, I think, that it was pointless for her to go on. After a while she made one last try: "Don't you trust me?"

"Why should I?"

She began to weep, frustration making fists of her fingers. I can't go on.

AUGUST 19   Rog has offered to quit.

This has never happened. Never, not since the day he arrived here. Yet I wasn't surprised. Somehow I have been expecting it—or maybe it is simply that nothing surprises me any more. I asked him why, only because he stood there waiting for me to ask.

His fingers seemed to curl before he spoke. At once I was reminded of J. during our awful scene. Curious. I asked myself, Is he angry? Frightened? Determined?

"Go ahead, Rog," I urged him. "You can tell me."

"I owe you the opportunity to free yourself of burdens. If I've become an encumbrance instead of an aid—which could happen without my even being aware of it—you should have the freedom to rearrange your household without having to be concerned about me or my feelings."

He was bluffing. As he made his statement, I felt a kind of relief. Better bluff than fear or grim resolve. I reassured him that I couldn't conceive of the household without him.

"But I must accept my share of responsibility," he said.

"For what?" I asked, as if I didn't know.

"The unpleasantness. The scenes. I know how painful it must have been for you, these last days."

"Well," I said, "your leaving will solve nothing. Nothing. In fact it will only make things worse for me. And what's more, you know it, so let's stop this nonsense. Now leave me alone for a while."

He reddened but said nothing, either in protest or in gratitude. He just turned and left me.

Question is, what does he know? It would be clear to an

idiot that the atmosphere of the house has been poisoned for days. Is he just trying to remind me of my dependence on him? That hardly seems necessary. Was it a polite gesture? Waste of time. Or is he telling me that he knows everything, about Seth, about me, about my words with J. the other day? That's most likely. At least it is if R. is as devious as Walter and Larry take him to be.

If he left the party—brawl would be more precise—that night and came to my room ostensibly to see if he might be of help to J. and me, then he could easily have heard everything. Everything. Then there would have been no necessity for him to sneak a look at my diary. I told her too much, more than I've written here. . . .

AUGUST 20   Lily came with cookies. I asked her why she had to stand and bake in this heat.

"It was an excuse," she said. "It gave me an excuse to come over and see how you're doing."

So she knows. She is not dumb, she must have sensed that when J. left, the morning after the party, it wasn't because of an assignment or a date in the city. But she is too sensitive to come out with it directly.

"Well," I said to her, "people are still fighting all around me. You'd think I had a million dollars from the way they're squabbling over my remains."

"You've got more than that," she said. "More than money."

And then she told me that Susie had had a fight with Seth. Another fight! I wouldn't have been surprised to learn that she herself had had a fight with Walter. In fact I told her so.

She smiled rather wanly. (She does not look too well—I don't think the hot spell agrees with her.) "On the way home from that gruesome evening, I told Walt I thought he hadn't helped any. We had Gabriel Gibbons along in the car, but I didn't care, I was very upset."

"What did he say?" I asked, more to be polite than out of any real curiosity.

"He said I didn't understand what was at stake."

Characteristic. It never occurred to me before, but I don't think Walter appreciates his wife.

Then I remembered what she'd said about Seth. How did she know about the fight? Susie had marched down the road to her, in tears, and "borrowed" enough money to "split." It all sounded funny, coming from Lily's lips, but I didn't want to be jocular at this point or to get off on tangents.

"Seth is still out there?" I asked her.

"As far as I know."

I could have kicked myself for asking, because it was a giveaway that he hasn't been in here to see me, and that I haven't talked to Rog about it. But Lily doesn't pick up on such things. Instead she told me Susie's story. She'd been upset with Seth (as J. had been with Larry) for his behavior that night. When she said he was not being "nice" to me, he told her to mind her own damn business—at which point she picked up and left.

"Walt has been trying . . ." Lily seemed to falter.

"Everybody's been trying," I snapped, and then remembered it was her husband.

"No," she said, "he's really been trying to bring people together. Mostly Seth and Larry. Larry's had to get back to Washington, but he's been on the phone to Gabriel and Walt."

"So now he's Gabriel? Do you bring him breakfast in bed?"

Lily replied with great dignity, "I believe he has been a moderating influence on Larry. Just as Rog has been with Seth."

"Everybody's moderating everybody, and they're all tormenting me. Don't you think I hear them out there arguing? I may be half-blind, but I'm not deaf."

"You're entitled to better, Sam," Lily said wistfully.

"I brought it on myself."

She looked at me almost fiercely. "That's not true!"

The way Jennifer used to talk. Would J. still say that now? I doubt it.

281

I looked at Lily out of the corner of my eye. "Do you know about Philip and Louise? And Seth?" I couldn't bring myself to be any more direct than that. I did add, I think, "And the checks?"

"Walt told me . . ." Lily paused ". . . about the checks."

"Seth was right to come here. He had the right to make demands. He sensed that I had perpetrated a great injustice on Philip and Louise."

Lily said nothing. She was sitting before me, hands in her lap; she raised them for a moment, then reclasped them. They are very fine hands, the hands of an aristocratic lady. She was holding herself in, holding herself together. But I couldn't stop either.

"Lily," I said, "you know about Larry and Jenny."

"What do you mean?"

"You know what I mean."

She got very red. People speak of her as being a progressive and remarkably free-spirited woman. But part of that is because she has espoused good causes in a direct fashion, often without regard to the consequences; she is bolder than her husband in that regard. But I have never heard her use a dirty word or utter a vulgarity. If she knows a lot, she says little.

Now she said, "Jennifer is a beautiful person."

"And Larry? What's your judgment of Larry?"

"You don't judge people who are that close to you. We've known him forever. He's just part of our lives, that's all."

"Well, it was I who pushed them together. Nothing would have happened without my connivance."

Lily got to her feet in great agitation. She stood with her back turned to me.

"You know how honorable they both are," I said. "You know how much they both love me."

"Well, they do!" She turned back to me defiantly.

"That's why I got such a kick out of it."

She stared at me. "I think I'd better go."

I said, "I thought you wanted to help me."

"I don't know that I can," she almost whispered. "What can I do?"

"I'm not sure," I said. "You see how they're all at me like a pack of vultures, don't you?"

After a silence she said, "Yes."

But I wasn't sure that she meant it. Maybe she was just placating me in order to get away, back to Walter and her rose garden.

"Do you still love me? Can I still count on you?"

She had never said either, not in all the thirty or forty years I'd known her; she hadn't had to. But now she said, "Yes," with her head low; and then she left.

After that I sat here, filled with self-contempt. If Jenny hadn't run off, I would have put the questions to Jenny. But she did run off, and here I am.

On the other hand, how could she have stayed and listened to what I was saying? It hurt her when I told her I didn't trust her, but that was nothing, nothing, nothing compared with what she must have felt when I told her that I knew in my bones every ounce of guilt that Larry had, I knew it and enjoyed it, I reveled in the guilty pleasure he took every time he touched her, I fantasized their coming together, their connection, I closed my eyes and let it roll over me in every detail, luxuriating in the knowledge that I was the agent of their lust and their guilt, that nothing would have come about if not for me.

She put her hands over her ears and ran out. And left me here.

AUGUST 22 Talk with Seth.

He stalked in and said without preamble, "I have to save myself from you."

"You mean you're leaving?"

"I've given that some thought." He smiled. "A lot of

283

people would like that. Maybe too many. So unless you want to evict me, I think I'll confound my enemies and stick around for a while."

"A while? Stay as long as you wish. You realize of course that you may be saved from me any day."

He glanced at me in some surprise. "Are you going away?"

"One of these days, for good," I said. Young people think they are going to live forever; they find it difficult to imagine that old people don't think that too. So I added, "I don't wish to sound dramatic, but I must point out that whenever I fall asleep I have no idea whether I shall reawaken."

"Ah well," he said, after a moment's thought, "death is a form of going away. And it happened to two of my classmates in Vietnam, did I ever tell you? At the time, you must have been over eighty."

I almost laughed at that dirty crack—he was really determined to get at me. But an idea entered my head, you might even say he put it there. Going away. I am going to hold on to it and turn it around from time to time. Ace in the hole.

Meanwhile there hung in the air his desire to get a rise out of me with the business of saving himself from me. As though there was anything I could do about that.

"I hope you don't blame me," I said, "for Susie's leaving."

"Oh, that," he said. "No."

"I liked her," I told him. "She's kind."

"Only when it doesn't involve any exertion," he said. "But that era is over. I have been wondering whether you had it in mind for me to change my name."

"To what?"

He stared at me as if I were demented. "Why, to Lumen, of course. It is my name, isn't it?"

"You got along without it for a long time."

He grimaced. "You have a way of . . . Listen, I came to tell you that I'm sorry about losing my head at Jennifer's party."

"Why didn't you tell Jennifer? Or Susan?"

"Because I wasn't sorry for them, particularly. Or for you."

284

"Don't tell me," I said, "that you're sorry for yourself."

"I blew it." A familiar phrase. "Brodie was making an ass of himself. I should have let him go on doing it. That's what I'm sorry about. I'm going to get him off your neck if it's the last—"

I waved him silent. "More threats? What are you building out there now, a coffin?"

"For someone who's on his last legs, you still hang on to your sense of humor."

"Do you want to strip me of that too?" I asked. "Is there nothing I can do to get you off my back too? Do you want me to say I'm sorry that you were born, or conceived? Is that it?"

"Just tell your foster son that I'm out there." He gestured out the window with his scarred and stained thumb. "And that I'm staying there—"

"With Grebner and Nadine?"

"—until I save us both from that guy's death grip. I'm going to live free, and if you're going to die, you might as well die free, not buried alive in a mountain of cement."

"Thanks," I said. "Thanks a lot."

But he was gone, and I doubt that he even heard my last words.

AUGUST 23   Ninety degrees. Still and hot as the tomb, on the porch. Came back in here, enervated. Would I have the strength left to go someplace cool? Where?

While I lay here perspiring, Rog came in with the mail and a cold compress for my face courtesy of Mrs. H. Every time I start hating her for stooging for everyone else around here, she does something thoughtful.

R. shuffled the mail. "There's a letter from Mrs. Lumen, in Manhattan."

I lifted a corner of the face cloth. "From Jenny? Read it."

He was a little hesitant. J. always phones, from wherever she is.

"Go ahead," I said, and I replaced the cloth, thinking he

285

might be less inhibited about opening my personal mail if we weren't looking at each other.

" 'My dear Sam.' " He cleared his throat. " 'I didn't trust myself to speak to you on the phone. But there are several things that have to be said.' " R. changed his tone. "Then she enumerates."

"That's Jennifer," I said. "Organized."

One. I have not seen Larry since the night of the party. Two. Even if I had, I should not have repeated to him anything that you said. If you wish him to know such things, you may say them to him yourself. Three. I did tell him on the phone that I was terribly disappointed in him. In his lack of self-control. He said he was disappointed in himself too, that he had let us both down. But that he had built his life and staked his life on you, and that he had no intention of turning back from his obligations. I asked him what he considered to be his obligations (forgive me if I am repeating something he may already have told you), and he said that personally they were to his children, and socially, to posterity. And that in both cases it was crucial that you and what you have stood for should be properly understood and appreciated. So I fear that for now he is unwilling to compromise with Seth, whom he seems to see as your evil genius. Four. I will do anything you wish in this regard that might be of help in reconciling those who feel they are doing what is right for you, but at present perhaps you are better served by Rog and Walter Honig. Your loving wife, Jennifer.

R. cleared his throat. "There is a postscript."
I waved to him to go on.
" 'I have been thinking about our honeymoon in England.' " R. stopped.
"Go on," I said through the cold wet cloth.

Not just the visits to Summerhill and the other schools where you were received so beautifully and with such honor and they were so gracious to me. Not even of the plays we saw that season, the Wilde, the revivals of *The Relapse* (at which you alternated between catnaps and bursts of wild joyous laughter), and of *Heartbreak House* (when you turned to me and said that if Shaw were as great as you'd thought when you first met him in the twenties, you'd have been reduced to tears now, rather than "merely fascinated" by the old Captain), and the rest. I have been consoling myself instead with our visit to Westminster Abbey, a tourist pilgrimage which at that time I confess I thought somewhat square, having done that bit ten years earlier as a teenager. You took me not to Churchill's tomb, or even to the Poets' Corner, but to the niche of Saint-Évremond, of whom I had never so much as heard. Instead of teasing me for my brash Sarah Lawrence ignorance, my glibness about Kierkegaard and Camus, Stieglitz and Steichen, which was really all that I knew, you said to me softly, "This is the man who said, 'I love therefore I exist.' " You told me how he had fallen in love when he was past eighty with the Marquise de la Perrine (I looked it up afterward, did I ever tell you?), and written, "The greatest of pleasures that remain for old men is living; and nothing makes them more certain of their life than loving." You held my hand in yours when you recited those words, and I knew then that I had done the right thing and that I would love you forever. That is what I cherish, and not what you choose to say to me now. J.

After that there was silence and I knew that the letter was over. But R. did not go on to other matters; he said nothing. Instead I felt his thin cool fingers on my wrist. He was taking my pulse.

"I'm still here," I raised a corner of the washcloth to look at him as he bent over me. He was crying.

"For God's sake, go," I said.

AUGUST 24   R. says Gibbons & Wells have come up with a date for the next episode in the life (and death) of Sam Lumen—something less than three weeks from now. More important, they want to shoot it in New York, at the apartment.

I smelled a rat. R. says he tried to stall them, as per my instructions, by telling them that I was suffering from heat prostration (perfectly true) as well as from the effects of that ugly dinner party. More calls, back and forth. Obviously Larry is masterminding the Washington end of it. The theory is that I can go to New York to rest up and prepare for it, and be actually more comfortable there than here, what with the air conditioning in the apt.

What they didn't say, although it is clear to me, is that in the apartment I wouldn't be subject to pressure from Seth & Co. Also that they could get the job over with in seclusion, quiet, and privacy, before I collapse from either the heat or the combined attacks from all quarters.

There was even an intimation (I think that's R.'s word) that the President would pay me a courtesy call at the apt. at that time or shortly thereafter. We would have a discussion about the Children's Center, and there would be a little formal thing, at the end of which His Excellency would present me with the keys to the building, or whatever. If I want, I can prepare a brief statement, or it can all be extemporized.

Not a word about Seth and the Children of Liberty.

Or about J. for that matter. Larry knows she is living there and not here. Does he assume she will welcome me there? For that purpose, I suppose he does; maybe she hasn't told him about us, since she did not tell him what I said to her about them.

Obviously they had decided to work through Rog. No other way to get at me. How can they be sure he won't go to Seth? Either they are confident that even if he does it won't make any difference, since at this point there is nothing Seth or his friends can do—or they have made some kind of a deal with R.

I can't ask him about it. If J. were here I could talk to her about it, but I queered that.

My head hurts.

AUGUST 25   Made a carbon of my letter to J. in case she tears it up, or R. never mails it to her.

Dearest Jennifer, When we married I couldn't tell you "everything" about myself, if only because there would have been too much to tell. You were eager to tell me all about yourself. The two affairs you had as a undergraduate, the guilt about your family, etc. I couldn't reciprocate, and maybe that tended to strengthen your fixed idea that you were giving yourself to a great old man, and not foolishly tying yourself (as I am sure wiser people must have warned you) to a desperate old man whose middle years had been divided between public good works and private dissipation.

I think I have told you that during those middle years I was practically at the mercy of my sex drives; and that although in a public way I "stood for" liberation and release, privately I was tormented by the things I allowed myself to do, particularly since they happened within earshot (and I fear within sight) of my son Philip. That is why I have never been able to tell you about Phil as a growing boy. Larry must surely have told you some of this, enough to convince you that my life has been filled with at least as much vice as that of any man I have known. More.

You write to me of Saint-Évremond. I remember the Abbey, and how we stood there hand in hand. But I remember Montaigne also, a far greater man than Saint-Évremond. Montaigne wrote about his old age, "in truth, we do not so much forsake our vices as change them—and for worse."

I quote you those lines not by way of expiation but of explanation. I don't think I ever fully understood them myself until I revealed my dark side to you as I did the other day.

If I live much longer—you may as well be prepared— I may do even worse. I can make no promises regarding Larry or Seth or anything.

With all this in view, would you accept me at the apartment? Rog and Larry can explain the reasons of state. I can only say now that I am hot and wretched here and could perhaps function better there, with the air conditioning turned on low. I would be grateful if you would allow me to come. I will understand if you prefer to absent yourself, or even to come back up here.

I love you dearly. I trust no one.

Sam

AUGUST 26 Decided to resolve problem of Rog and Seth and the TV interview, while waiting to hear from J.

But before I could do anything, Walter showed up. Calm, almost grave, but I know him well enough to see that underneath he was *molto agitato*. He sat around making small talk, like a man visiting a friend in a sickroom, until I had to take the initiative and ask what was biting him.

Even then he continued beating around the bush. I had the feeling Lily had warned him not to get me upset. He was torn. Finally I got him to bring up what was on his mind.

"Did you talk to Seth about the plans for the next Wells interview?" When Walter tries to be casual it puts me in mind of a whale disporting itself in mid-ocean—a memorable experience.

I told him that I had been thinking about it, but had not yet gotten around to it because I wasn't sure of the best way to broach it to him. Which was true.

"Then there's been a leak," W. said somberly.

I said he sounded like a security officer at the Pentagon.

"Maybe you won't laugh when I tell you that Grebner and

his friends have been threatening dire things if Gabriel Gibbons goes ahead with the scheduling."

"Dire things?" I asked. Sometimes W. is positively Victorian.

W. didn't want to get into the details just yet. "First things first," he said. He wanted to know how they knew.

"You think Rog tipped them off," I said.

"Doesn't it seem likely?"

"Call him in here," I said. I found myself wishing that Lily had come along, to restrain Walter and to shield me from further bickering.

When R. came in he and W. greeted each other politely, and W. got right to it.

"You are aware," he said, "of the negotiations and arrangements for a final interview session. To be held in the Lumens' New York apartment."

R. nodded. "Yes."

"You disapprove of them."

"I have had reservations. I expressed them to Mr. Lumen many months ago. Since then I have come to feel that the final decision had to be his." He smiled as coldly as Walter, I must say. "I limited my involvement to an attempt to insure—mainly through conversations with Mr. Lumen— that he'd have full opportunity for a thorough expression of his deepest beliefs."

"Are you going to claim now that you have not been involved in the conspiracy of Grebner and the others to prevent Mr. Lumen from completing that telecast interview, by blackmail, if necessary?"

"Mr. Honig," R. said patiently, "I don't have to claim it. It happens to be the simple truth."

"You introduced them into this house, into this study."

"Only because I know that Mr. Lumen likes to keep abreast of all the currents."

"And more recently?" W. pressed on, as if he were going to get the witness to reveal himself.

"Only because of the special relationship of Seth Fox to

both parties. I have spoken to absolutely no one but Mr. Lumen himself about the current situation—I have the impression he hasn't even made up his mind himself about the final taping and the meeting with the President." He turned to me, not pleadingly, but simply inquiringly. "Isn't that so?"

"If I've made up my mind," I said, "I haven't told anybody."

"Sam," W. said firmly, "I don't want to do anything behind your back. There's been enough of that. I don't want you to feel that I'm involved in intrigue."

"But?"

"Now that I've talked to Girard, I want to question Seth."

"Well," I said, "let's all go."

There were protests from both men. The more they protested, the more they talked of the strain and of having Seth come up here, the more determined I was. So I picked up my walking stick and went off with them, leaning on R.'s arm.

Seth was there, alone. He dropped the knife with which he had been whittling and rose to greet us. "A delegation?" he asked.

"More like a commission of inquiry," I said. "May I sit down?"

"It's your house."

"Seth," W. said to him, "Mr. Girard asserts that he has not spoken to you about the next interview of Sam by Dick Wells."

Seth smiled. "You mean the one they're trying to set up in New York?"

W. glanced at me meaningfully. "Then you do know about it."

"Sure."

"Are you denying that you learned of it from Mr. Girard, here?"

"Is it supposed to be a secret?" No question, Seth was enjoying himself. "As a matter of fact it was Dr. Brodie who informed me."

"What?" W. was flabbergasted. "That's preposterous."

"Want to see his letter?" Seth was playing it to the hilt. "First one I ever got on White House stationery."

"Why should he write to you?"

"Ostensibly," Seth said coolly, "to warn me not to interfere. But I wouldn't try to fathom his real motives. From all I know of him, it has to do with advancing his career in some way."

W. said doggedly, "So you promptly passed on the news to Grebner."

"I don't see, Mr. Honig," Seth said, "what business you have in querying me about my business. It's been a long time since you stopped sending me those monthly checks."

W. flushed. I was the only one who had sat down, and from my rocker I could see that old Walter was being humiliated, first by the fact that his suspicions of Rog were apparently groundless, second by all this private family linen being washed in front of Rog.

"I've been Sam Lumen's friend and counselor for a long, long while," W. said, struggling to keep his composure. "Since long before those checks. I have an obligation now to see that he isn't harassed."

"You ought to take that up with Larry Brodie," Seth said. "Right, Rog?"

R. closed his eyes for a moment. He did not answer.

"At the moment," W. said grimly, "I'm talking to you and not to Larry Brodie. Would you be willing to tell me, in front of Mr. Girard and Sam, just what it is that you have in mind?"

"Well look," Seth said, not just to Walter, but to me. "You seem to know already what Grebner is up to. And he isn't even here, he's gone to the city. So why the courtroom manner?"

"I'd like Sam to hear it from your lips."

Seth laughed. Not an unpleasant harsh laugh. Not a bark. More of a chuckle. "I want Sam," he said, "to fire the shot heard round the world."

If W. was baffled, I wasn't. And I had the sense that R. wasn't either—his antenna is finely tuned for nuances in ideology and terminology. Well, Larry's too for that matter: L. would have known at once what S. was talking about. In fact he already knew it, that's at least partly why he wrote him that preposterous letter telling him to lay off—he sees himself as locked in fraternal combat with S. for my immortal soul. I am afraid S. sees it the same way.

"There's no need to be cute, Seth," W. said with a certain asperity. S. was making him testy. "Can't we talk to each other plainly, without indulging in all this revolutionary rhetoric of the Children of Liberty?"

At that S. turned on him. "I'm talking Foxy Grandpa's language." W. winced at this, so did R., but there was more to come. S. was really flashing fire now. "Maybe you haven't been listening to all this rhetoric all these years, maybe you just tuned out. Well I didn't. I think I got it in my mother's milk. Louise Fox was a disciple, wasn't she, even before she met Philip? She bought all that stuff about Sam Lumen being in the direct line of American revolutionary action. Well, when it came my turn, so did I."

"I don't see what all this has to do—" W. protested.

"You asked me, so I'm telling you," S. said. "Sam's own grandpa, Sam Lumen the first, was born in New York in 1789, the year George Washington was inaugurated. Don't tell me you haven't been reminded of that a million times. Old Sam waited until 1836 to produce Philip the first. Philip the first waited until 1886 to produce this Sam, who waited until 1924 to produce his Philip. Sam, Philip, Sam, Philip, a direct line from the Revolution, from that revolution to this. Three generations for Sam Lumen, not from shirtsleeves to shirtsleeves, but from revolution to revolution. I'm a kind of misnomer, an offshoot, a byblow, but I think I belong in there, in the catalog, at least as much as Larry does."

The genealogical litany fell like a series of hammer blows to my heart. I felt myself sinking down in the chair, unable to respond to a volley directed as much against me as against Walter. And Seth was implacable.

"For a long time in a long life," he persisted, "Foxy Grandpa has persisted in trying to have it both ways, revolution and respectability. Punch one button and out comes his Grandpa, Sam the first, and 1789. Punch another and out comes his prison sentence for subversion in 1917."

"1918," I said.

"You see? 1917 or 1918, it's still a long way from there to 1976. Next year comes the big celebration, Sam is ninety, and we all throw our hats in the air with a huzzah. He's made it, we've made it, and the Lumen Building is there to prove it. But that's not enough, you see?"

W. asked, "Who are you to say that's not enough?"

That was a bad mistake.

"Who am I?" Seth laughed. "Now that's a funny one. Let's just say that I've been in the process of finding that out, with Sam's help. Perhaps twenty-odd years from now I'll know for sure, and I'll be ready to produce a male heir. Right, Sam?"

I was shivering, despite the heat. I was in no mood for this kind of banter. Rog had withdrawn to a dark corner, like some watchful animal; I felt that if I were to snap my fingers he would trot to my side and lead me away, back to the safety of my room and Mrs. Hoskins' grumbling but careful ministrations.

Walter by now was aware that he had set off a train of events beyond his control, like touching a match to a fuse at the end of a string of firecrackers. There was no way he could shut off Seth, and he did not even try; with folded arms he regarded him, occasionally glancing over at me as if to see whether I was still, in my huddle, aware of what was happening.

"If my rebelliousness is legitimate," Seth was saying, "it means that Sam's was. And if that's the case, it's worth another shot. Grebner thinks it'll be heard round the world. But even if it's not, for my own selfish sake I want to hear it. I want to hear Sam assert himself and justify once more our being on this earth together." He said to me directly, "Do you deny me?"

"No," I mumbled through parched lips, "I don't deny you."

Walter said stubbornly, "But he's not going to deny Larry Brodie either. If you have this kind of feeling in your heart you would not ask him at his age to make such a choice. He should be allowed room for everything, for everyone."

"That kind of liberal cosmic acceptance is not what Sam was all about," S. asserted with a kind of dogmatism. "It's what they make statues and marble buildings out of, but it's not what I read in his rebellious bitter old heart. I see instead a half-stifled desire to free himself at last, to say no, one last time, to tell the children that the world will be theirs only if they turn their backs on the shit and press their claim to something better—even if it hasn't been born yet."

"Come on," W. said to me roughly, extending his hand to help me to my feet, "let's get out of here." He was not rude, just shaken.

AUGUST 27   The phone kept ringing and ringing. R. has the bell turned low and my door was closed, but still it was maddening. I was dozing, and it seemed to me that my sleep was punctuated by the sound of the bell.

Strange dream: I was in our makeshift gym in the School's barn, teaching Philip how to box. He was thin, shifty, fast, adept at avoiding my punches. So much so that I kept muttering to him, "Come on, Phil, let's mix it up." I told myself that it was because I wanted to show him how to block a punch, how to take one, but Larry, who was refereeing, was bouncing around us in his sneakers, muttering to me from the corner of his mouth, "Don't draw blood, he's doing fine, what do you want?" After a while I began to get a bit winded, and it seemed to me that Philip was taunting me, not just avoiding my flailing swings, but deliberately wearing me out. Hoping that the bell would ring so that I would have the excuse to trot off to the showers with Philip and his friend, I pressed on, as if by crowding Philip I could bring on the bell and hasten the end of the "lesson." Suddenly he tripped on a wrinkle in the mat, he could not retreat, and my up-thrusting right fist caught him on the chest and glanced up off his smooth, hairless jaw. He tottered and fell back as his legs gave way. I remember the feeling as I stood over him, watching him collapse, watching Larry bend down to help, watching the shock and pain take hold and spread across my son's sweating boyish features. My arms hung down like an ape's, the tightly laced balloonlike gloves were heavy as stones at my sides, and I was swamped, simply swamped, with gloating triumph and sick self-disgust. Then the bell rang, and I said half-aloud, "You're ringing too late."

It was the telephone yet again. I lay there atremble, wondering if it had ever actually happened. I could not be sure that it hadn't. How seldom I dream of Philip, how infrequently he visits me in my sleep, by contrast with little Sophia, Luba, Hester, the women of my past! There are times when I have drifted off almost wishing that he would return to life in my mind just as he was when he was small and I was proud. And now this. The irony is that, unlike Larry, Philip always hated contact sports. He hated violence, and so he died violently, after having me for a father.

When R. tapped at the door and stuck his head in tentatively, he looked almost frightened; my expression must have been quite unpleasant.

I sat up as quickly as I could, passed my hand over my face, and slipped on my dentures. I don't like people to see me toothless and gummy; it seems to me somehow shameful. Bad enough to be long in the tooth and mottled with liver spots, without displaying your skinny shanks, shrunken cheeks, and dangling sack to the world.

I suppose I sounded annoyed, too, when I said, "That

damn phone has been driving me crazy. It's as bad as hearing you all bickering out in the hallway and the living room."

"It's an extension of the bickering in a way," R. replied. "There have been calls from Mrs. Honig, Gary Grebner, and Dr. Brodie. Oh, and of course Mrs. Lumen."

"What do you mean, of course?" I demanded. "Why didn't you put me on?"

"You were asleep."

"That's what you think. How could I have been, if I heard the bell always ringing?" I realized I must sound petulant, so I asked him what Jennifer had wanted.

"She said not to disturb you." R. smiled with a discreet victoriousness. "She said to tell you the apartment is ready and waiting, whether she's there or not."

"Now what does that mean?"

"I take it she's not sure of immediate plans—she may have to go to Washington."

Washington? That reminded me of L.'s call. I hesitated to ask about it for fear of being too obvious, but R. went ahead anyway without seeming to notice my hesitation.

"Dr. Brodie will be arriving tomorrow by car. He says we should be prepared to drive to the city with him."

"Oh he does?" I didn't like being rushed—on the other hand, I did rather like the idea of Larry's concern and of what it implied about him and J.

"The limousine is air-conditioned and he promises you you'll be comfortable."

"That's kind of him," I said, "but he, of all people, should know better than to make promises like that. If I'm determined to be uncomfortable, I'll be uncomfortable."

R. smiled. "That reminds me," he said. "You have plenty of clothes in the New York apartment, but as I recall they're all winter things. Should I have Mrs. Hoskins put some summer shirts and slacks in a valise?"

"Don't rush me," I said. I had thought R. would be reluctant about the apartment, with all it implied, and his seeming eagerness confused me. Was he making a deal with Larry and the others?

It struck me that all this might have to do with the other goings-on, the other phone calls. I asked him what that was all about.

"Grebner was phoning from Boston. He's been meeting with his group."

"So?"

"Their expectation is—that's the way he put it—that Mr. Gibbons and you will honor the commitment."

"Commitment?" I said. "I don't remember any commitment. Wells said he'd be glad to ask me questions about new groups like the Children of Liberty, and about how they squared with my notions of . . . what? Radical rejuvenation? Youthful revolt?"

"Something of the sort," R. said. "At any rate, he said he'd already informed the network. And if the commitment isn't honored, they'll feel free to act as they see fit."

"You know," I said, "one of the problems of these people is that their spokesmen tend to sound like the symmetrical opposite of the Establishment spokesmen. I suppose there's no way out of it."

"Seth would argue," R. pointed out, "that that's precisely why we have to break the cycle, so we can get out of the linguistic and cultural bind that ties us together so tightly with our enemies."

"You argue it almost better than he does," I said. "It may be true. But I still don't like to hear Pentagon language coming from the lips of pacifists."

"Grebner says he has ways of learning what will take place. If they are defrauded—I think that was the word—he'll hold a press conference."

That sounded a little silly. "To do what?"

"To announce that you are being held captive."

By whom, I thought, by the President? But it's not completely silly, they can make a case, particularly if they enlist

Seth. They can turn my last days into a hell. Which is what S. says Larry is doing to me, whether or not I acknowledge it.

I couldn't bring myself to talk about it any more. I waved it off. "What did Lily want?"

"She would like you to come to lunch tomorrow." He added, "I'm to phone her back. I told her Dr. Brodie would be coming, but that won't be until late in the day."

"Tell her," I said, "that I accept with pleasure."

Of course, I'd no sooner said it and he'd gone on about his business (after telling me Walter would be by to pick me up at noon) than I began to wonder whether W. hadn't put Lily up to it. Another custom we've picked up from the Establishment—doing the dirty work over a dinner table. Or a modest country luncheon.

We'll see tomorrow.

AUGUST 28 Walter pulled up in the driveway promptly, as always, at high noon. Stick in hand, I was ready and waiting so he wouldn't have to get out of his car.

"Hello, Nurse," I said to him, teasing, "how's my old nurse?"

"What's this?" W. asked suspiciously. "What's all this?"

"Don't you bring me a potion? Tonics? Elixirs? And punctuality? Remember what Mercutio said to the Nurse—'the bawdy hand of the dial is now upon the prick of noon'?"

W. shook his head disapprovingly. "You're a dirty old man."

"The Nurse didn't say that," I told him. "She said, 'What a man are you!'"

"Comes to the same thing," W. said. "I never saw anyone like you for remembering the smutty parts."

"I was a good teacher of Shakespeare in my time," I reminded him. "At least I didn't turn the kids off. They loved the smut."

"You set them to looking up the words in the dictionary."

"At least I got them to reading. Ask Larry."

Rog had hurried out to help me into the car. Getting in and out is the hardest part for me now. Once I'm in I like the driving, even when Walter is at the wheel. He drove slowly, as if reluctant to get back home, after he had arrived at my place with such punctuality.

Actually I was wondering what he had been asking Larry. I was certain they had been putting their heads together by long distance. If nothing else, W. derives a professional satisfaction from meddling in this stuff, scheming and planning. He tried to keep the conversation away from the current problems, but he is so transparent it leaks out in ways he cannot control. For example:

"I hope you haven't been talking like that with Wells," he said gloomily. "You know, you can't get away with stuff like that on the air."

"Oh, smut!" I said rudely. "Walter, don't you realize that's a four-letter word that's practically gone out of circulation? And don't you realize that you're dying to talk about the Wells interview, even though you hoped to put it off until after lunch? You're so obvious!"

"I suppose you think you're devious, calling me Nurse and all that."

"All right, Walter," I said, "let's get to it. You put Lily up to inviting me for lunch so you could soften me up for something. For what?"

"Lunch was Lily's idea," he insisted. "It's immaterial to me whether you want to talk business now or afterwards."

"Business?" I had to pick up on that word. "So there is business. Why not during lunch—do you want to spare Lily's sensibilities, or are you afraid she'd take my side?"

"I thought that's what I've been doing," he rebuked me quietly.

By then we were at the Honigs' anyway, and there was the business of getting out and into the house and greeting Lily, and having the ceremonial glass of sherry before we settled

301

down to the salad. Lily had remembered to leave out the radishes—she knows so many little things about me.

So we were practically through before W. told me that he had gone off and gotten injunctive relief against Grebner & Co.

I practically dropped my dessert spoon; and I had been trying, I must admit here, to make a good impression on Lily, just as she had knocked herself out to make a nice meal and a pleasant atmosphere for me, in which I could relax and be at my ease as in the old days.

"An injunction?" I said. "For Christ's sake, what is all this, Walter?"

"Calm yourself," he said. "It's quite simple really. An ad interim restraining order to prevent those people from interfering with your movements."

"How could you do that without consulting me? Did you hear what he said, Lily?" I asked her.

Walter waved her quiet. "This was simply to prevent them from doing unspeakable things—"

"You mean smutty things?" I asked him.

"—and I emphasize to you that it's temporary."

"You've become a willful and arbitrary old man," I said. "I want to get out of here. I want to go home. Lily, can you drive me?"

She was so badly shaken that I felt almost as bad for her as I did for myself. I hesitated; and as I saw the agony on Lily's face I suddenly found myself weeping. It was humiliating. I had to turn and face the corner like a dunce. I was groping here and there, in every pocket, my stiff fingers refusing to function, until finally they came up with a half-shredded hunk of Kleenex that had already been through the washer.

Behind me, Walter was pleading. "Please, Sam, don't misread me. I didn't act whimsically or capriciously."

"Oh, I'm sure you got good advice," I said. "No doubt you've been consulting with the Justice Department."

"As a matter of fact, I have," he said. "There's a former student of mine—"

"There's always a former student, isn't there? They're as bad as brothers-in-law. How about my former student, Larry? What have you been cooking up with him? Did he serve as liaison?"

"Come on, Sam," W. wheedled. "Don't make it sound as though there's something underhanded about my keeping in touch with Larry. Whom else would I turn to at a time like this?"

"And whom else would he turn to but you? I see the whole thing now. You're supposed to feed me and hold me here and soften me up while Larry comes rushing to the rescue. I bet you've been getting calls from his limousine phone on his way up here."

To my surprise, I saw by the stricken look on W.'s face that my wild charge was true. It enraged me, the vision of Larry encased in glass with the telephone to his ear, like a general or a president, issuing instructions about me.

"For God's sake, Walter," I cried, "why must you people go on tormenting me?"

"Protecting, not tormenting."

"Against those foolish kids? Using the majesty of the state, the law, money, power, influence? It's like turning a cannon on a mosquito."

"What they threaten is not a mosquito bite. They want to control you and, if need be, to humiliate you. All I'm doing is seeing that if they interfere they get their just deserts." Walter's lips were pressed; his sententiousness was one more bit of fuel on the blaze.

"Polonius," I said in a fury, "remember what Hamlet warned you: Use every man after his desert, and who should escape whipping?"

"Shakespeare day," W. said. "I can't compete in that department. Your memory is extraordinary."

"So maybe I'm not senile, after all," I told him. "So maybe you should have consulted with me instead of with Larry. It isn't Grebner I care about, it's Seth. You can't do this to him, he's my flesh and blood."

"Turn the sentence around," W. said. "Haven't I gone to plead with Seth? Isn't he allowing himself to be used by those people for their own ends?"

"If so, he has his reasons," I said. I was afraid I was going to start to cry again. "Come on, Lily, what do you say to driving me home?"

"Sam, I don't want you to be angry with me," W. insisted. "I think I know what Seth means to you. If you don't believe in my friendship at this moment, think for a moment of what Lily and I would have given . . ."

"Are you going to use that gambit now?" I couldn't look at Lily. "That's even more unfair."

"If you can just ask him to promise you, even a verbal promise, that he'll get them to lay off, I swear I'll—"

"You'll do what?" I asked. "Get Larry and the Justice Department to lay off? Once upon a time," I said, "there was a man named Dean Rusk."

Walter stared at me wordlessly.

"He had this nervous habit, like a tic, of repeating compulsively year after year, 'We just want them to stop doing what they're doing.' "

"Sam," Walter said, "just answer me one thing. Do you want them to go on doing it? Do you want to make Seth happy by making a fool of yourself and endorsing them? Do you want to break Larry, after almost forty years?"

"No," I said, "I don't want to do that. I want to go home."

But when we got out to the driveway I had a sudden desire to prove myself to Lily. Also a fear that the drive would last only two minutes, and that then she'd turn the car around and speed back to W. So I asked her if she'd be willing to walk me back instead.

"You haven't walked it in quite some time," she said, smiling a little for the first time since I'd showed up. I felt she knew what I was up to.

"What's the matter," I teased her, "are you afraid you can't make it both ways? You can rest up at my place, and if you're still tired I'll have Rog drive you back. Or you can phone up Walter."

"I don't like leaving Walt alone," she said.

That was preposterous. Besides, we were already walking down the drive, with her on my arm. What she meant, I told her, was that she didn't want W. to feel she was walking out on him after he'd gotten into the argument with me.

"Well, he is upset," she protested. "He loves you like a brother."

"How about you?" I pressed her.

"You shouldn't have to ask me," she said, "and I shouldn't have to tell you."

"We celebrated your seventieth birthday two years ago," I reminded her. "By this time you shouldn't feel inhibited about expressing yourself. Do you think it's right, what they're doing?"

She replied fervently, "I think it's all wrong."

I actually felt my heart thump. "Then you have to say it to Walter. You have to say it to Larry too, when he gets here. He's the instigator."

She stopped at a big quartz boulder that glittered in the sun on the edge of the meadow. We sat down together. She took my stick from me and turned it in her hands for a moment, reading over the inscription on it as if she'd never seen it before.

"Larry's not an instigator," she said, "any more than Seth is. I think what Seth's friends are doing is all wrong too."

"I do too," I told her. "Believe me, I do. I just can't take sides the way everyone is pressing me to. Lily, I think my only hope is to go away."

"To New York?"

"That'll precipitate the whole thing." An alternative began to seem possible, for the first time. I heard myself saying, "No, I mean someplace else, where they'll all have to leave me alone, because they won't know where I am and they won't be able to get at me."

She shook her head sadly. "Sam, that's impossible."

"Why? Am I in prison? Can't I make my own decisions? I may be physically dependent on others, but you'll see, my life itself is still my own, to do with as I wish."

I found that I was speaking to her as I address these sheets of paper, as a kind of extension of myself. Therefore: No point in setting it all down and courting exhaustion. I do think I made it clear to Lily that if my loved ones and friends will not leave me alone, I will have to take things into my own hands in order to insure that I am left alone.

R. would be the logical one to help, Lily saw that herself (and how furious W. would be if he heard her say it!), but can I really trust him all the way? He might be inclined to help me escape if only because he would then be the one with my fate completely in his hands—they would *all* have to deal with him then, willy-nilly—and also because he would then be the sole repository of my confidences, he'd know things no one else does, he'd become the authority on my last days.

Am I being unfair to him? In any case, I do not think I dare ask him for help. The probability is that the very request would frighten him. He has enjoyed involving me, engaging me, and so scandalizing the old folks. But I think now that when he went so far as to bring Grebner and the Children of Liberty into my life he was frightened by his own audacity and the possible consequences.

I remember the day he and I had that discussion and I brought up the matter of his never having married, devoting his whole existence to me, etc. While he hopes to reap the benefits (and in fact there's no reason he shouldn't—I do owe him a lot), it makes me wonder whether he'd go the whole distance with me. He is a committed man, he believes in his causes unflinchingly; but at the moment his main cause is me, and if something were to happen to me in the course of his helping me to get away, they would hang it on him—and there'd no longer be any benefits for him to reap. So because he is basically a calculating man, I don't think I dare take the one last chance with him. The odds are too great.

There remains J. I can't be sure whether or not Lily actually uttered her name. Doesn't matter. It hung there between us. If not Rog, then why not J.? Have I wounded her too deeply? Is she too committed to Larry in ways that I don't even know about? This will have to be resolved before I make my move.

Anyway, all this got me quite exhilarated. I pulled Lily to her feet and walked on home at what I must say was quite a clip—she was impressed, I don't think she'll be saying again that I can no longer make it on my own. She wanted to walk back after a glass of my cold spring water, but I insisted on R. driving her since he had things to mail anyway. She looked flushed and excited when she left, really quite pretty. I can see, she begins to feel she is my accomplice.

I took a little nap (well, a long one) before getting up to write these pages. No dreams. I must look ahead.

Now I am waiting for Larry to arrive.

AUGUST 30   Skipped a day. Day after tomorrow is September!

Larry. Came tooling up not too long after I finished that last entry. Hopped out of his air-conditioned hearse looking cool and comfortable, if a little rumpled. I had Mrs. Hoskins do her mother act with his government chauffeur—bottle of beer and a cold bird.

L. did not seem eager to settle down on the porch or anywhere. He began to prowl around me like a high-strung, restless dog. I asked him why he didn't sit down.

"I'm ready to take you to the city," he said.

"But you just got here. You've been driving all day."

"Not driving. Just sitting in the back seat. Anyway," he laughed, "I don't fuck around, I'm a big bureaucrat."

"Do you talk like that to your boss?" I asked him.

307

He laughed some more. "On occasion."

That was when I told him I wasn't quite ready to go, wasn't packed, hadn't even made up my mind. He had the grace not to be annoyed, not to remind me that he had left his desk and his work and driven some hundreds of miles in order to be at my disposition. I guess he saw that he was in for an evening of discussion before anybody went anywhere.

We disposed of the weather first. I told him that the worst of the heat wave appeared past, and that in any case I didn't seem to be suffering from it as I had a few days ago; I was feeling better, and not eager to expose myself to the whir and freeze of the air conditioner in the apartment—to say nothing of the isolation from the real world, hanging behind double glass windows eighteen stories over Washington Square Park.

"Jennifer likes it there," I said. "Not me."

By easy stages L. worked his way around to the broadcast, or telecast, now scheduled to be held in the apartment.

"Doesn't mean I have to go there tonight or tomorrow," I asked, "does it?"

He supposed not, but meanwhile he had broached the dread subject, and he hung on to it all the way through Mrs. Hoskins' cold turkey plate.

Finally I told him that I didn't enjoy being pressured.

He said innocently, "But, Sam, it's not a matter of pressure. You've made a commitment to complete the interview series. I gather Wells and Gibbons would prefer to do the next segment in the apartment for technical reasons. But that's not what's at issue. They want to set the date, and so do I."

I don't know if he realizes—he should, after all these years—how that fake guilelessness gets my goat. I waved it all away, told him I was referring to the muscle he'd been using on the Children of Liberty, and indirectly on me, to get the Children's Center thing wrapped up while the restraining order was still in effect against Seth's friends.

He saw by then that he was in for a siege and suggested

that maybe we should call it a day and go over the whole matter in the morning, when we'd be fresher.

"I'm as fresh as I'll ever be for the rest of my days," I told him. "I had a three-hour nap in anticipation of your arrival. So let's talk."

"Sam, you're indefatigable," he said.

"You're the one that's overanxious," I told him. "What do you want to do, put me to bed so you can rush over to Walter's and plot some more? Or get on the hot line to Washington to see if you can get those kids thrown into a concentration camp until after the boss shakes my hand?"

He said, "You're being unfair. Remember one thing: I'm no more zealous in your behalf right now than I've been all my adult life."

So we got down to it. It was not easy for either of us, because it involved not just bringing up the past, but talking about things that you generally, with those you are close to, don't probe too deeply for fear of opening wounds that may never heal.

I felt I had to get him to admit, to say in so many words, that the Lumen building, the presidential meeting, all that, was as much for his benefit as mine, as much to advance his name as to preserve mine. Not because it was wrong—I don't think I ever charged that—but because it was essential to be honest to get things in the right perspective.

The result was that Larry talked to me as he had not for many years, not since the Sophia days when he used to come and ask my advice about graduate school and careers and girls and job choices. He was throwing himself at my mercy. Sitting there and listening, I felt a mixture of paternal pride and, I must confess, a kind of glee that I could still get my faithful student, my favorite old boy, to humble himself before me even in his middle years, with his waistline thickening and his curly hair turning. The cruelest thing about me is the pleasure I take from being cruel—sometimes even from thinking about how I am going to be cruel.

He was the one who was crying now, dabbing at his eyes

309

as he apologized for all the misery he'd been visiting on me in his effort to immortalize me and my works. As he unburdened himself, he unbuttoned himself—threw his jacket on a chair, yanked open his tie, ignored his shirttail as it worked its way up over his belt.

"It's true," he said, "this is the climax of my life, in a way. I've been in the White House for years now, I've cut myself off from the academic community in a functioning way. It's true I could go back to it, in fact I probably will, but you know what it means when people stop thinking of you as a fruitful research worker and start labeling you as an adroit administrator, a smooth paper-shuffler and person-shuffler. The Lumen Center will be the living proof that I haven't wasted these years. I can walk away from Washington in triumph, not as just another guy, another presidential advisor put to pasture in a lecture hall or a foundation office."

"I expect," I said, "that if you wanted to, you could run the Center, couldn't you?"

He didn't deny that, or that he'd been dreaming of staying in Washington and running the national child development program. "It's what my life has pointed to," he said. He didn't have to remind me that he'd busted up with his wife over the whole business of leaving academia for the power and the glory. (According to him, Courtney was afraid of being a hostess and meeting celebrities at parties; according to her, he was selling out what he'd devoted his life to, for three administrative assistants, the White House business address, and a monthly session with The Boss.) Or that I had told him to go ahead, it might be fun for a few years and, who knows, he might even get something done.

Well, this was what he had been getting done. And now I was throwing a monkey wrench into his carefully constructed machinery, and he was begging me not to; there was even the intimation that Courtney would gloat if he stumbled and fell, and would be unable to keep from saying I told you so to their kids.

Would you really fall?

"A lot of these things," he muttered, sweating, tie askew, "you don't verbalize in Washington. There are intimations, hints, things that simply hang in the air. Do this or else . . . Don't do that or else . . . Because of the intense publicity," he said intensely, "because of the bicentennial, the celebration, your ninetieth birthday, the erection of the building, there has to be absolute certainty before he takes the final step."

"Before he anoints me," I said.

L. gulped. "I don't have to tell you, as far as I'm concerned you'll be anointing him. But that's it, yes. And I have to say clearly what I tried to intimate a long time ago: If there's any indication that you've gotten involved with endorsing spooks, the indication has to come before the point of no return. They can still name the building for you, but the President has to be in a position where he's above it, uninvolved, you see?"

When he said those last two words it was as if he were a kid again at the School, tugging at my arm, pleading to be first in line on the nature walk.

"And if you get him involved," I wound up for him, "if you commit him to something, even if it's on tape and still able to be killed or aborted, it's your responsibility and you have to pay the price. You swore the old man was safe and he turned out to be softheaded, so then you have to write the letter of resignation, and it's accepted with great reluctance and you slink out of town with your tail between your legs. Is that the scenario?"

Larry was in a misery. "It isn't a question of your being softheaded or silly. Everybody knows how sharp you are. In a way, that only makes it worse, it makes me look softheaded. You can see that." His face was all twisted up. He cried out, "For the life of me, I just can't see why you'd want to do this to me!"

He stopped without adding, After all these years, after the

311

way I've devoted myself to you, after I've kept you before the public, after I've tried to crown your life with laurels.

"Do you really think," I said, "that all this comes of my deliberately trying to mess things up for you?"

He forced a smile. "Only in my more paranoid moments. But why, then? You can't take those kids seriously. You can't be taken in by the flattery of that little crowd."

"It has very little to do with them either," I said. "It has more to do with . . ."

He said it, the word he'd been avoiding since he rolled up in the limousine: "Seth."

Once he'd said it, the tables were turned. I was the one who had to do the sweaty explaining now. I owed it to him. So I tried to be honest, I said, "Not him even, so much as Philip. And Louise."

"Sam, don't you think I know what it meant to you to have their son turn up after all these years?" His face was glistening. "Phil was my best friend in the School, I'd be happy to be of help to his son, but you have to draw some reasonable line, some—"

I said, "Seth isn't his son. He's mine."

"I can even understand that," Larry said.

"You didn't hear me," I insisted. "I committed an act of aggression against Louise. In fact I think you must have suspected this—don't tell me it never crossed your mind, you know me too well."

I had expected, I don't know, some further outburst, either a denial or a cry of pain. I was astonished to see how quietly L. took this. Maybe he did know, had known, maybe he was still so fixed on his own pain that he couldn't see mine, maybe he just . . . I don't know, I just don't know. Perhaps I should simply put down what he said:

"Your terminology is spooky." That's what he said. Then he added, "But if you insist on it, I have to remember that you've been paying reparations for a long time now." So he knew about the checks. "So long that some people—like me —might think you've done your share."

312

"If you think there's ever such a thing as adequate reparation," I said, "you're more insensitive than I'd have thought. Or more concerned with having things go your way and not Seth's." I made the mistake (I can only mitigate this by observing that, as I've tried to indicate, L. too had been making mistakes with me) of adding oratorically, "You'll never know the burden of guilt I bear. Neither will Seth—or if he does, I credit him with not taking advantage of it."

"But that's exactly what he's doing," L. said in exasperation. "If he knows, it's simply abominable."

"No more abominable than what you're doing. And maybe he feels as guilty in his way as I do in mine. Have you ever thought of that?"

"I've thought of a lot of things," L. said. "I keep pretty busy, but it doesn't seem to stop me from thinking, especially at three o'clock in the morning." He turned away and said through his teeth, "I've abused your hospitality, your generosity . . ."

When I realized what he was talking about I could not keep from laughing. Maybe my laughter came out more like a senile cackle of relief that he was not going to berate me for what I had confessed, or try to take advantage of it. Maybe it was the incongruousness of it; the language of his confession seemed as funny to me as mine had to him. Spooky was his word.

L. was startled by my laughter. Frightened. He turned back to me, to see if he had misheard. "Sam," he said, "I'm talking about Jenny."

"I know that," I assured him. "You could never have done anything, or even started anything, without my unspoken collusion and even encouragement. Right? You're both too honorable for that. But while you've been congratulating each other on what a wonderfully understanding old boy I am, I've been getting my own kicks from being the author of your pleasure." He was gaping at me. "Don't tell me that never occurred to you. But now . . . I've outsmarted myself. I didn't count on the two of you joining, not just for mutual

313

gratification based, among other things, on your guilty connection with me, but for a common attack on me through
Seth."

"That's one thing that hasn't happened. Sam, I swear to
you—"

"Don't swear. I've already told you, it's not becoming."

"Please listen. I have never attempted to enlist Jennifer in
anything like that."

"I don't believe you." He flinched. "You're not that much
of an honorable damned fool."

"Ask her."

I was about to say I wouldn't believe her either; but suddenly I realized a trap had been dug for me and was ready to
be sprung. If I said aloud that I trusted no one, not even my
loving wife any longer, I'd be proving that all of them were
right, starting with L. Senile dementia, justifying their
frenzied activities in my behalf.

So I had to temporize. Besides, it did hurt, his having to
plead as if he were still a kid and I was still his schoolmaster,
with the unspoken accusation that I was perversely turning
on him at the most critical moment of his professional life.
He did have the right to certain claims on me, certain expectations perhaps beyond those of any other person. With the
exception of Seth.

We talked some more and finally agreed to tell Mrs. H.
and the chauffeur to go to bed and to do likewise ourselves.
L. was still hoping to get me into the car in the morning and
continue the discussion, as he put it, on the way.

Next morning.

No, I am too tired. Will put down the rest tomorrow.

AUGUST 31 At breakfast L. had recovered his
aplomb. He accepted Mrs. H.'s suggestion of blueberry pan-
cakes, had three cups of coffee, joshed me about our mutual
confessions of the night before.

Then he said something interesting.

314

"You tried quite hard last night," he said, "to convince me that you're as weak and corrupt as any of us, me included. If I spoke of my vanity and my careerism, you reminded me of yours. If I confessed my guilt, you came back with yours."

I told him I thought he might have the order reversed, but in any case I didn't see what he was driving at.

"You were saying, Stop looking at me as a saint. See me as I am, a sinner. I think you wanted to shock me into letting go."

As soon as he said this I knew there was no use. He wasn't going to let up, the stakes were far too great, he'd bet his whole life on me. Even if he were to read every line I've typed here, he'd interpret my confessions as one more mark of greatness. I didn't even have to listen to him going on about the way I deprecated myself needlessly, how he was well aware of my hesitations and turnabouts, my various appetites and the way I'd gone about satisfying them. I don't even know whether he believed me about me and Louise; it just didn't make all that much difference to him.

I've been giving myself away, and I can't even find any takers. Only the Children of Liberty threaten to expose my dark secrets. What would they do if they knew no one was interested?

Maybe that's a way out.

There was nothing for me to do but tell L. that I had changed my mind for sure and was not going to the city. I apologized about the chauffeur and the wasted trip, but he waved that aside good-naturedly. He'd have the chauffeur drive him to Bradley Airport and he'd grab a plane back. We'd be in touch.

"I'll keep up the pressure," he said, laughing, "but in a nice way."

So he recouped, at least to the extent that he left without making any concessions. And he left me with the impression that he simply couldn't afford to make any, he had too much riding on me to let anyone get in his way. Including me.

Three hours after he left, Jennifer was back.

September

SEPTEMBER 1 She had been shopping. Not just for herself, although she was as beautifully turned out as ever; she had bought me a cardigan, underwear, a sweatshirt, some large-print books. Nice, but not to the point.

Always before when she left and returned it was as part of her, our, life pattern. She shopped, she photographed, she saw Larry, she got assignments, she visited relatives; but always I was here (or in the apartment), "in her mind and in her heart," as she put it. And I believed her.

Now she had done the things that a free and busy woman does—visited the gallery about a show of her work, bought supplies, seen two publishers about assignments, purchased the gifts I've mentioned. But behind it had been the possibility of no return. Then why was she here?

She claimed it was simple, a matter of what she had already written me, that no matter what, she had done the right thing in persuading me to marry her, and would love me forever.

"You were shocked by what I said," I reminded her.

She didn't deny it. In fact she added, "I didn't think you were capable of that kind of cruelty. It took me a while to get accustomed to the idea of that. But now I am, and I've come to the conclusion that it doesn't change anything."

Cool. Poised. My old Jennifer.

What was I to do? Accept a return to the status quo ante? There ain't no such animal, and I told her so.

She wanted to know what had changed. Remarkable how the young refuse to acknowledge change, unless it is one they themselves have precipitated or helped bring about. And if I told her they were closing in, if I said I could no longer trust her any more than I could Larry, if I complained of

319

being isolated by her flight far more than by her previous periodic departures—I would reawaken her worst suspicions. She would come to feel not just that I am capable of unsuspected meannesses, but that there is in me the deterioration and decay that I feel in my relations with others.

Have to be careful. I said that to myself, I know I did, I remember it, and yet something goaded me on. Cruelness (her word) perhaps? I really don't think I am all that cruel. I think others—whether from the best of motives or not—are cruel to me.

I believe I wanted to give her another chance, to try her out, to see. . . . I asked her if she would still do anything for me, as she had so often asserted before the revelation of my darker side.

She laughed and nodded, but I thought I detected a flicker of the eye, the faintest nervous throb. So many things are a blur, how can I be sure of these fine movements?

"Supposing I wanted to escape," I suggested. "Would you help?"

"Darling," she demanded, the smile still on her composed countenance, "what do you want to escape from?"

"You know," I said.

But she wanted me to say it, the way some people during sex want to, have to, say "dirty" words. I had shamed and degraded her once; now if I wanted her help I was going to have to beg for it.

"For shorthand," I said, "I have to escape from Larry on the one hand and Seth on the other. You once answered, when I asked you something regarding Larry, But I'm your wife. It was beautiful, the way you said it, it rang in my heart."

She seemed to flush a little. "You're speaking now," she said slowly, "of the entire situation symbolized by my foolish dinner party."

"In a way."

"Then I don't know what you mean by escape. As I wrote

you, you could have come to the apartment. It seems you've decided against that."

"The weather has turned around," I said. "Seth would stay away, Larry would stay away if you requested it of him, but those television men, Gibbons and Wells, would come. That means Larry's boss, which in turn means harassment from Seth's young friends. So that's no solution, is it?"

J. frowned, not at me apparently, but in honest puzzlement. "I don't see," she said, "I honestly don't see how you can avoid that. There are some things you can't escape, aren't there? Some things you have to face and get over with."

That was when I tried another tack. The reason I set it down here is that it came out so unexpectedly, not just for her, but for me too. It was the last thing in the world I had expected to say, certainly to her.

"I want to escape *to* something," I said, "not just from a nasty situation."

Of course she asked me, To what? and I said abruptly, "To children."

There was a long silence after that. J. sat looking down at her hands, consideringly. Finally she said, "Truly I've been under the impression that after a lifetime of working with children you wanted this peace and this quiet. That you wanted to think about them rather than be with them." She lifted one hand and moved it vaguely. "The constant demands, the sheer physical wear and tear."

"You're describing what it was like," I told her, "when we met almost ten years ago." Once again, she couldn't see that things had changed or how they had changed; then we had been a very old man and a young girl, now we were an ancient and a young woman. Nothing was different, just more of the same, I had my contemplative doze (to put it politely), she had a rich and varied life. Everything but children. Why complain?

"Maybe I made a mistake," I said. "Maybe you made a miscalculation."

Fear entered her face. "I don't understand."

Neither of us had any way of knowing at the time of our marriage, I observed, that I would be around this long. True, we hadn't uttered it aloud, but in the back of our minds must have been a feeling that we would at best have a few years together. "If you had known then," I asked her, "that you'd be condemned to childlessness, not for a few years in your early twenties, but for all this time . . ."

She stared at me. "All this time? Is that how you define our marriage? Don't you think I've been happy?"

"I hope you have been," I said, "but look ahead. You wouldn't have the guts to go and have a baby while I'm still alive—and who knows how long that will be? I keep threatening to wake up dead one of these mornings, but I haven't made good on it, have I? And who knows how long it will take for me to get around to it?"

"Are you threatening me that you'll stay alive?"

"Until your youth is gone. It's possible. Meanwhile I want to be where there are children's voices."

Hysteria bloomed in her cheeks. For a minute I think she hated me. Wild, wild, I could read it in her eyes, a wild old man to charge me with depriving him of the company of children, as if I were the old woman and he the young husband.

She bit it back. "Sam, the Children's Center is going to be practically your second home."

"It's going to be a mausoleum for me, is that what you mean? How many people do you think drop in to Grant's Tomb?"

"I'm not sure I understand what you're after," she said carefully. "You know perfectly well the Center won't be one of those bureaucratic hives—you trained Larry too well for him to allow it to degenerate into anything like that. There'll always be more children in it than adults, and if you don't want that, then . . ."

"For one thing, it isn't finished yet. I may be finished

before it is. For another," I said, "I don't like the idea of buying my way in. I think maybe the price is too high. When I asked if you'd help me to get away, I meant from Larry as well as from Seth. It sounds to me as though you're still in Larry's corner."

"I'm sorry," she said, "if you interpret it that way. I was only trying to be, well, responsive. I guess I simply don't understand just where it is that you'd like to go."

"I don't either," I told her. "Not yet anyway. But I feel the need suddenly very, very badly." And I was not lying, either."

"Well, she concluded with a kind of forced cheerfulness, "we can discuss it some more later."

We can, but I don't think we will.

SEPTEMBER 2   Awakened from a horrible nightmare by Rog. He had to shake me, apologizing while he did so, and ducking away from my flailing arms. Shameful. Like having to be dragged off the stool with your pants around your ankles.

Might as well set it down here. Anyone who has read this far will probably be less sickened and disgusted than I was. It began quietly, sweetly actually, as nightmares sometimes do—as if the only way they could entice you into the underbrush was through the perfume of their false flowers.

I was leading a group of children on a nature walk through the forest trail of our school. It was a glorious summer morning, the sun filtered through the dogwoods and the tulip trees, bees hovered over clumps of naturalized hibiscus mallow, monarch butterflies fluttered in pairs over the heads of the laughing children. Some of the younger ones clung to me, but others were more adventurous and tended to wander off despite my warnings to them not to go too far from the group.

Suddenly one of the boldest came running toward me, her

dark eyes round and large. She was my own Sophia. I was not in the least surprised to see that she was one of my group, only happy that the business of her death had all been a crazy misunderstanding on the part of Luba and me. Sophia said nothing, in fact she held her chubby little fingers to her lips in childish imitation of her teachers and dragged me forward to the edge of the clearing, a kind of glade.

There she indicated that I should put to my eye the large wooden-handled magnifying glass with which I had been displaying to the children the mysterious undersides of ladies' slippers, jack-in-the-pulpits, and love apples, and the erotic interiors of drooping day lilies, from which bees had been drinking. I followed her instructions, crouching forward and peering through the parted bushes in the direction Sophia was indicating with a smile of childish delight and wonderment.

Before me, so grossly enlarged by the glass that at first I simply could not make out what it was, thrashed some large pale hairy object. I thought it might be a wounded animal, wounded and impaled in some way, and struggling to free itself from whatever held it down, but it was too white even to be a pig, and it was then that I saw it was a man copulating in the grass, his white buttocks plunging up and down irregularly, prodded forward from time to time by a pair of heels which engirdled him and drummed him on.

As I knelt there, breathing heavily myself and listening to the gasps and moans, the wet slapping sound of sweaty flesh clapping together, I seemed to know instinctively, as though this was the entire reason, the goal and aim, of the nature walk, that the buttocks were those of Seth, and that I was having the joy of watching him fuck his Susan in the open air. I wanted to see her ecstasy, I was dying to see her come, and I pressed forward heedlessly like an explorer peering over a precipice. Suddenly Sophia began to giggle convulsively at my side; I heard her whisper, "Susanna and the Elders."

324

Seth jerked his head about angrily. To my astonishment and horror, the girl he was topping was not Susan. It was Jennifer, her face wet, red, and ugly, her mouth open as she gasped for air.

I wanted to shriek. I tried to make him stop, I threw the magnifying glass at him, I lunged forward, my arms clawing.

He became Rog, of course, holding my thrashing arms until the rage and terror had subsided.

"I'm sorry," he said. "But I thought I'd better wake you."

"Was I yelling?" I asked, falling back on the pillow.

He smiled in his innocence. "You were making sounds," he said, "choking sounds. Are you feeling better now?"

"One of these days," I muttered, "I'll die in the midst of a bad dream. What a way to die, frightened to death, like some idiot in a horror story." I had to get to the bathroom.

"Seth wants to see you," R. said. "In fact he says he has to see you. I told him you were napping, so he's waiting on the porch, but when I heard you . . ."

Somehow I got to my feet. "He'll have to wait," I said. "Where is Jennifer?" The dream still possessed me so, I half-expected to be told that she was out there with Seth.

"I believe she's gone over to the Honigs'," R. said.

Finally I got out to the porch, where S. was pacing.

"I suppose you realize," he said, "that Brodie and his people have gone too far for me to feel any compunctions about what happens next."

"I had nothing to do with it," I told him. "I'm not apologizing, I'm simply telling you."

"That's like saying," he said, "that you have nothing to do with Brodie's plan to get that building named for you. So I'm simply telling you."

I don't know if he loves me or hates me. Does it make any difference which? Does it make any difference? I asked him if he had been discussing things with Jennifer, and it seemed to me that he looked at me strangely. "Why?" he asked, and I didn't have any answer, I could only change the subject.

That made him look at me more queerly. I had a suddenly panicky, naked feeling, as if he had divined the subject of my nightmare—had Rog told him of shaking me awake from it, while they waited for me to come out of the john? I don't doubt it.

He asked me if I was sure I felt all right.

"No," I said, "and I don't expect to. I never will again, and I don't think there is any way I could explain it to you that you would find understandable."

He and R. exchanged glances. I am not dreaming this; when S. and I broke off inconclusively I went on inside—but from the hallway window I watched him wait out in the driveway for R., who walked slowly with him back toward the guesthouse. They were deep in conversation.

I don't like that.

SEPTEMBER 3   J. brought Dr. Harrison in to see me this morning. "How are you feeling this morning," he asked, "fresh and chipper?"

What a boob. I was about to tell him that I'd been feeling all right until he showed up, when I remembered Seth's question of the day before. J. was standing in the doorway, her arms folded, looking—what's the expression?—as if butter wouldn't melt in her mouth.

"I'll leave you two alone," she said.

"That sounds like a line from those doctor movies," I said, but she was gone. People always seem to be walking out when I talk to them.

Harrison sat himself down and commenced what I suppose he thinks of as a nice little chat.

"You're about as subtle as an avalanche," I told him. "Who sent for you?"

"I just thought I'd drop by on my way to the hospital," he said, "before I start on my rounds."

I told him he was being evasive, and he looked hurt, in his inert, doglike way.

"You guys don't even make house calls to write death certificates," I said. "Who put you up to this?"

He was insistent that nobody had, and I let it go. I thought I might get a clue in the way he handled himself, and me, but no, he just rattled on, presenting me with a series of inanities while he opened his satchel, like a Fuller Brush man proudly displaying his line of goods. He had the nerve to tell me that he had a vested interest in keeping me going because I am so famous, and my continued existence redounds to his professional credit. Jocular.

"Like the kindly country doctor and the Dionne quintuplets?" I asked, and he took that absolutely straight, with a straight face.

"Well," I said, "if you're going to sneak in an examination you might as well get it over with. Just make it snappy, that's all."

He took my blood pressure, etc., tapped, palpated, and so on. Finally I wouldn't let him do any more.

"What the hell do you expect to find?" I asked him. "I'm breathing, right? What more can I ask for at my age?"

A trace of irritation at last. "I have the obligation," he explained, as if reciting something he'd memorized, "of determining whether you are fit for the tasks you persist in taking on."

"What tasks?" He really did have me baffled. "All I do is answer letters and questions and odds and ends like that. Sometimes I see the people that Rog sorts out for me. The rest of the time I take naps. Do you think napping is an onerous task for a man pushing ninety?"

"I was referring," he said, "to your public involvements. To your commitment to the new generation."

"Harrison," I said, "that's too general. It doesn't take any particular energy to be committed."

"It takes energy to meet public figures at your time of life," he replied with some briskness. I was teasing it out of him. "To say nothing of being interviewed by Dick Wells."

I had it out of him at last. I could hardly wait to get him

out of here. Whoever had put him up to it was not just concerned with my blood pressure. That was a blind. All his chatty nonsense was designed to see if I knew what day it was, who he was, who I am.

Who am I? I am someone who has to get away.

I called out for Jenny, as loud as I could, after Harrison's car pulled out of the driveway.

"I resent very deeply," I said to her, "having that idiot called in and let loose on me. He's incapable of diagnosing a swollen pastern joint, much less—"

"What's a pastern joint?" she asked. She was going to try to make light of the whole thing.

"Don't give me that," I said. "You were one of those girls who went out with horses before you heard about boys. If you felt that my mind was failing, you could at least have done me the honor of bringing in a man of some distinction, a specialist in geriatrics or whatever. Or does that come next, after Harrison turns in his report?"

"I don't know what you're talking about," she insisted. "You make such a fuss over an ordinary checkup. In any case, it wasn't my idea to have him stop by."

"Then whose was it?" I challenged her. "This was no ordinary checkup. In his clumsy way, he was pumping me to see if I could follow his line of patter. Who put him up to it? Walter?"

Jennifer closed her eyes, then opened them. She was telling herself to be calm. "That's utterly ridiculous," she said. "Walter was just saying to me yesterday how remarkable your memory is for things like Shakespearean quotations."

"So you were talking to Walter about me and my mental state. Now that you've conceded that much, tell me who else was behind this—Gibbons? Is he worried that I may not recognize Wells? Or remember him? Or that I'll fall asleep during the interview? Or insult the President?"

"Sam," she said, "you can really be exasperating when you put your mind to it."

328

"At least you believe I still have a mind. I get the impression that everyone is writing me off."

"Now listen," she said. "If they were, why would they be so anxious to lionize you? Wouldn't they be trying to ditch you instead? Come on, think about that."

Well, I did. Taken straight, it could mean that it was the *others* who had gotten hold of Harrison. Would they go to such lengths to keep me from appearing, from being heard, from being taken seriously if what I had to say didn't meet with their approval? Or was J. simply trying to plant such suspicions in my head?

"All right," I said, "Larry will be glad to hear that I have a clean bill of health, won't he? Now we can go full speed ahead and damn the torpedoes."

When I asked J. to send Rog in on her way out, she seemed relieved. I guess sometimes she must wonder why she bothers to come back here.

When R. came in he told me there were several strangers asking for time with me—a couple of kids who had hitch-hiked out from Boston, some local liberals asking for an endorsement for their scheme to aid retarded children.

"Let them wait," I said. "I want to know if you asked Harrison to come and examine me."

"I wouldn't do that," he said, "unless it was at your request, or—"

"That's not true," I said. "You've called him in before."

"Well, in an emergency."

"Do you think I'm in an emergency now?"

"Certainly not." He stared at me, puzzled. "I hope he didn't upset you."

"I'm always upset these days," I said. "It doesn't take much. Has Seth had anything to do with Harrison?"

I could see the wheels going around in R.'s head. He drawled, "Well . . . when Susan was with him, she was feeling under the weather, and he asked me whom he should call. I suggested Dr. Harrison."

"What happened to her?" I asked. "Did she trip and bruise a pastern while she was doing an anti-event?"

He had no idea what I was talking about, nor what had been wrong with the girl. "But you must recall," he said, "we paid the bill."

I didn't want to admit that I didn't remember. I don't want to admit anything. I said, "I want to see Seth."

"I believe he's gone off for the day."

I know it was silly, but I felt suddenly enraged, as though I knew for a fact that Seth had gotten Harrison to come and cluck over my poor wandering brain, and then had run off himself so as not to have to take responsibility.

"Look here," I said. "When he gets back I want you to give him a message. Tell him that nobody who was losing his faculties could have sat here as I have, and written long entries in his diary day in and day out as I have. Doesn't that make sense to you?"

R. did not find it easy to answer. If he agreed with me too enthusiastically it would look funny, almost as if he had been reading these pages after all. His nod and smile were very uncomfortable.

"That's something to think about," I demanded, "isn't it? That in this desk drawer sit hundreds of pages of proof of undiminished mental capacity."

"That kind of proof is hardly necessary."

"Well," I said, "when he gets back, you just remind Seth that it's there." And I was going to add, "And it's dynamite too," but I had already said far too much, so I sent him off to the waiting visitors, hardly able to keep from shaking his head as he went.

SEPTEMBER 4 They are closing in. Telephone ringing, driveway full of cars. R. came in and said, "Three newsmen are waiting to see you."

My heart sank. They wanted to find out if there was any

truth to rumors about cancellation of Wells's interview. Who started the rumors? No one ever knows. Why should it be canceled? According to some reports, my ill health. According to others, pressure from outside sources. I said I wouldn't talk to them. R. said, If you don't ask them in they'll conclude that you're ill. I said, Let them conclude.

But I saw that no matter what I did I'd be on the spot. Which is what they want. It's not a matter of my being a coward, it's more that I feel as though I'm being driven into a corner. Is that what I get for living so long? I've done a lot of things I regret, but what did I do to deserve this?

Finally made a compromise, after several more journalists had shown up. Told R. to herd them out onto the back lawn. When they were all out there I grabbed up my stick and went out onto the back porch, waving it at them in what I hoped was a cheerful gesture. (Maybe they took it as defiance or anger or something else.)

"Ladies and gentlemen," I said to them, while they stood gaping up at me, "forgive me for not inviting you into my home. I have been very busy and I am not inclined to involve myself in one of those formal press conferences."

They looked restive and began muttering. I decided to liven it up so they would have something to take back to their bosses. "If you were curious about my continuing existence, you can see for yourselves that I am still among you, even if I cannot promise for how much longer. If you are curious about my opinion as to the state of my health, I can assure you that I haven't felt better since my eighty-ninth birthday."

That got a laugh out of them—but it also opened the floodgates. They began yelling up at me, questions about my family, the program, rumors. . . . I had to get out of there, and I moved as fast as I decently could, although I didn't exactly feel dignified, hobbling away from them, waving off the questions with one hand and clutching the stick with the other until I was safely back in here.

I have to do something.

SEPTEMBER 5   The irony is that never before have I had such resources, so many people presumably attached to me and eager to be of help or at least in my good graces, and yet never before have I been so powerless. When I was younger it was quite a thing to leave home on any kind of voyage; railroad timetables to be pored over, hotels to be written to, horses to be fed and watered and hitched up to the buckboard. Now, all you need is a tankful of gas for the getaway and a credit card for perpetual motion.

And yet I am immobilized. I haven't driven since our marriage, when I put J. and me in a ditch and had to be towed out by the Hendricks boys. I don't think I even have a credit card, and if I did I wouldn't be able to cope. I don't think I could see where to sign for things.

Why must I be so dependent? And whom can I trust?

With all the physical difficulties of getting about in the old days, it was exhilarating for me to get out into the world. I loved going to exotic places, difficult ones, learning things, meeting people, yes, even being recognized, if only as a reckless American or a good-hearted one. It was an adventure always, saying goodbye to the ordinary and the humdrum, and setting off for the unknown.

All that faded. The journey to Biafra was the last. I could hear my bones cracking as I bent over and crouched in those airplanes rushing in and out of the equatorial darkness with food for the children. I didn't really feel excited, I couldn't see that well; I felt infinitely depressed.

And so it reached the point where R. brought the exotic to me, read me the news, introduced me to the people whom I would formerly have met on my own, going out into the world instead of having it brought to me in measured spoonfuls. A dose of young people, a teaspoon of educators, a draught of radicals. No wonder that when S. lured me into his pickup I was frightened and uneasy, wary of a trap like an old lion half-aware that the cubs are laughing at him and finding him useful only as bait. Could that be the same man who used to go everywhere, heedlessly, eager for experience, thrilled by the very sensation of motion?

Yet it cannot be all gone. I had good reason to be beguiled by Seth's friends. They offered me one last glimpse of a chance-taking life, of growing out to others instead of in upon myself like the nails on my toes and the hairs on my cheeks. Wrong or right, was that really at issue? Wasn't it rather a matter of whether I could somehow summon up the courage to be a fool one more time? My son, my son, you asked too much of me!

But if I cannot do that, especially when the offer is made under the threat of a kind of blackmail, especially too when it would amount to destroying Larry, I persist in the thought that I can save myself, renew myself, by one more flight into the unknown. The will is there, in me, I know it, I can feel it, I am ready to go out and greet the children.

I think then I could die. The children would live.

Who will help me?

SEPTEMBER 6   I think I have it!

Must move fast.

Lily is going to visit her younger sister in Mankato, Minnesota. The sister was married to a businessman who died last year of heart failure; she has been in a state of depression and refuses to come east to visit with the Honigs. Walt won't go out there (he says he can't, he has too many things pending here, which seems strange for a retired man and makes me suspect that he is spending more time messing about with my affairs than he is ready to admit). So Lily is preparing to go on her own.

W. will drive her to Bradley. She'll take a plane to Minneapolis and then drive a rented car to her sister's, where she'll stay for some time. She has already talked to Mrs. H.

about coming over and "doing" for Walter while she is away. J. assured her that would be all right with us; in fact added that she herself would stop in to see that all went well with the garden and the watering of the house plants, and that she would be inviting W. over here "to water him too."

Now! I made Lily swear to me (don't swear, I always say to Larry, but this was on our sacred friendship, and I didn't feel guilty, not when I saw the thrill of guilty pleasure on Lily's face) that she would tell W. *nothing* of what I was about to confide in her.

Once she swore, she was drawn into it willy-nilly—I don't think she ever realized that. But I did, I did, and I pressed on. The more she sees it as our joint conspiracy against the world, and her sacrificial act in behalf of her oldest friend (in both senses), and also as a rescue operation of a helpless man from the clutches of grasping men—the more all of these things, the less she will be inclined to nit-pick or to tell me that it's out of the question, or scary, or loony.

I want her, I said, to reserve two seats instead of one. When we're in Minnesota we can get in the car that's waiting for her, and before she goes to her sister's she can drive me where I want to go.

That's where she gets the shakes. She finds it hard to imagine wandering around with me in an unknown state (when she said that, I was unsure of the sense in which she was using the word "state"—I suspect she was, herself). It seemed "wild" to her. I had to talk fast.

I am not used to talking fast. Persuading Lily was like— it makes me smile to think of the analogy—persuading the Board of Trustees of the Sophia School that they should trust me to guide them into uncharted waters. I pressed on, driven by the knowledge that she was my last, best hope, and that I was justified in using the tattered, shrunken remnants of my "sex appeal" if that was what it would take to enlist her as a willing volunteer in my dash to freedom.

What a challenge! Just to see the gradual changes in her eyes, on her face, from incredulity to doubt to excitement to a kind of guilty glee. . . . I couldn't awaken those responses in J., she is on the one hand too young and on the other too sophisticated; and besides, Larry stands in the way. Put there by me but nevertheless (or maybe for that very reason) in the way. . . . Who would have known that I still had the power, that it hadn't entirely atrophied!

As I talked on, as I stared compellingly into Lily's fine and shining eyes, I began to feel how I was succeeding at persuading not just her, but myself—which was perhaps even more important—that I have it within myself—the initiative, the intelligence, the directing force, the power and the vigor—to resolve this hellish dilemma. To escape from the trap, to find refuge and shelter.

"But then what?" she demanded. "Then what?"

I was improvising as I went along. There is a school for orphaned Indian children in that part of the country, I know, run by one of the Catholic fraternal orders. Not only am I on their immense mailing list for their annual fund-raising appeals; the father superior, or whatever he is called, has written me personally more than once, I remember, asking for an endorsement, a statement they can use in their campaigns. I don't recall what I answered or had R. answer for me— perhaps that I made it a policy not to make such statements without personal awareness of the entire learning situation and the total environment of the children. "In any case, that's the least of it," I said to Lily. "That doesn't make any difference."

"What do you mean, it doesn't make any difference?" In her mind, I had gotten us as far as Minnesota. But she couldn't see what came next, what I would do, what good it would do, how she could keep from being charged with some nameless crime of complicity by everyone from her husband to the television networks. She asked, her voice starting to quaver with doubt, reflecting terror of the incalculably unknown, "They may not even take you in. And even if they did, then what?"

"They'd be delighted to have me as a guest. And if I wish

to stay for a time, an indeterminate time, in privacy and meditation, in communion with their charges . . ." I came out with it triumphantly, "there is the sacred principle of sanctuary. They would be morally bound to honor my request. Lily," I said, staring into her eyes, "I don't wish to be immodest, but don't you think they'd feel honored?"

She faltered. "I didn't mean . . . But you couldn't stay there forever."

"I could stay indefinitely, that's the key thing," I said. "And if you didn't speak, there'd be no way of knowing where I was until I chose to speak out."

"That's just it," she said. "If Walter and the others . . . How long do you think I could remain silent, with all that pressure?"

"Just long enough," I said, "for me to exert pressure on all of them to compromise."

That was the point at which it all became clear to me, so clear that I knew I would have no problem persuading her. With me physically absent, each side would be deprived of the very base of its argument. It would be almost as good as if I were dead (Lily shuddered at this, but I said we had to think in realistic, practical terms), in fact, in a way even better—because from my sanctuary I could demand that if they wanted me back, the bickering, the blackmail, the injunctions, must come to an end.

And what was more, I should be in a perfect position, among those Indian children, to make my demands of the television people, of Larry, of Seth. Why? I pointed out to her that one of the young women who had been a member of the Children of Liberty's first contingent was herself an Indian orphan. "She came by that path," I said. "She traveled that route. She'll listen."

When I saw that I had Lily sold, persuaded, at the very minimum, of the possibility of success for the daring scheme of what you might think of as *going home,* I felt that I could raise the logistical problem that for me was paramount: How could we get Walter out of the way? How on earth would it be possible to have her pick me up and drive me to Bradley Airport without Walter being along to see her off and bring the car back home? I could see no way out of that.

To my astonishment, Lily was airy about this. Airy! I shall never cease to be amazed at the ease with which women deceive their husbands. And not just about their love affairs. I should be willing to bet that Lily had never been involved in such a thing, never. Nonetheless, as soon as I put the problem in terms of hoodwinking Walter, she saw it as one that could be readily resolved. Indeed, my fellow conspirator was smiling at me in a chiding way, surprised that I should regard her husband as any kind of serious obstacle, once I had overcome that presented by the Indian orphanage.

Lily said with calmness, even aplomb, that the answer lay with me, since W. is currently 100 per cent involved in my problems and my welfare. "All you have to do," she said, "is think of something connected with all this back-and-forth activity, something that will take Walter away for a day or two. Then what I'll do is, I'll tell him that instead of driving our car to the airport and leaving it there, which would be a great nuisance for him, I'll rent a car from Joe Hendricks' cousin down at the garage and turn it in at the airport." Simple.

Well, it is simple compared with the job of selling I had to do on Lily herself. I still can't believe I have enlisted her for the duration. In fact I wouldn't believe it, I would have to suspect her of leading me on, entrapping me with the intention of betraying me, if it were not for one thing: Before she went back to W. she said, with a display of emotion and handkerchief-twisting I have never seen from her in all these years (I think I am quoting her correctly), "Dear Sam, you are the only person in the world for whom I would dissimulate like this."

I remember thinking, in one of those flashes, Not even your own husband? and then asking myself, No, she can't even conceive of old Walter ever asking her to lie. Maybe that's one reason I got her to agree: the novelty of it! And she'll fly away with me!

She made herself say, in a tremulous way that made my heart ache for her, that she had always loved me, had always felt that life had been unkind to me, and that after I had given so much of myself it did not seem right that those "nearest and dearest" to me (her phrase) should be the very ones to make me feel like a prisoner who has to plot his escape from the very ones who care for him so deeply.

Now, ninety per cent of my chances lie with the capacity for guile and cunning of this sweet, frail woman. The remaining ten per cent is up to me. And if I cannot outsmart W. and slip past my keepers I deserve to rot here and be pulled to pieces by those who love me.

SEPTEMBER 8 No one must see this before I am gone. I am ready.

It was so easy! Walter snapped at the bait. I could see his nostrils dilating when I told him this morning that Seth had phoned me from New York, about a meeting with the Children of Liberty.

"Well?" he demanded. "Well?"

"They're ready to discuss terms."

"You see?" he asked. "No one likes being placed under restraint. I hope you didn't make any commitments."

"I thought I'd talk with you about it first," I said.

I was worried that such unwonted humility would make W. smell a rat, but no, he was too pleased about being vindicated. He wanted to know what else Seth had said. I told him that they were planning on getting in touch with Gibbons for a meeting with Wells, at which they wanted some assurance that I'd be fed a "non-hostile" question about their group and their goals. "They've all gotten together at the Algonquin," I wound up.

At once W. said, "I'd better get down there, if you'll give me your authorization to speak for you."

I said cautiously, "Well, you can ring me up from there, if you feel like making a special trip, and we can discuss it on the phone."

Then he said, "Damn, I've forgotten all about Lily's trip. I'm supposed to drive her down to Bradley first thing in the morning. I know, I'll leave the car there and grab a plane to New York after I've seen Lily off to Minnesota."

I had outsmarted myself! For an instant I was tempted to explain it all to W., to say, Look here, old man, if you do that you'll wreck my scheme to get you out of the way. How many husbands have wanted to ask their wives for their co-operation in planning to deceive them! It is a sign of affection, after all; I know.

In a split second I had recovered myself. I told him Seth had not merely opened negotiations, he had given me a deadline to respond.

"When?"

"Tonight. That's why I rousted you out so early this morning."

"I see." W. didn't question me at all; he was too eager to be in at the kill. "Well, I'll have to get home and talk with Lily before I run off. Maybe she can postpone her trip for a day or two, until I get back."

I held my breath. How would Lily handle that?

"Trouble is, she's so worried about her sister. She has all her reservations, plane and car and everything, and she's determined to leave tomorrow morning."

I thanked him for all the trouble and apologized for making a nuisance of myself. He patted my back and said it was nothing, and for a moment I felt real compunction at sending him out on a fool's errand at his age, making him chase all the way down to Manhattan to stand helplessly in the Algonquin lobby. But by the time he's tracked down Grebner, talked to Gibbons, gotten to Larry in Washington, etc.,

I'll be out safe. That's what counts. Someday he'll realize that I had to do it, that it was not from perversity, and that really this was the best way he had of helping me . . . through his wife and his own departure.

Now I have to pack a small bag without Mrs. H. nosing around and catching me, while R. and J. are out. I'll be up and out at dawn, walking down the street toward the Honigs' so Lily won't have to drive in here and chance waking up the household.

Tomorrow at this time I'll be entering my sanctuary. I'll be with the children, away from all this madness.

Who knows if I shall ever write in this diary again? I am going to leave it here, locked in the drawer. Let them look. It won't help any of them, once I am out of their clutches. I stick out my tongue at everyone!

SEPTEMBER 15   I found the date on the big wall calendar. I am surprised. I have lost track of the days. A week since the flight.

I was determined to write nothing more, but today I said to myself, Why not, why not finish what I started last spring, when I wrote that first naive entry about my Venetian birthday celebration as a little boy. After all, I have learned a lot since then. Who says you can't learn when you're ninety years old?

Lily kept her word. She was there, on the road, motor warmed up, at 6:45. By this time of year it is chilly at that hour. The ground was wet underfoot, the leaves were turning on the maples, and here and there some were curling and dropping to the moist grass. In the distance a dog was baying at a rabbit, yipping nervously, awakened from its warm sleep. I felt myself shivering a bit, even in the warm cardigan Lily had knitted for me three or four years ago.

But she was radiant as she climbed out of her car to open the door for me and stow my bag in the back. "You're wearing my sweater!" she cried. "How nice!"

To tell the truth, I had not remembered it as hers when I put it on; I was looking only for something that would protect me from the chill. For her it was a special sign, setting the seal, I suppose, on the elopement.

She turned on the heater for me, and when I had thawed out a bit said, "It's going to be a beautiful day. Don't you think that's a good omen? Did you find out anything more about the Indian school?"

She was both excited and uneasy; only natural. I assured her that I had found the stuff in Rog's files, and in fact had a map of the place they'd sent me, which would come in handy when we picked up the other car.

That reassured me. But after a while she ventured, somewhat timidly, to assert that there was just one thing she didn't fully understand. Why hadn't I taken Jennifer into my confidence? Jennifer was young, yes, but wasn't she utterly devoted to me?

I knew how much effort it had taken her to bring this up. I know Lily, and I know she wasn't fishing for gossip about J. and L. I didn't want to talk about that anyway, but I did feel Lily was entitled to an answer; in fact she was entitled to just about anything, given all she was doing for me. So I told her I had more or less hinted broadly to J. that I wanted to break loose, to get away from everyone, to go someplace where I could be the master of my fate instead of its servant.

"What did Jenny do?" I said to Lily. "She went running to that fool Harrison."

"She was worried about you, Sam."

"I don't deny that," I said. "I know she's devoted to me. But there is a final measure of trust . . . it's like the willing suspension of disbelief. I wanted her to read me like a novelist, and she chose instead to read me like a nurse."

Lily had no ready answer for this, and we drove in silence for a long while, until we had gotten onto Route 91 and were buzzing along at a steady sixty, being passed only by an occasional truck or early-bird salesman. In another few minutes, though, the highway would be aswarm with the station wagons of returning vacationers and the car pools of people heading for their jobs.

It was than that she turned to me and said, "I feel like singing."

I challenged her. "Why don't you?"

She laughed. "Just because I'm so excited is no reason to terrify you. I guess I haven't sung in twenty years. That's a confession of sorts, isn't it, Sam?"

I put my hand over hers on the steering wheel. It seemed that everything she said this morning touched me deeply. I had completely forgotten that many years ago, back in the twenties, she used to sit at the piano and accompany herself while she sang Favorite Arias from Grand Opera, and Songs the Whole World Loves; that was when I first knew her and she and Walter had only recently been married. He used to listen to Lily doing Meyerbeer and Offenbach, in her light soprano, with great pride—and incomprehension, no doubt. He had bought her the piano for a wedding present. I think she still plays it, but only when she is home alone. And I suppose the little bird in her died with the menopause.

She wanted to know if I was as excited as she. And I told her, Even more so. "I'm afraid," I said to her, "to tell you how excited I am. It might unsettle you. I'm too dependent on your steadiness."

"You're sure," I remember her asking, not nervously but as if she simply wanted to hear it from me in my voice, "that you're doing the right thing? I don't mean leaving like this— I can see why you felt impelled to it, even if it is disturbing to everyone who loves you, including me."

"Then what, if not this?"

"Choosing to go out there, to the Indian school."

"I'm sure about it," I said. "I am happy in my mind. I only wonder why I didn't think of it earlier. In a way, I suppose I should be grateful to everyone for forcing me to the decision."

Lily said, "As you grow older, it's harder to push yourself,

342

to risk discomfort and strangeness. It's one of the things about you that I've always admired, your readiness to brave the unknown."

But that was just it, I didn't see myself as braving the unknown this morning. Rather, I was returning to the children I should never have left.

The sun was higher now, striking through the windshield, reminding us that it was still summer, as we rolled on toward the airport. I think it was at this point that I asked Lily if she remembered her Victor Hugo.

"Oh, goodness," she said, "I must confess I probably haven't read him in half a century or more. Should I?"

I had to laugh at the way she glanced at me, ready to be advised. After nearly half a century of friendship, Lily still looks to me for a kind of guidance.

"I guess people don't read him any more," I said. "When I was running the School, the kids still adored him. Even the reluctant and the slow readers got caught up in those romantic stories. I was just thinking, while we were talking about the Indian school, of Jean Valjean saying to Cosette in *Les Miserables,* 'When you are old, you feel like a grandfather to all small children.' I feel that now, I understand it as I don't think I ever did when I used to read *Les Miserables* to the children."

Lily's eyes were so flooded with tears that I feared for her driving. She reached for a Kleenex from the box that lay between us. After she blew her nose she was smiling again, and ready for what the next hours would bring.

As I think back on it now, I marvel at the fact that throughout the whole drive, all the way down 91 to the turnoff for the airport, Lily never once chided me for the trick I'd played on her husband, in fact never expressed any regret for what we'd done in terms of misleading her husband. It was almost as if she took for granted, not that he had it coming (Lily has never been vindictive to anyone, least of all to her marriage partner), but that he would be able to cope, and would bear no grudge when it was all over and he came to understand that we had had no alternative.

All of her concern was for me, my well-being, my having the chance to realize, this last time, the control of my own destiny. As we pulled off to the approach road she said in her most businesslike way, "I am going to pull up to the departure gate to let you off and to drop off my bags. You can wait for me right there while I turn in the car, and I'll come for you as soon as I can."

She brushed aside my offer to accompany her as unnecessary, and rolled up to the curb. Before I could move, a skycap, an elderly black man, had opened the door and was helping me out and reaching in for my bag. He took the keys from Lily, opened the trunk, and lifted out the bags she was taking with her.

"You just wait right there, Sam," she called out, "and I'll come for you as soon as I can."

I apologized to the skycap for not being able to help him with the bags. He laughed, not patronizingly, but in a nice way, and assured me that he was used to it; he stacked the bags onto a dolly and rolled it off, explaining to me that he would check everything in for us.

After that I stood there by the pillar as Lily had instructed me. The air was noisy and fume-laden, what with all the cars and taxis pulling up, discharging people and bags, and then roaring off in a series of ear-splitting blasts. The sun came up over the edge of the building across from where I stood, and suddenly it was summer again. I felt blinded and hot. I unbuttoned my sweater and stepped around on the other side of the pillar, afraid to go too far lest Lily miss me when she returned; yellow and green circles were forming in front of my eyes.

A middle-aged lady came up to me and said, "Excuse me, sir, but can I help you?" She started to say something else, but I was afraid she was going to ask me if I was lost, so I cut her off.

"No, no, that's all right," I assured her, "I'm waiting for

344

someone." And I pulled out my pocket watch to glance at it impatiently, by way of showing that I was on top of things. Fortunately the woman had no way of knowing that I could not make out the numbers on the dial.

It seemed to me that an awfully long time had passed, and I began to get worried. I thought, well, maybe the lot was full and she had to park all the way at the far end and then walk the long distance back to the terminal. But then I remembered that it was a rented car, and I started worrying all over again. I thought she might have run into some complications turning it in. I didn't know the name of the rental agency. I was afraid if I went to look for it she might not find me.

A woman, not Lily, was peering at me strangely. I don't think it was the one who had asked me if she could help, but in a short time I had the feeling that others were doing the same thing. I felt conspicuous, and a little sick and dizzy from the sunlight. Suddenly I had to pee something awful, and I was terrified of an accident in front of all those people.

I thought if I could find a men's room it would give me some relief, and that when I got back maybe Lily would be there. I turned and walked up the rubber carpeting, reaching out for the glass door, not thinking that it would open automatically at my approach. I stumbled and managed to right myself, and entered the freezing building. I was trying at the same time to button my sweater and to read the signs on the doors.

Finally I came on one that I thought said Gentlemen, since it was just next to a drinking fountain, but when I pushed it open I found myself in a big, almost vacant room, nothing in it but a table on which some men in uniform, or at least uniform jackets, were sitting, smoking and reading the morning paper.

"What's up, Dad?" one of them said, and I told him I was looking for the men's room. By that time I was near desperation.

He took me by the arm and led me through another door

to a row of urinals. "Can you manage now?" he asked. I didn't know if he was teasing or being serious, but couldn't take time to find out.

I think I made something of a mess, since I tangled up between my zipper and my cardigan buttons, but I was distracted from all that by a new voice calling over the loudspeaker system. It was different from the one that kept announcing arrivals and departures at the various gates, and it sounded very much like my name being paged.

I turned to ask the man who had brought me in, but there was no one there any more. I thought to myself, Lily must have missed me at our rendezvous, she must have panicked. But I had no idea where she was. I listened again and I thought the voice said, Please report to Gate 22, the boarding gate for our flight. That sounded logical, so I set off.

But I took two wrong turns, even after asking at the newspaper counter, and by the time I got headed in the right direction I was very tired. The numbers moved by odds, 7, 9, 11, but at great distances from each other. At 13 I decided to stop and catch my breath; it had an area lined with empty benches, and a young man in a blazer who ignored me when I sat down slowly on one of the benches. Nothing there but stand-up ashtrays, some flung-aside newspapers, and a Coke machine. I didn't know any more if I was shivering or sweating. I closed my eyes to rest them for a moment.

Next thing I knew I was surrounded. Absolutely surrounded, in absolute confusion. I heard the voices, familiar voices, and I opened my eyes. Walter, and Jennifer. Also Seth, was that possible? And Larry? And Rog, holding Lily by the arm. She was crying, "Sam, Sam, I didn't do it. I swear!"

I told her not to swear, and I heard them asking me how I felt, touching my forehead, and ordering a wheelchair from the man in the blazer.

"No wheelchairs," I said.

I let them lead me back. I let them bring me home, pushing aside yelling people, men with cameras, trucks, station wagons. It was almost good to be back, and I did not find it worthwhile putting up a fight when Harrison was brought in to go over me.

All I said was that from now on I wanted to be left strictly alone, except for food and medicine.

And that's it.

SEPTEMBER 16   I have read over these pages with a mixture of fascination, disgust, amusement, and boredom. When I began reading—a slow process—it was not only to see how much I had set down, but to restore to my own mind what others may have been surreptitiously peering at, before I placed it beyond their grasp by destroying it.

A life. Yet it seems to me that destroying it would be, paradoxically, to place too much significance upon it. Too much solemnity. After all, if I learned anything from these last six months or so, it is that I was the one who engendered the atmosphere of constant crisis as much as anyone. I took myself too seriously. How we deceive ourselves! Ourselves first of all, when we think we are being shrewd, manipulating others.

I convinced myself that I was trying to dissuade both camps from deifying me, from being unfair to me, when in truth I was being unfair to myself as well as to them, and trying to extract from both the most flattering notions of what I had been and presumably still was.

As if it was possible at this point to change myself into a virtuous man! What arrogance! Once upon a time I memorized Montaigne: "It is almost better never to become a decent man than so tardily," but I never understood him, did I? He warned me, that old man writing about the approach of deafness: "You will see that when it is half gone, I shall still be blaming those who talk to me." And all I knew how to do, as my own blindness increased, was to chuckle at what I thought was mere wit.

To chuckle, and to rage at those around me. Now I see, or

347

I think I do, that it's far too late for anything I do to make a difference in how I am regarded by posterity. I have had ninety years in which to make an impression. What alteration could my final squirming and twisting effect, one way or the other?

To the very last, stumbling around that airport, I deluded myself into believing that I was being decisive, courageous, wily. But supposing poor Lily and I had made it all the way, how could I conceivably have changed the popular view of what I am?

Thanks to a good constitution, I have survived these destructive episodes. Now, pushing ninety and preparing for the unavoidable celebration, I have even managed to achieve a certain good humor, if not exactly a serenity. While I am waiting, I will do what is expected of me by all hands. No more sulking. If it is looked on as contradictory, so be it. No more explanations. It no longer matters to me what kind of figure I will cut for posterity. Posterity is here. Hello, from this old boy! Take it away!